Air Ready

Love and death decisions

When big-market broadcast reporter Elizabeth Danniher arrived in rustic Sherman, Wyoming, she struggled to adjust to wide-open Wyoming, a small-town TV station, and a betrayal that left her questioning career—and romantic—choices.

After investigating a series of murders, Elizabeth is drawn to both enigmatic rancher Thomas Burrell and her former KWMT-TV colleague Michael Paycik. But Mike has career aspirations of his own, and Tom's feisty daughter, Tamantha, is definitely Team Dad.

Now KWMT is for sale, everyone's job is in danger, no one's answering Elizabeth's messages for information, and she's about to be asked to look into something she's never investigated before. Can murder—and love—be far behind?

Caught Dead in Wyoming series

Sign Off
Left Hanging
Shoot First
Last Ditch
Look Live
Back Story
Cold Open
Hot Roll
Reaction Shot
Body Brace
Cross Talk
Air Ready
Holiday Bullets
Cue Up

"While the mystery itself is twisty-turny and thoroughly engaging, it's the smart and witty writing that I loved the best."
—*Diane Chamberlain, New York Times bestselling author*

More mystery from Patricia McLinn

Secret Sleuth series

Death on the Diversion
Death on Torrid Avenue
Death on Beguiling Way
Death on Covert Circle
Death on Shady Bridge
Death on Carrion Lane
Death on ZigZag Trail
Death on Puzzle Place

The Innocence Trilogy

Proof of Innocence
Price of Innocence
Premise of Innocence

AIR READY

Caught Dead in Wyoming, Book 12

Patricia McLinn

Cover design: Art by Karri
Cover image: Nicolaus Wegner

✧   ✧   ✧   ✧

DAY ONE
FRIDAY

Chapter One

"I, UH, THINK I'll go home now."

That's how I announced the midafternoon end of my workday in KWMT-TV's newsroom. For good reasons, including, but not limited to, that I'd worked enough extra hours lately to challenge a calculator.

First, in resolving a murder, along with several cohorts. Most of those cohorts, joined by more KWMT staffers, then worked with me to produce a special.

That was just the beginning of the extra hours.

As a result of the murder investigation, newsroom staffing had gaps.

I can't say we had a vacuum in leadership ... though our previous leadership *did* suck.

What they left behind was more like a dustbuster with a dying battery.

But they had filled chairs.

I'd been available for substitute chair-filling over these weeks because the backlog of segments of *Helping Out!* with E.M. Danniher could dam the Mississippi River.

As far as my non-regular beat went, I figured we were due a long, quiet spell with no more citizens of Cottonwood County, Wyoming, killing someone or getting themselves killed.

We don't have that many residents to start with. We can't afford to lose more.

As tired as I was, I'm sure I would have noticed a murder, so I felt safe saying, so far, so good on the no murders front.

All in all, I could use a short day and a nap before tonight's session of Contributions and Inventions of Native Americans, a community college course I was auditing. That was no reflection on instructor O.D. Everett.

It was the result of devoting too few of my sparse non-working hours to sleep.

A lot of things on my mind.

The station in Sherman, Wyoming—in case you couldn't guess, the smallest TV market in the country—was on the sales block and the leading candidate to buy it was renowned for closing newsrooms.

Leading candidate? The *only* candidate I'd learned of.

Ideally, someone would have responded to my going-home announcement with *sure, go home, get some rest, you deserve a break, nobody deserves it more.*

I wasn't surprised nobody did. The waiting and not-knowing meant the newsroom bullpen was not a fun place at the moment.

I was surprised Jennifer Lawton said to me, "You can't. Someone's coming to talk to you."

Jennifer's officially a news aide and unofficially a whole lot more, especially within the small group of us who've dug into a number of mysteries in the past year and a half.

"Who?"

"You wouldn't know her name."

"What does she want to see me about?"

"She'll tell you. She should be here any minute." In other words, Jennifer didn't want to tell me why this mystery woman—at least I knew the gender of *someone*—was coming to talk to me, which did not bode well. And in more other words, Jennifer didn't know exactly when this woman would arrive.

"Have her make an appointment for tomorrow."

"No."

Jennifer turned her back to me and resumed her work.

No and a turned back are among my least favorite things in the world. Right up there with Brussels sprouts.

It's decidedly personal with Brussels sprouts. With *no* and the turned back it's professional.

It's my job to ask questions. Then, as a TV reporter, to make sense of the answers and bring news and useful information to viewers.

I'd done that while my TV journalism career traveled through Dayton, St. Louis, Washington, D.C., and New York before crash-landing in—you guessed it—Sherman, Wyoming, for complicated reasons involving the shallowness of TV news, my once-considerable salary, a personal betrayal, pitfalls in my network contract, and the machinations of my vindictive ex-husband. Mostly my ex.

The size of the market doesn't change the value of questions. They are how we find out things in this world. Especially things other people don't willingly tell us.

That's where my dislike for *no* and the turned back comes in.

These past weeks I'd discovered I also dislike being *asked* questions when I don't know the answers.

Make that singular.

When I don't know *the* answer.

To *the* question behind whatever my co-workers said.

What's going to happen?

To KWMT-TV.

To them.

Owner Val Heatherton put KWMT-TV up for sale because she didn't want to be tied to embarrassments associated with the station, even though she'd laid the groundwork for the embarrassments. As far as I could tell, embarrassments tangled with murder didn't bother her. Personal embarrassments dinging her ego did.

The two-pronged *what's going to happen?* became more pressing in the past two days since newsroom staff learned what I'd known for weeks. The only known contender to purchase the station was a religious network notorious for closing news departments.

I'd kept that part quiet while trying to discreetly work sources in my scant spare time.

No sense keeping my source-working quiet now.

I had more than a dozen calls out to learn about the network and to plant seeds with potential bidders that a station in Sherman, Wyoming, could be a good buy for a non-news-crushing organization.

The weird thing was it could be, because of an ads market with little competition.

Which reminded me, I needed to ask Needham Bender, the owner, publisher, and editor of the *Sherman Independence,* if his advertising was as lucrative as KWMT's. I'd assumed he ran on a shoestring—shame on me.

But I wasn't calling him now. First, he'd ask a lot more questions than he answered, and we've already covered how I felt about that.

Second, I was very busy.

All these return calls to *not* answer.

I'd started with a carefully crafted list of potential sources. Not too high up. Not too low. Not likely to dismiss KWMT as not worth discussing. Not likely to feel so sorry for me working in a news shop about to be obliterated that I couldn't stand it.

After a day of no one answering or responding, I expanded the list.

By today, I stretched it to just about anyone I'd ever had contact with in the news business.

Not even Wardell Yardley—who never missed a chance to gossip about the biz—called back. Okay, as White House correspondent for a major network, he was traveling with the president in Africa.

If not even Dell would gossip about KWMT—

No.

He was working. Hadn't picked up my messages yet. Had picked up a woman (anyone from a member of the host country's cabinet to a fellow correspondent to a molecular biology post-doc who delivered hamburgers to the media pool as her part-time job. Dell had a knack.)

But what reasonable explanation could there be for Mel Welch not getting back to me?

Mel became my agent two years ago. My former agent proved more than china gets divided in a divorce and chose the network exec staying in New York over the one-time rising star reporter whose burnt-out shell landed in Sherman, Wyoming. Go figure.

Mel, who had never agented before, but has an enviable rep in Chicago legal circles, stepped in. He's married to my mother's cousin's oldest daughter and—even more useful—is terrified of my mother. Most people are.

He did not have great connections in the biz except through me.

I take that back.

He'd had one hard-to-beat connection in knowing deep, dark Heatherton family secrets. With them no longer secret, there went his connection. *Pffft.*

Although, he'd bonded with a woman in the Heatherton conglomerate who'd overseen aspects of KWMT from afar. I hoped he could work that source for insight to potential buyers.

He hadn't called back.

Along with every other person I'd reached out to.

Like they were avoiding me.

I am not paranoid.

Not even about coworkers whispering in corners, which might or might not be them wishing I'd kept my nose out of figuring out who committed murder, which then cascaded into this uncertainty.

Nobody said it to my face.

They did ask—repeatedly—what the heck was going to happen, like I had a direct line to all the *Jeopardy* questions.

It felt like we were in—rather than on—*Jeopardy* and I not only didn't know the questions to their answers, but I was sure my buzzer didn't work, even though I'd had no cause to use it, because— remember this part?—I didn't have the questions to answer their answers.

Which led to the dialogue I ended by saying I was going home.

That exchange started with Jennifer saying to me, "Elizabeth?"

"I don't know. Okay? I don't know," I said loudly. "Not any better than any of you. Just because I helped figure out what our station owner didn't want figured out doesn't mean I know what's going to happen. Not to mention, why aren't I asking you, Jennifer? You helped figure it out, too."

"I was going to ask if you want coffee. Dale's on a run to Hamburger Heaven," Jennifer said.

The room had gone still and everyone looked at me. *Everyone* in the KWMT-TV newsroom bullpen didn't constitute many people.

I deflated like a pinata hit by a tank. "No. Thank you, Jennifer. I, uh, think I'll go home now."

Before I snapped anyone else's head off.

That's when she pulled out the *somebody's coming to see you* ... threat? Bribe?

The Hamburger Heaven coffee Dale brought me was mostly gone when the interior set of double glass doors from outside opened and a young woman walked in.

She wore rugged jeans, work boots, a cowboy hat, and a winter jacket that would have told me she did ranch work even if the rest of her gear didn't. Ranchers rarely wear ski parkas, puff jackets, lined trench coats. Have never seen one in a car coat or overcoat. They favor tough, multilayered jackets with—most important—multiple pockets.

Her pockets displayed lumps and bumps of essentials kept handy for a job with unpredictable demands.

The KWMT-TV doors led into an open walkway, with the news-room bullpen to the left. The closest thing to a receptionist was Jennifer or a fellow news aide at the point where the hallway made a diagonal turn to the left, slicing out a space grandly called the break room.

Newcomers advanced well into the building before anyone greeted them. Most walked slowly or stopped to get their bearings.

This young woman went straight to Jennifer. No hesitation. Yet something was off about her walk. An old injury? Recent soreness?

Jennifer greeted her by name—Hailey Newhall.

What was the world coming to when Jennifer Lawton told me she didn't know who someone was when she did?

No...

Wait.

Boy, was I ever off my game.

I asked Jennifer *who* was coming to talk to me and she said *You wouldn't know her name.*

She was right. I'd never heard of Hailey Newhall until Jennifer said her name.

By the way they greeted each other, I knew they weren't friends. Not enemies, either.

Jennifer gestured to my desk, then escorted the young woman toward me.

I flashed back eighteen months to Tamantha Burrell standing by this desk and ordering me to clear her dad of murder.

Tamantha must be on my mind from a recent trip we'd taken. That was the only explanation for this connection, because in our first encounter, Tamantha had been a second-grader with wispy hair down the sides of a square face, intense brown eyes, and features not yet in tune with each other.

This young woman in her mid-to-late twenties had wide cheekbones, a strong chin, and slightly larger than average nose. Her features and thick hair with natural streaks of lighter and brighter amid glossy dark brown hit all the right notes.

Unlike Tamantha's faded plaid shirt and blue sweater, this woman picked jeans and shirt to fit precisely. Unless she was one of those women who walk into a store and find everything perfect for her.

Everything ... perfect. The words jangled discordantly even as they formed.

Because of her eyes.

Not their shape or color. Those fell under the perfect column.

What was in them.

Everything *not* perfect.

Jennifer introduced us, gave me a quick look, then left.

"I need your help," Hailey Newhall said.

That cut her connection with Tamantha, who favored orders over requests, as I'd come to know well.

"If you have an issue for *Helping Out!*..."

"I know it's not something you'd usually look into. But it's important to people around here and it doesn't make sense. Why would somebody—Anyway, I thought I'd try."

She looked at me. I waited for her to say more.

After several beats of stalemate, I gave in. Though I didn't break completely. I lobbed the ball back in her court.

"Try what?"

"To get you to find out who cut off my horse's tail."

Chapter Two

I SWALLOWED THE *Excuse me?* that jumped to my lips, but she might have seen it in my expression.

"It's not the first time there have been horse-tail thefts. Other areas of the country have been hit. Nobody sees a pattern. Not in the horses they hit or where or when. We had several here going on three years ago."

"Several instances of people cutting off horses' tails?"

"Yes."

"You said *thefts,* so they take the tail?"

"Of course they take the tail—as much as they've cut off," she said impatiently. "You think they'd cut off a horse's tail and leave it there?"

I'd never contemplated the question. Possibly because I'd never thought about a horse's tail being cut off. I had a vague idea those beer horses in the ads had short tails. Beyond that? Nothing.

"What do they do with the tail?"

"Sell it."

"There's a market for horse tails?"

"Several."

Questions piled up in my head. I stuck to the basics. "When did this happen to your horse?"

"Last night. You should come see him now. It's not far."

Tamantha rarely softened her edicts with *should* or *not far.*

The germ of an idea started in the back of my brain. And it did not involve me going to look at a horse without a tail.

"Have you called the sheriff's department?"

"No. Those other thefts here, they never found out who did it."

"You should call them, get it on the record." There'd been big changes at the sheriff's department in the year and a half I'd been here. "I can ask around, but it's your world. You know who to talk to—"

"I've talked to them. First thing I did. We've all talked to each other. Everybody knows Fred White and—"

"Fred—?"

"My horse. Fred White. Everybody knows him and they're almost as upset as I am—or pretends they are. Somebody not from our world could see things clearer."

She played dirty without even knowing it.

How many times had I said an outsider could see things more clearly under a lot of circumstances?

Now I was caught by my own argument.

Almost caught.

"I'll think about it."

She grimaced. "That's what parents say to kids right before they say no."

I wasn't *that* much older than her.

"Best I've got. But we can get the word out wider about this happening. We could do an interview tomorrow or—"

"No offense, but your *Helping Out!* pieces hold a long time before they're on air. No help."

It didn't offend me. For one thing it was mostly true.

What it did do was snap that germ of an idea into full bloom as a potential way to deal with this without committing myself.

After all, I had all these not-returned calls and messages to not answer. Busy, busy.

Besides, I'd heard the lineup for the A blocks of tonight's newscasts at five and ten o'clock. We could use something fresh and local not involving a KWMT-TV staffer and murder.

"Where's your horse now?"

"At our place."

She named a road I knew from passing it on the way to Michael Paycik's house.

The former NFL player and KWMT sports anchor had rented out the land since he bought the ranch a few years ago. Since he'd recently moved to Chicago, where he did sports on a network affiliate, he was looking to rent out the house.

Other thoughts connected to Mike, I sternly quashed.

They had nothing to do with this conversation.

Not even the part about not keeping him as updated on the station's situation as I knew he would want to be.

Instead, I calculated drive time and how long good daylight might last, while automatically asking, "Who's the *we* in *our place?*"

"My brother and me. My fiancé lives there, too."

"Uh-huh." I pitched my voice to reach the edge of the bullpen. "Jennifer, is anybody near—?"

"Jenks. On his way back from an assignment and he'll go right by there."

Diana Stendahl would have been my first choice, but Jenks was a more than decent cameraman.

"Is Audrey—?"

"Got her on the phone. Switched to you."

With Jennifer's last word, my phone rang.

The assignment editor was in a vehicle. I briefly outlined the story and said Jenks was in the vicinity and if Audrey didn't have another assignment for him…

"Hell, yeah. Tell him I'll get him in the A block. Thanks, Elizabeth."

She disconnected before I could say she should be the one to call him.

With Hailey Newhall watching me, I debated how to handle this— preferably by getting out of it—for two beats, which was all I had before Jennifer announced. "Got Jenks. Coming to you."

My phone rang again.

Jennifer and I needed to have a talk about her cutting my get-out-of-something time to nothing.

Me giving orders, including assignments, had been loaded with all sorts of baggage—think of a paper suitcase loaded willy-nilly with shatter-prone glass—under the recently-departed newsroom regime.

On the other hand, the regime *was* departed. And I'd be following Audrey's orders.

"Jenks, it's Elizabeth. Audrey's out of the newsroom, but she told me to tell you…"

Without any sign from him of glass-like fragility, we covered logistics, aided by a certain uptick of interest in his voice.

That call finished, I turned back to Hailey. "You need to leave now to meet our cameraman at your place. And call the sheriff's department."

"You're not coming?"

"No. I have another assignment." Actually, my class this evening, but no need to explain my off-hours life to her. "This will get your story on-air tonight. That way we should hear quickly if there have been other occurrences."

"You'll start investigating tomorrow?"

Pushy, but not compared to Tamantha, who wouldn't have settled for anything other than right that minute.

"We'll see."

Chapter Three

"YOU'RE GOING TO look into the theft of her horse's tail?" Jennifer asked before Hailey Newhall cleared the parking lot on her way to meet Jenks.

"We'll see." It worked on Hailey, so—

"What are you waiting for?"

"For starters, to hear what Jenks gets today and what we hear after the story runs. If horse-tail thefts are rampant in Cottonwood County—"

"They're not. I checked with the sheriff's department while you two were talking."

I gave a *See, you just strengthened my point* grimace. "—that would be a different matter from her horse being the only one recently affected— or afflicted. In fact, you can help by researching horse-tail thefts."

"On it."

Having distracted her with an assignment, I relaxed enough to ask, "How do you know Hailey Newhall?"

"I know who she is. She doesn't know me. She was years ahead of me in school. When I was going into middle school, she was like queen of everything. And if she wasn't queen, she was president. But she wasn't a—" She veered away from a word. "You know. She was even good at *that.*"

That I interpreted as meaning *nice.*

"She remembered your name," I pointed out.

Jennifer's face lit up. In this instant, I saw her as her younger self. Talented with and fascinated by computers, IT, communications—she had a worldwide network of friends and devotees. Yet not fitting in with a lot of her classmates. Looking at the older, popular girl who probably appeared to do it all with ease and aplomb. Simultaneously knowing it wasn't that simple, yet not then possessing the tools to defeat the resentment she could barely remember now.

"I guess she did. Maybe from my working here. Anyway, like I said, she wasn't mean. A few people didn't like her because she had all those positions and things and she *wasn't* mean. But nobody could be jealous of her after."

"After what?"

She gazed at me incredulously for a beat. "I forget you haven't been around forever. It *seems* like you've been here forever." She meant it in a good way. I was sure she did. "After her parents died.

"About two and a half years ago, her dad shot her mom, then killed himself. I'd started as a news aide here by then and it was a *huge* story. The biggest one until Deputy Redus disappeared in the fall. You know about that."

I did. Even though the disappearance happened before I arrived in Cottonwood County.

But my thoughts stuck with Hailey Newhall.

Poor kid.

That explained the eyes.

Those were my first reactions.

Followed by, *and now some jerk has cut off the tail of her horse.*

It fell way out of my area of expertise, but I supposed I *could* ask questions.

Besides, asking questions about the theft of a horse's tail had to be better than getting no answers to what was going to happen to the station, my fellow employees, and me.

✧ ✧ ✧ ✧

O.D. EVERETT EASILY kept me awake during class at Cottonwood County Community College, despite a failed nap making me more sleep-deprived.

Failed even though I'd been absolutely comfortable on my bed, under my favorite napping coverlet. Shoes kicked off, head on pillow, phone turned off, dog on the rug beside my bed.

Everything perfect.

The phrase flashed a picture of Hailey Newhall behind my eyes.

Everything perfect.

Except ... Someone stole her horse's tail and her father killed her mother, then himself.

My version of *everything perfect except* was much more mundane, with my brain going tickety-tickety-tickety.

Nearly every tick involved the newsroom of KWMT-TV and its fate.

Nearly every tick...

In case you didn't get my earlier references, the newsroom was abruptly and severely shorthanded. Add in chronic under-staffing and there weren't many bodies to fill gaps.

Yet we had risen to the challenge.

We is not the entire staff.

The handful of Thurston Fine loyalists did as little as humanly possible, an ongoing emulation of our former anchor's non-work ethic.

Another small group stuck strictly to their usual work schedule and duties, as if the extraordinary circumstances didn't touch them.

But several people I'd expected to fall into that category stepped up. Like the part-time producer I'd never done more than say hello to, who slid in next to me in an editing bay and took over to finish a wire piece for the Ten weeks ago, so I could get back to the special on the solved murder. I grinned at him. He grinned back.

And then there were the stalwarts, Jerry, Jenks, Walt, Leona, Dale, and, of course, Audrey, Jennifer, Diana, and me. Even Mike contributed a couple times from Chicago by writing copy in a pinch for us.

With the exception of Mike, these people stood in jeopardy of being kicked to the curb with a sale to this news-phobic network.

I swung my feet off the bed, earning a disapproving look from Shadow, and made another pass through all the people I'd contacted earlier.

With the same results.

Then I added one more call.

Michael Paycik.

He knew about the station's shorthandedness as a result of the solved murder. He didn't know about the sale of the station.

Why hadn't I told him?

Partly because he'd want to fix it for his former coworkers, for his hometown. It would hurt him that he couldn't.

Partly because the previous time we talked one-on-one—as opposed to speakerphone in the bullpen—he talked about soul-searching, important life decisions, and planning to come back here to talk to me in person.

Yes, I was chicken.

He'd spoken of his feelings before, including trying to persuade me to join him in Chicago, working for the same station.

I'd declined that proposal.

"Is this a bad time?" I asked him now, knowing I'd caught him in his newsroom preparing for broadcast.

"Nah," he lied.

"I'll talk fast. It's about KWMT. Val Heatherton is selling."

For most of my time here, I'd considered the Heathertons the poster family for absentee owners. Had never met Val. Had never met her son-in-law Craig Morningside, the nominal general manager. Now she'd sell, take her money, and forget the pesky TV station she inherited.

Mike whistled.

I explained. Then, because he hadn't said a word and maybe I wanted to cheer him up, I told him about a conversation with Wardell Yardley before this recent upheaval.

Along with being a familiar and impressive figure (not solely because of his wardrobe, although it didn't hurt) on the screens of viewers, Dell was a colleague, frequent tormentor, mostly friend, and sometimes purveyor of advice, little of which I took.

Dell's theory on promotions in the news business said those who go about their work in a professional and unhistrionic manner are least likely to be rewarded.

Yet he held out a shred of hope.

Mike latched onto the shred. "Hey, by Dell's theory, KWMT's management could be replaced by people who recognize initiative in a crisis and reward it."

I didn't say anything. First, trying to adjust to his cheerfulness in contrast to the mood at KWMT. Second, realizing it probably resulted from my not giving him the whole story. Third, feeling guilty for not giving him the whole story.

"Listen, Mike, why don't we talk later. After you finish for the night and—"

"I've still got time. You don't think KWMT will be that lucky?"

Not telling him the scope of the bad news was harder and harder. "I suppose it has to be more possible with new management than with Les and Thurston, but…"

"And ownership, since attitude starts at the top. Replacing the Heathertons will be a step up."

It just became impossible to not tell him.

"Mike, I've looked at the ownership group in line to buy us and it's bad. They close news operations. Every time. Then they pay the remaining employees with prayer. In fact, prayer is the only hope their employees have of surviving."

"That's bad."

His response tore me in two between being ticked at him, because he sounded almost cheerful, and suspicious, because he sounded almost cheerful.

Mike was making good money, adding to an impressive nest egg he'd accumulated and multiplied during his NFL years. But I didn't believe he'd become so detached from KWMT's people or pay scale.

"Mike, I'm not sure you understand how—"

I heard sounds on the other end, while someone talked to him.

"Damn. Sorry, Elizabeth. Now I do have to go. Listen, tonight's not good. But I'll talk to you tomorrow. Promise."

So, I arrived at the Contributions of Native Americans class with an additional row of bags scalloped beneath my eyes.

I kept expecting code talkers from World War II as a topic, but like any good storyteller, O.D. made his audience wait.

Tonight and during previous sessions, he'd judiciously sprinkled in tales of items like canoes, corn, hammocks, lacrosse, and pain relievers. He'd explored the use of plants for medical aids, including syringes and contraceptives, then added that Iroquois and other tribes used a bear gut with a bird quill as a nipple for a baby bottle.

In an earlier class, students spouted out geographic names from Native American languages, compiling an impressive list. I contributed several from my Illinois roots, including, of course, Chicago, Peoria, Kankakee, Waukegan, and Illinois itself. In each class since, students added more.

Tonight, though, I had something else to mention to O.D.

Two other students and I accompanied O.D. to the main doors, then paused there to wrap up our conversations before going outside. One student, Paytah, was O.D.'s grandson. The other was Aleek, a young man studying for advanced EMT certification.

"If I miss any remaining classes, know it's not by choice," I told O.D. "I'm enjoying it. But we're shorthanded at the station."

"It is not apparent to your viewers. To turn on the TV and watch the local news is better now than ... before," he concluded with a subtle twinkle.

"Thank you." I agreed, but it was good to hear it. "Folks are stepping up. Like Jenks' story on horse-tail thefts."

As long as I hadn't been able to sleep, I'd watched the Five. Jenks let his camera do most of the reporting ... and Hailey Newhall do the talking.

Despite Leona D'Amato's hatred for the anchor chair, our part-time *society* reporter did a fine job. As long as the rest of us wedged in hard news, which she hated even more than anchoring.

None of my three current companions responded to my horse-tail thefts overture, so I nudged the topic along. "I'd never heard of horse tails being stolen. Is it common?"

A new element dropped into their silence, rippling out with significance I didn't understand.

None of them looked at each other or at me. Aleek said,

"Wouldn't say common."

Without warning, but unhurriedly, O.D. Everett raised a hand in brief farewell and pushed out the door.

That was his way—not a lot of easing into or out of a conversation. Yet this had a different feel to it.

I looked at Paytah and Aleek. Their closed-off expressions informed me they weren't going to explain the difference. Sometimes I remembered what an outsider I was.

"Suppose I should get going," I offered in a brilliant segue.

Both dropped their heads in the smallest confirmation they'd heard me.

"Good thing about the horse-tail theft was Thurston Fine didn't do the story," Aleek said.

But he said it after I'd pushed open the outer door, so I didn't know if it was meant for me to hear.

Nor did I know if I was supposed to hear Paytah's response. "That's the good thing about every story now."

DAY TWO

SATURDAY

Chapter Four

SHADOW DESPERATELY WANTED to get free to greet the man standing in wan morning sunlight outside my back door.

Before Shadow recognized the man as Tom Burrell, my dog's desperation had been to get free so he could protect me. Now he wanted to get free to see Tom.

Because I had him wrapped in a bear hug.

Sort of.

Like a small bear trying to hug a grizzly, who thought the small bear had lost its mind yet remained determined not to hurt the small bear, even as the grizzly did its best to get free.

I didn't mind that this standoff delayed Tom coming inside.

Not because I didn't like the lanky rancher, but because I did.

How much and in what way ... Those made Hamlet's *To be or not to be* quandary rank with adding tomato or blue cheese to your burger order from Hamburger Heaven.

Shadow heaved a sigh and went limp, apparently deciding that was the only way to deal until the small bear—I—regained its mind. He closed his eyes.

Without looking up at the man outside my back door, I said, "You can come in now, Tom."

Unhurried, Tom opened the door, entered, and leaned against a section of wall.

He looked entirely at ease, even though we had unfinished business ... that I was in no condition to address.

"What are you doing?" Tom asked quietly.

In the same tone, I said, "Working to get Shadow to relax."

He looked over the dog, then to me. I decided to watch Shadow.

"I think your work is done, Elizabeth. What about you?"

"What about me what?"

"Relaxing. You look tired."

Temptation to snap out *Thanks for noticing* died. Not only was he right—I couldn't avoid every mirrored surface—I *was* tired.

"I was watching dog training videos late last night."

"Because...?" he invited.

"I want to be a good owner for Shadow."

"You two have done fine. You don't need videos."

"You don't because you've had dogs at the ranch. I do."

To prevent my neck from spasming, I'd lowered my head, which put my mouth next to a particularly fluffy portion of Shadow's ruff.

"You said your family had dogs when you were a kid."

"Yeah, but Mom did all the training. If you haven't had a dog as an adult, you don't know what you're doing wrong. Especially a rescue. The dog's already been through trauma and now he's stuck with *me*. After you rescue a dog, then you have to *heal* him—or her, or they for non-binary dogs."

Slowly, I released Shadow. He opened one eye. So, not asleep. He rotated his head to see Tom, but didn't otherwise move as I stood.

"Non-binary dogs," Tom repeated. "How many videos did you watch last night?"

"A lot. Including ones about feeling their feelings and by doing so letting them release those feelings, especially fears and anxieties."

He looked at Shadow. I knew what Tom was thinking. He was thinking this dog didn't mess in the house, destroy my belongings, fight with other dogs, lunge at people (except bad guys), bark his head off, cower or shudder in a corner, or any other behaviors on those videos. But how did I know if Shadow didn't suffer from *hidden* fears and anxieties I could rid him of if I connected with him better.

I did not say that aloud.

Tom Burrell means ... a lot ... to me. Exactly what variety of *a lot*, isn't clear. Especially since, the same day I learned the station was for sale with news-killers the likely buyers, he told me he couldn't stay away from me.

And then he'd pretty much stayed away from me.

There had been brief greetings when Tamantha, Mrs. P, and I left on a weekend girls' trip, then on our return. We did *not* talk about *I can't stay away* with that audience.

He and Tamantha continued visiting Shadow—mercy missions while I worked so much. But to me, not a word.

Until now.

"Elizabeth, you're doing fine with Shadow. You're worried about something you can't do anything about—and can't find videos on TV stations sold out from under its employees—so you find something you can do something about *and* watch videos on.

"Or," he continued, "is watching dog training videos all night letting you avoid something else?"

His expression didn't change, yet I knew Tom had just shifted from KWMT and my dog, to whatever the heck was going on between him and me. Which tangled quickly with his concerns for his young daughter Tamantha and her expectations.

It didn't get any less knotty because of Mike Paycik and whether there might be anything between the former KWMT sports anchor and me.

Or *could have been anything* if Mike weren't in Chicago, climbing the ladder to success. Or possibly *could have been anything* if I'd gone with him to Chicago, as he'd wanted.

See what I mean about complicated?

Aloud I said, "Maybe it is about the station being sold."

The lines around Tom's eyes folded deeper in amusement.

He said, "Any news about the sale?"

"None. How's that for irony? No news about a news operation being sold to a company that tosses out people who've made it their life's work to try to be fair and accurate and get vital information to the populace. Toss them out into the cold—and I do mean cold, since

Wyoming doesn't fool around when it's November and—"

Tom gripped my forearm. "Elizabeth. Go get changed. I can't do much about your lack of sleep, but I'm taking you for breakfast. When was the last time you had a real meal?"

"I'm going to lunch at Linda's today." Linda Caswell, one of Cottonwood County's prominent citizens, was a mutual friend.

"That's future. I asked when was the last time—No, don't bother—"

I appreciated the reprieve, because I couldn't remember. There'd been the Hamburger Heaven coffee yesterday afternoon and cookies on the drive to class ... Tom wouldn't count them as sustenance, though I did.

"—no matter when, it was too long ago. We're going to breakfast. Now, go."

Only after I was upstairs, did I assess my attire. Pajama tops and bottoms did cover me adequately. Topped by an ancient sweater to my knees for when I'd let Shadow out. Accessorized by bulky socks and my hair in a listing scrunchie. All topped by a coating of dog hair.

It was a miracle the man didn't swoon at my feet.

✧ ✧ ✧ ✧

WHEN TOM, STANDING in my back yard several weeks ago, said he couldn't stay away from me, that was a change. He'd earlier said he was done dating me because it confused Tamantha.

Before I could ask him about *can't stay away*, an acquaintance arrived with the news about the station being sold.

Tom gave a crooked smile and said he'd see me later.

I knew logically he left because he knew I'd instantly gone into journalist mode.

Not so logically, it made me think of how, after the first murder I'd helped unravel, Thomas David Burrell showed up at my then-front door, kissed me, then walked away.

He wasn't getting away with that twice.

If he'd stuck around in my back yard those weeks ago, I'd have pinned him down with questions so perceptive and probing he'd have explained exactly what he felt, wanted, and thought.

And while I was at it, those questions would have clarified everything I felt, wanted, and thought.

What would I have asked to accomplish that?

The best questions flow out of the moment. In other words, I don't know.

Possibly, *What the hell, Burrell?*

Maybe the station's future wasn't the only reason I hadn't been sleeping.

And now?

This was not the place—Tom had chosen the Haber House Hotel dining room for breakfast—to discuss *can't stay away.*

Even the few people who didn't stop by and say hello, watched us closely.

Between hellos, Tom said, "Whatever's going on, you can't take it out of your hide."

I was chewing on bacon, so I couldn't raise the possibility of taking something out of his hide as an alternative.

Bacon swallowed, I parted my lips, caught sight of a woman I recognized as a fellow shopper at the Sherman Supermarket, and closed them.

"Not sure this is the place to talk about that," I said, letting him think I meant KWMT.

He slewed his eyes to one side, taking in the fellow shopper. "Right. Something else you want to talk about?"

"Going to Fort Phil Kearny with your daughter and Mrs. Parens."

That weekend had been my one respite—if you can call it that—in these weeks of unanswered questions and overwork.

"I've heard a considerable bit from Tamantha, but I'd be interested in your take."

"What I want to talk about is how you held up, letting her out of your sight. Two whole nights."

Tom's protectiveness is why I hadn't thought the trip would happen. A while back, he'd let her go to an event in Cheyenne for top students, but those kids had more security than the vice president of the United States.

Sure, Tamantha had a will of granite, but where do you think she got it from?

I should have known the trip would happen once Mrs. Parens decided it should.

And Tom wasn't the only string she pulled.

The site normally operated during the summer, with limited May and October hours. That didn't stop Emmaline Parens. We were slated for a personal tour of the grounds and related sites, plus a visit with a descendant of Sioux warriors who shared oral history of the fights against those at the fort.

"I let her out of my sight," he said. "Overnights and—"

"*Two nights*," I emphasized.

"—staying with my sister."

I scoffed at those offerings. "Where you could get to her in an hour. But this was hours away and with only Mrs. P and me."

"There are no two people I'd trust more."

I snorted. Very ladylike.

I gave him my edited account of the trip and ate, until noticing the time.

As we headed to our separate vehicles in the parking lot, he said, "I know you're going to the station and you'll work all day, but you need to—"

"You say how tired I look one more time and—"

He interrupted with a laugh and we waved good-bye.

Only as I headed east toward the station did I wonder what he'd been doing in town this morning.

Chapter Five

DIANA STENDAHL DROPPED into the chair beside my desk. She's KWMT-TV's best cameraperson and my good friend.

My desk chair does not turn in the direction of where she'd sat. To face her without neck-twisting damage, I had to make a three-quarters turn in the opposite direction.

"Don't get too comfortable," I warned her. "I've been summoned to Mrs. P's. She didn't say why. Any ideas?"

Her message instructing me to come to her house in O'Hara Hill awaited me when I arrived. For a second, the presence of a message— any message—fluffed up my spirits.

I wondered if Mike's Aunt Gee knew I was coming to Mrs. P's today.

The two women, next door neighbors through long widowhoods, had both a close relationship and a deep rivalry.

Nobody knew Cottonwood County better. Emmaline Parens from a long career as a teacher and principal, Gisella Decker from years as lead dispatcher for the sheriff's department.

"No idea," Diana said about this summons. Then she added, "How disappointing."

"I know. Still no news."

I might have been talking about the response to Jenks' story on the horse-tail theft. There *had* been outrage, relayed to me by the on-duty news aide, but no word of another horse subjected to that mistreatment. Which meant no fodder for a follow-up.

But we both knew I meant news about the sale of the station.

I'd called my mother, to check that nobody in Mel's immediate family had died or gone into intensive care—the only two explanations I could think of for him not calling back. Though even with intensive care I would have expected a message.

Maybe not if *Mel* had gone into intensive care.

Mom eliminated that possibility. She'd talked to Mel's wife the day before and all was well. She promised she'd find out why he wasn't calling back.

I felt a twinge of guilt for siccing my mother on Mel. The twinge passed.

"News on the station's status would be nice," Diana said, "but I meant you."

"Me? I'm disappointing?"

"I heard you and Tom were out for breakfast."

I produced a cautious, "Yeah." Clearly, she was making a point.

"Separate vehicles, but that's not definitive," she said.

She raised her brows, waiting for me to get what she was not saying.

I raised my brows back.

She exhaled noisily.

"I had hoped," she said after replenishing her oxygen, "when I heard you two were out for breakfast that it was a follow-up to being together the night before." Her point hit me directly between the eyes. "But I can see by your face it was just breakfast."

"Oh, for heaven's sake." I might well have said something less genteel. We were, after all, in a newsroom, surroundings not known for restrained language. "If—which we aren't. And won't. Because Tamantha. Plus ... other things."

"And other people," she supplied with a spurious air of helpfulness.

Her oblique reference to Mike wasn't helpful.

"We have far more important—and pertinent—things to talk about."

"Can't think of anything more important and not much more pertinent."

"The selling of the station."

"You said there was no news, so what is there to talk about?"

I hate being defeated by logic.

Casting about for a topic far, far away from whether Tom Burrell and I spent the night together—which we didn't, wouldn't—

Find another topic.

"I got a strange vibe last night from O.D. Everett, his grandson, Paytah, and another guy from class," I said. "They'd said the news was better without Thurston, then I mentioned Jenks' story on the horse-tail theft. They got silent and distant, then O.D. left quickly."

"Oh."

I grimaced. "Great. Now I've got you going all knowing while not explaining a thing. That's exactly what they did. Next, you'll leave abruptly."

"I will have to leave abruptly. I have an assignment. But I'll explain first. They might have felt you were saying more than you intended. Last time there were horse-tail thefts, they were accompanied by rumblings in some quarters that tribes were responsible. Several of the tribes' crafts use horse hair."

"Jenks' story never mentioned tribes or crafts."

"Didn't have to. Everyone around here—most everyone—" Her correction acknowledged me as the exception. "—knows it. It was understood, the tendency of some to blame tribes built into whatever Jenks reported."

That was one of the frustrations of reporting. The audience came with all sorts of biases—largely unrecognized by themselves, though they saw other people's fast enough—and whatever tint their bias-colored lenses presented, they shaded anything and everything reported accordingly.

"Jenks' story mentioned the horse's tail hair can be used for bow strings for musical instruments. Why not blame them?"

"Uh-huh. Heard about any rogue cellists around here?"

"Not that I know of. Besides, how would you know if a cellist went rogue? Or if they were using a bow with stolen horse hair."

"Same thing holds true for crafts done with horse hair. Tough to track the provenance of the materials. On the other hand, might be easier to spot tail extensions for show horses."

I side-eyed her. "Not easier for me. And I'm not going to start learning. Hanging around the rear end of strange horses does not appeal. Especially since I think you're pulling my leg."

"I'm not."

"Tail extensions for horses? Really?"

"Really. Not working horses. As I said, show horses. Also mane extensions and forelock extensions."

"Forelock...? You've shattered my illusions. I feel like my brother Rob did when he discovered women dye their hair and add, ah, enhancements to their figures. I'll never trust again."

"Sorry. We won't talk about Santa until you've recovered."

"Thank you. Okay, so crafts, bows for musical instruments, extensions, which have got to be expensive. I couldn't believe it when Jenks said horse hair can sell for more than five hundred dollars a pound, higher for light hair."

"I can. It can take a couple years for a horse to grow back its tail. That's why you don't find horse owners volunteering hair. Although I've heard of donations to a horse with a condition, but it's a little from a lot of horses. Not cutting off a tail. That can change the horse. They get depressed."

"Vanity?"

"Nature trains species that looking a particular way makes you a prime candidate to reproduce. That's deep in the DNA. Also, for a horse, the tail expresses emotions—interested, irritated, angry, curious, excited, alarmed. These thefts take away communication. Plus there's the flyswatter aspect."

"Now that makes sense."

"Also, it must feel like an attack to the horse. Think how you'd react if someone came up behind you and cut off your hair. Previously friendly and curious horses become standoffish and wary."

"What about those horses in beer commercials? They had short tails," I said.

"Draft horses. The argument for docked tails for horses drawing carriages or wagons was they couldn't get tangled in the harness. Supposedly, horses were less likely to bolt, so safer for humans, too.

"Other arguments said long-tailed mares could rub and cause lesions on stallions mating with them. Never heard anyone who'd *seen* lesions, just that it could happen. I say, wrap the mare's tail. Besides, if stallions who were free to choose for centuries had skipped long-tailed mares, there wouldn't be long tails.

"Tail-docking's not in favor now," she said. "Veterinary groups are against it and it's outlawed or restricted in a lot of countries. Sure can't see somebody docking their horse's tail in the dead of night then reporting it as theft."

"Hey, I didn't suggest Hailey Newhall did that. Just asking questions. Did Jess and Gary's horses get hit in that previous rash of thefts?"

"No. But the horse of a girl Jess is in drill team with had a section taken."

"Elizabeth," Audrey called from her desk, "is the lead-in to the recap on the California wildfires air ready?"

"Five minutes." I said to Diana, "One section? They left the rest for flyswatting?"

"More likely they abruptly realized standing behind a horse's rear legs and sawing away at its tail wasn't their best idea. That horse is a kicker."

She said that with considerable satisfaction.

AIR READY IS a multipurpose phrase in broadcast journalism.

Some use it to refer to the talent—also called talking heads by the production folks. In that case, air ready is whether reporters about to go live or anchors in studio are prepared to broadcast.

It can also mean an entire package is complete, set to put on the air at any time. Or it can be used for the component parts of a package. "That's an air-ready script." "The graphics are air ready."

It can also be a threat, as in, "You have five minutes to get the California wildfires lead-in air ready."

I made it.

So Audrey did not object when—after another round of fruitless messages—I opted to head to Mrs. Parens' house early.

Even reporters inured to the frustrations of unreturned messages have limits.

Golfers get the yips, mostly involuntary wrist jerks when putting. Baseball and other sports borrow the term. Gymnasts call it the twisties when they lose the ability to orient in the air. Quarterbacks get happy feet, dancing around anticipating a sack instead of focusing on the throw.

It's not the same for reporters, though equally crazy-making.

My buddy Dell—while maintaining it never, ever happens to him—calls it a personal blackout.

If you've expanded your calls to connections of connections of the people you need to talk to, then checked and re-checked your devices are working, plus looked up symptoms of your phone and computer being jammed, you've experienced a personal blackout.

I might be experiencing a personal blackout.

I made a quick call—which *was* answered. Yes, Hailey Newhall would meet me at her property.

I could pretend I had something semi-useful to do before seeing Mrs. Parens.

Chapter Six

HAILEY NEWHALL'S HORSE was kept at a property with a barn, several outbuildings, and fenced corrals. Those were on one side of a cottonwood-lined creek, with a shoebox-shaped house as an afterthought on the other side.

It took me a while in Wyoming to adjust to not seeing mostly red barns, with a few white ones thrown in, as I did growing up in Illinois.

For an elementary school project on why barns were red, I learned New England farmers in the 1700s applied a homemade varnish the sun turned red. By the time paint became readily available, the tradition was set. Plus, red paint cost less.

In Wyoming, they largely left barns unpainted.

Farm fences in Illinois included white or black painted, unfinished wood, barbed wire. Wyoming goes mostly for barbed wire and unfinished fence posts used as-is from nature.

In Illinois, fencing and buildings stripped of paint and staunchness by weather and time signal desertion.

Spot a similar scene in Wyoming and it could be the busy hub of a thriving operation, a getaway for an eccentric billionaire, or—yeah—someplace deserted.

This property had a worn, hunkered down, appearances-don't-matter air.

On the other hand, the horse in the pasture closest to the entry road, appeared sleek and well cared for.

Also wary.

Though I couldn't give the horse my full attention as I drove in, because a once-white pickup was exiting at the same time. It hit the pickup trifecta—old, dirty, rusty, with bonus points for dents on the back quarter panel and one mismatched tire.

I caught a snapshot of the driver—high school boy, sharing enough attitude with Hailey to guess they were related.

His face was taut with underlying tension—like a low-grade fever, rather than a raging hundred and five.

He sure wasn't on edge about driving, because he swung past me with the casual disregard for close quarters of someone familiar with the ranch road's potholed surface.

When I got out of my SUV and walked slowly toward the fenced enclosure, the horse sidled to the far side, keeping me in sight.

He had a reddish coat I'd call chestnut, but much lighter mane and tail—from what I could see.

I wondered if the lighter color made his hair more valuable.

Hailey came out of a shed and joined me at the fence. The horse didn't come any closer, but some of the tension in its stance eased. I caught a slightly better look at its unevenly truncated tail.

"His coloration's striking," I said after succinct hellos. "I didn't know palominos could be so red."

"You don't know much about horses." A statement, not a question.

"I'm learning to ride." Although my informal lessons with Tom went on hiatus along with our dating.

"Learning," she repeated, as if I'd said I was learning to breathe. "He's not a palomino. He's a flaxen chestnut. They have the blonde mane and tail."

I didn't ask if that increased the value to horse-tail thieves—I didn't think she'd take well to the monetary consideration.

She turned toward me, challenging. "Are you really interested in pursuing this? Or—"

She bit it off. As if I couldn't fill in —*are you here to quit?*

I answered words spoken and unspoken. "I don't know. No one's contacted the station about being victimized recently. Unless you've heard—?"

"No."

"Have you talked to the sheriff's department?"

"Yes. A sergeant sent a deputy out. Richard Alvaro."

Interesting. Alvaro was as close to a protégé as I could imagine Shelton having. Did sending him mean Shelton took this seriously? Maybe. Or he might have wanted to give the young deputy something to handle on his own or a break from the office or something less benign. No telling with Shelton.

Not privy to my deconstructing Sergeant Wayne Shelton's motives, Hailey went on. "He knew what he was talking about."

As opposed to me. Yeah, I got it.

For someone who'd come to me for help, she was not scoring points with her attitude.

That didn't mean I'd bail.

There was the journalist's creed to uphold—*Try to find out everything*—and its corollary of *Whatever someone doesn't want you to know is the best stuff to find out.*

"Anything else you've thought of to share with me?"

"We found something I'd missed before. A scrap of fabric— denim—caught in the top of the fence. We spotted it while we were putting up a camera in that corner of the shed roof." Following the direction of the jerk of her head, I caught the glint of a lens. Not hidden, but not glaringly obvious. "I gave the fabric to Deputy Alvaro. Don't know what good it will do, unless he makes suspects present all their jeans to look for holes."

She did sarcasm quite well.

Recalling Diana's comment about one victim of the earlier thefts, I asked, "Would your horse kick someone cutting off his tail?"

"Probably. Maybe," she amended. "Hard to know how he'd react out here alone."

"You put up the camera yourself?" I shaded my eyes to scan the roofline.

"Multiple cameras. With motion sensors. My brother helped," she said shortly. The kid who'd passed me? Definitely some of the same tension as I'd seen in his face now showed in hers. "He helped me connect them. If this ever happens again, we won't be wondering who could have done it. Don't put it on-air that we've put up cameras. I don't want to scare somebody away."

"More likely they'd destroy the cameras."

Grimly, she said, "That would freak out Fred White even more. You can see how unsettled he is. Was even that way with Gavin—" Presumably her brother, possibly the guy I'd seen leaving. "—and the deputy. Even edgy with me awhile."

All of whom knew a whole lot more about horses than I did. I got it.

"I've got to go, Hailey. Stopped on my way to an appointment in O'Hara Hill."

"Why bother? You didn't do much."

I had an odd flash she was pushing me as a sort of test. It didn't make sense, but I'd learned not to ignore flashes. They weren't infallible, but useful often enough to respect them.

"Wanted to see the scene," I said mildly, purposefully leaving off *of the crime.*

She raised her hands in a modified flap, pivoted on a moderately worn boot heel, and walked away.

"Bye, Hailey," I called after her.

No response.

Back in my car, even though I'd left the phone on while talking to Hailey, I immediately checked for messages. None magically appeared.

Nor were there any awaiting me when I called the station.

I couldn't have logically expected any, since I'd left my phone number as contact.

Logic disappeared during a personal blackout.

Like a bookend to my arrival, a pickup truck drove in as I pulled out.

They were mismatched bookends, though. With this one only a couple of days away from a shine and no more than a year from the dealer.

The drivers also constituted a mismatch, beyond both being male and wearing ball caps. This guy, not a teenager, but difficult to pin, slowed to a crawl and looked at me closely.

That gave me a chance to see he had dark hair and beard. The hair longer and the beard more neatly trimmed than usual in Cottonwood County. Above sunglasses dropped artfully down his nose, dark eyebrows stood out, even against a fading tan. They tilted up toward the middle, giving him a distinctive look.

I'd remember him if I saw him again.

Considering his study, he could say the same of me.

Chapter Seven

EMMALINE PARENS WELCOMED me warmly but with restraint. She was not a woman to gush.

She did not even glance toward the next driveway.

I already had.

Gisella Decker's car was not there. Most likely at work as dispatcher at the Sheriff's Department outpost in O'Hara Hill.

My being here would require some sort of evening-up in their complex and unspoken scorekeeping. It was times like this when I really missed Mike, because he took the heat off me. Especially with his aunt.

Times like this—and other times—I really missed him.

Mrs. P ushered me into the front room of her small house. It could double as a museum, but she ran it as a classroom. Class photos covered a full wall and progressed down another. The rest displayed photos and maps illustrating the history of Wyoming.

She gestured me to a straight-backed wooden chair—no cushion—and sat in another, her posture making the chair look like a slacker.

She came right to the point.

"I understand Hailey Newhall has sought your assistance in a puzzling matter."

I understand was Mrs. P-speak for knowing every detail and nuance of not only what we'd each said, but what we'd thought.

Notice that, to the public, I had no connection to the horse-tail thefts. Jenks did the story. I appeared nowhere in it.

But Mrs. P didn't need TV news to know what was going on in

Cottonwood County.

"You're going to tell me you know why people cut off horses' tails in order to steal them?"

I was kidding. Mostly. It wouldn't completely shock me if she did know.

"I do not have an explanation for that behavior. There have been points at which cutting off—or docking, as it is more properly called—a horse's tail became popular. Indeed, *de rigueur* in some circles, especially in England and with particular breeds. Some historians maintain the English wanted their horses to look different from French horses. You are familiar with the painter George Stubbs, who rendered anatomically correct equine subjects?"

Couldn't say we were best buddies, but I recalled paintings of gleaming horses, posed in profile, often with a groom or owner holding the reins. "Sure."

A certain look in her eyes told me to get comfortable.

"The history of art has known any number of those who specialized in one subject or style. In this region, as might be expected, the favored subjects involved the landscape, the indigenous people, the wildlife, the ranching life.

"In many instances, the most widely known artists merely visited our region, while residing in the east, including Frederic Remington and Thomas Moran. One exception was Charles Russell, who worked as a cowboy before making his living as an artist. Are you familiar with early female artists of the western region?"

"Georgia O'Keefe."

Not bad for a pop quiz.

Mrs. P's reproachful look stopped my self-congratulations cold.

I said, "She has to qualify as Western from her years in New Mexico. So what's your objection? O'Keefe's not early enough?"

She didn't answer directly. "There is a historical myopia that afflicts the majority of the population." She amended her statement. "A historical myopia that afflicts the majority of the population that evinces an interest in historical topics. That can be a distressingly small percentage of the wider populace."

Having forthrightly faced distress, she continued with her usual calm. "This myopia causes members of any generation to see the accomplishments of its generation clearly, while their view of previous generations becomes increasingly blurred."

"Not early enough," I muttered.

She pretended not to hear me.

"That applies to gender as well as period. It could qualify as speculation, although not hyperbole, to say that women numbered among the cave painters. Females certainly have been creators of art, as well as utility, in textiles and in pottery. Logic guides us to a likelihood that women also created in other media.

"In the world of painting, we have written history of women in the mid-1500s achieving the level of fame that preserved their works so they can be verified as those of an individual creator. For example, Flemish Renaissance painter Caterina van Hemessen was known for female portraits starting in the 1540s. Or consider Sofonisba Anguissola."

I could honestly say I had never in my life considered Sofonisba Anguissola.

Could say it.

Didn't.

Not to Mrs. Parens.

She continued. "She was a child at the time Caterina van Hemessen was active. Sofonisba Anguissola grew up in an aristocratic family without means in Cremona, Italy. One of her portraits caught the eye of King Phillip II of Spain, who called her to his court when she was in her early twenties. However, she was not there officially as an artist, but as a lady-in-waiting tasked with teaching the queen to draw."

She nodded and I realized I'd grimaced at Sofonisba being constrained with the lady-in-waiting job.

"Furthermore, it was not seen as fitting that she be paid for her paintings because of her nobility. Presumably gifts of appreciation were sufficient to support her, because she lived into her nineties.

"Another Italian woman, Lavinia Fontana, born in Bologna at approximately the time Sofonisba Anguissola went to the Spanish court, was not burdened with nobility. The daughter of a painter, she is generally considered within written history to be the first professional female artist. Her painting supported her family and she worked through eleven pregnancies."

"*Eleven?* Her husband must have really liked her painting. Or... Was there a husband?"

"He was her agent and some say her assistant. When they moved to Rome, she obtained commissions from popes and the nobility, which could be viewed as proof of his ability in what today might be termed marketing, as well as proof of her talent, of course.

"For these women to be included in written history, which frequently demonstrates multiple forms of myopia, is both an achievement and a logical indicator that many more women painted before and during their time.

"As I noted, the preservation of an artist's works, the recording of them, and the passing of them into wider knowledge has been a particular obstacle for women. Even when not born to an upper-class family, a woman was not considered womanly if she sold her creations. They might stay within a family or be presented to friends. If they were preserved at all, it was often without recognition of the painter.

"That handicap continued across time and geography. However, looking at the western United States, we do have records of women artists' achievements in judged shows, especially in San Francisco, starting in the 1850s. No doubt that represents a small percentage of the women painting in that time.

"Beyond the period's conventions, women in our region worked under additional handicaps. Consider a woman then living in Wyoming or Montana facing the twin difficulties of procuring training and supplies."

"Must have been tough," I said.

She assessed me with a look, then said, briskly, "You know of the trappers who came to what is now our state of Wyoming well before the push of what we flatter ourselves to call civilization?"

I perked up. This I knew.

"Jim Bridger," I said promptly. Then, to show off a bit, I added,

"John Colter. Left the Lewis and Clark Expedition on the return trip and came across—among other things—an area now in Park County named Colter's Hell after him."

She nodded, but didn't waste time complimenting my knowledge.

"James Bridger and John Colter were, indeed, among those men. During that period a limited number of another type of man came to this region, seeking to thrill themselves with a hunt unlike those they previously experienced, as later generations embarked on safari in Africa. In this region, they often organized these hunts with such a man as Bridger as their guide. These wealthy hunters sought trophies, both of the animals they killed and of experiences they could expound on once they returned to the East.

"One such wealthy hunter ventured to our region and was said to have formed a liaison with a Native American woman associated with his guides. He became quite enamored with the woman, leaving her with a token of his affection—" Mrs. P indulging in almost-sarcasm? This wealthy hunter better hope she never encountered him in the afterlife. "—in the form of a daughter, born after his departure.

"He never returned. Indeed, he died while that daughter remained a child. What was quite unusual for that time was he made a bequest to the woman and his daughter in his will. That bequest included three horses and a considerable store of art supplies. The woman was renowned for her skill in the more customary art of the tribe. What he provided the child were supplies from his world.

"According to what I have been told, his daughter never used them. But her daughter did. That daughter's name was Carey Maight."

"Oh." The sound came out without my giving it the okay.

It appeared to please Mrs. P.

"Have you encountered her work?" she asked.

"There's a painting at the Western Frontier Life Museum, by Carey Maight. It doesn't say any more about the artist or painting, including who donated it." I'd never asked the museum curator, Clara Atwood, about it. As if, as long as I didn't mention it to anyone else, it belonged only to me.

It had taken me a while to pin down why it appealed so strongly.

In other places I've been, air is largely remarkable only when it conveys an extreme—steamy with heat, sharp with cold, smelly with garbage, aromatic with perfume. Air can even be used as a metaphor for nothingness, for something easily dismissed.

Not in Wyoming.

Sure, it can be steamy, sharp, smelly, aromatic. Even when it's none of those things, though, it makes itself known.

The wind, absolutely.

But a more subtle movement, too. It ... it *breathes* for lack of a better explanation. It comes over the Rockies from the west and expands across the Big Horn Basin like it revels in finally spreading out and taking up as much room as it wants.

This breathing gives a sense of unending movement, even as the mountains, the land give a sense of never-ending stillness. Neither tells the truth. Yet, together, they get at something integral to Wyoming.

That small painting by Carey Maight hanging in the museum caught this as no other representation I'd seen.

Mrs. P said, "I stipulated that there be no further information on the plaque when I donated Midnight on Circle Creek."

"You donated it?" I repeated it because I doubted I'd have given up that painting if I'd owned it.

"I did. It was given to my parents. They bequeathed it to me."

"Did you know the artist?"

"To my regret, only in passing. My parents did, however, and held Carey Maight's abilities in high regard." Without changing anything about her upright posture, Mrs. Parens gave the impression of releasing her shoulders. "You have quite different things on your mind now, do you not, Elizabeth."

Not a question.

"You mean someone hacking at Hailey Newhall's horse's tail?" I didn't give her a chance to answer. "Without other people being affected or other developments, there's nowhere for the story to go."

"Isn't there."

Again, not a question.

Before I could respond, she added "What of other matters on your mind?"

Finally, a real question.

"The station. I don't know any more than you do." Possibly less.

"You must be patient, Elizabeth. Sometimes you must wait for the answers to come to you."

✧ ✧ ✧ ✧

IF DELIVERING THAT message had been Mrs. Parens' purpose in my visit, I didn't think much of it.

Journalists don't wait for answers to come to them. They go after them the way a rodeo roper goes after a calf galloping out of the chute—chase, rope, bring to the ground, tie-down.

Then raise our hands over our heads to signal to the judges we're done and invite the crowd's admiration. Yes, I was thinking of Wardell Yardley.

I did my best to hide any of that sentiment from Mrs. Parens, pegging my departure to the driving time to reach Linda Caswell's ranch for lunch.

Like Tom, Mrs. P knew Linda well. Without the three of them, ninety percent of the activities, committees, and events in the county would shrivel up.

On the surface, Mrs. Parens accepted my departure with complete understanding and wished me an enjoyable meal with Linda. Yet something didn't sit right.

It struck me halfway through the drive that Mrs. P had steered me away from further discussion of Carey Maight.

A surprising impression, considering it followed the impression she'd led me there in the first place.

✧ ✧ ✧ ✧

ON IMPULSE, I detoured to the Western Frontier Life Museum in Sherman.

The museum is west of the county courthouse, which meant going through the center of town to get to Linda's place, instead of skirting Sherman as I'd planned. That might give the impression I devoted a lot of time to the detour. Nope.

Going through or around Sherman doesn't make that much difference.

The stop in the museum could have taken longer, but the painting
wasn't there.

The small plaque with the title and artist's name remained.

I looked around and saw a sign announcing an exhibit of western
art planned for the new year.

On my way out, I stopped at the reception desk to say hello to the
volunteer stationed there.

Possibly also to ask a few questions.

After hellos, I slipped in a non-question question by saying, "I see
there's an exhibit coming in January."

"That's right. A real coup and it all came together fast. Clara's so
excited," she said. "We just got these advance brochures and postcards."

I picked up a full-color brochure from the pile on the reception
desk.

I recognized Edward Borein's drawings, then works by E. William
"Bill" Gollings, with cowboys and horses as their subjects. A third
artist's work brought the drawing chops of Borein and the vivid
coloring of Gollings, but this artist's landscapes were sparer, the
humans and animals fewer. Character studies, rather than crowd
scenes.

The painting donated by Mrs. P and now missing from the museum wall wasn't shown in the brochure, but the artist was the same.

Carey Maight.

"I see you're particularly interested in our local artist." The volunteer beamed at me. "We have two reproduction postcards of her work
from the brief time when they weren't controlled by the family. The
original postcards are quite rare. Even these reproductions are a strictly
limited run."

The reproduction process or the original postcard or both mud-
died the landscapes compared to the one by Carey Maight I'd seen
displayed.

I bought two postcards anyway.

Chapter Eight

EVERY TIME I drove into the gates of Cottonwood Drive, the Caswell family ranch, I heard the old *Bonanza* theme in my head, despite its newer, symmetrical front façade hinting at East Coast roots.

Must have been the back of the building, hinting at Ponderosa-like origins, triggering the tune.

I particularly liked the room Linda Caswell led me to. She used it as her office, with a huge desk taking center stage. Book-filled walls, a cozy sitting area in front of a fireplace, and the piecrust table—now set for lunch—with two wing chairs by a large window overlooking cattle grazing beside a creek raggedly slashing the land, made it far more than an office.

"Want to start with dessert?" she asked. "You look like you could use an indulgence."

Somewhat better than Tom's comment, but the same gist.

"I'll resist temptation, no matter how bad I look."

She clicked her tongue, but didn't bother with soothing words. I liked her for that.

She gestured for me to choose a chair, which she always did. I took the one I always selected.

One way, it looked out the window at the grazing scene. The other direction gave an angled view across the room, then out the open hallway door to a portrait of Rupert Caswell, Senior, founder of Cottonwood Drive, named after his arrival in the region with a herd of cattle from Texas, thus beginning the Caswell fortunes.

We chatted about county doings not involving KWMT or the

Heathertons.

An excellent source once told me the family had always been important in the county, but unlucky in love. I think Linda broke that unlucky streak with rodeo cowboy Grayson Zane.

I hoped so. I liked them both.

That excellent source was Penny Czylinski.

Officially, she works at the Sherman Supermarket as head cashier. Unofficially, she is an acute observer of her customers, their habits, and their emotions. Though interpreting her observations often took considerable parsing.

Except the last few times I'd been in—to buy Pepperidge Farm Double Dark Chocolate Milano cookies—she had not been hard to interpret at all. She'd flat out said I needed to buy real food. She didn't even dangle unattached pronouns in her declaration.

There might be something in what she said. I hadn't added any to my sleep total, yet after Tom's breakfast and Linda's lunch, I felt more energized.

Also more relaxed, as we ate excellent chocolate pie. Even remaining relaxed when Linda brought up the fate of KWMT.

I asked about the for-now owners. She'd previously shared details of the Heathertons' dysfunction, but I was looking for more. Especially vulnerabilities in the owner.

Don't get me wrong. I'm all for a woman being in charge. As long as I pick the woman, for example Linda.

Also no problem with a man being in charge. As long as I pick the man.

Now, though, I was digging for a lever to keep Val Heatherton from selling to this news-hating network. I sipped excellent coffee as I tried reassembling the shreds Linda gave me into any kind of lever.

Linda's voice ended my fruitless mental efforts.

"Do you know you stare at that painting every time you come here, Elizabeth?"

Paintings must have been on my mind—the part not occupied with KWMT. Though this large canvas was entirely different from the small, now-missing landscape painting Mrs. Parens and I discussed.

"I didn't know, though it is stare-worthy."

"You have a thing for my ancestor?"

Rupert Caswell Senior wasn't a handsome man, but ... arresting.

The driver of cattle, men, and family, the founder of Cottonwood County because he made other people get out of his way, a terror to homesteaders and sheep raisers to his dying day.

For a beat, it seemed I knew all that from the portrait, instead of lessons in local history.

"Not only does it look like his face would crack if he tried to smile, but he's been dead for what? A century? More? No, definitely not a thing for him. Though, I might have a thing for the artist."

"She's dead, too. Not as long as him, but a long time. Her name was Carey Maight."

So it *was* her work. And—Linda said—I'd been caught by it each time I'd been in this room. Interesting.

"We have records of Rupert Senior sitting for the portrait," she continued. "Not only financial, but comments in his planning diary. He noted all sorts of things about the ranch every day for decades. Now and then he added personal and family items. Certainly could tell his priorities. Anyway, he commented about sitting for her multiple times. Not very graciously."

"Because the finished portrait reveals him too much?"

"Ah. You feel that way, too? Apparently, it became the fashion to have a portrait painted by Carey Maight at the time. But I look at some paintings and wonder why the sitter didn't burn them. One in the office at the First Church of Sherman of the founding minister makes me shudder. It screams that, underneath the sanctimony, he was not the man of God you'd hope for."

I tipped my head for a new angle on Rupert's portrait.

"Like she painted Dorian Gray portraits, only hers didn't need to be hidden in the attic, so more people saw the real person behind the portrait?"

Linda looked at me a moment in what I decided to take as admiration for my insight, before saying, "Rupert Senior wasn't wildly enthusiastic about the finished portrait. A couple very ripe comments in his diary. He wouldn't hear of having it hung in the courthouse."

I snorted. "Didn't want the public seeing it. Wonder why he didn't bury it."

"I think he considered it. A line in the diary said *if she weren't so talented* ... then never finished the thought. Though he instructed it be hung in the house and bequeathed from generation to generation."

"Recognized the artistic value. Didn't like the accurate reporting."

"I think you've read Rupert Senior well, though you didn't mention ruling with an iron fist. I felt quite daring when I moved his portrait from the formal dining room to this spot."

"Smart. Wouldn't want him disapproving of my dessert."

"Or champagne." Her chuckle died. "But as much time as I spend in this room, and going past the portrait several times a day ... I'm thinking of moving it to a guest room where I'll only put people I don't like."

I smiled, but said, "One plus of where it's hanging now is great lighting. Coming down the hallway from the north, plus lots from the windows in here, but softened, adding to the split between reality and unreality."

"Split between reality and unreality?"

I gestured toward the painting. "He's a real person. Solid. Specific. Yet it's almost like he's coming at you from out of mists. As if the world around him obscures his reality and it can only be seen in this portrait. A sharply focused view of one instant caught here, but mostly caught behind fog. You know what I mean?"

"Yes, I do know what you mean, but I've never been able to express it in words. You did."

I looked at the portrait. He wasn't a warm and cuddly man, but he certainly was real. Yet with those mists.

Because we all tried to pull protective, obscuring mists between ourselves and others?

If so, and if Carey Maight not only saw through them, but caught what she saw in paint on canvas for all viewers to see, not to mention posterity ... "She could not have been a comfortable woman to be around."

"I suppose that's why he was ambivalent about the sittings. As for the portrait, not so much of a philistine he didn't recognize its merits, too much of an egotist to like it."

"You don't do half bad expressing what you think, Linda."

An absent smile nudged her mouth. "She also painted landscapes. You have to see those. Or have you?"

"The one at the museum. No others that I know of and I think I'd know."

"Yes, you would." Subtext overflowed and dripped down the sides of that statement.

Trying not to let annoyance into my tone, I said, "Looks like they'll have some in the exhibit in January. I'll look forward to seeing more landscapes then."

"Uh-huh," she murmured. "If other opportunities don't come your way sooner."

Now she was being purposefully mysterious.

When I turned to frown at her, though, she wasn't paying any attention to me. Despite needing to lean forward to accomplish the trick, her gaze was back on the painting. "There are so many stories about Carey Maight. She had an interesting life. Not an easy one. But interesting. Mrs. Parens knows a great deal about her."

"Uh-huh. The art supplies from her white grandfather."

She nodded, still looking at the painting, but with a different head-tip for a new angle. "I've always wondered how much her use of pony-hair brushes influenced her work."

"Her what?"

"Pony-hair brushes. That's what they call them. No trouble saying hog or boar, so why balk at saying they used horse tail hair—"

"Used *what?*"

This time my tone penetrated her abstraction. "Some artists use horse-hair brushes, from the mane or tail. I understand it holds the paint well, so they don't need to dip the brush as frequently."

"Still? Now? I mean, current artists do this?"

"I don't know. Carey Maight is the one known for it. At least in my limited art knowledge." Caution replaced her abstraction. "Why?"

I stood and walked out of the room, across the hall, until the tip of my nose nearly touched the painting, looking at the brush strokes. "Do you know artists currently using horse-tail brushes—pony brushes, whatever they call them."

Following me, she shook her head "I wouldn't know..."

She knew movers and shakers, especially in the non-profit sphere of the art community. But she didn't know the artists.

This didn't betray snobbery. It reflected her interests. With charities and arts programs, she made sure they ran well to serve the most people the best way possible.

When it came to horses, ranching, rodeo, she knew everybody, including folks who slept in their trucks between picking up day work mucking out stables. She mucked out the stables beside them.

"Could you find if any area artists currently use horse-hair brushes?"

I saw her temptation to ask why and her decision not to. "I'll see what I can find out. No guarantees."

"Tell me about Carey Maight using them."

"You'll hear different things from different people. Sometimes different things from the same person. About whether the original brushes from the grandfather wore out or if Carey Maight made a statement of her connection to her heritage by using horse-hair brushes. Either way, it was integral to her technique."

"I have wondered if it helped her capture the light, the movement somehow."

As we returned to the table, we saw I'd tipped over my bag and the postcards had slid out onto the table.

"Are these the postcards for the show?" Linda asked.

"They are. Tell me—" I stopped myself. My phone also had slid out of the pocket, showing the time. "Thank you for a lovely lunch. I need to get to the station. If you hear something about the sale, the new owners, or—"

"I'll be in touch."

Chapter Nine

AFTER CHECKING IN with Audrey Adams and hearing today's broadcasts were in better shape than expected, I returned to my desk and placed my phone and reporter's notebook on it in the blighted bullpen of the KWMT-TV newsroom.

Not a single message returned.

Blighted.

It fit.

Blighted by aged and mis-matched furniture. Blighted by gray-green walls. Blighted by desks not claimed because the bones of a skeleton staff didn't stretch to fill them. Blighted by the Heathertons.

And now it would all be gone.

Was it possible to be nostalgic for blight?

My phone rang.

I answered without checking the caller. At this point, I'd take a spam call.

It wasn't spam.

It also wasn't about the sale of the station.

Or the theft of a horse's tail.

It was my next-door neighbor, Iris Undlin.

"Elizabeth, you better get home right away. Zeb heard water running in your house. If there's a leak, you know how fast damage can—"

"I'm on my way." I'd stood at her saying my name, dropping the usual accoutrements back into my bag.

I was out of there in two minutes flat, including the seconds to tell Jennifer where I was going and why.

I mentally reviewed leads on plumbers during the short drive. Only as I turned onto my street did I wonder why Iris' husband, Zeb, hadn't let himself in to turn off the water. He was remarkably handy. They had my key—they pinch-hit on the care and feeding of Shadow if I was held up at work. I suspected at other times, too, which was fine with me and more than fine with Shadow.

On the other hand, it was darned presumptuous of me to expect Zeb to take care of the issue. I was fortunate they'd heard and called.

At the house, I rushed in, then stopped to listen over my dog's greeting.

I developed a sensitivity to the sound of water running in my childhood home, when it cued getting a shot at the bathroom between my older brothers' showers.

I didn't hear a thing.

A sense of movement behind me made me turn.

Another man stood outside my back door.

Another man my dog was dying to greet.

Not Tom Burrell.

Not Zeb Undlin, either.

❖   ❖   ❖   ❖

MIKE PAYCIK SWEPT in, ruffling Shadow's head, then wrapping me in a hug.

I hugged back. Hard.

In this moment, questions without answers didn't matter. He was *here*. And hugging the heck out of me.

I gained enough room to refill my lungs with air and to demand, "What are you doing here, Mike?"

"Heard you had a water leak and might need help."

"You heard—? There's no water leak, is there. You wrangled Iris into calling me? You sneaky, deceiving, lying—"

He chuckled. "Missed you, too, Elizabeth."

"This is what *Talk to you tomorrow* was about on the phone last night? You knew then you were coming?"

"Yeah. Wanted to surprise you."

"Well, you did. But why the secrecy? And why lure me away from the station instead of—" Suspicion grabbed me. "You don't think you're coming back to work here in a quixotic effort to save the station—?"

"Quit in Chicago? Come back as sports anchor here? No way."

I believed him and breathed more easily—an effort aided by both of us easing up on the hug.

"Good, because it wouldn't save us from the news-hating network. It would just add you to the roster of the unemployed." Still, there was a reason he'd come to my house instead of the station. "But then what—?"

I broke off. Remembering his words from a few weeks ago, *soul-searching* and *life-changing* and *need to talk to you in person*...

I swallowed.

He grinned. "You didn't think I'd leave you all in the lurch, did you? I came back to see my people."

"In our hour of need? No, I shouldn't say it flippantly, like it's not the hour of need, because it is. I'll be okay. Diana and Audrey and all of them won't be."

He followed my lead into seriousness.

"Maybe there's a way the employees wouldn't have to worry about being paid in prayer, the way you described it—"

"That's the best-case-scenario, Mike. Everything I've found out—which isn't much with people not answering my messages—says this network guillotines the entire news operation immediately. It's what they've done at every station they've bought."

"Leave that aside a minute and let me finish. There could be a way the employees wouldn't have to worry about being paid in prayer, plus a whole lot better chance for people who step up in crises being rewarded, like you and Dell talked about—if staffers have a say in the running of the station under the new ownership."

"Staffers have a say? Hah. Did you hear what I said about the network? Their offer's supposed to be inches away from officially being on the table. At which point, the Heathertons will snatch it up, so they can fly the coop. Actually, they've already flown the coop, pretty much. You think the Heathertons are going to wait for another buyer, much less anyone who'd involve the employees? Not going to happen."

"It might."

"Mike—"

"More than might. It *is* going to happen. With me as majority owner."

Chapter Ten

"RIGHT, MIKE. YOU just bought KWMT." I turned away to reheat coffee left over from this morning.

"Pretty much. I'm finalizing the minority ownership, so if you're interested…"

I turned back, carafe in hand, and gaped at him. "You're serious?"

"Yes."

"Not pulling my leg or thinking this is funny?"

"Not pulling your leg, though I am starting to think your reaction is a little funny."

"You mean it. But Mike—" How, when, why, where, and a few other questions fought to get to the front of the line. What came out was, "*You?* But the religious network's on the verge of buying."

"There's many a slip between on the verge and ink dried on the contract … or some saying like that."

"Not any saying I ever heard of."

"It will be. It will spread far and wide as an example of the acumen of the new majority owner of KWMT-TV."

"I doubt it. Too muddled to catch on."

"Hey." He took the carafe from my hand. "How old is this stuff?" He poured it out and started a new batch.

"Never mind that. Paycik, is this a quixotic gesture, because—"

"Not quixotic. A practical, well-thought-out business move."

Rather than stating my doubts, I went for open-ended. "If you're majority owner, you need minority owners. Is that another many-a-slip-before-the-ink-dries?"

"Shouldn't be. I have enough minority ownership lined up to make it a go, but I'm hoping to edge some out by offering an employee ownership share package."

That meant his minority ownership wasn't cemented in, which meant they could back out, which meant—

My thought train stopped cold at his next words.

"Mel's been working with me and—"

"Mel. *My* Mel?"

"Yeah. No need to shout. After you put me in touch with him when I first got back to Chicago, we hit it off. He and Peg have been real welcoming."

No less than I'd expect. Have Mike over for dinner, help him adjust a bit in the move from Sherman to Chicago—though he already knew the city from years playing football for the Bears. But this ... this was something totally different.

"This didn't come up while Mel and Peg were being welcoming."

He cheerfully dismissed my semi-accusation. "Nah. I went to him as soon as I heard the Heathertons might put the station on the market. Which was way, way before *you* got around to telling me, by the way. Heck, if I'd waited around for you—"

"You wouldn't be doing this crazy thing."

"Not crazy. Didn't you listen? Practical, well-thought-out business move, working with Mel. I have a guy who knows ins and outs for regular finances and NFL stuff. But he doesn't know anything about TV, sure doesn't know KWMT, and he wouldn't approve of this investment—"

"There's a reason for that," I said darkly.

"—because he doesn't know what's important to me."

"But he might know a TV station can be a money pit."

"Can be. Doesn't have to be. Told you the Heathertons have worked it as a cash cow."

"Because they ran the operation—especially the newsroom—on a shoestring. I know you, Michael Paycik. You will pay the people what they're worth and you will buy equipment that's not secondhand from an elementary school in a third-world country—and there goes the budget. There goes your profit. There goes—"

"Now you sound like Mel. He warned me, too, until I showed him the numbers—even before we got a better price." He grinned. "The religious network knew how much the Heathertons wanted to sell and kept squeezing down the price. Then we slid in with an offer a shade over the religious network's and a fast close. Mel's offer was a masterpiece. Anyway, he said there's room to increase expenditures for people and equipment—not just in the newsroom—and still have a profit. If I do it smartly. If I have the right people in place. Mel says—"

"Ah, yes. Back to Mel. My friends-and-family agent."

As well as his being my to-the-rescue agent, I'd known and loved the man most of my life.

None of which changed the veracity of what I said next.

"I'm going kill him for not telling me."

"I'm a client. He couldn't tell you my business."

"I'll still kill him."

"Huh. That's exactly what he said—you'd kill him," he said. "He seemed resigned to it. He also said if you complained to your mother, she'd kill him, too."

There was a thought. Leave it to Mom to punish Mel for keeping me in the dark. She'd do it better and I could look like the reasonable one.

Then another aspect struck me.

"We can make this a double execution, because Mel's not the only one who's kept secrets from me."

"I wanted to surprise you."

Was that the only reason? "You said this isn't finalized?"

"Nope. So you can't say anything to anyone."

"I won't, but what do you have in mind for minority ownership?"

"Three groups. Ten percent ownership for locals, with small enough shares ordinary people can invest, but never enough to think they can boss the newsroom. Twenty-five percent ownership for employees. Ten percent outside ownership. So even if all three groups get together, I'd still outvote them with my fifty-five percent."

"I'm impressed. I knew you weren't the image of an NFL player who blew through his money, but this is far more mogulish than I expected, Paycik."

He confessed, "Mel."

"Figured. So, where do you want me? Employees or outside?"

His face lit up, but he said seriously, "You're sure you want to be involved?"

"I'd usually say I want Mel to look at it first, but since he's structuring it, yeah, I'm sure."

"Can I wait to decide which group? You could go in any of the three and if one comes up short, it sure would be nice to have you where needed."

"Sure."

"In fact, talking about where we need help … I want you to be general manager. We haven't really had one with Craig Morningside doing nothing. And you know Haeburn didn't pick up much of the slack. It can be—"

"No." My mouth said it before I knew the word was on its way, but hearing the sound of it, I knew it was right.

"You'd be great, Elizabeth. Don't say no because you haven't done it before. I can't imagine anyone I'd have more faith in—or want more as top boss if I worked for the station. Think about it and—"

"No. No thinking. Because my answer isn't just no, it's hell no. It's not my skill set and I don't want it to be."

He studied me for a beat, a second, a third. Then streamed out a breath between his lips. "I hoped … Okay, I won't badger you about general manager. News director, then. With needing to fill both positions, you can make it what you want—"

"No," I said slowly, which gave him a chance to open his mouth, so I slipped in another "No."

"I'm not taking no for an answer. We'll come back to it later."

"Mike—"

"Really, we'll come back to it later. I'm a station owner now— nearly—you have no idea how much I have on my mind."

I snapped a kitchen towel against his upper arm. "If you're going to go all management on me, we have nothing more to talk about."

He grabbed for the towel. I kept it out of his reach by turning my back to him in best playground fashion.

My maneuver did not fool the former NFL player. In a second, he had both arms around me and used one hand—showoff—to pull the towel, bringing me along with it.

It seemed natural and comfortable to turn it into a hug. Him hugging me, me hugging him.

Natural and comfortable and if one of us moved our head—

A knock sounded at the front door.

Neither of us jumped back. No reason to. Even if it hadn't been a natural and comfortable hug.

I eased out of it and went to the door.

It's not much of a trip from the kitchen to my front door, but long enough to note neither of us had moved our head.

I opened the door to Tom.

Had I known he was there?

No. How could I?

But I wasn't surprised.

Clearly, neither was he at seeing Mike, coming up behind me.

Was that why he came to the front door this time? Leaving Mike and me privacy at the back of the house?

They exchanged casual hellos. I would have expected more after several months.

"You knew he was coming to town," I accused Tom. Then turned the accusation on Mike, because I knew Tom wouldn't rat out Mike. "Because you told him you were coming when you didn't tell me."

"I wanted to surprise you." He showed no sign of being cowed by the wrath of a Danniher.

I turned back to Tom. "You knew this morning. Making sure I could take the shock?"

"Making sure you had a decent breakfast."

I looked from one man to the other.

As a kid, Mike looked up to Tom, then a high school basketball star. Mike's athletic success later far eclipsed Tom's, who'd left college to run his family ranch and a road construction business.

But in these past eighteen months, they'd formed a bond of mutual respect and friendship. Even while both expressed—*had* expressed—interest in me.

I squared off with Mike. "What else have you told him and not told me?"

"You mean about this trip?"

My suspicion spike would have taken down the entire West Coast if it had been a power surge. "About anything."

He shook his head. "Disqualified question. Far too broad."

"Paycik—"

He raised both hands in assumed innocence. "Honestly, can't think of a thing."

"Who else knows you're here?"

As if on cue, my phone dinged with a message from Jennifer. With raised eyebrows, I read aloud.

"Have you found the water leak?"

Before I could send back a reply, the phone rang. Also Jennifer.

"I'll be over as soon as my shift's done to help you with the water leak."

I realized her use of water leak was caution against anyone in the newsroom hearing mention of Mike.

"Don't you want to know the answer to your question?" I asked.

"It's yes, isn't it?"

"Yes, but—"

"Jennifer, bring dinner when you come," Mike called out. "You'll go right past Hamburger Heaven and I should be back by then."

"Back from where?" I asked.

"Tom's taking me to talk to James." James Longbaugh was a lawyer in town. A good lawyer. And trustworthy. "He and Mel have been lining this up. He'll go with me tomorrow morning to meet with the Heathertons." He grinned. "I think Mel was too afraid of facing you to fly out here with me."

"What time?" Jennifer asked through the phone. "And for how many?"

Mike counted off to Jennifer. "You, me, Elizabeth, Tom—"

"Can't. Picking up Tamantha after we finish at James'."

So he was attending that meeting, too. No doubt representing the community's interests.

"Bring her, too," Mike said. "She won't tell anybody I'm here if you tell her not to."

Amusement lit Tom's eyes. "No, she wouldn't. But maybe, instead of hitting her with it right away, we ease her into the idea you're in town."

"Oh. Yeah."

Tom and Jennifer chuckled.

Mike and I didn't.

Tamantha had the idea the reason her father and I were not together was Mike. The girl could make her displeasure known.

What did it say about this fourth grader that her reaction to Mike's return—temporary as it was—got mentioned before how the staff would respond to him being the buyer? Although, in fairness, KWMT-TV's staff was pretty darned likely to be delighted, while Tamantha's reaction was up in the air.

"Now that's settled," Jennifer said, "what have you gotten done today, Elizabeth?"

Mike and Tom raised their eyebrows at me for an explanation of her question.

I made a never-mind hand gesture.

"Talked to a few people. Nothing concrete," I told her. Boy, that was an understatement.

I was saved by a voice in the background calling Jennifer.

"Gotta go. See you all later."

"What was that about?" Mike asked immediately. "An investigation?"

"Not the kind we've done before."

"The horse-tail theft on the news last night?" Tom asked.

"Yeah, but—"

Mike interrupted. "Horse-tail theft? Like the ones a few years ago?"

"How do you know about those? You were still in Chicago."

"I kept up with the news around here. There've been more? How many? Whose horses?"

"One theft, one horse, belonging to Hailey Newhall," I said.

"Newhall. Related to Kim and Lewis Newhall?"

"Their daughter," Tom confirmed.

In those few words I caught the weight of sorrow in both men.

"Did you know the Newhalls?" I asked.

"Yeah," both said. "Nice people," Tom added.

"Never would have believed—" Mike cut off his own words. "And now somebody's stolen her horse's tail and she's asked you to catch the thief. How are you approaching it?"

"I'm not. Not now."

"Why not?"

"Not only do I not know anything about horse-tail thefts—"

"Hasn't stopped you before."

Tom's murmur earned him my most withering look.

He withstood it.

"—there's too much going on at the station. Even though it's great news—"

"So what?" Mike asked. "If you're saying no to GM and news director, that's got to mean you want to keep doing what you've been doing. So do it."

My hands dropped "That's not a half-bad point, Mr. Station Owner."

"Of course, it isn't—in fact, it's a whole, good point. It's a mystery and we can help this girl. Tell us—No, wait. Can't now. It's time to see James. Over dinner?"

I smiled up at him. "Sure."

Chapter Eleven

BUT THE CONVERSATION at dinner never reached the horse-tail theft, as we all attempted to catch up. Not so much with news, because we stayed in touch, but with the pleasure of being together.

Most of the evening we avoided the topic of the station, too, perhaps feeling superstitious before signatures were in place. Until, with the evening nearing break-up, we sorted out a few ideas.

Then, I raised a specific point nagging at me.

"Why'd you involve Tom?" I asked Mike as he and I cleared the kitchen of debris from our Hamburger Heaven meal.

"You mean besides wanting someone who could listen to what James said from a wider perspective than the newsroom? I needed a ride from the airport from somebody I could trust. I need to keep things quiet until it's finalized, then tell folks at KWMT first."

"Good idea, but—"

"That's why he's staying in the Bunkhouse, too," Diana said, bringing in another plate. Not far from the ranch house she shared with her two kids, she had an efficiency apartment everyone called the Bunkhouse. I knew from experience it was very comfortable. "James will pick him up in the morning for the meeting with the Heathertons."

"They're in town?"

"Flying in from Cody for the signing," he said.

"You could stay here," I suggested. "Would save James the drive north to Diana's, then back down to Cody."

"Too easy for him to be spotted here," Jennifer said. "Neighbors too close."

"Iris and Zeb are the closest and they already know."

They weren't listening.

"What time do you think you'll get to the station tomorrow?" Jennifer asked Mike.

"Lunchtime, maybe? I'll message when we leave Cody or if anything goes—"

"It won't." Diana added to her firm redirection by saying to Jennifer, "Message me when you hear from Mike so I can try to adjust my assignments to be in the newsroom when he gets there."

"Yeah. I'll get other people there, too ... without them or Audrey knowing why."

Tomorrow being Sunday wouldn't make a big difference. Weekends can be the busiest time for journalists. Throw in our shorthanded status and it was all-hands-on-deck.

Jennifer was the first to leave, with an early shift the next day.

"About that horse-tail theft," Mike said as he snared a French fry from the bottom of a bag before he crushed it, "did Jenks' story cover it well?"

"Yes. He did a very good job. And seemed to get along with Hailey."

"You don't?"

I sketched out her prickly moments.

Diana said to me, "Jenks covered it, there's no additional information, and Hailey hasn't been exactly a joy. Tell me again why you're doing this."

Recognizing the truth of the words as I spoke them, I said, "*Why* is why."

"Why people are stealing horse tails? Jenks covered—"

"Not why horse tails are stolen. Why Hailey Newhall came to me. She knows I'm less suited to find the answers than people who know her world. So, why come to me?"

Mike looked back at me, silent a moment, then said, "Because she wants something else. Asking you to look into the horse-tail theft was an entry point for—"

"Don't say it," Diana said. "You haven't been around, Mike. You don't know how much we need a rest from ... Let's stick with the horse-tail theft for now."

As Mike and Diana left, I hugged him again. Hard.

DAY THREE
SUNDAY

Chapter Twelve

DESPITE WORKING MY seventh day in a row, arriving at KWMT-TV was a lot more pleasant than yesterday or the weeks before it.

Except I'd forgotten most staffers didn't know what I knew.

I ping-ponged from being dragged down by their mood, to holding onto my excitement, to concern over anything going wrong.

This ping-ponging explained why I didn't notice Hailey Newhall's arrival until she stood beside my desk, followed by greeting her with possibly too much enthusiasm. Think of a puppy let out of a cage.

In the process of sliding off her jacket, she side-eyed me with re-flexive—and understandable—alarm. Then her partial retreat stopped abruptly.

The alarm transferred to me, because I saw my response spawn false hope in her before she spoke.

"You found out who cut off Fred White's tail? Already?"

"No." I said it too sharply and backtracked. "Why don't you sit and we can talk about it."

She sat. She looked at me expectantly.

I played for time. "Fred White. That's an interesting name."

She didn't smile, yet it was like the underlying structure of her face time-traveled to when she was even younger than she was now.

"That was Gavin. When I got Fred White, Gav was still little. First time he saw the horse, he was so excited and he tried to say the horse is *red and white*. But it came out Fred White." Her momentary time-travel snapped back to the present. "What have you found out?"

"Nothing concrete. Early on like this, the biggest achievement is gathering information. That's what I've been doing, along with—"

Learning of the salvation of KWMT-TV News and the employment security of a slew of people I care about. Possible salvation. Unless something went wrong.

"—background on the thefts of horse tails. As I told you, I'm starting from scratch, so this will take time—"

Especially with much of my time and attention devoted to working on the new KWMT if the sale to Mike went through or despair if it didn't.

"—so I understand if you want to reconsider having someone already familiar with the subject—"

Even if Jennifer does hold a grudge about me dropping this inquiry. Heck, she's leaving after the holidays for Northwestern for a special program. I could survive her disapproval that long.

"No," Hailey said.

"Okay. Then I'll keep at this."

Not hearing from Mike meant they hadn't left Cody. What could be taking so long? Especially, what could be taking so long that didn't mean something went wrong?

"I thought after you came out to the place yesterday and your expression just now…"

"Sorry. Sometimes the smallest thing can spark a journalist's enthusiasm. So small it wouldn't mean anything to anybody else, but it's a tiny step toward finding the answer."

"I understand. I guess."

She stood, pulled her jacket on. Then she stopped, with her back to me. She went so still I thought she might be holding her breath.

I waited.

Without facing me, she spoke, her voice low. "There's something else."

Bingo for Mike.

If she'd been facing me, I'd have let the silence grow, maybe raised my eyebrows. Instead, to move this along, I said, "Oh? About horse tails?"

"No." She jerked around, dropped the jacket off her shoulders, and sat again, not looking at me. "About my parents. All right? My parents. You must have heard about that, being a big-shot reporter and all."

"I've heard a little," I said mildly.

"And all of it wrong. Because nobody's heard what *I* have to say. Nobody wanted to hear it. Nobody would let me say it. From the start, they were so damned sure what happened. Murder-suicide, they call it. Like that wipes out it was a mass murder—her, him, me, my brother, our family, our memories. All of it. Murdered."

She was on the verge of shattering.

I pulled her back from it.

Not because I haven't let people I've questioned shatter— sometimes I actively pushed them to it. But I knew the stakes with those people. I didn't with this young woman.

"Your brother—older or younger?"

"Younger."

"Was that him leaving when I drove in yesterday?"

"Yeah."

"He'd been there to help you with the cameras. That's nice. I have brothers—all older." Her breathing steadied, quieted. "How do you get along?"

"Fine." Her gaze flickered and I knew there was more, but she wasn't ready yet.

"How much younger?"

"Ten years."

"What's his name?"

"Gavin."

"What's he like?"

For some reason that jolted her. "Does that matter?"

No, in that I'd asked the question to keep her talking.

Yes, in that she hadn't answered.

Questions people don't want to answer can actually benefit the question-asker, because, with the answerer guarding against one particular question, others don't seem so bad.

"What made law enforcement think it was murder-suicide?" I

asked.

"They said all the evidence pointed that way. The deputy—the one that disappeared later and then they found dead?"

I nodded confirmation I knew who she meant. "Deputy Foster Redus."

I had good reason to know the name of a man who disappeared well before I arrived in Sherman. Investigating what happened to him wrought major changes in my life.

Hailey—understandably—stuck to her life-altering associations.

"Deputy Redus said Dad had a gun on Mom. His own gun. She was moving forward—toward him—when he shot her." Her voice deepened with the gravel of tears but she didn't spill them or falter. "Then he turned the gun on himself. He—the deputy—said the forensics proved it, including gunshot residue on Dad's hand."

"That's—" I rejected several word choices and went with bland. "—interesting detail the deputy gave you."

"He wanted to shut me up. To stop me from saying Dad wouldn't ever have shot Mom."

She likely had read Redus' motivation correctly.

That didn't mean Redus wasn't right about what happened.

On the other hand, from what I'd learned of him, he wouldn't have strained himself to follow the evidence or investigate thoroughly. Instead, declared himself right and hurried off to keep to a complicated schedule of women.

"What did he say about a motive?"

Her upper lip lifted. "That you never knew what caused someone to snap."

"Did he ask about strains in your parents' marriage?"

"No. He also didn't listen to me when I said they were happy. That wasn't what he wanted to hear. But were there strains?" Her voice went raw as it rose. Another reporter turned toward us. "Yes, there was a strain in their marriage. One strain—*me!* I was the strain in their marriage. Me."

That last word edged toward a sob. But no sounds followed it. That might have been because she had her lips pressed so tightly together nothing could come out.

But something more needed to come out.

"In what way were you a strain in their marriage?"

She parted her lips enough to draw in a breath through her teeth.

"The usual way. He wasn't my birth father. Mom had me before she met Lewis Newhall. He adopted me. My birth father's dead."

"It can be difficult to have a stepfather," I said carefully.

I won the parent lottery with Catherine and James Danniher and most of the time I know and appreciate it. (The other times? Come on, I'm human and so are they.) So my knowledge of being a stepchild is second-hand and observational.

Maybe that makes me *more* aware of the diversity of stepfamily dynamics—I recognize the myriad possibilities because I'm not viewing them through the tight focus of a relationship I'm in. At the same time, I can't feel what it's like to be a stepchild.

"He wasn't my stepfather. He was my father. My dad. *Daddy.*"

If she had been Tamantha Burrell, I wouldn't have resisted the urge to wrap my arms around her. But Hailey Newhall came to me for something far different from consoling.

Still, I needed to acknowledge what had me wanting to wrap my arms around her.

"You loved him very much." Inane, I know. Not even a question to move this conversation along.

"He loved me very much."

She'd pulled herself together. From the near-sob on the word *Daddy* to a restrained statement of fact, despite the emotional import of the words.

She continued in the same strain.

"Mom loved me, too. She loved all of us. Dad, Gavin, me. And so did he." She jerked her head to one side, suddenly impatient. With me? With herself? With something else? "This isn't about a family that hates each other. Hated each other. We got along. We had fun. We enjoyed each other. We didn't fight—"

She broke off.

She hadn't said *There's something else* because she had a sudden urge to tell me her family's tragedy. She wanted something.

And then she said, "Happy. Truly happy. And yet they're dead."

Hailey Newhall's next words came out clear and certain.

"Because somebody killed them both."

Chapter Thirteen

I WASN'T SURPRISED. Logic didn't leave a lot of wiggle room once you ruled out murder-suicide, as she did. It was pretty clear a suicide pact also wasn't on her list of possibilities. Plus, if Redus was right about the forensics—

I sat back in my chair. Mistake. It produced the squawking sound of a rusted gate.

"Is this the real reason you came to see me Friday?"

"Partly, I guess."

"If your horse's tail wasn't stolen, calling—"

She jolted. "It *was*."

"—the sheriff's department wasn't your best move."

"You *told* me to."

"Because I thought that's what you were really interested in." Without a pause, I jumped back to what she'd avoided before. "Your brother. Do you have a picture of him?"

Hailey thought she wasn't going to respond. Decided that was stupid. Still hesitated.

She pulled out her phone. Found a selfie photograph of her with two adults and a teenaged boy in front of a Christmas tree. I saw that much upside down.

I took the phone from her hand, even when her grip tightened on it fractionally.

Now I could see it better.

Kim and Lewis Newhall were pleasant-looking, middle of the road attractive people. Gavin had an athletic body with a baby face that blended his parents' looks. Hailey must resemble her birth father.

The tree, the furnishings, their clothes, all pleasant and ordinary.

Their smiles, though, were winners. Genuine, relaxed, completely untroubled. If this was their last Christmas together, what happened between then and the following July?

I handed it back. "Send me a copy."

That request rocked her. Like she was handing over her family's fate to me, but she produced a passable, "Okay."

As if recognizing she'd betrayed her warrior woman stance, she overcompensated with harsh words.

"I didn't make up an attack on my horse to have an excuse to come to you. I wanted to see you in person, talk to you before I said anything about ... I don't even know why. You're not raring to go on investigating what happened to Fred White, so why I would think you'd bother with the murder of my parents—"

I cut off her slide toward melodrama. "Because you're not an idiot."

That jolted her into an, "Excuse me?" delivered as a rebuke.

"You have other choices to look into the theft of your horse's tail. People you know and who know a lot more about the background than I do. But how many choices do you have for someone to look into what happened to your parents? Sheriff's department's declared the case closed. Sherman police? They turn anything complicated over to the sheriff's department. There's no PI in Sherman. You could try one of those true crime podcasts, but what are the chances they'd take on your story?

"You've probably followed investigations KWMT has done, seen me and others on TV, and started thinking we might be your answer. But it's not easy broaching the subject. Especially when you're thinking that if I say no, you're out of options. So when your horse is defaced—" Not the best word, considering it was the other end, but assaulted, abused, attacked, all had other associations. "—you take the opportunity to assess me."

"What if I did?" She gave me no chance to answer before adding, "*Will* you look into it?"

Jennifer arrived off to our side, remaining quiet but making no effort to hide she was listening.

I kept my focus on Hailey. "I'll poke around to see if I think there's something to look into. That's as far as I'll commit."

"That's not going to find out who killed them."

"That's what I have to offer."

She tried to level me with a glare.

I'd long ago built up my glare resistance. Though Tamantha could get through it with unnerving speed.

As long as Hailey was glaring, I added, "Understand we ask a lot of questions. Questions you won't want asked, much less answered. You have to be prepared."

"If that will get the person who did this—"

"It's the only way I know that *might* find the truth."

She considered it. Considered it seriously.

"Okay."

I was more ambivalent.

If she'd said no, I could have—we all could have—concentrated on the monumental changes at KWMT.

...And left the question of whether Lewis Newhall killed his wife and then himself to gnaw at the back of my brain.

Oh, hell. Probably just as well to continue.

Jennifer broke into those thoughts, saying sternly to Hailey, "To have any chance of knowing what happened, we dig into a lot of things. I need your permission to access your parents' records. Financial, phone records if there's still access to them—"

"There is. We've kept the same plan, Gav and I. The password is FredWhite9, one word. For the others, I'll have to check, but I'll give you whatever you—" She included me. "—need to get this done."

Jennifer had acquired an *open sesame* for her skills, without resorting to hacking. Smart kid.

Okay, not such a kid.

She nodded and returned to her desk.

Hailey stood again. Also again, she stopped with her back to me.

A shorter pause this time, before she looked over her shoulder and said, "If you're any good, you'll find out they were murdered."

Not bad, I thought as she walked out with her head high, but still with that weighted walk.

Was it all from sorrow?

✧ ✧ ✧ ✧

SHAKING OFF LEFTOVER questions about Hailey Newhall, I went to Jennifer's desk.

I didn't look at her screen, because part of me wanted her tackling Newhall records immediately, part of me wanted her devoting time to KWMT. I wasn't going to be completely happy either way.

"I can't believe there's still no word."

"I sent you articles on the Newhalls' deaths." Her fingers didn't slow. "They're on their way. You're supposed to meet them at the café in ten minutes. He wants to talk to you first."

"What?" I said it loud enough to turn a few heads. "Why didn't you tell me? I was sitting over there sweating whether the whole thing blew up."

"What blew up?" Leona D'Amato demanded.

She hadn't been there a second ago. It was a knack of the best reporters—as opposed to media personalities, which are not the same thing at all—and she was a good reporter.

"The story about the horse-tail thefts," I said immediately.

She leveled a skeptical stare at me.

"Which," I added, "now turns out to have been a blind. Hailey Newhall believes her parents were the victims of a double murder, rather than her stepfather killing her mother, then committing suicide, which is what the sheriff's department concluded."

That was intriguing enough to momentarily capture even hard-news-hating Leona. "Ah. The Newhall deaths a couple years ago."

"Exactly. What am I supposed to do with that? Especially—"

"What you always do," Leona inserted. "And it wasn't the sheriff's department, it was Foster Redus concluding."

"—after more than two years since—"

Jennifer didn't insert, she rolled over my words. "What you're supposed to do is be on time for your meeting. You need to go now."

I blew out a breath. "All right, all right."

I wasted no time getting my bag and outdoor gear from my desk and heading out.

If Leona realized she'd been misled, Jennifer had to handle it—a just reward for leaving me in the dark.

AT THE CAFÉ, Mike was jubilant and nervous. James was calm and cautious, reminding his client there was a lot left to do to set up ownership the way Mike wanted, not to mention the application to the Federal Communications Commission for its consent.

Granted, that was likely to be accepted with just short of a rubber stamp, considering KWMT's miniscule size.

Mike now was on the hook for an amount of money I'd reported many times without a qualm, but made my head swim attached to someone I cared about.

He hardly seemed to think about that as we said good-bye to James, who wasn't accompanying us to the station. He would be around when we got the full staff together.

Or maybe Mike did think about it during the short drive, because when we exited our respective vehicles in the KWMT-TV parking lot, he grasped me by the shoulders and spoke solemnly.

"Elizabeth, you've got to change your mind. Be general manager. I'd know everything was in safe hands while I was in Chicago. And it could make all the difference attracting talent here."

"Mike, we went through this. You truly don't want me. Not as general manager and not as news director."

"Yes, I do. Not only do I *want* you to do one of those jobs—either one, your choice—I *need* you to."

"No, you don't. Because I'm not the right person. You want people who can teach new hires and existing staff to do it all. You need people who are up on all the technology. We both know that's not me."

At the end of my spate of words I caught my breath, which gave me the opportunity to notice his silence.

"You might be right."

Being right soothed the perverse pang of not being wanted or needed, despite being the one who'd pointed that out. "Of course I'm right."

"But I still want—the station still needs—what only you can give us. You'll be a special consultant on major decisions, personnel moves, special projects, the daily meeting—"

Apparently reading my expression, he quickly amended to, "The daily meeting when you choose to attend."

"I don't want to be strictly behind the scenes. I'd miss reporting and—"

"Oh, this would be in addition to your regular job," he said, as if offering a special treat. "No way would we pull you off reporting. Like with the horse-tail theft story you're going to pursue. Might—"

"About that—"

But he was intent on his argument, thinking I was making one against what he was saying.

"—as well test from the start having you keep on doing what you've been doing."

"There better be additional pay for this extra work." I'd tell him about Hailey Newhall's other issue soon. For now it was too much fun pulling his chain, especially since a little back-and-forth would settle his nerves.

"You know, you're underutilized, so—"

"No way, Paycik. No management tricks from you."

"Okay, okay. But cash flow will be tight at first with all the things we want—need—to do. I could sweeten the pot with a few more shares, maybe. We should get inside and—"

I stopped him with a palm to his chest. "Are you sure you're not giving away more shares than you own?"

"Mel wouldn't let me," he said simply.

He was right.

✧ ✧ ✧ ✧

WE WALKED IN together, but I peeled off toward my desk to be sure Mike had the solo moment he so richly deserved.

Also to drop off my outdoor clothes. That is not a small consideration in Wyoming, where the not-so-funny joke is there are two seasons—winter and the Fourth of July. It was past mid-November and clear which season we were dropping ever deeper into.

Standing by my desk, I watched staffers rush up to say hello to Mike—unaware of the bigger surprise coming.

Diana came over to my side. Companionably, she bumped her shoulder against me—not against my shoulder, because she's not tall enough.

Newsroom staff clustered around Mike even faster than mosquitos cluster around me in July. I saw Jennifer had lured a good percentage of the tech/operations day shift, too.

"Hold up, hold up. I've got something to say." He held his hands up. They quieted. "We'll have an official statement with the usual details and boring stuff later today. I wish we could tell everyone at the same time, but this being a newsroom and all, we have folks on assignment... Anyway, I wanted to get as many of you as we can right now."

He had their complete attention.

Unobtrusively, he pulled in a deep breath.

He also looked over the heads between us to meet my gaze. That wasn't as unobtrusive. I saw Leona follow the direction of his look, then her gaze sharpened.

"I'm going to hit you with the headline right off—I'm the new majority owner of KWMT-TV."

Chapter Fourteen

I HAVE A number of newsroom moments forever stored in my memory. Many having to do with the first instant a huge news event broke. A few coming later in the cycle of a major story, especially of backlash from one vested interest or another against the reporting of the truth. Several from announcements of Peabodys or Edward R. Murrow Awards won. Three for colleagues lost.

Those other memories might fade. This never would.

"...meeting in a couple days so we can get as close to the full staff together as possible. And some things will take time to see exactly how they work out, including details of the ownership structure. But I'll tell you it's my intention to have all of you involved in the ownership."

That infused added juice to the murmurs of pleasure, relief, interest, curiosity.

Not trusting my voice, I bumped Diana back, bending my knees.

"Uh-huh," she said, neither of us taking our eyes off our colleagues gathered around Mike.

Oh, a few were kissing up to the new owner, but most were genuinely glad to have Mike Paycik be that owner. And all were hugely relieved.

Except Leona D'Amato.

After a couple minutes, she marched through the cluster with elbows out, making her way directly to Mike, unimpeded. She grabbed one side of his shirt collar—I'm sure she would have grabbed his tie if he'd been wearing one, but with more casual styles, she had to make do—and yanked. That brought his head down to a few inches higher than hers.

"You will get me off the anchor desk, you hear me, Michael Paycik. And you will do it fast."

"Leona, you've been doing an amazing job—"

"Don't give me that bull. Off the anchor desk and fast. Back to my beat. Back to part-time."

He swallowed and muttered something.

"And what about Elizabeth?" she asked, still belligerent toward The Man. "You should make her general manager. Or news director. Or both. Haeburn basically did both and God knows Elizabeth would do it better."

"I would if I could," Mike said. "She said no. To both. To either."

That swiveled all the heads toward me.

"That's right," I said, pitching my voice to reach across the bull-pen. "I'll be a sort of consultant, but otherwise, I keep doing what I have been doing. So we'll need a general manager and a news director for starters. And they'll have to be people I can work with." That drew chuckles. Maybe a couple held an edge.

"Then you'll have to help hire them," Mike said.

"That's doable. Now, tell them the next piece." We'd been through this last night, so I wasn't springing anything on him.

"Audrey gets promoted," he said.

I couldn't see her in the tight group, but heard her small gasp and saw the motion of multiple hands patting where I thought her shoulders were.

She wouldn't be news director yet, but on track. If the added experience gave her a better crack at securing the job elsewhere she'd been chasing, so be it.

Mike was going on. "We also hire two new anchors, with another reporter being trained as backup—people already here get to try out first. And we hire more staff overall. Anything I'm forgetting, Elizabeth?"

"Equipment to replace the stuff we have now that must have been bought at a fire sale."

"A fire sale after the Chicago Fire of 1871," Jennifer said bitterly.

Mike said, "I can't promise state of the art, but definitely better."

"Hard to be worse," someone muttered.

"And the new ownership will train everybody on all the equipment they want to learn," I said. Some looked interested, others skeptical. "Start working people toward being multimedia reporters so their skills are marketable elsewhere."

"Hey," Mike objected, but with a grin, "you want me to pay people while I'm training them to leave?"

"Just like the minor leagues. It's the way to get more people with potential to come here. In fact… Mike, you tell it."

"We're considering an intern program like Artie—" A beloved news director from before my arrival here. "—used to have, even more ambitious, and we name it after Artie."

"Oh." That's all Leona said. It was plenty.

"C'mon, Mike, commit to it now, Leona's crying," I said.

"I am not crying."

She was.

Mike put an arm around her shoulder. She thunked him on the chest.

"On one condition, Elizabeth. You're in charge of the program. You don't have to do all the work, but you have to guide it."

"Deal. If—"

"Oh, c'mon, you're killing us here with the horse-trading," Jennifer complained. "Finish this up."

"If," I repeated, "Jennifer does a section on digital researching without getting on the wrong side of the law."

"Tie my hands behind my back why don't you," she grumbled, but then she said, "Deal."

And we had the first rough outline of the new KWMT-TV.

We also had newscasts to put out at five and ten.

It's why journalists seldom celebrate during the day. Though we often make up for it at night.

❖ ❖ ❖

I PULLED MIKE and Diana aside for a few minutes after the happy furor died down and reported Hailey Newhall's new request.

Mike was exultant, and not just at being right. Diana sighed, sounding weary, but said she wasn't surprised and of course she was in.

More than an hour later, Jennifer summoned me from across the newsroom. "Elizabeth, come see this."

She gestured toward her screen.

Despite the invitation being addressed to me, Leona, Diana, and Mike, pinch-hitting as a news writer for today, followed me.

"You called me over for this?" I complained as soon as I saw her screen.

"You mean Thurston? No. Wait."

Waiting meant the weirdness of watching our departed and unlamented anchor in action.

On-screen, in the minimal space left beside Thurston Fine, a headline of *Tragic Murder-Suicide* showed above an image of the Newhall house I'd also seen in the *Independence* articles Jennifer sent me right after Hailey left. The date on the replay made this a second-day story.

Thurston hatcheted the intro, calling the family New-shell. He added one piece of information—assuming he got it right—when he said the couple had been found by a friend of the family visiting from out of town.

When Thurston threw the story to Walt, doing a live shot by the house, it added another layer of eerie. Walt had Deputy Foster Redus as his live interview.

While Thurston was merely dead to all of us, Redus was actually dead.

But what made watching this old replay truly eerie to me was Walt's expression.

I knew what that expression felt like from the inside.

Thurston had told the viewers everything Walt expected to present as breaking news in the interview, leaving Walt hollowed out and livid, while struggling to reveal none of that to the audience or interview subject.

Walt asked Redus if the sheriff's department had any further information.

The members of the sheriff's department I dealt with now would have said *No*. End of interview.

Redus did the opposite, which was almost as bad. Clearly loving being on camera, he repeated all the basic information. Not only day-old news, but Thurston had spouted it, too, making it repetitive old news.

When Redus got to the part about the couple being found by someone who *described himself as a friend of the family,* though, Walt demonstrated his veteran status by saying quickly, "Yes, and we have that friend of the family here with us right now. Wylie Easley."

As he spoke, he turned away from Redus and reached out with his non-microphone hand to draw another man into the frame, aided by the camera operator subtly shifting focus.

Wylie Easley was about five-seven, judging against Walt's height. Broad shoulders gave him a square appearance, borne out when the camera took a full-body view later in the interview. Short legs heightened the effect.

The core of the interview was Wylie Easley found Kim and Lewis Newhall dead—no surprise, since Thurston and Redus had said the same thing.

Still, it was interesting to see and hear the man.

"Kim and I were going to go for coffee. I stopped by to pick her up. And ... It was horrible. The worst thing I could ever imagine. Horrible."

He swallowed hard, then cleared his throat.

"Had you known the Newhalls for a long time?"

"Not him. Just met him this past week. But Kim..." Another swallow. "We went to school together. We were good friends. Real good friends, a group of us. Real close."

Walt asked a couple more questions, but the man shot a glance in Redus' direction and said nothing useful.

Walt did get more from Easley on how he grew up here, moved to Tucson, but was back visiting the area.

"Seeing family, old friends." The man choked up on the last word.

After that, nothing for Walt to do but wrap it up. Between

Thurston and Redus, this exclusive was a dud.

Though Wylie Easley's apparently genuine emotion added a human touch far outside Thurston's range.

"We're very sorry for your loss," Walt said in closing. "*I'm* very sorry for your loss."

The revision was not lost on any of us watching now. Some viewers might have missed it completely, while the meaning behind the change didn't register with others. But a fair number would have absorbed it—even if subliminally—when the camera cut to Thurston's blatantly uncaring expression.

Walt made sure there was an expression of sympathy Thurston's attitude couldn't undercut, so he'd separated his condolences from the more generic expression on behalf of the station.

Jennifer froze the screen on Thurston's face. The next flick of her fingers sent it to black. We all let out a breath.

"I'd already forgotten how bad he was," Leona muttered. "Is this about—No. Don't tell me. Bad enough reading the stuff on-air. I am not getting involved with you people chasing it down."

"Speaking of reading it on-air," Audrey interrupted from nearby, "you all better get busy or there won't be anything for Leona to read or our viewers to see tonight."

It wasn't subtle, but it was effective.

Chapter Fifteen

THE FIVE STARTED and those of us not on-air watched the lead story on monitors hung from the newsroom's ceiling—Mike's purchase of KWMT-TV.

When I said air ready means the entire package is ready to air, I left out that in the best news shops, it's not just a package pressed and crisp enough for airing, but one *worthy* of being aired.

That's worthy in two senses.

For the first, think of it as the TV journalism version of seaworthy. A piece that's not air ready will sink.

For the second, it's a piece that represents why the best of us got into the business.

Not a tough standard to live up to for a package—or whatever else the term's applied to. Nah. Not at all. Easy-peasy.

Just the ideals that got us into the biz in the first place.

The package on Mike buying the station was air ready. In all senses.

Following Mike's instructions to continue on as before, I took a few minutes to call Hailey Newhall, as the Five continued.

"I need your brother's contact information."

"Why?"

The defensiveness brought me up short. Particularly since that was my easy intro to smooth the way before asking a specific question. In fact, asking her *why?* Though my rendition of the word wouldn't be sharp with defensiveness.

Was her *why* protectiveness of her younger brother?

I certainly couldn't say anything to him that would be close to what already happened to his family.

Resisting temptation to say *why* should have been self-evident—I wanted to contact him—I said, "To set up a time to talk to him."

Hailey's next words remained sharp, but I didn't hear protectiveness in them.

"It won't help any. He wasn't there, either. The only good thing about the whole … He wasn't there. He didn't find them. Talking to him won't help you."

"We gather lots of views, impressions, doubts. They all help."

"He doesn't have doubts. He's sure Dad killed Mom."

That only stopped me for a quarter of a beat.

All the more reason to talk to him.

If this was a wild goose chase, better to know soon.

As if she'd heard my thought, Hailey added, "Whatever he says, I won't quit. It took me a long time to get to this point and I'm not stopping. No matter what he thinks." She sucked in a breath. "I don't understand him at all. He knows—knew—them as well as me. How he could think—? But even if he has doubts, why can't he be like Clayton?"

Her challenge implied I should have an answer instead of wondering who Clayton was. "What does Clayton think?"

"I'm not saying he's all for this. He keeps coming back to saying the sheriff's department investigated and they're experts, so listen to them. But they're *not*—not experts about Mom and Dad. About *us*. Besides, the point is he doesn't say I'm crazy or refusing to face reality or—He supports me, no matter what. That's what a fiancé should do. That's what family should do."

Was Clayton the fiancé the dark-haired guy in the newer pickup arriving as I left her place? Could be.

Hailey added, "He says I gotta do what I gotta do. He understands."

He didn't sound greatly enthusiastic about her quest, but maybe compared to her brother it felt that way.

Which brought me back to my question of *why,* before hers sidetracked us.

"Hailey, why are you pursuing this now?"

"Because that guy's back in town." No defensiveness. She was perfectly willing to talk about this.

"What guy?"

"That Easley who found Mom and Dad."

Wylie Easley was in Sherman—that was news. Before I could get more details, she had more to say.

"He was here before they died, circling around Mom, like—" She bit it off. "And he went to the house that day. He said he went there to pick her up to go for coffee because they'd been friends as kids."

"Do you know him?"

"Never heard of him before that week."

"Did you talk to him after your parents' deaths?"

"No. I—" She bit it off. "Maybe. I don't know. A lot of people said things to me at the funeral. I don't remember what they said. I don't remember who was there. I don't remember much. Except for burying them together. And I didn't care what anyone said about that being wrong and how could I and all that rot. Dad didn't do it. They loved each other. They'd have wanted to be together.

"But I kind of wish I had talked to him—Easley, I mean. Or remembered it if we did talk. He and Mom and my birth father and Clayton were all close friends."

That popped my eyes open. Clayton the fiancé was a contemporary of her parents?

Hailey was still talking, not encumbered by doing a rough age-gap estimate in her head.

"Mom told me about my birth father, but she stuck with facts. Clayton will talk now and then, but it makes him sad because he was with my birth father when he died. Highway wreck," she answered before I could ask. "So I don't like to ask him. I'd like to ask Wylie Easley. And to thank him for one thing."

"Thank him?" A second ago she'd sounded like she considered him a suspect.

"If it hadn't been for Wylie Easley getting there first, Gavin would have walked into the house alone and seen ... more than he did see.

Everybody said Easley hustled Gavin right out. So, yeah, I would thank him."

"You haven't talked to him since he came back this time?"

"No."

"Or any time since your parents' deaths?"

"No, unless…"

"Right. The funeral. Do you know where he's staying or have a phone number for him or—?"

"No."

I stifled a sigh.

"Okay. But you do have that for your brother, Hailey."

She sighed without stifling.

But she did give me Gavin's contact information.

I LAYERED UP to venture off to the Sherman Supermarket.

A news aide had been sent out for dinner for the crew staying to put together the Ten, but I didn't want to abuse the new owner's generosity by detouring the aide on a cookie run for me.

That could wait until the new owner wasn't so new.

Walt reached the station's exterior door ahead of me and held it open.

"Quite the day, huh?" He casually added his layers as we exited.

"And just the start, I think."

We grinned at each other.

"Hey, Walt, we watched your interview with the friend of the family who found an apparent murder-suicide couple from about two and a half years ago."

I drew breath to add identifiers. No need.

"The Newhalls. Kim and Lewis," he said immediately. One of the benefits of living in Wyoming—events like that were rare enough to be remembered years later. Then, Walt grimaced. "Classic performance by Thurston."

"It was. You did a good job despite it."

"Thanks, Elizabeth." He looked at me from under his brows. "You don't stint on compliments, but I don't see you digging up a years-old interview to give me an *attaboy*."

"Nope. Do you remember anything more about him—Wylie Easley—or the interview than made the air?"

He did a TV reporter trick of talking on the surface, while his brain accessed memories and impressions filed deeper. You filled in to give yourself time to mine for nuggets. It was a useful skill to avoid the dreaded dead air. I wondered if he could teach it to young journalists. He certainly could model it for them.

Doing the listening version of that trick, I made a mental note to watch for examples on-air.

"Wylie Easley. His family's had a garage in Sherman for generations, over by the Alley bar?"

I nodded that I knew the location.

"He knew the wife—Kim—from school. His older brother took over the garage. There was a family blow up. Wylie moved away, made a success of a car dealership in Texas—no, Arizona. Tucson. Was back in town, looking for a summer place. Said he was supposed to take Kim to coffee to get her opinion on possibilities before a real estate agent took him out looking."

His attention snapped to me. He'd reached the deeper information.

"He made a point before we went on air about how he'd met Kim and her husband at the café earlier in his visit. Said it a couple times. Thought at the time it was nerves. You know how some people talk and talk when they're knocked sideways." I um-hummed. "But it could have been to register with Redus that he was friendly with both of them, so he wouldn't be viewed as a suspect."

"Why do you say that?"

"Because you're asking about him," he said immediately.

I snorted. "Not everybody I ask about is a suspect."

"Most of them."

I didn't push the argument—I might have lost.

"Was there more that didn't make the air?"

"Isn't there always?" He didn't wait for my agreement. "A neighbor who'd chatted with Kim that morning said she wasn't enthusiastic about seeing Easley again."

"*Wasn't enthusiastic.* That could go a lot of ways."

"Yeah. Not afraid of him. I asked and the neighbor said no. More like an inconvenient obligation to a long-ago friend."

"Any gauge of how her husband viewed it?"

He'd started nodding as I asked. "Also not enthusiastic. Neighbor thought that contributed to Kim's lack of enthusiasm. But she—the neighbor—was adamant there wasn't friction between husband and wife over it. She was one of those saying no way did the husband do it."

"Were there many saying that?"

"Several. Redus drowned them out, then buttoned up the case fast. You don't hear many people now saying outright that the husband didn't do it, but you also don't hear many people saying he did. Like they've accepted it's something that will never be known."

Not accepted by Hailey Newhall.

"How'd Wylie Easley strike you overall?"

"Shaken. Badly. But accustomed to being in charge. Of himself and his surroundings. Trying his damnedest to grab back hold of being in charge and being in control.

"Can't blame the guy. They were all friends from school. Kim, him, the daughter's biological father who died around the time she was born, and another guy."

Clayton. Now engaged to that daughter.

"Remember anything else, Walt?"

"Easley ended up buying a place outside Jackson." Walt limited his facial muscles to a micro-expression, but it was recognizable as disdain for the rich guy making the obvious, even clichéd choice.

"Not around here," I muttered. "Did you know he's in town now?"

"Had no idea. I wonder why."

So did I.

❖ ❖ ❖ ❖

TALKING WITH WALT put me behind schedule.

Yes, because I needed to get back to the station to work on the Ten.

More important, because I needed to protect my claim to my dinner order. Or it would be gone, with only packets of catsup, mustard, and salt left for my sustenance.

Along with cookies, assuming my current mission to the Sherman Supermarket succeeded. There was an excellent chance it would, since Penny kept backup cartons of my favorite cookies in case of supply chain conniption fits. Bless her.

As I defrosted in my SUV—heated seats are one sign the collapse of civilization is not imminent—I saw Needham Bender, editor and publisher of the *Sherman Independence*, called while I talked with Walt.

He hadn't left a message. He didn't need to.

Nor did I need to identify myself when I called back as I drove.

He answered with, "And here I thought I'd about gotten rid of you pesky competitors."

"No way. Besides, you know you love us."

"Passably fond of you, maybe, but the rest of that lot? Nah."

We both laughed.

He said, "You know I called Mike before you. Set up a time to interview the station's new owner—could even say savior."

"I'd expect no less of you, Needham."

His voice turned serious. "He's a good kid—made sure we timed the interview so I'd have it for the next edition."

Which also wouldn't hurt the station, since we broke the story tonight.

There'd be a honeymoon period for Mike, generating a lot of good will as the local boy who'd made good, but didn't forget his roots.

"Not so much a kid," I said, partly in response to my own thought of *local boy*.

"Maybe not these days, but he always will be somewhat of a kid to me. So will Tom."

Whether Needham meant to or not, connecting the two of them slathered on more of that subtext that kept cropping up.

I could resent his subtexting into my personal life, but he and his wife, Thelma, were friends. My time in Wyoming's helped me relearn the lesson about letting people in. Part of that was not resenting their subtexting into my personal life.

Besides, his next words took this a different direction.

"You don't think—That's an awfully big financial commitment, even with the ownership structure he's looking at." Which Needham already knew about, of course. "I'd hate to see him…"

"He's looked into it carefully. He's also working with a very experienced lawyer in Chicago—"

"Your relative."

"Distant, yeah. Also my agent. Mel has great connections. And he's smart enough to know what he doesn't know, so he finds people who do. Mike and Mel are also working with James Longbaugh here."

Needham breathed out. "That's good." He shifted from serious to needling. "So what's your job going to be? Queen of the newsroom?"

"Why, Needham, I already am. We might go for Empress."

Chapter Sixteen

I RUSHED TOWARD the cookie aisle. Where I would turn into my happy place, stood a familiar figure. Right in my path.

As if he'd been waiting for me.

I could have gone around him. But it was so rare to spot Sergeant Wayne Shelton outside of a crime scene or the Sheriff's Department office, my curiosity kicked in.

Okay, it rarely kicks off. In this instance, it hit a higher gear.

Before I could get out a greeting or question, he made a statement, glowering up at me.

"You're sticking your nose into the Newhall deaths."

Maybe he *had* been waiting for me, just to fire that off.

"Why, Sergeant Shelton, how nice to see you, too."

He growled.

It's one of my favorite sounds. It meant Shelton knew I hadn't crumbled before the natural and positional authority he packed into a short, stocky frame.

Seeing him now made me think of Wylie Easley on the clip Jennifer found, though nothing was out of proportion about Shelton. Just short.

I stood up straight to maximize my height advantage ... which he never seemed to notice.

"And here I thought you'd be more interested in the change of ownership of KWMT, not only allowing reporting of local news to continue, but strengthening it. I thought for sure you'd celebrate that."

He snorted.

Not an entirely unfriendly snort.

In our ongoing and intricate negotiations between peace and hostilities, it was a concession.

"Newhall case is closed," he said.

That wasn't.

"Did you close it?"

"Not my case."

Not the same thing.

With someone else, I'd press the point, aiming to get them to say more.

Shelton would not be pressed into saying what he didn't want to say—not if I got a commercial laundry press, wedged him into it, and turned it on full throttle.

"I know you weren't. It was Foster Redus' case. Suppose he was pleased to close it so quickly."

"Newhall case was part of Redus' hot streak," Shelton said with a twist of his usually inexpressive mouth.

"What hot streak?"

"Never mind."

"A legit law enforcement-associated hot streak? This is the first I heard of him having a hot streak that didn't involve women."

"Just keep thinking that way, Danniher."

He wouldn't answer if I asked. But with enough needling—say, enough to supply the fashion industry—I might get something to slip.

"I know Redus shared gunshot residue evidence with the daughter of the couple." One needle inserted.

"Shouldn't have done that."

That could cover me knowing it, Hailey telling me, or Redus telling her. Or all three.

Then, Shelton surprised me by adding, "Gunshot residue was incomplete."

"Incomplete in what way?"

"How is that your concern?"

He so rarely asks me questions, I needed a half beat to respond.

"Hailey Newhall first asked me to check into the theft of her horse's tail—a reprise of a series of thefts from a few years ago. Apparently, the sheriff's department's at a standstill on those thefts and the current one. Standstill sounds better than baffled, don't you think?"

"Leave it alone."

"Perhaps seeing no progress on those matters made her rethink acceptance of the department closing—"

"The Newhall deaths are—" he started.

"—her parents' case. She is unwilling to leave it closed. She's asked us—KWMT—to look into it."

He walked away with another growl.

It didn't matter. I took away something valuable, beyond the reward of that final growl.

The chances this inquiry was a complete wild goose chase resulting from a young woman's pain had dropped precipitously.

Because Shelton had referred to the *Newhall deaths* or the *Newhall case*. If he accepted it being closed as a murder-suicide, why not say it?

I SCOOPED UP cookies and hustled to the checkout lane.

The checkout lane because it was the only one operating at this hour. More important, it was womaned by Penny Czylinski.

I used to think I had her schedule figured out. I was wrong. There might be underlying regularity to her official hours as laid out by the store manager—whom she called *the boy*—but she swapped shifts at such a prodigious and unpredictable rate, it was obliterated.

She didn't work all the time. But when I came into the store and she wasn't here, it felt like the universe had become misaligned.

"Bye now," she said to the person leaving her line. "Well, hello there, Elizabeth. Real food. Three meals. Breakfast with him, lunch with her, still leaves dinner."

No surprise she knew my social calendar. "Two out of three—"

"She did a good thing telling her to sell to him when—"

"Linda? Linda told Val Heatherton to sell the station?"

"—it could've been a lot worse. Doesn't often get told sense. Listens to it less. Good thing she listened this time.—"

As interested as I would have been in Val Heatherton selling the station a few days ago, I now had the luxury to try to steer Penny in another direction. "What do you know about Hailey and Gavin Newhall?"

"—and opened the way. Best she ever did for this county is leaving it. So sad. Like grease."

For some reason, that connected in my head with Shelton's comment about incomplete gunshot residue. Would grease block the residue? I'd think it would make it stick more, but—

"Him more like John Travolta than her like Olivia Newton John. Not as—"

Grease, the musical. Not grease, the gunk you scrubbed off bacon pans. Solving that didn't advance me much.

But I did enjoy the respite of proper names instead of free-floating pronouns. Wished I could trade them in for names I was interested in.

"—blonde. Different worlds. But came together and that was that. In the end—"

Was she talking about Hailey falling for Clayton? Though she wasn't blonde. From the family photo, her mother was.

"—she blended the two of them together, better than they ever did. Time changes and some don't have the sense to see it. Twittering about what never had been so how could it start again? Couldn't. She's a good girl, seeing them at the café—"

I perked up. Her niece, Tansy, worked at the café, and was Penny's protégé.

"—said they were like two saplings after a windstorm. Him leaning toward her, her leaning away." She lifted her hands long enough to present them to me palm to palm, about four inches apart, then tipped them both to her right.

"He might want, but she never would. So there was no reason. No reason for them saying he snapped like a bean. Most ask about him—"

That had to be Lewis, didn't it?

"—trying to get to believing it against their own good sense, because they think it's tidy when it's not. Never would've done that. Not sayin' people can't surprise you now and then—"

She meant that literally—people could surprise *you*, but not *her*.

"—but never could've done it that way. From—"

"Because he loved Kim?"

"—the first they came in here, saw all the way through his bones how it was. Holding her tucked up against his shoulder—"

I struggled to imagine an embrace in the Sherman Supermarket where Lewis would hold Kim tucked up against his shoulder. In bed, yes, but how—?

"—and any fool could see. Blood doesn't make a father."

Ah. *Hailey* tucked up against his shoulder.

"Take a bullet, yeah. Not fire one because of the after. If—"

"The after?

"—he shot her—which he didn't—he'd never have left it for him to find. Neither him nor her. Not to leave any chance at all. Some don't give it another thought, but would've yanked him right out of the doing of it if he ever thought of it at all, which he didn't. No reason to. He knew he might have wanted to but she wouldn't. Not ever. Bye now. Well, hi there—"

Ejected from Penny's line and sent on my way with my bag, I had her words, unattached pronouns and all, to sort.

Sitting in my SUV, I thought the last part was that whatever Wylie might have wanted, Kim wouldn't have and Lewis knew it.

I felt more confident interpreting another of Penny's points.

Lewis Newhall would not have shot his wife knowing their son would be the one to find their bodies.

But why did Penny think Gavin would have been expected to find them, when Wylie Easley had?

✦ ✦ ✦ ✦

ON THE WAY back to the station, I called my parents. Both to share the good news on the station and to call Mom off Mel ... More accurately to redirect her from why wasn't he calling to how could he have kept the secret from me?

"That's great news, Maggie Liz," my dad said, using the childhood nickname inverting my names. "Though I'll miss seeing Mike on-air here."

"He's going to continue to work in Chicago."

"Hey! The best of both worlds," Dad exulted, also celebrating because Mike's connections provided him tickets to occasional sporting events.

"You'll be working a lot more with Mike now?" Mom asked. *Subtext, oh, subtext.*

"I'll be working for him, officially. He'll come back here frequently, but that will be for business."

"Uh-huh. For business."

It took some doing, but I got off the phone only a couple minutes after parking in the KWMT lot.

Conversations with my parents are meant for Chicago commutes, not Sherman commutes.

I entered the newsroom barely in time to snatch my dinner order from the always-hungry jaws of Dale, a news aide, who is tall and thin and can consume more calories than a panel of competitive eaters.

I'd like to say we spent the rest of the evening in high-minded contemplation of KWMT-TV's future role in television news excellence.

We mostly sprinted through putting together the Ten.

I also had a glut of returned messages from all those who hadn't answered previously. All wanting the inside scoop on Mike buying the station.

Almost all.

I messaged back to friends Matt and Bonnie Lester in Philly that, yes, this was the best news and thanks for their good wishes. They were newspaper people. Neither covered sports or the media beat. They were genuinely reacting to what it meant for me.

After the Ten, Leona said she was going home to bed. "It's been a long day. Even longer for you, Mike, and you have to drive out to Diana's."

Mike and I looked at each other.

"She's right," I said. "See you all tomorrow."

✧ ✧ ✧ ✧

I HAD FOUR messages when I checked after bringing Shadow in from last call then reading the coverage of the Newhalls' deaths.

Mike's said, *Gang together tomorrow night for case?*

Jennifer's said, *What next?*

Tom's said, *Happy?*

I answered *yes, don't know yet,* and *yes & relieved.*

Then I sent Krista Seger, who owned and ran the Wild Horse Bed and Breakfast, a message. *If I came by at breakfast time, would I have a good chance of seeing Wylie Easley?*

DAY FOUR

MONDAY

Chapter Seventeen

YES.

Krista's reply awaited me when I woke up.

She ran a B&B. No wonder she was up way before I was. On the other hand, she hadn't been awake receiving and sending messages last night.

I'd been conscious of not asking her directly if Wylie Easley was a guest. That might break a B&B-keeper's oath. But it was a good possibility he was there.

The Haber House Hotel was historic and clean, but the style wasn't to everyone's taste. The other choice in town was the Do Sleep Motel. No one with the money to stay elsewhere made that choice.

I hurried Shadow through our getting-out-the-door routine, earning me several has-she-lost-her-mind side-eyes, because my preferred way of dealing with morning is waiting until it's over.

On the way out, I saw Zeb already in his garage, wearing a jacket that looked older than him and a hat with ear flaps. Raised for now, but poised for ear-warming action. He was doing something to his pruners to keep them ever-sharp after decades, while the ones I'd bought this year were already dull.

"You're out and about early. Anything wrong?" he called in the verbal version of Shadow's side-eyes.

"Lots to do. Did you hear—?"

"About Mike buying the TV station? Sure did. That's real good."

He grinned and I grinned back. "It is. Real good. Gotta go, see you later, Zeb."

"With all you have to do today, Iris and I could stop in and see Shadow, if you'd like."

"He'd love it. Thank you."

Mike buying the station didn't mean there'd be less to do today than there had been the past few weeks. But I was making this side trip to the B&B before anyone would expect me at the station.

I knocked at the back door and acted on Krista's *Come in* call.

No sign of her husband, Dirk. But Krista didn't volunteer statements on the state of that relationship and this was one instance when I *don't* ask a lot of questions.

From the smells, Krista had the breakfast half of B&B all set.

She said hello, shifted her eyes to a solitary man seated at a small table, then went to a couple preparing to leave and walked with them toward the front hall.

In other words, *that's him* and *you're on your own*.

She added an epilogue with a wave toward a plate on the counter with fresh-baked Danishes.

The only thing good to be said about morning is you can eat pastries and it's considered a meal.

I plucked a Danish, a plate, and a napkin.

With extra cheer, I said, "Hi. Wylie Easley? I'm E.M. Danniher of KWMT-TV. I—"

"I know who you are. I've seen you on TV."

How? I hadn't been here when the Newhalls died. Hailey hadn't said how long he'd been in town, but I hadn't been on-air the past few days.

Apparently pleased at surprising me, he gestured over a plate overflowing with fried eggs, hash browns, fried tomatoes, and bacon for me to take the chair opposite him.

Maybe he needed all that food to fuel those shoulders, which I now saw were not only broad, but deep from front to back.

"I stay on top of what's happening in Cottonwood County. Even if

I didn't do it to keep up with old friends, there's a family business here, though it's only part of my holdings." A not-so-subtle snub of the Easley garage his brother ran. Making Easley the kind of man who had to come out on top? "Got a guy to fix up a KWMT feed for me."

Jennifer did something similar for my family in Illinois, as well as Mike and Mel. I needed to bring this up to Mike. Packages for displaced Cottonwood County-ites might be an additional revenue stream.

"What can I do for you, E.M. Danniher?" He smiled at me.

I could see why he succeeded as a salesman.

"Hailey Newhall would like to thank you."

"Thank me? For what?" He sounded both confused and wary.

"If you hadn't been there first, her younger brother would have been the one to find Kim and Lewis Newhall dead two and a half years ago."

He grimaced. "Had a devil of a time keeping him back."

"So you were actually inside and…?"

He nibbled at that fill-in-the-blank bait. "Not all the way in."

At my artfully confused look, he plunged into full explanation mode, while still eating.

"I went to the back door. Most of us do around here. Plus, I'd pulled in the driveway and it was closer than the front door."

He gave a little shrug that struck me as practiced. It took planning to restrain a shrug with those big shoulders.

Although it and the words could be practiced only from repetition over the years.

"I knocked. Didn't hear anything inside. Waited a bit." Bite of bacon. "Knocked again. Waited again." Another bite. "Then I tried calling Kim. I could hear her phone ringing inside. Seemed weird. Don't know why, but I checked the door and it was unlocked.

"I opened the door, doing that *hello, hello, anybody here?* thing. I was about two steps in when I sort of saw Kim. And I could smell—"

The shoulders gave a twitch that didn't seem practiced. But whatever he felt didn't slow his eating.

"I was frozen there, when I heard steps coming up the outside steps and then the kid was there. Her son. Asking who I was, what I was doing, where his parents were. And when I didn't answer fast enough—what do you say?—he tried to push past me to get inside."

He paused for several more bites of egg and hash browns.

I didn't ask anything. If his tale was practiced from repetition, might as well let him get it all out before trying for fresh material.

"Finally brought me out of my freeze, him trying to get in and knowing what he'd see … I blocked him. Said we had to get out. Said he needed to call 911. It took a while to get him out, get the door closed and stand against it so he couldn't get by. He called then, all right, said I was an intruder.

"Wasn't until the deputies arrived that I said what happened, what I saw. I guess the kid overheard, because he started trying to fight his way inside again. Thought one deputy, the one who took charge, was going to deck him. I tried to calm the kid down, but of course he didn't know me, even though..." His gaze flicked away as he took another bite of egg. "Anyway, not long after, they took both of us to the sheriff's department. Don't know what happened to him from there.

"I was questioned for hours. Gave my statement. They still kept me. Finally heard that deputy out in the hall, telling someone it was murder-suicide. I said I wanted a lawyer. He let me go instead."

"You said you sort of saw Kim when you first entered?"

His gaze went unfocused and his fork stopped in mid-air. "I don't know if I really saw her that first time or not. I saw both of them when I was trying to push the kid out. And I keep seeing that." He swallowed. "One of the deputies asked why I didn't call for help, get a doctor. Hell, I had all I could do to keep the kid out. It all happened fast. And, besides, I knew … There was no way either of them was alive. No way."

He pulled in air through his nose, then looked at me again.

"You said Hailey wanted to thank me. You're friends? Or—? No, you introduced yourself as being from the station. What's your connection?"

He asked as if merely curious.

I answered the same way. "She came to us about an incident she hoped we could look into. I don't know how long you've been in town—"

"The horse-tail theft story the night before last. That was Hailey? I still think of her as a baby. I only saw her briefly at the funeral and I wasn't—I heard the name on the TV report, but thought it was one of Newhall's younger cousins. Poor kid. As if she needed any more trouble in her life."

"You saw it on your special feed?"

"No. Here. Drove over from Jackson the day before the story was on."

While talking and without sparking the word *shoveling* in my mind, he had dispatched the mound of food.

"Tell Hailey I appreciate her thanks. Maybe someday soon we can talk in person. I'd like to meet her again. Without ... In better circumstances."

Unhurried, he stood.

It was a jolt. Despite seeing him on camera, sitting across from him like this, my unconscious brain must have calculated an expectation of his height based on his visible torso.

He picked up a cowboy hat—a new, expensive one—tipped it toward me, then settled it on his head.

"Nice meeting you, E.M. Danniher. Good morning."

I nibbled on the Danish, listing facts.

Wylie Easley had been in town when Fred White's tail was stolen.

Wylie Easley had been in town when Kim and Lewis Newhall died.

Wylie Easley had been at the scene where Kim and Lewis Newhall died.

And I could now recognize a cowboy hat as new and expensive at a glance.

I chomped down on the Danish.

"IS THAT ANY way to consume a delicate confection? One must enjoy the mingling of flavors and textures. You're mangling it."

I pivoted as far as the chair back would let me to behold one of the most recognizable African-American men in the country according to a recent poll, as he'll tell you, given half a chance.

"Dell, I had no idea you were back from Africa. Or—"

"You need to keep up with the news, Elizabeth."

"—coming to town," I added with an overlay of accusation.

"Got in last night."

In other words, he'd gone straight to Clara Atwood's place.

I wondered sometimes about the museum curator and Dell.

She didn't tolerate meandering discussions in the guise of an interview nor of friendly conversation. She got to the point. While Dell would chat to a fence post if nothing with ears presented itself.

On the other hand, maybe he liked getting to the point with her.

He and Clara had a liaison going that seemed to suit them both. He showed up in town now and then, usually when something took him from Washington, D.C., to the western half of the country. Less frequently, she left her beloved museum for a few days and they met wherever worked for them.

Not that he'd told me that.

For an inveterate gatherer of gossip, he kept his personal life close to the vest.

"What are you doing here, Dell?"

He raised one eyebrow, incredulous I had to ask.

"I know, I know. To see Clara. And maybe you'd have gotten around to saying hello to me eventually, too, but I mean here, at the B&B."

"I come for breakfast. Clara has many fine qualities—" His glinting look made it clear which ones he had in mind. "—but she is an execrable cook."

"You could cook yourself."

"Why?" he asked simply. "Krista makes a wonderful breakfast."

"I thought you couldn't bear to be here after ... you know." Somehow it seemed indelicate to bring up dead bodies to him in this moment, though I'd been fine talking to Wylie Easley about them. Part of the famed Wardell Yardley aura?

"Krista has done a commendable job of eradicating those memories—before you raised them."

I skipped the accusation at the end and said, "You mean with her cooking. And baking—I highly recommend the Danish."

"Bring me one and join me." As I obeyed orders, he added, "The new anchor you have is quite impressive. When I say *new,* I don't mean—"

"Whatever you mean, don't say it to Leona. Not any of it. Not that she's an anchor, not that she's new—or not new. Just back carefully away from the topic entirely. But there's bigger news. Michael Paycik—"

"Bought your little station."

"Of course, you caught the Ten last night, when you saw Leona."

"I was otherwise occupied at the time of your newscast. However, I had heard a murmur of the impending sale." Part of what made him such a good journalist was he couldn't bear to be beaten on any story. It could also make him a pain in the ass as a friend. "How exciting for all of you, considering the alternative."

I whacked his upper arm with the back of my hand. "You heard *a murmur* and didn't tell me?"

He didn't flinch—not from blow or complaint. "Darling, Elizabeth. You know one cannot risk one's credibility by sharing murmurs. One needs confirmation."

"You didn't answer my calls."

"I feared the temptation," he said earnestly. "I so value our friendship, I could have been tempted into exactly that—risking my credibility."

"You ever do that again and you'll risk something even more important to you than your credibility—I'll wring your neck."

"Such violence, Elizabeth. You mustn't—"

"Wait a minute." I regarded him between suspicion-slitted eyelids. "Are you here to do a story on Mike buying the station?"

"Really, Elizabeth, what—?"

"You are. You fiend. You heard your *murmur.* Saw it as a chance to get here to see Clara, sold your bosses on it being one of those human-interest stories they always want you to do to warm up your image and you fight against like the devil unless it suits your purposes, like getting into Clara's bed and—"

"Take a breath."

"—you must have had a track or something on Mike. Knew he flew here and chased right after. And now you think you're going to break the story before his station in Chicago can."

"Well, if they're slow off the mark—Where are you going?"

I'd stood as Krista arrived from the front of the house and turned on a stove burner, asking, "How do you want your eggs today, Dell?"

Not waiting to hear that momentous decision, I waved a *thanks* at Krista and said to Dell, "To call Mike to get somebody from his station out here."

✧ ✧ ✧ ✧

STEAMING—THOUGH not as much as I might have been with someone else because this was part of the Wardell Yardley parcel—I sat in my SUV and called Mike.

I covered the necessities in four succinct sentences. What Dell planned to do and what he—Mike—needed to do.

"Dell's in town already?" Mike said.

"You *knew* he was coming?"

"Well, I figured he would. I'd picked up word he was asking questions about me. But don't worry about it. I didn't do this behind my bosses' backs. They're sending a crew out tomorrow. After, I'll give Dell an interview, too. Keeps his trip here on the up-and-up with his bosses. Can't hurt the station. And it might help."

"About that. I have an idea. I'll tell you when I get to the station."

"Won't be in for a while. James and I have a breakfast with the county commissioners."

I chuckled. "Ah, the joys of being a mogul. But you know who else you better have a meeting with before much longer?"

"Aunt Gee and Mrs. P," he said immediately. "Got it covered. Lunch at Ernie's. Want to come?"

Chapter Eighteen

MIKE ARRIVED AT the station just in time for us to leave for lunch in O'Hara Hill.

In the interim, I'd put in three hours editing wire stories, helping Audrey with the preliminary block assignments, and making phone calls for a follow-up on the theft of Fred White's tail.

Headed north in Mike's luxury SUV, I told him about Wylie Easley getting a feed of KWMT-TV and my idea of offering that to others.

"You mean I'd have to pay to keep getting the feed on my own station?"

"You and everybody else. I'll give it to you as a Christmas present. And my parents and Mel—no, not Mel. You give it to him as a business expense."

"You know what I'd rather you do? Keep working on this Newhall case. If it wasn't a murder-suicide, that's a heck of a story."

Despite the tickle of Shelton never using the term murder-suicide, I said, "A very big *if.*"

"Won't know until you dig into it more."

"You want to pursue another investigation while you're here in town because you miss it."

"That, too, so we have to wrap it up before I go back right after Thanksgiving." He fought down his grin. "But, really, Elizabeth, it's important. For their kids, most of all. But for a lot of people. Everybody thought they were such a strong couple, such good people. Makes everyone question if they know their neighbors, their friends, their family. Maybe even themselves. That's tough on a community.

Especially one like this, where a lot of people are spread out and you need to rely on the ones you know."

AS MIKE AND I reached the back door of Ernie's restaurant in O'Hara Hill, Jack Delahunt exited, settling his cowboy hat in place. He immediately tipped it to me. With Mike he exchanged a handshake that would have put my fingers in splints.

Jack could have been the model for the old Marlboro Man ads, though one who didn't smoke.

He's the long-time foreman at a very large ranch that spreads from Cottonwood County into its neighbor. You would think he might be isolated from Cottonwood County's jet stream of gossip. Nope.

First thing he said after the hellos was to Mike: "Glad you're taking on the TV station, keeping it going for all of us."

Not wasting time waiting for a response, which might have gotten into ooey-gooey thank you stuff, he said to me: "Good you're helping out Hailey Newhall. She's a good kid."

"How do you know her?"

"She worked for the outfit. Summers while she was in school, like Mike did, then up until her parents' deaths. After that, with her kid brother to look after, she couldn't do it full-time. Though I get her to come out now and then. Hard to beat her way with horses. She's brought a couple back to full health the vets gave up on."

He looked at me from under the brim of his hat. "Got the idea money's tight for her."

Then he nodded, satisfied I'd received the message.

"Hear you got your aunt and Mrs. Parens coming for lunch, Mike. Ernie's setting up the table up front as befits those two fine ladies." His grin flickered into existence. "And the pair of you, too."

He then did one of those conversational shifts that's smooth and natural in the speaker's mind, but left the listeners trying to connect the dots.

"I never knew any of these people. But gossip around here isn't considered past its use-by date just because it's a century old. Officially,

Mrs. Parens' father employed Carey Maight and her mother—" Had mentioning Mrs. P been what brought this to Jack's mind? "—though the joke among old-timers was he paid Carey Maight to paint, because she didn't do any work around the place. Guess he helped support her and her family when the money from her paintings dipped low. Best get going now."

Unknowingly, he'd filled in one gap for me—the painting Mrs. P donated to the museum after inheriting it from her parents likely had been given to them by the artist. As thanks or payment or both.

Though his segue from the Newhalls to that history replaced it as a mystery.

Ernie had, indeed, prepared the favored table in front for us. As you entered from the front, it sat on the right side by the window, with no other tables near it and the bar starting beyond it. The other tables staggered down the left side, close enough for easy eavesdropping.

Mike went to the front door to hold it for the arrival of his aunt and Mrs. P.

It was no surprise they came together, despite the rivalry. Mrs. Parens didn't drive and Gee chauffeured her neighbor.

The first half of lunch was all about Mike buying the station. Mostly congratulations, with a side order of concern from both women that he not put his finances in jeopardy.

He assured them he wouldn't, pulling out Mel Welch as his economic guardrail. But they didn't know Mel the way I did and they had known Mike since he was born, so they said all the right things, and still worried.

Perhaps to evade their worry, Mike tossed me to the lions for the second half of the meal.

"…and one of my first acts as owner was to tell Elizabeth to continue looking into the deaths of Kim and Lewis Newhall."

"I thought you were trying to find whoever stole the tail off Fred White," Gee said as if she didn't already know about the other task, which she clearly did.

"That, too," I said. "Hailey's hoping for more answers on her parents' case than she received from Foster Redus."

Gisella Decker was in a quandary. Under the current sheriff, she considered the department not in need of any assistance from non-law enforcement. She didn't quite call us amateurs, but the word hovered on her lips. As did orders to leave this alone.

On the other hand, her opinion of Redus as a disgrace to the profession was public record. Which was why I'd used that angle.

But I knew better than to press her for direct information on the case. Much better to let Mike work his wiles in private.

I redirected the conversation toward Mrs. Parens.

"You talked about obstacles women wanting to pursue art in this area faced a century ago and more. Were you thinking of Carey Maight?"

"She was among those with no formal training I had in mind. How she obtained supplies has become part of her legend, especially making her own horse-tail brushes. She collected carefully and combined characteristics of tail and mane to serve specific purposes. Always she took great care to harvest strictly limited amounts. Many owners came to view it as a compliment to their horse if Carey Maight included its hair in a brush."

A far different approach from whoever took Fred White's tail.

"She faced a further obstacle."

"Because she was a Native American," I supplied.

"She preferred Indian, as many do still, but yes. From our perspective now, it is not difficult to imagine prejudices she faced from the white world. For anyone outside her life, however, it would be difficult to understand how it was for her to face rejection and criticism from both inside her tribe and outside it.

"There was expectation from both that she would express her art in the form of crafts. Attire, footwear, belts. Those were among the accepted practices for native women's art."

Did Carey Maight use horse-hair brushes as a nod to those crafts? Or a declaration of how she was different?

"Then, too, she used the white man's easel, paint, and canvas to create what her tribe viewed as white man's art, while most white men of the artistic establishment saw only that she was a woman and a native."

"She must have been lonely," Mike said.

"Such an assessment would be difficult for anyone to make, Michael," Mrs. P said. "In addition to her art, she married twice, had a child and grandchildren. In addition, she formed bonds that might now be termed a mastermind group with women photographers in our area.

"Without the tradition of centuries of institutions and expectations built by men, photography, as a new form at the time, allowed more latitude for women pursuing it. As examples, have you heard of Evelyn Cameron or of Lora Webb Nichols, Elizabeth?"

Mike released an audible breath at being spared this question.

I shook my head.

A glint of disapproval showed in her eyes, but mostly determination to get on with the job of eradicating my ignorance.

"Each was a photographer of acumen, Cameron in Montana, Nichols in Wyoming. Cameron came from a quite well-to-do background in England. She and her ornithologist husband took their honeymoon in Montana and returned to make their home there. Trying to ranch, they had financial difficulties, including bankruptcy. She took up photography to help their ends meet.

"Nichols came from quite a different background. She was raised in Encampment, Wyoming. One could say she pursued what you young people refer to as the gig economy. She began a number of businesses. As might be expected, one was a photography studio, which developed film, as well as lending cameras to customers. She also opened a newspaper and an ice cream shop."

"Combined, these two women left an archive of tens of thousands of photographs of their and others' lives in Wyoming and Eastern Montana at the end of the Nineteenth Century into the first decades of the Twentieth Century.

"Carey Maight, too, left an archive through her portraits and landscapes, despite the handicap to hers that copies are not readily made. In addition, hers remains mostly in private hands, which makes it all the more impressive that Clara has won agreement from some holders to share their works in the exhibit."

Before I could ask more, Ernie arrived with the bill.

✧ ✧ ✧ ✧

MRS. PARENS AND I walked out together, leaving Gee solo time with her nephew.

Living on the edge, I asked, "Why don't you just tell me things, instead of all this cloak and dagger?"

I knew some of it was a firm stance against gossip, but not all. And it was frustrating.

"As a reporter, you tell your viewers. I, however, am an educator. Those who find information for themselves remember the information far better than those who are told it."

I produced a half smile. "In other words, our viewers would remember better if we made them work harder for the information?"

"If your goal was for them to learn and retain information, as well as improve their ability to find such material for themselves in the future, then I would say yes to your question. However, your goal is to inform your viewers."

"True. And my goal in gathering information—including by talking with you—is finding the truth."

"In general, a worthy goal, indeed, as is the goal of education."

I got the message. She wasn't changing her ways.

Chapter Nineteen

AFTER OUR LATE return from lunch, Mike retired to the news director's office.

KWMT had no office for the owner and the general manager's office had been turned into a storage closet years ago. Mike could have taken over Thurston Fine's office—the nicest room in the building. But over the past weeks we'd used it as a break room, since it was bigger than the official one, had a better fridge and microwave, and boasted a comfortable couch.

I checked in with Audrey, who had the Five and Ten in good shape for this hour of the day. My vagueness about leaving to get background on a potential story didn't bother her at all. Another sign she had things lined up.

Jennifer, on the other hand, perked up and practically pushed me out the door.

I drove west, through Sherman, then out the other side to the high school.

It was a good thing I hadn't lingered in the office. The football team managers and coaches were already on the field, preparing for practice, when I found an open gate where I could intercept one particular player when he emerged from the locker room.

I caught a major break and a minor one.

Major? They didn't have their helmets on yet.

Minor? Gavin Newhall was on the side of the path where I stood, so I didn't need to cross over to snag him.

In light of Hailey's description of her brother's attitude, I'd decided springing myself on him in person gave him less chance to refuse to talk to me.

I recognized him, nearly at the back of the pack, from a photo Jennifer pulled for me from last year's yearbook. I'm not sure I would have recognized him from the family photo Hailey sent. Almost three years make a big difference in a high school boy.

So did your parents dying and you accepting the official report that your father killed your mother.

He sure wasn't smiling now.

He was a few inches taller than me. More slender than bulky, so likely not a lineman. He was attractive, but in a different way from his sister. Lighter hair and skin, blue-gray eyes to her dark brown.

The resemblance was strong when it came to their expressions, though.

Troubled.

His might also *be* trouble.

"Gavin," I said, stepping in front of him. "I'm Elizabeth Margaret Danniher."

I skipped the official E.M. and station affiliation. Even so, a few other players eyed us curiously.

"Your sister's asked me to talk to you." Close enough.

If I'd thought mentioning his sister would serve as my bona fides and make him comfortable, I was wrong.

He jerked to a stop, but thrust his face toward me. "About Fred White?"

"No." Quietly, I said, "About your parents."

He must have expected that after I'd eliminated the horse-tail theft as a topic.

When you brace for something you don't want and then it comes, it often brings a get-it-over-with relief. He seemed to ease all over. Except his voice, which retained full belligerence. "Is she on that again? When is she going to let it go?"

"Not until she's satisfied."

"She's never going to be satisfied because she's living in a fairy tale that we were a happy family." He hawked. I prepared to evade a forceful stream of spit until I realized he hadn't ejected an excess of phlegm but expressed disdainful amusement.

"Did you think you were happy at the time?"

"Too stupid to know the truth," he said immediately.

He'd thought about this. Reconciled what had been before the shooting with what the shooting said. Worked it out. Had his answer ready.

"My father shooting our mother has got to be a hint it wasn't a happy family. Even to Hailey."

"Why do you think he did that?"

He jerked one shoulder sharply. "My father snapped. Got out a gun and shot our mother."

Hailey Newhall's declaration that her brother didn't have doubts took the edge off shock at his coldness.

A deliberate tactic on her part? That would be fairly sophisticated, but not outside the realm of possibility.

I'd heard this level of anger before as a journalist. It was how some people reacted to grief.

He kept talking, but—like Easley's practiced shrugs—his words were ones he'd used before. They were worked over. Not raw. The emotion behind them, though ... For all his assumed cynicism, the emotion remained raw.

"We aren't the first ones this has happened to. We're not special. Murder-suicide happens all the time. The guy kills a woman he was supposed to love, then kills himself. Like the coward he was."

"You think that's what happened?"

"I know that's what happened. That's what everybody knows happened, except Hailey. That deputy told us the first night. Haven't you read the case file? Some kind of reporter you are. It's all there. The scene, the gunshot residue, how Mom tried to stop him and that's what led to the trajectory going up, how he shot her anyway, how he turned the gun on himself. Contact wound." He threw those two words out like a weapon against me. "Let Hailey explain that away. She can't, even though she's been trying since—"

"*Newhall! Here. Now.*" The male voice boomed over us all the way from the field.

Voice like that must be quite a benefit for a football coach.

"We'll talk again," I said.

"I have nothing to say. And you tell Hailey to leave me the hell out of whatever she's got going."

"Tell her yourself. I'm not—"

He was gone before I finished expressing my unwillingness to carry messages between these two.

I LEFT.

Not with the impression of him I'm sure he'd intended.

He wasn't baldly stating facts as he saw them. A clear-eyed adult recognizing the truth, in contrast to what he presented as Hailey's childish beliefs.

I didn't know which of their beliefs was more right—pretty good chance each of them was partly right and partly wrong.

What I did know was he was not a clear-eyed adult.

He was a kid seething with anger he refused to let out.

But there was more to be gleaned from what he'd said.

The shooter was *my* father, the victim *our* mother.

He was a blood relation of the killer, Hailey was not. He'd settled the burden of grief and anger on his own shoulders.

HALFWAY BACK TO my SUV, I recognized a familiar uniformed figure coming out of a side door of a classroom wing, this one not short and stocky.

Deputy Richard Alvaro.

He'd gotten better—or worse, depending on your point of view—at the expressionless cop face since Shelton took an interest in molding him. At the moment, spotting me, he didn't appear to know which expression to adopt. Friend, foe, something between?

"Hey, Elizabeth."

"Hi, Richard." We don't usually go in for such chit-chat, since I'm usually trying to get information out of him and he's usually trying to hold it all in without being overtly impolite. Which is more than I can say for some of his colleagues. "What are you doing here?"

He cracked a grin. "Not on a case. Did a presentation for my niece's class."

Hard to believe he had a niece old enough to be in high school, considering he looked like he'd graduated yesterday. Older siblings could explain being a young uncle and he was among the youngest of a large family.

"What are you doing here?" he asked.

I opted for the truth on the chance it might spark something from him.

"I came to talk to Gavin Newhall."

His face did that not-sure-what-direction-to-take thing again. "I know you folks at the station have had a good amount of upheaval, but if you're doing sports…"

"Very funny, Richard. I wasn't here to talk to him about football."

"The theft of his sister's horse's tail? That's a weird one, isn't it."

Of course he knew about that—he'd taken a report from Hailey and seen Fred White himself. So, why did he sound *off?* Off in a way that made me think he didn't believe the horse-tail theft brought me here.

"Have you matched that piece of fabric Hailey found?" I asked him.

"A piece of denim? No, we haven't."

"No lineups to see if someone's missing a bit from the seat of their pants?"

"No. Is that what you were talking to Gavin about?"

"What else could it be?" I asked with wide, innocent eyes.

We stared at each other for one beat. Three.

"Their parents…" He stopped, cleared his voice. "The deaths of their parents. Was one of the early times I was out with Redus."

My antenna twitched. Richard had told us about another time he'd ridden with Redus. At real risk to his career if the then-sheriff had learned of it. Richard's information helped us reach the truth.

If he was thinking along those lines now…

He grimaced. "My first time on a death scene. It was … tough."

"You knew them—the Newhalls?"

"To nod hello to. Not real well. Hailey was a year ahead of me in school. I saw her there at the family house that day, of course. She didn't remember me from that when I talked to her about her horse's tail being taken."

"Not surprising."

"No," he agreed. "She was totally broken up about her parents at the scene. Guess they'd had arguments and she felt … But it wasn't like it was her fault. For sure she felt real bad their last conversations ended the way it did."

Watching him, I felt entirely confident in saying, "The empathy does you credit, but that's not what bothered you the most at the scene." Bothered him enough to be on the verge of telling me more than strictly necessary, despite Wayne Shelton's influence.

"No, that wasn't what bothered me most. I mean, it did bother me. Nice people, family torn apart. Yeah, that bothered me. But the scene…"

After that intriguing start, he wound down to silence.

What about the scene? would be the automatic question. But this turtle could draw his head back into his shell at a very un-turtlelike speed. I'd seen it before.

He needed a bit more encouragement.

"Hailey Newhall said she was told it appeared her mother was moving toward her husband when she was shot," I said.

"Yeah," he drew it out to about five syllables.

"She wasn't?"

"Oh, yeah, sure appeared she was. Only with him being so much taller than her and the angle of the shot that killed her being … well…"

Mom tried to stop him and that's what led to the trajectory going up, Gavin said just minutes ago.

I resorted to the direct. "What about the angle?"

"It didn't seem right to me. Some downward or level made more sense, him being taller than her and where she was hit. But it was upward."

I imagined the two figures from that family photo facing each other in a moment of rage or sorrow or something else that drove Lewis Newhall to this act.

If she'd seen the gun and tried to reach to him...

But would she have jumped up to be taller than him?

Not likely.

"If he drew from the hip?" I said aloud.

"That's interesting." Richard sounded admiring. If so, it was admiration for my imagination. "But the GSR—gunshot residue," he explained kindly, while I stilled the snap-back that I'd known what GSR was since he was learning to read, "—on his clothes wasn't consistent with a hip shot."

"Hesitation on his part. He let the gun drop from a natural position."

"Maybe." But he didn't believe it.

"What did Redus say about it?"

"Said I was making a big deal out of something real simple. The husband shot her, then himself. Period." He shifted his feet. "But there's something else."

He stalled.

I waited.

He remained stalled.

I raised my eyebrows.

At last, he tipped his head slightly and focused on a patch of gravel that had come loose from the paved parking lot.

"That gunshot residue," he murmured.

"Right, the gunshot residue," I encouraged.

Drawing Richard along was worth the effort. Even if what he said ended up not getting us anywhere.

Shelton had his points, including being a good cop and all that entailed. But his other points frequently jabbed me in the ribs or an eye.

So, yeah, I enjoyed a moment of triumph at Richard Alvaro telling us things Shelton wouldn't like him telling.

"Redus put a lot of store in the contact wound on Lewis Newhall's head and GSR on his hand that held the gun."

Something in his tone told my antenna there was a flaw. "Which hand?"

He looked at me directly for the first time in a while. "His right."

"Was he right-handed?"

"I see what you're thinking. But, yeah, he was right-handed. That fit it being a murder-suicide. The angle of his wound was a little weird, but the medical types said it can be in a suicide. Emotions don't make for the best aim. No, that wasn't it."

"What was it?"

"The gunshot residue was incomplete."

Shelton had said that, too.

"Redus didn't wait for testing to be completed before closing the case?"

If the test contradicted his conclusion, even Redus—

No, Foster Redus wouldn't have reassessed. And no way then-Sheriff Widcuff would have overruled him.

"Oh, the test was completed," Richard said, proving I'd jumped to conclusions based on Redus' and Widcuff's characters or lack thereof. "But it wasn't all over Lewis' hand. At least it wasn't the same amount all over his hand. Some variation's normal, sure, but this was like the GSR didn't reach parts of his hand.

"I tried to ask Redus about it and he cut me off. Cutting people off was his specialty, especially cutting them off at the knees."

"Did you ever talk to anybody else about it?"

His eyes went dark and his mouth rueful. "You know what it was like then. Who would I have told?"

Shelton, I almost said.

Except Richard hadn't really known Shelton at that point.

"Are you doing something about this for on-air, Elizabeth?"

Was it a coincidence Richard Alvaro asked that a day after Shelton's less genteel inquiry? (Or accusation. In Shelton-speak they were the same thing.)

Could Shelton have sent Richard to get more from me on whether we were looking into the Newhalls' deaths?

Yes.

Except even if Richard hadn't delivered a talk to his niece's class—far too easy for me to check up on—he couldn't have known I'd be here now to talk to Gavin Newhall.

I produced my most earnest tone. "With all the stuff going on at the station? How could I possibly have time?"

One side of his mouth lifted in a disbelieving smile. "Well, if time's all that's stopping you, you could be real efficient by asking O.D. Everett for insight on his granddaughter and her family at the same time you take your class."

His granddaughter...?

Oh.

Hailey's birth father. The fourth member of the group Easley talked about.

I added a bright smile to my earnestness. "You're right, I could. I'll do that. Thanks and see you later, Richard."

I waved and walked briskly to my SUV.

Chapter Twenty

AWARE OF RICHARD watching me, I didn't hit speed dial until I was out of his sight.

"Is Hailey Newhall related to O.D. Everett?" I demanded of Diana.

Yes, I already knew it from Richard—why would he lie? But I wanted it confirmed by a reliable source I knew was on my side.

"She's his granddaughter. Why—?"

"Why? I'm the one asking why—specifically, why didn't anyone tell me?"

"Because we forgot you didn't know would be my first guess. Because we had no idea you'd be interested comes in a close second. Besides, if we told you how everyone here was related to everyone else, that's all we'd talk about. It's not a secret or anything."

"Clearly not, since Richard Alvaro just let it drop."

"Richard? Where'd you see him?" Diana asked.

I recapped quickly to get back to what I wanted to talk about. "Now, tell me. Hailey's birth father was O.D.'s son? Were he and Kim Newhall together? Or a one-time—?"

"Together. Of course she wasn't Kim Newhall then. They met right after she graduated high school, I think. They were an unlikely pairing, but seemed to really love each other. That's looking back, though. Neither family was happy about it at the time. A lot of their friends, either. But they formed this self-sufficient group with Wylie Easley and Clayton Rayger. Wylie had been tight with Kim since they were kids. Clayton was Isaiah's sidekick. Definitely supporting cast to the main couple."

"How does O.D. figure into this?"

She humphed. "He and Isaiah weren't close to start with, whether from ordinary father-son conflict or more, I don't know. O.D. didn't approve of Isaiah being with Kim. Didn't exactly melt the barriers when she got pregnant. Not with her family, either, by the way. Then Isaiah died. I—"

"How?"

"Self-inflicted drunk driving. The miracle is he didn't kill Clayton, too. Just the two of them in the car. Hailey was a newborn. Kim refused to go out with them that night. Wylie stayed with her. Good thing or they and the baby … Anyway, as far as O.D. and his grand-daughter went, I don't know what all was involved, but there must have been a meeting of the minds between Kim and O.D., because he was part of their lives. Not right in the middle, but there for birthdays, other celebrations. Why are you so interested? Anything beyond the fact that you didn't know and you don't like not knowing."

"Yes," I said promptly. "Because I don't like missing the explanation for a mystery."

"What mystery?"

"O.D.'s reaction about the horse-tail theft."

"I told you—"

"Yes, and I bet the tribes getting blamed without proof last time is part of it. But there was something else. Hailey being his granddaugh-ter explains it. He must not have known and it hit him hard. He left abruptly to go talk to her."

"Okay, but does this have anything to do with Kim and Lewis Newhall's deaths?"

"Don't know until I ask, do I?"

My automatic driving brain—we all have one. It's like a lizard brain for behind the wheel—must have known our conversation's destina-tion, because as I said those words, I pulled into the main drive to the low, long shape of the Cottonwood County Community College.

❖   ❖   ❖   ❖

O.D. EVERETT'S OPEN office door let me see him sitting at his desk, looking at something in the corner of his office, masked from my view by the door as I came down the short hall.

He had a black desk set off-center, to block less light from the window behind him. A yellow wall added to the room's brightness.

"Hi, O.D."

He looked around to where I stood in the doorway. "Elizabeth. Come in, sit down."

As I did both with outward ease, I realized he'd been looking at someone, not something, behind the door.

His grandson, Paytah, sitting on the ledge that divided deep cabinets below from narrower bookshelves above.

I said hello, he nodded. Not masking that he wasn't happy. With me for interrupting a conversation? Or with his grandfather over the substance of their conversation?

I'd heard no voices from the room as I'd approached. Though, I'd been walking fast, so I might have missed what came before a thoughtful—or angry—pause.

"I hope you are not here, Elizabeth, to tell me that your burden of duties won't allow you to continue our class. I hoped the news of Mike Paycik leading a new ownership team would result in allowing you more open time."

"Not if he has his way—which he won't." His faint puzzlement was understandable, but I didn't feel like explaining about Mike pitching the GM and news director jobs. "Most of us worker bees are much happier about the station's future with Mike as owner, but we're not working any less. Short-term and maybe longer we'll remain quite short-staffed. So, I can't say yet whether I can finish the course. I hope to."

"I hope so as well. And I was glad to hear you took time from your duties to visit Emmaline Parens, even before the good news of Mike buying KWMT," he said. "That was nice of you."

I didn't even bother to raise my eyebrows that he knew about my visit. If I'd produced any expression at all, it would have been an eye-roll. Word spread in this county about everything and anything, no matter how innocuous.

"Can't claim niceness for going to see her. I was summoned." The other two made knowing, faintly amused sounds, as I'd intended. "I heard the brief, underrepresented history of women artists, leading to an odd foray into and an even odder foray out of the history of a local artist. Carey Maight."

No amusement now, but another abrupt stiffness.

If I hadn't still been short on sleep, I might have interpreted that better. As it was, the only thing that came to mind was they'd reacted to my coming even that close to criticizing the icon of Cottonwood County who was Emmaline Parens.

"Sorry. That wasn't gracious, when she was kind enough to invite me. Along with being shorthanded, I'm short on sleep."

"The lack of sleep does not show," O.D. said gallantly, though mendaciously. Also, possibly, gratefully at the shift in topic.

Paytah pushed himself up. "Got a class. Goodbye, Grandfather. See you later, Elizabeth."

O.D. nodded. I turned to say bye.

I saw something Paytah had blocked while sitting.

Against the back wall of the shelves, with books cleared well to either side of it and a small art lamp dispelling shadows, was a painting. It showed a red hill, fuzzed by sagebrush, melting into the surrounding land under blue sky, like an ice cube under the sunlight. No sun showed in the painting, yet the sky seemed to shimmer with it. It was that evocation of the light, the air—

"It's by Carey Maight," I said aloud.

"It is," O.D. said.

"I've seen some of her portraits—"

"Those are not the paintings of hers to admire," Paytah's words came sharp from the doorway.

"You prefer the portraits to the landscapes?" O.D. said.

Thinking of the painting from the museum, I couldn't agree. Still, there were points for the portraits.

Before I could express either sentiment, Paytah said, "I prefer the results when she devoted her talent to freedom instead of to those who stole it from us."

He walked away, clearly feeling he'd vanquished all before him.

I stood and walked toward the painting, then discovered I preferred a bit of distance. It wasn't best seen from nose-against-the-paint distance, but from where O.D. sat.

"You must know all about Carey Maight," I murmured.

Had their stiffness come because they thought I'd criticized Carey Maight?

"Most in this area know some."

As mild as his words and tone were, it felt like a Keep Out sign.

I wouldn't. Not permanently. But I came here for another purpose. Accomplish that first.

I returned to my seat, then spoke with deliberation.

"Has your granddaughter taken your class? Or, perhaps, she doesn't need to, covering all those topics through her association with you?"

"I have more than one granddaughter. However, I will not pretend confusion over which granddaughter you mean. Hailey has not taken any class I teach. Nor does she know anything of our ways, our history, our culture."

"Why not? Having you as her grandfather surely exposed her to—"

"It did not. Her mother was why."

After a noticeable gap, I asked, "Was that Kim's reaction to the disapproval—from her people and his—of her relationship with Isaiah?"

"When that was their largest trouble, I can believe she did feel that way. It would be understandable. After his death … She cut herself off from her people, who did not share her grief. She also wanted nothing to do with the tribe. She blamed it for Isaiah's death, exposing him to what she called the infectious disease of alcohol. Especially drinking and driving. She blamed me, too. For not being a stronger factor in Isaiah's life. For not keeping him away from the drinking, the recklessness.

"And she was correct. I should have done more."

As he did for Paytah? His other grandchildren? I knew he was involved in their lives, as well as being a tribal leader.

"Yet Kim included you in Hailey's life," I said.

"Her good heart would not let her cut me off from Hailey, as long as I came as *grandfather* and left *tribe* outside their door."

"By being in her life as her grandfather, you left open the possibility of teaching her about *tribe* eventually."

His expression gave me nothing. Neither did his silence. Still, I'd take the bet that I was right at almost any odds.

"You said Kim Newhall's good heart. Does that mean you were the exception and approved of her relationship with your son?"

"I did not know Kim until after my son's death."

"But you knew of your son's relationship with Kim before he died. Did you approve?"

"I was not asked for my opinion. I did not express it to my son or anyone."

"Did you approve?"

"I did not."

"Then they knew it. You're not as difficult to read as you might like to think, O.D."

I'd amused him now.

"Whoever said you were a stupid woman was mostly wrong."

I chuckled. "But not entirely wrong."

"We are all stupid at times." His amusement disappeared. "Know this about Kim. She never once raised to me that I had tried to stand between her and Isaiah. She took me as I was then. A man who had lost his son. A man who wanted a chance to know that son's daughter. She wanted that for her daughter as well. She saw a difference between the tribe and the individuals in it. As she did with her own people. It was her greatest gift."

It was a valedictory comment, meant to close the door on this conversation and send me on my way.

I stayed seated.

You know what they say about when one door closes...

O.D. Everett regarded me with only the mildest of interest.

In a casual, nearly disinterested tone I hoped matched his expression, I said, "Someone once told me about an artist who did mezzo-tints based off a portrait of the prince who became King George IV of England when he was young and considered quite handsome. The print artist came back years later to update the prints after a self-indulgent life caught up with the royal figure.

"The later edition of the print could serve as a warning against that kind of life."

"Hah," he said in soft amusement, likely connecting the observation to Carey Maight's portraits of county leaders, as I intended.

"And I said to the person telling me this," I continued, "that the artist must have been brave, to show the king as he was. But the person telling me about these before and after prints said, in fact, the later prints showed pencil marks, apparently based on measurements, that would have made the afters far, far less flattering than the finished product was. The artist showed some change, but not as much as reality."

"Hah." This time the sound added understanding to amusement.

"Exactly. So the artist was somewhat brave—an artist with no bravery and no integrity could have portrayed older royalty as he'd been as a young and handsome prince. But the artist also was cautious."

"And so was able to continue feeding his family."

"Yes. An important ability," I confirmed. "I'd imagine that held true for Carey Maight as well."

"It was of utmost importance to me, since I would not be here if she hadn't fed her daughter."

I tried not to gawk at him. I failed.

"You're Carey Maight's grandson?"

Chapter Twenty-One

CAREY MAIGHT'S GRANDSON and Hailey Newhall's grandfather.

Which made Hailey the great-great-granddaughter of the artist.

My brain tried to sort tangled strands—including this family tree— in real time.

Pieces of Mrs. Parens' conversation fit better now. Carey Maight wasn't a Wyoming history lesson out of the blue. She connected to Hailey Newhall.

But at that point, Hailey had told me only about the horse-tail theft. Even if Mrs. P believed Hailey wanted another investigation and intended her information as background—deep, deep background considering her foray into Renaissance Europe—on the deaths of Kim and Lewis Newhall, how could Hailey's great-great-grandmother figure in?

I resisted the urge to rub my forehead.

At least now I understood Jack Delahunt's segue from Hailey's situation to Carey Maight being supported by Mrs. Parens' parents.

"I am her grandson," O.D. confirmed without emotion.

Questions jammed up in my head. I snatched one to keep him talking. "Everyone uses both her names. Not just her first name like a lot of people do for Charlie Russell or her last name like they do for Frederic Remington."

"She said it took both names to identify her," he said. "I wondered if she also liked that people—the white art world, in particular— couldn't know if she was a man or woman, couldn't know if she was of their world or not. She never responded to anyone who called her Mrs.

Maight. Wouldn't let anyone call her grandmother or aunt or mother. She said she was not to be defined by her role in other people's lives."

I could see strength in her emphasizing herself as an individual— insisting on it. But sadness also. Refusing to be defined by her roles at least partially denied the relationships.

"Women can feel invisible inside those roles, as if there's no core of a real person."

"You will never be invisible. You don't require the mirror of other people's opinions to make you visible. Many rely on others to tell them who they are."

O.D.'s turning my words around to spotlight me silenced me.

Not an accident.

Not a time for subtlety. "And Carey Maight? It sounds like she refused to be invisible. But she wouldn't have had to work so hard at it if others didn't try to make her invisible."

The slightest shift of his shoulders acknowledged without full agreement.

"She painted people to make her living, to feed and clothe and shelter her family. Her other paintings, those of the land, those of her people, those were of her soul."

"Portraits went to the sitter—the buyer—but how were the landscapes dispersed?"

"Carey Maight gave them to those she most favored."

"You?"

"I received a few. But to live was to fall out of her favor." His eyes narrowed in thought. "To live and to grow. She did not like people changing. She could forgive—she did see it as requiring her forgiveness—as she became accustomed to the new person the old one became. My mother said it was like a snake shedding its skin as it grew. Carey Maight preferred the existing skin to what came next ... until that was the existing skin. She was most comfortable with babies, coming into their first skin, and old people, changing slower and slower.

"With those going through challenges and changes, she could be short, distant. When I was getting my first degree, she barely looked at me. Talked to me out of the side of her mouth.

"I asked if she resented me going away for schooling because she could not. A cruel thing to say if true. A stupid thing to say if not. The look she gave me said I was a child not to have seen both. That look. I was humbled as never before or since. I was very much in that state of shedding a skin and growing not just one, but multiples I could shift to for what I was doing, where I was, *who* I was."

He nodded. "I see you think that would not be comfortable. You are correct. I learned to keep parts of many skins in order to form one. You did that, as well. But here, it has been the opposite for you, Elizabeth. Leaving behind portions of skins from your past. Paring down to those you want."

This was becoming very uncomfortable. And not only at the nerve-crawling concept of shedding my skin and pulling on new. Or all the mentions of snakes.

Had it been a similar experience for those who sat for Carey Maight's portraits? How did painting people and landscapes differ for her? Because, in a way, she got beneath the skin of landscapes as well ... while simultaneously exploring their air.

I'd crossed from artsy fanciful to downright weird.

"She followed her way to her death. Many of her paintings went to her first great-grandchild, a baby at the time. *Because* he was a baby." His breath deepened for two cycles. "He died before he could scatter them to the winds of his whims, of his desires. He died without a will, but with a daughter—Hailey Newhall."

My eyes popped wider.

"She owns the largest collection of Carey Maight's works. Though we have now established ... safeguards. That—"

"Wait a minute. Go back to Hailey. You didn't approve of Kim and Isaiah. What about Hailey and Clayton Rayger? And you know she's asked me to look into her parents' deaths? Why am I asking? Of course you do. What do you think of that."

His eyes nearly closed. "A man capable of learning does not cut off his second leg."

Having been wrong about Isaiah and Kim, he was not prepared to risk being wrong about Hailey and Clayton and lose his relationship with his granddaughter.

"As I was saying, we established safeguards to the legacy of Carey Maight. Our concern was that without such safeguards the paintings would disperse into nothing."

As Mrs. P described happening to many women painters.

But there could be other factors.

"That also keeps the market for Carey Maight paintings very low on supply and prices go up."

He jerked a shoulder, revealing impatience. "We are not collectors leveraging the market. We do not look to capitalize on ownership of these paintings."

Was that true of all the people hemmed in by those *safeguards*? And just how far did they go?

"The exhibit Clara at the museum is putting on next year, are you lending any paintings for it?"

"I am. As are others."

"Hailey?"

"No."

"Why?"

"For that, you must ask her."

"Is she part of the group with these safeguards?"

"Yes. After my son died and those paintings went to his infant daughter, a number of us agreed that anyone interested in selling would first offer it within our group, Friends and Family of Carey Maight.

"We had gathered in my living room to create a written agreement, when came one more knock. In walked Kim. She said she'd heard about our meeting and as Hailey's guardian, she wanted to know what was going on. She was among the first to sign the agreement.

"That was my first true interaction with her. I came to respect her. I had thought she was bad for my son. As time went on, I saw it was the opposite. She had been good for him, though he might not have been good for her. Lewis Newhall was.

"It is a hard truth to know your son would not have been as good a husband to his woman, as good a father to your grandchild as another man became."

DIANA CAME IN my front door with a mild grumble.

"With two of us out at my place, the center of gravity shifts. We could hold these brain trusts at my place like we used to when you lived in the bunkhouse, Elizabeth."

"Easier to come here from the station," Jennifer said.

"For you," Diana pointed out. "Not for Mike and me."

"This way we don't disturb your kids. School night," I said virtuously.

She scoffed. "Have you tried to wake those kids up? A bomb might do the trick. Nothing short of it. But I know when I'm licked. Think about it, anyway."

I didn't raise it as a reason to gather at my house, but Shadow would miss the extra attention. At the moment, he was being petted at one end by Jennifer and the other by Mike.

That stopped only when Diana placed a bag of goodies on the coffee table, distracting Mike. She took a chair close to the fireplace, where a modest but sturdy fire chugged along. Central heating did the trick for warmth, but the fire added something a thermostat never could.

I set out glasses and mugs on the kitchen counter for hot or cold drinks. In my small house, they could serve themselves in the kitchen and hear everything said in the living room.

As I rounded the counter to join them in the living area, Mike said, "So, tell us all, Elizabeth. Seems like you're the only one who knows anything."

"Oh, I suspect Jennifer does."

"No, I don't. All I knew was Hailey Newhall called and asked to talk to you."

I slanted my head for a different angle on her. "Had you heard about her horse's tail being cut off and stolen?"

"A little."

"You knew her parents died two years ago last July."

"Everybody knew that. I—"

"Except me."

"—didn't pay attention to details."

The articles hadn't been thick with details, either. "Diana, I meant to ask, were you at the crime scene or—?"

She shook her head. "I didn't catch those assignments. Was aware of it because Gavin was at the high school with Jess when it happened. Still is. Didn't know Hailey. And before you ask, didn't hear about Fred White's tail until a friend texted me mid-morning."

"Do you really think there's something in this—I mean the parents, not the horse's tail?" Mike asked.

I told them about my encounters with Shelton and Alvaro. "I might be making too much of Shelton's semantics with not calling it a murder-suicide, but Richard truly seemed troubled."

"Shelton told you to leave it alone." Jennifer said, clearly considering it an inducement.

"Defying Shelton is not all that's needed to commit to an all-out effort," I said. "Especially not with what's going on at the station."

"Don't give it another thought. I'll have a word with the owner," Mike said airily. "You think Shelton's having his usual fit over us looking into a murder?"

"Maybe."

"It's not a new case he's investigating where we keep getting ahead of him, so it shouldn't bug him as much."

Jennifer's assessment of our always being ahead of Shelton and what might bother him both struck me as overly optimistic.

I settled for, "Maybe."

"I'd think Shelton would be more peeved about an old case being resurrected," Diana said. "If we're saying the sheriff's department got it wrong—"

"Redus got it wrong," Jennifer said.

"True. But, still, a case they thought was settled," Diana persisted. "And we'd be saying all they got right was that Kim Newhall was murdered. Not who killed her, not that Lewis committed suicide, and of course not who killed him. The more I think about it, the more I'd expect Shelton to give us a hard time."

"Getting in my way when I'm buying cookies is plenty hard enough for me."

They all laughed.

I asked, "Any of you remember anything *before* the Newhalls' deaths involving Foster Redus?"

Mike said, "I was still battling delusions of my knees carrying me through another NFL season. Retired before regular season and came here. Plenty of talk about the deaths, but the case was closed."

"No," Jennifer said. "Why?"

Diana repeated, *"Anything?"*

"A case, an incident. Something to do with his job."

"Until I met you," Diana said, "I did not memorize criminal events, nor all activities by the sheriff's deputies of Cottonwood County, despite those activities being considerably more limited than they are now."

Mike preempted my rebuttal. "What makes you ask, Elizabeth?"

"Shelton said closing the Newhall case was part of a *hot streak* for Redus. Does that mean anything to any of you?"

Diana and Jennifer shook their heads.

"I can search Redus' name in the *Independence*, see if Needham reported something that could be part of a hot streak," Jennifer offered.

"Good, Jennifer."

"What else can I do?"

That was a challenge. I challenged back. "Find more about the thefts of horse hair."

"I will." Challenge accepted.

Mike said, "Which brings us back to you being the only one who knows anything, Elizabeth. Start talking."

Chapter Twenty-Two

IT WAS SUCH meager fare, I found myself including not just what Hailey and Gavin and Wylie Easley said, but also Mrs. P and O.D. and even Linda on Carey Maight.

I pointed out O.D. never answered my question about how he viewed Hailey asking us to investigate Kim and Lewis' deaths.

When we got to the part about the group of Kim, Isaiah, Easley, and Clayton, Diana explained the relationships.

I told them about Hailey now being engaged to Clayton.

Jennifer said, "So what if he's older? It's not like he's after her money. They were together before she inherited from her parents."

"Did she inherit much when her parents died?"

"I don't think so," Diana said. "They sold the house—understandably—and she and Gavin moved out to that ranchette."

"And Clayton," I inserted.

"The biggest inheritance has to be the Carey Maight paintings," Mike said.

Diana shook her head. "She inherited them when Isaiah died. Kim had control as guardian, but that ended well before the shootings. Although everything I heard indicated Hailey, Kim, Lewis, all were good with having the paintings stay in the space he built for them, especially with Hailey away at school, then living mostly on the ranch while she worked for Jack Delahunt."

"If Clayton didn't know she already owned the paintings—?" I started.

"Oh, he knew. Everybody knew."

"She could have written a will that leaves him all the paintings," Jennifer said. "Although why he'd kill her parents when she already had the paintings…?"

Diana said, "And if that was his goal, why is she still alive? So that points away from him. Clayton and Hailey … I don't get that pairing, even though it is Emma and Mr. Knightley-ish."

"Emma and Mr. who?" Jennifer asked.

"Don't let Mrs. P hear you ask that. Emma Woodhouse from the Jane Austen novel *Emma* and Mr. Knightley was her family's neighbor and … her brother-in-law's brother. Yeah, that's right." She focused on Jennifer. "You must have read it. It was required in Mrs. P's classes."

"Oh, yeah. I just forgot."

Diana, who'd been looking at Jennifer, turned to me. We had reached the same conclusion.

"You never read the book, Jennifer," I said.

She started to puff up to deny it, then sank back. "Don't tell Mrs. P." Earnestly, she added, "I did watch the movies. There were three really, really old ones like all out at the same time, except in one she had a different name."

"*Clueless*," I filled in for her, despite the *really, really old* description. "That's the movie, not the character."

"I know *that*." She added, "How are Hailey and Clayton like that story?"

Apparently, the movies hadn't deeply affected her.

Diana said, "Emma grew up with this guy being like an older brother—"

"Or, in this case, another father figure," I inserted.

"—until she abruptly realized her feelings were not sisterly."

"Or, in this case, daughterly."

"Okay, I guess I get that," Jennifer said. "But weren't there other people in the movies who made her jealous because the guy started getting interested in them?"

She'd retained at least that much.

"Yes, there were." Diana approved more generously than Mrs. P would. "That's an interesting point. Could Clayton have had someone from his past who wanted revenge on Hailey for taking him away?"

"Pretty extreme," Jennifer said.

"It would be," I agreed. "To kill her parents as punishment for stealing her guy? And it didn't do any good because they're still together."

"I meant extreme for anybody getting that worked up about any guy." She tipped her head.

Diana, with her usual equanimity, said, "Maybe. But I'm going to ask around. In the meantime, anything else?"

Mike cleared his voice. "I did see Aunt Gee today. She came to town for sheriff's department business and I took her to lunch."

"What did she say?" Jennifer demanded.

"Hardly anything. She was really tight-lipped. About that case, anyway. She had a lot to say about other things." A look crossed his face, and he added hurriedly, "The only thing I got out of her was the gunshot residue dispersion pattern was *unusual*."

"In what way?"

He shrugged. "When I say tight-lipped, I mean it. Said it was unusual, then clamped her mouth closed. You weren't kidding about her being protective of the sheriff's department. Practically bit my head off."

I resisted asking how she'd done that with her mouth clamped closed.

"Even though this was Redus' case and under Sheriff Widcuff's watch?" Diana said. I suspected she approved of Gee's no-talking policy now that the department was under Sheriff Russ Conrad.

"Yup."

I said abruptly, "Shelton said incomplete."

"Incomplete what?" Jennifer asked.

I didn't answer immediately because I was remembering Alvaro said the same thing. But Shelton was the one who mattered.

"Shelton said the gunshot residue evidence was *incomplete*."

Mike leaned forward. "What else did he say?"

"Nothing. He literally said *gunshot residue was incomplete*. I asked incomplete in what way, he didn't answer. I should have followed up more. I should have asked—"

Mike cut me off. "He wouldn't have answered. Not if he'd decided not to tell you."

He was right. I still should have asked. "What's interesting is he didn't say *inconclusive*, like he'd say if it didn't give them an answer one way or the other, but *incomplete*."

"Not finished?" Diana suggested.

"Then how could they close the case? And why would Redus cite it to Hailey as proof her dad killed her mom."

"Because he was an asshole," Mike proposed.

"Valid possibility," I acknowledged. "Still, that word *incomplete* bothers me. Let's see what we can find out."

"I'll try Aunt Gee again."

"Good. Richard also said the trajectory wasn't what he'd expect." I explained that.

At the end, Jennifer said, "There was another thing you said Redus told Hailey."

Diana supplied, "You mean him saying Kim was moving toward Lewis when she was shot, right, Elizabeth?"

"That's what Hailey said Redus told her," I confirmed. "She said he said the gunshot residue showed that. Though exactly how that could be told from gunshot residue ... But maybe that's the only other detail she remembered and she's combining two things he said. Or the only details Redus gave her. Other evidence he didn't share could have made him conclude Kim was moving toward Lewis."

Diana frowned. "Moving toward him could mean a lot of things."

"Almost anything. Attacking, pleading, trying to get the gun away, trying to go to his aid, reflexive—"

"Trying to go to his aid. That's an interesting one," Diana said. "Why did you say that?"

"I was thinking the murder victim in a murder-suicide could try to come to the other person's aid by stopping them from committing the act. Not only trying to save her own life, but save his, because she knew he'd kill himself next."

Jennifer said slowly, "That would say a lot about their relationship—even as he held a gun on her she wanted to save him."

I gusted out a pent-up breath. "Or it could be any of the other things I mentioned and a lot I didn't and each of those could mean a lot about their relationship. We're flailing around in the murk. All we really know is how Hailey viewed their relationship."

"Also the brother's impressions," Mike said.

"We have those mostly second-hand through Hailey until we talk more to him. What I got today was he's angry. Very, very angry."

Diana said, "Interesting you used the word murk."

"You think murkiness is more common? That doesn't make murk wrong."

"I wasn't assailing your knowledge of words. I was thinking murk in slang, including hip-hop, can mean to kill someone."

"Since when do you know hip-hop slang?"

"Since I have teenagers. They might be ranch kids, but it doesn't mean they don't have ears. Or eyes."

In her rueful tone, I heard all she wished she could protect Jessica and Gary Junior from, along with the knowledge she couldn't. She *could* aim to give them tools to protect themselves.

How had Kim and Lewis Newhall felt they'd done with Hailey, sending her out into the world, engaged to a man they'd considered a friend, yet were against her marrying.

Solely because of the age difference? Or more?

Talk about murk.

Hailey's mother and stepfather had another child, nowhere near as far along the launch continuum as Hailey.

"We need to talk to Gavin," I said.

"We need a lot of things." Diana held up one hand. Her fingertips were orange, so maybe we didn't take her next words seriously. "We always do at this stage. But this time..."

That sobered my response immediately. "I see us having two major handicaps. The lapse in time." Nods all around. "And the original investigation—"

"Being done by Foster Redus," Mike completed.

"Exactly. If we were looking at this in real time, what would we want to check?"

"Alibis," he said.

"Timelines," Jennifer added. "I have software I've been wanting to try, but it's so long ago…"

"Motive," Diana said. "Sort of. I mean, if there'd been a big, glaring motive like financial disaster or she was dying of a painful disease or—I don't know, but something easy to find, even Redus would have found it. Instead, it's like most people—except Hailey—"

"And Penny."

"—accept Lewis killed Kim, then himself, but can't say why."

I felt myself nodding as she finished. "Excellent. We know the means—no question about that. So, what we're talking about are motive and opportunity. With alibis and timelines a huge part of opportunity, it's tough because of the time lapse. Hard to check after more than two years, especially since Redus didn't check them in the first place."

"And if asking questions got us to the motive, it seems talk would have gotten there a long time ago," Diana said.

"Maybe. But the talk hasn't been combined with the rest of it, including questioning the investigation, delving into what was going on in their lives, reconstructing their emotional landscape."

"Like those recreations of crime scenes, only about their emotional lives," Jennifer said.

"Very well expressed," Mike said.

As I added, "Exactly," my mind followed another track. "You know what would really help would be a copy of the report."

"Yeah, right," Mike said. "Why don't we see if we can have a sé-ance with Foster Redus and get it direct from him."

He grinned. It faded as he looked around at the rest of us.

"You want me to ask my aunt for a copy of the report?"

"Sure would save us time and effort."

"You know what the chances are? If slim and none were each cut in half, then cut in half again…" Another look around at his listeners. "Fine. I'll try. But we probably would have a better chance with the séance."

DAY FIVE

TUESDAY

Chapter Twenty-Three

MIKE GRABBED ME by the arm as I walked into KWMT.

That might otherwise have been painful, since he's a strong guy and appeared to be worked up about something. But my November layers provided padding. Not quite kid-in-a-snowsuit padding, but close.

"I need you, Elizabeth. It's an emergency."

Far too early in the day for a newscast emergency. "What's up?"

"I got a call from the station—my station—my station in Chicago." Life was complicated when you had to clarify which TV station you meant. "There's a huge snowstorm there."

"Hah. And you're here in Wyoming with no more than flurries."

"Yeah. Not the point, though. The team that was coming here to interview me is stuck at O'Hare. They can't get here. They can't even get back to the station. I hear they're sending good stuff from the airport, but..."

Even through my morning fog, I got the significance. "They can't do the interview with you before Needham interviews you. The Sherman *Independence* will scoop your home station."

"I can't let that happen. And there's Dell."

"Forget Dell and delay the interview with Needham."

He grimaced. "I promised. Both of them. And it would mess up Needham's deadline." Reliable and considerate. Hard not to love this guy. "But I swore to my bosses that owning KWMT wouldn't screw things up there. And here's the first thing and..."

"Not your fault there's snow in Chicago." Having grown up in Illinois, I figured the blame went a lot higher. "They've got to be used to that. What did you tell them when they told you the crew couldn't get here?"

"That I'd take care of it. That you'd interview me."

"What?" I took back the hard-not-to-love-this guy. "I'm not—"

"And Diana's going to shoot it. C'mon, it'll be fun. And it will save my ass."

He did have an ass worth saving.

"I get to ask you anything," I bargained.

"Sure, sure. I just don't have to answer. It'll have to be later this afternoon. I have employee meetings."

Mike had started one-on-one meetings with all station employees. One benefit of being short-staffed.

Rather than working through the hierarchy, he had Sheila in administration draw names randomly. They posted the time slots and let people swap for their convenience. My spot was third-to-the-last, which suited me fine.

"And I have business calls in between. I'd invite you to join them, but Mel made me promise you wouldn't. You really need to let him off the hook. The guy's shaking in his boots."

"Later." Maybe much later.

MIKE HAD BARELY closed his office door when, phone in hand and Diana in tow, Jennifer ordered us into the KWMT ladies' room.

Accosted twice and I wasn't even to my desk.

The ladies' room was relatively private because no one could open the door with the three of us in there.

"I have background on the horse-tail thefts," she announced.

I'd hoped for something juicier, but okay.

"You already know there have been thefts all over the United States and Canada, back to 2004—"

"I didn't know that," I said.

The other two ignored me. "—and I found references to thefts in New York in the late Nineteenth Century and St. Louis in the early Twentieth Century. Also current reports of thefts in the UK and Switzerland and Australia."

I whistled.

Jennifer continued, "In some incidents, the horse's tailbone is bruised or even broken."

Diana shook her head. "Fred White got off relatively easy."

"Tell that to Hailey," Jennifer mumbled, then returned to her reportorial voice. "Even without such injuries, thieves can be charged with animal cruelty, a criminal attack, criminal mischief, and trespass. *If* they can be caught."

"Are people caught?" I asked.

"I've found no reports of arrests. But I have the guys digging deeper." *The guys* were online friends of hers. Their computer skills might rival Jennifer's. My concern was their ethics didn't. "Most of the reports talk about how hard it is to catch anyone. The thefts happen at night or when nobody's around. More people are putting up cameras. The thieves move on. Because there *is* a market."

"So someone else in the area could get hit now that Hailey's put up the cameras. Keep checking with—"

"The sheriff's department. I am. I found lots of uses for horse hair. It's durable and strong. Great for cleaning and shining leather.

"But it's soft enough to clean jewelry and silverware. One blogger got excited about how it got into the filigree of her family's sterling silver tableware without scratching." She gave the impression of a tourist who'd visited a strange land and lived to tell the tale. "Lack of scratching's also why it's used for polishing jewelry.

"And you can make jewelry with it—horse-hair bracelets are all over. Along with what's listed as pow wow regalia."

"Why O.D. reacted the way he did," I murmured.

Jennifer kept going, "And there's the market for mane and tail extensions for show horses. A mane extension, far less than a pound, can retail for $500 and up. Plus…" She drew it out, ensuring she had our full attention. "Human wigs and extensions."

"Human ... That's..." Clearly Diana didn't have words to follow up.

Still, she had more than my "Ew."

"But where would you sell any of this stuff?" Diana asked.

Jennifer tapped at her phone and up popped a well-known marketplace.

We crowded around her screen as she scrolled. "See? There are bracelets in different colors." Braided and chevron patterns slid past.

"Slow down, slow down." After several seconds, Diana added, "I see people selling horse hair or horse-hair brushes or the rest of it, but not a lot of buyers rating them."

"Would they be selling if someone wasn't buying?" I asked.

"And this is the open-market tip of what all the sources say is a black-market iceberg," Jennifer said. "That's some of what the guys are looking into."

Diana pointed. "Look, an antique lady's sterling silver brush with horse hair for sale."

"Wonder if the lady used it on her horse-hair wig," I muttered.

Still looking over Jennifer's shoulder, Diana continued, "Look at the prices on these things. They could be a lucrative cottage industry."

"But first they need horse hair, including from horses being slaughtered." Jennifer's face darkened. "There are reports people get horses slaughtered for the money—hair and the rest—rather than adopting them out."

I felt sympathy for Fred White's confusion and discomfort, but he had Hailey looking out for him. I spread a lot more sympathy to animals who landed in the wrong human hands.

Echoing my thoughts, Diana muttered, "*People*. Sometimes the bad ones block my view of the good ones..."

"No kidding," Jennifer said. "Okay, so, we're covered on research on horse-tail thefts? You don't want any more?"

She'd already opened the door to the hallway. Diana and I followed.

I said, "I suppose, but I can't guarantee—"

"Good. Because I'm going to be busy with something else. And so are you, Elizabeth."

"What?"

"For me, phone and financial records. Got a start but there's a lot more."

"The station—" Diana started.

"The rest of them can take care of that. Audrey's got things in hand. I know you're helping with consulting and the intern program, but that stuff won't happen right away."

"What do you think I'm going to be doing instead, because—"

Jennifer tipped her head toward the hallway behind Diana and me. I turned and saw Hailey Newhall coming toward us.

Before she could give voice to the demand I saw in her expression to know if we'd solved and resolved every question in her heart and mind, Jennifer said, "Thanks for coming, Hailey. Elizabeth would like to talk to you."

I didn't even have time to give Jennifer the dirty look that maneuver deserved before Hailey responded.

"You said I had to come. I stopped to tell you I can't. I'm taking Gav his lunch. There's nothing in the house and ... Anyway, I can't. Besides, I'm meeting Clayton for lunch at the café after."

Not the two of them together, when that would seem to be a natural combo. Solely because the times didn't mesh? Or Hailey and Clayton wanted time alone? Or...?

Well, now I had to know.

"Great. I'll tag along and get to talk with all of you." I presented a big, fat smile in answer to her less-than-enthusiastic reaction.

She didn't have the nerve to say no to that smile.

Was Fred White hurt when his tail was taken?" I asked, as Hailey drove us through town toward the high school.

Her truck fell between the two I'd seen at her place. Not new, not fancy, but kept up well.

"Horses need their tails for all sorts of—"

"I know." Thanks to recent education in the matter. "But physical injuries?"

"No. Deputy Alvaro said that was fortunate, considering some of these thefts. And Clayton keeps pointing that out. Trying to cheer me up."

"What does Clayton do?"

"He works at Pen and Ink in town."

"The print shop?"

"Yeah. They do framing, too. That's mostly him. Store should have been his. When the previous owner sold, this guy swooped in and bought it out from under Clayton. And then he didn't even make Clayton the manager, even though he's been there longest and has the most talent. Brought in somebody else who works with photography, because the shop also repairs and sells cameras. As if that's more important. Clayton does things for the museum, too. The guy in charge of cameras doesn't."

"What sort of things?"

"Working with the art," she said vaguely.

"How long have you two been together?"

"It'll be three years at New Year's." Just after the family photo she'd shared. "We'd known each other forever. He and my birth father were close. Clayton was always there when I was little. Even after Mom married Dad, Clayton came around. I took him for granted.

"Then, that New Year's Eve, we were both at this party on our own, you know? No dates. And we got talking. Really talking. It was like we hadn't ever looked at each other before. One minute we were like we'd always been ... and then we weren't. We were so much more."

"What did your parents think of you dating someone so much older?"

"Mom was a couple years older than Dad. Besides, in twenty years it'll hardly make any difference at all."

Those sounded like arguments she'd raised to her parents, which meant...

"What did they say about the two of you dating?"

"They were awful to him, to us. It made him so miserable. They said they wouldn't make me choose, but in reality they did because of how they made Clayton feel. I chose him. I love him."

She said nothing for a moment, but it wasn't exactly silent, because of the whooshing whisper of her thoughts and self-arguments, including that she'd loved her parents, too. And how much she regretted they'd died possibly thinking she didn't.

One strain—me! I was the strain in their marriage. Me.

"Did both your parents feel the same way?"

She opened her mouth. Frowned. Closed her mouth.

I waited.

"I was going to say Mom was more against me being with Clayton than Dad was. But they never said that."

"We often pick up a lot of information without consciousness of taking it in."

"I guess." She was not interested in the theoretical. Only the practical. And personal.

"Can you think of anything you saw or heard that helped you toward that feeling?"

She shook her head. "I told you, Mom knew him from before and he'd always been a friend of the family. So why she got so weird about it...

"And then when she and Dad ... died, he couldn't have been kinder and more loving to me. It was like all his friendship for them came back, along with him loving me, and he understood, like nobody else could."

She fell into a silence.

I let it develop to see what might come out of it.

We were nearly to the high school turnoff when she spoke again.

"You asked what he's like. My brother. What he's like now is not what he was like most of his life. A sunny kid. Smart, funny, athletic. Got along with pretty much everybody."

"And now?"

"Surly. One of his teachers used that word to describe him. If he weren't so good at football, he'd probably be suspended or quit school. I don't know what's going to happen when the season's over. But he's

not even as good at football as he used to be because of his attitude.
Too many penalties. The coach pulled him from one game. Told him
he was off the team if he didn't get straight."

Chapter Twenty-Four

WE'D STOPPED AT a fast-food place close to the school and Hailey ordered nearly half the menu. No wonder they had no food in the house if that's how this kid ate.

Despite the tempting aromas, I opted to wait for the café lunch with Clayton I'd invited myself to.

Almost before Hailey backed the truck into a spot so we faced the school, Gavin Newhall strode across our windshield view.

"You're late," he accused his sister, not acknowledging my presence as he climbed into the back seat.

I might have passed it off as a bad case of hangry, except it seemed to be permanent.

She passed the bag over the seatback to him.

He dug into it.

I swung around with my back against the door so I could keep both of them in view.

"You know your sister wants to reinvestigate your parents' deaths."

Gavin kept eating, didn't look up.

"And we know what you think happened. But if you're basing that solely on what Deputy Redus told you, I recommend you look up the reporting on him after his murder. He was not a reliable source. Make up your own mind. That's what we're doing. Finding the facts and letting those tell us the truth."

He met my expectations by continuing to chew.

I said to Hailey, "Let's start with what was going on in your lives in June, the month before your parents died."

Hailey tipped her head, thinking, but shook it at the same time. "It was all pretty normal. I was at the ranch a lot, working and bunking there four or five nights a week. Seeing Clayton when I could. Gavin was in summer school and working out for football. Mom and Dad were working, gardening. We celebrated Dad's birthday on the twenty-third."

She shot a look toward her brother he didn't return.

"Really, the only thing was Mom being worked up about a missing key. She said it disappeared the week before Dad's birthday. But she must have been wrong or it got mislaid. Because they were in the silverware drawer when we packed in the fall."

"What key?"

"To the painting closet," Gavin muttered from in back.

"What's the painting closet?"

"A room—a large closet—Dad built between the house and the garage," Hailey said. "It was heated in the winter, stayed cool enough in the summer. He built racks, too, to hold the paintings upright. That's what the expert he consulted before he built it said. Never expose the paintings to extreme heat, cold, humidity, or sunlight—"

"In other words, don't have them in Wyoming," Gavin muttered.

She ignored him.

"He used to take me in there when I was little and tell me all the ways to take care of them. Be careful not to lean a painting against sharp surfaces, including corners of furniture or anything that could stretch out the canvas, even tear it. Don't let it get super dusty because that can dry out the paint. But only a gentle brush, because cloths can catch the surface.

"People think it's special treatment to preserve them, but it's more not doing things. Don't use household cleaners or spray or water on them. Mom showed me how when I got older. I do it for the paintings now."

Another grumble from the back seat. "They have their own bed-room."

"What are you griping about? You want that room? It's smaller than yours, but if you want it—"

"With the windows covered up? No thank you. I don't—"

"Stop." I surprised them enough that the word worked. I focused on Hailey. "You said *they*. *They were there in the silverware drawer*. But you first said your mom was upset about *a* key missing. Was there more than one key to the painting closet?"

"No. That got mixed up. The key to the painting closet Gavin mentioned came later. The key Mom was upset about at Dad's birthday was the one to the gun safe. She didn't say anything about the one to the painting closet being gone and she definitely would have. But after ... after what happened, the painting closet key wasn't there when the deputies wanted to get in. Then, when we packed to move, both keys were there. They must have been in the silverware drawer the whole time, under an upside-down serving spoon."

I felt like I should hold onto my head to keep it from launching.

"Let me get this straight," I said more calmly than I felt. "A key to your gun safe went missing a few weeks before the shootings and nobody saw it again until you were moving out of the house in the fall."

"I know what you're thinking," Hailey said, "because I thought the same thing—that was proof Lewis didn't shoot Mom and himself. But he had his own key and Deputy Redus said he must have used it and put it back in the bedroom."

My head ached. Redus' explanation was Lewis got the gun out of the safe, then put the key neatly away before shooting Kim and himself?

"The missing key was the key kept by the back door with lots of other keys."

"Including the key to the painting closet? And it went missing at the same time?"

"Not at the same time. Mom didn't talk about that one being missing and she would have. When Redus said it wasn't where I told him it was, he wanted me to look. But I couldn't go in the house. Not then. It was hard enough to pack later."

For a second, sister and brother's gazes almost connected. Both looked away.

"Redus said they searched the whole house and couldn't find it. They said they had to inventory the paintings, to be sure nothing was taken. They broke in the door to the closet, then we had to pay for a new lock."

"Did the inventory match your records?"

"Yes. O.D. checked what the sheriff's department listed to be sure it was right. We did another check when we moved them from the house to where we are now. I didn't really care about any of that for a long time."

"So the key you found in the silverware drawer in the fall—"

"Keys. One to the gun safe and one to the painting closet were there, under a turned-over serving spoon. We hadn't been in the house, much less used things in the drawers, so they must have been sitting there the whole time. But you'd think the deputies would have found them."

Yes, you would.

"Anything else? Even the smallest detail out of the ordinary—"

"Mom talked about someone calling her, asking if she'd sold any paintings."

Unexpectedly, that came from the back seat. Gavin's tone said it was less than small, it was trivial.

"She was telling Dad. Sort of clicking her tongue, like it was a spam call. She said she told the caller the paintings weren't for sale and if any were, family would have the first chance to buy them."

"Did that caller call back?"

He shrugged.

"Did your mom get the name of the person?"

Another shrug. "Why would she? Mom told the person none of the paintings were for sale."

Hailey started to say something, until I made a quick, short gesture with my hand—in her line of sight, but below her brother's. I saw something more bubbling to the surface of his memory.

"She sort of grumbled the woman didn't know what she was talking about, saying Carey Maight landscapes were on the market. Said she sure wasn't giving out how to contact you."

We waited, but he added nothing.

"Anything else? You were going to summer school, Gavin. Was that unusual or—?"

"Did it the year before, too. They said making sure my grades stayed up was more important than getting a job."

"I told you the other unusual thing," Hailey said tautly. "I was arguing with my parents. I love Clayton and I wouldn't change that if I could, but there had to be a better way—"

"You think he snapped because of you? That's bull—" Gavin completed the term. "You think you're so important it was all about you?"

"That's not—"

"Why can't you let it go? Why can't you listen to everybody else and just let it go? You always know best. You haven't listened to anybody from the start. Clayton doesn't agree with you, you know. And that deputy didn't, either. He said it was murder-suicide. He was the professional."

"A professional screwup," Hailey shot back. "Look at all the stuff that came out about him after he disappeared." She turned to me. "You and those other people from the TV station dug up stuff about him. You know."

Before I could respond, Gavin said with a sneer, "Oh, yeah? O.D. thinks he was okay. I saw them, sitting in O.D.'s truck and one would talk and the other nod and then they'd switch. Talking and nodding like they were in sync. That was after—After. And O.D.'s always said you need to accept and move on."

"He doesn't know anything about investigating a murder." We all heard the weakness in Hailey's retort.

With grim satisfaction, Gavin pushed his advantage. "Clayton, too. He was always talking about Redus said this and Redus said that."

"That's because Clayton talked to him for me. He's protective and makes sure no one takes advantage of me. That Redus seemed familiar at first and I thought he was nice, but he wasn't. And I didn't want anything to do with him. Clayton kept me updated on the investigation. Something you never wanted to know about."

A spasm crossed the kid's face.

Even more than not knowing, he didn't want to think about it. Any of it. Which was why he'd gone the opposite direction, with his cut-and-dried stance that his father did it and deserved nothing but a direct trip to hell.

Hailey continued, telling me how Clayton had been the buffer between her and Redus, between her and the rest of the world when she needed it most.

I couldn't tell if she knew she was tormenting Gavin.

After a reference to Clayton taking care of her at the funeral service, when a relative of her mother's confronted Hailey about burying her parents together, Gavin interrupted abruptly.

"They were ready to accept the two of you."

Hailey turned toward him without comprehension, as if he'd spoken in another language.

"I heard them talking about it the night before. In the morning, before I left for school, Dad said to Mom, something about they agreed on it and they should tell you and Clayton without wasting anymore time, so the family could get back together."

He stumbled over the last couple words.

"But ... But you've never said anything about this. Why?"

"Guess I forgot."

She didn't believe it. I didn't either, and I barely knew the kid.

"Why didn't you tell me?" she said. "Why did you let me go on thinking—"

"Because you made them miserable. You ruined everything. We were a real family and you screwed it all up. So why should you feel better?"

"You—You—"

"Besides, they thought once they stopped fighting you on it, you'd get tired of him. It wasn't like they were really happy about you screwing a guy old enough to be your father."

If they'd been face-to-face, would she have slapped him?

She sure would have thought about it.

She did pivot around in her seat and glare at him.

Digging for something to keep them talking, which in this moment meant throttling back on the tension, I said conversationally to Gavin, "Have you ever gone over the timeline of what happened that day?"

With no throttling back, he scowled at me.

"I got up like normal, had breakfast like normal, said good-bye to my parents like normal, caught a bus for summer school like normal, went to classes like normal, came home on the bus like normal—"

"Not like normal," Hailey interrupted.

I was grateful enough to her for stopping the building tension toward the so very not-like-normal deaths of his parents that it took a beat to patch that together.

"How wasn't it like normal?" I asked.

Gavin remained sullenly silent. Another good word for him. Sullen and surly.

Ignoring him for now and remembering Penny's words about who would have been expected to find the bodies being absolute proof Lewis didn't shoot Kim and himself, I prodded Hailey. "You said you were grateful Wylie Easley found your parents instead of your brother, which means there was good reason to think he might have found them. Why didn't he?"

"He was late getting home from school. He was taking summer school, getting a couple classes in ahead of time so there'd be no danger of his grades falling during football season." She snorted softly, conveying that seemed a quaint concern now. "He took a different bus, then walked home."

"Why?"

"I don't know." Impatience snapped that off. Or maybe concern.

"You never asked?"

"I—*we*—had a lot more important things to worry about than him being a little late. What does it matter? He didn't take his usual bus. That's why Wylie Easley found them. Otherwise—"

"I should have found them," he ground out.

"That's—"

I talked over Hailey, addressing Gavin. "Would your father have shot your mother, then himself, knowing you'd be the one to find them?"

"I wasn't the one. That guy was."

"You would have been if you'd followed your regular schedule. The one your dad knew about. He couldn't have known you were going to take a different bus home unless you told him."

His mouth slowly sagged open. He hadn't told his parents.

Hailey jerked upright. "He wouldn't have done that to you, Gav. You know he wouldn't, not ever."

"Somebody else could have gotten to the house before I did." It was almost eerie hearing their voices stripped of anger for this moment. Almost ... like normal.

"He wouldn't have risked it being you. Think, Gav. *Think*. He knew your schedule. Even if you think he went crazy enough to actually do it, he would not have left you to find them. Not ever."

He said, "Or you."

They agreed. Lewis Newhall wouldn't have killed his wife then himself, then left either of his children to find their bodies.

Air streamed out of Hailey at her brother's words until she looked limp. That confirmed my guess it was the only chink in his armor he'd displayed to her since that July day.

He had the opposite reaction. He jerked upright, crushed the empty fast-food bags together between his hands, then shoved open the door.

"Gotta go. Class."

He'd slammed the door behind him and appeared through the windshield, walking away from us fast.

Chapter Twenty-Five

HAILEY SAID NOTHING during the drive except to answer my question about if she had a will with a distracted, "No."

Remembering Jennifer's musing about Clayton inheriting, I figured I'd cover that point while she wasn't really paying attention.

Inside the café, she went right up to a man about to sit in a booth and flung her arms around his neck.

No big surprise, he was the dark-haired man who'd driven the newer pickup into Hailey's place as I'd left Saturday.

He wasn't as tall and lanky as Tom nor as built as Mike, but fell in the middle—a spot surely attractive to a lot of women. I happened to prefer the two ends.

During their embrace, I moved past them, taking the far seat and leaving open the one with its back to most of the room.

He sat, bringing her down with him, since she still had her arms around his neck.

"Clayton, you've got to hear what Gav said. We were talking about how if he'd followed his regular schedule—Oh, this is Elizabeth Danniher. I told you about her. Elizabeth, this is Clayton. Clayton Rayger, my fiancé."

I returned the man's nod, then watched them together.

In excitement and relief, she tumbled out patches of the conversation with Gavin. I couldn't see how Clayton Rayger could possibly assemble them into a coherent whole.

As he listened to Hailey, his eyebrows angled up over his nose and down at the sides. Quizzically puppyish? Or questioningly philosophical? Probably depended on the eyes of the beholder.

His hair flopped artistically over one eye in the style of long-ago teen idols.

His beard was interesting. Lighter in density on the sides, leaving a thicker and darker goatee and beard in the center.

The mustache, also thicker and darker, turned down at the corners of his mouth, making him look more serious than he might have been. The combination with the eyebrows made me think of a singer being particularly soulful.

He and Hailey made a striking couple.

Hailey wound down enough to say, "Elizabeth's here to ask you questions."

"What about?"

"I told you—"

"Right, right. Though I really wish you wouldn't worry about that stuff, babe."

"I know you do." She smiled up at him. "You're always looking out for me."

Before the mood of this gathering could change, I asked if he knew of any enemies the Newhalls had, heard any arguments between them, noticed anything unusual around that time—no, all around.

Switching to questions requiring more response, I asked how long he had known about the Carey Maight paintings—from early in his friendship with Isaiah—and that Hailey inherited them—all along.

His answers carried no hint of reluctance.

Hailey jumped in and asked if he remembered Kim being upset about a key missing when they went to the house for Lewis' birthday dinner toward the end of June.

His eyebrows tented again. "Something about a key, but I didn't pay real close attention. Told you that, Hailey, when you and O.D. were asking."

"That was the painting closet key. This was earlier and the one for the gun safe. Remember?"

He nodded, apparently acknowledging her distinction between the two. But when it came to remembering, he said, "No."

"Was it common for keys to go missing?" I asked.

"No," Hailey said.

"Well," he temporized. "The one to the gun safe that Lewis kept, that one he usually knew where it was. The ones by the back door ... You've gotta admit, babe, they were in a tangle. Not to mention, anybody going in or out could grab one. Carpet cleaners they had in, the guy who fixed the microwave, the woman who made curtains for Kim and Lewis."

"Not without Mom realizing it," she said stubbornly.

He shrugged, acquiescing.

Was his beard's color a little too even? Couldn't blame him if it was. Especially not with his fiancée being so much younger. Though, I would not have pegged him as the same age as Wylie Easley.

"Have you connected with Wylie Easley while he's been in town?" I asked.

"He's in town?"

Not sure I believed his lack of interest.

"Hailey didn't tell you?" It was the reason she'd cited for renewing examination of her parents' deaths.

"Oh, yeah, of course. Sorry, babe. It just went out of my head."

Gavin could be right that Clayton didn't really back her efforts. Or Clayton could know Easley's return wasn't the motivator Hailey said it was. Or a couple dozen other possibilities.

"Hailey, you said Wylie Easley was circling around your mom before the shootings. What did you mean?"

They exchanged a look.

It might be a stretch to guess he was her source for that, but for sure they agreed on it.

"Calling, wanting her opinion on things, taking her for coffee like he said he was doing that day."

I said to Clayton. "I'd understood you were good friends with Wylie, along with Kim and Isaiah."

"Wouldn't say that. He had a crush on Kim, I'd been friends with Isaiah since we were kids. Didn't make Wylie and me close."

"You think that crush was still alive at the time of the shootings?"

He twitched slightly at the overtness of the question.

"Wouldn't be surprised. But can't say for certain."

Hailey started to add certainty, but I cut her off.

"Hailey's sure Lewis didn't shoot Kim. What do you think, Clayton?"

He raised the hand not enmeshed with Hailey, turned it slightly, then dropped it back to the table. "Doesn't matter what I think about the shootings of Lewis and Kim. If this is what Hailey wants, I support her all the way."

But that gesture said he didn't think much of it, undercutting his support.

Hailey didn't appear to notice.

I produced more believable enthusiasm than he did. "Great. Do you have any insights to help us with this?"

Again, that hand raise, flip, drop back to the table.

"Wish I could give Hailey what she wants, but I don't have anything that would help."

He thought that would stop my questions? No way.

"How did you find out about the deaths of Kim and Lewis?"

"I called him," Hailey said. "He left work early and came right away and stayed by my side, but like I said when we were talking with Gavin, Clayton talked to the deputy over and over, so I didn't have to, not after that first time when he was spouting all his *facts*, about gunshot residue and trajectory and telling me I just had to accept it that I didn't know my own parents and it was murder-suicide."

"What else did Deputy Redus say?" I asked Clayton.

He grimaced. "Once he closed the case, he didn't want to revisit it. Pretty much, he'd say Lewis and Kim got shot, it was murder-suicide, and the case was closed. Hailey would ask more, I'd go to Redus, and he'd say the same thing."

"It was so frustrating," Hailey said. "And then he disappeared and there wasn't even him to ask. After the new year, I went to the sheriff's department and wanted to know more and the guy behind the desk wouldn't tell me a thing."

My urge to ask if his name was Ferrante came in second to my not wanting to detour this conversation ... even if it didn't seem to be going anywhere.

"He said nobody could talk to me except Redus. I said he'd been missing for months and he said I was out of luck. I didn't know what else to try. I gave up for a long time."

I understood. I'd done something similar after my divorce and career implosion and with a lot less reason than she'd had.

I wouldn't fall into the same trap now. Even with everything else that was going on.

You get no answers, you keep asking questions.

If I couldn't get anything from the time of the Newhalls' deaths...

"Clayton, tell me about when you were friends with Isaiah and Kim."

Hailey interrupted. "I told you, he doesn't like to talk about that."

"It's okay, Hailey. It's okay. She's doing this for you, isn't she? And if this is what you want, I'll answer her questions."

Was I being overly sensitive or was that meant to make her feel guilty, so she'd say, no, it wasn't what she wanted, he didn't need to answer more questions, and forget the whole thing about looking into whether her parents' deaths had truly been a murder-suicide.

In case she was tempted, I briskly said, "Thanks, Clayton. I appreciate that and I'm sure Hailey does, too. Now, I understand you were good friends with Isaiah?"

"From way back, yeah."

The sun came out when a cloud, chugging across the sky like a long freight train, finally cleared it, and spotlighted his face from the side through the window, until he adjusted his hat.

The moment of spotlight revealed the foundation under the beard. Let's say his chin and jawline weren't strong. The darker goatee and the rest of the beard masked it. He had one heck of a barber.

Not to criticize him. Women have been giving ourselves cheek-bones for decades with trompe l'oeil.

"When you four were all—" I stopped before adding *young*. Not politic. "—together, you and Isaiah and Kim and Wylie—that must have been strange, one woman and three guys. How did that happen?"

"Isaiah and Kim," he said. "We went into the ice cream shop and there was Kim, working behind the counter. Her first day, we found out later. Isaiah started trying to work her for free ice cream. She didn't fall for it for a minute. Stood right up to him. I'm here to tell you, no other girls did. And that was it for the two of them."

"You and Isaiah had been close friends until then. A lot of times, in those situations friends drift apart, resenting the girl who came between them."

"I can see that. But, like I said, I'd been friends with Isaiah a long time." Almost reluctantly, he said, "Same for Kim and Wylie. They'd been friends from first grade or something like that. If he wanted to keep on being her friend, he had to fit himself into them being a couple."

"What about you? Was it hard?"

He chuckled, no tinge of resentment. "I had it easy—liked Kim from the start and already friends with Isaiah. Wylie had to try to get along with Isaiah who didn't like having someone around who'd known Kim longer and maybe better than him."

Wanting to knock him out of his placid answers, I considered him for a moment before saying, "You looked up to Isaiah, but you loved both of them, Kim and Isaiah."

"I guess I did. Nothing weird," he added quickly.

"After Isaiah died, did you think you could step in and be with Kim? I bet she didn't want someone who reminded her of Isaiah."

"That's—"

I didn't look away from him at Hailey's irate interruption. And I didn't stop talking. "Not you, not Wylie. That would have been going back and she wasn't going to do that. The only way you could keep from being closed out was to take the role she let you have. Friend of the family."

"That worked for me. Happy to be there at Kim and Lewis' place with all of them and—"

"On the edges. Watching her until—"

"Until Hailey." He smiled as he said her name.

She put her arms around his neck again, pressing her cheek to his, her eyes almost closed, but with enough opening that I caught her challenging look toward me.

"I was thinking about earlier," I persisted. "When Kim stayed on her own until she met someone very different from Isaiah and fell in love with Lewis Newhall."

I thought his smile flickered. It was hard to tell under the turned-down mustache.

"Lots of guys fell for Kim. Maybe she settled down with Lewis, but she always loved Isaiah. Wylie hated that. As if Kim would ever give up Isaiah for him."

Penny's voice sounded in my head. *She blended the two of them together, better than they ever did.*

Click.

Not Kim blending Clayton and Wylie together, but Hailey blending Kim and Isaiah.

In Hailey, Clayton Rayger had both Kim and Isaiah.

Not evidence, but a new understanding of the past.

And I suppose there are worst foundations for love.

"Tell us about the night Isaiah died."

"No," Hailey started.

"Jennifer and I told you there'd be difficult questions. If you don't want—"

"I didn't say that. But—"

Clayton talked over both of us. The advantage of a low voice. "Babe, it's okay. I'll answer her questions. For you. Unless you don't want me to..."

She subsided.

I repeated, "Tell us about the night Isaiah died."

"It was bad. Real bad. The baby—Hailey—wasn't very old. We were all at their place and we'd been drinking—me the most. Isaiah said he had a meeting with somebody and Kim wasn't happy about it, asking what kind of meeting happened at that hour. He wouldn't tell her anything. First fight I'd seen them have. He said if she didn't trust him, she could come with. She said he was crazy. It was snowing hard and she couldn't leave the baby.

"She had a point, but it made him madder. The only thing to do when he got like that was go along with him. Trying to talk sense to him—" He shrugged. "—got you nowhere.

"Easley stayed with Kim, of course. We got outside and it was snowing hard. Really coming down. I told Isaiah he was an idiot, but that made him even more stubborn. I was so far gone myself, I crawled in the back seat and fell asleep."

He drifted in a momentary silence, both Hailey and I respected.

"No idea what happened until someone found me a distance from the car, passed out. They say I couldn't have been thrown clear—not enough injuries. That I must have gotten myself out. They could tell from drag marks that I tried to help Isaiah. I don't remember any of it. But it wasn't any use. His ... his neck was broken. I sure don't remember any of it."

Hailey made a sound.

"It's okay—"

"No." She stopped Clayton, scowling at me. "Why are you doing this to him? Can't you see how it hurts him? And it has nothing to do with my parents' deaths."

"It's okay, babe." He put his hand over hers. "If it helps you to understand better, it's worth it to me. You know that. I'll look out for you like always."

Not done scowling, she said, "I want to talk to Clayton alone."

Hailey talked about Clayton taking care of her. What I knew from this brief encounter was she looked out for him at least as much as he looked out for her. And did it fiercely.

He put a hand on hers. "Babe, it'll be okay—"

"I haven't ordered yet," I protested.

"You, either," he pointed out to her.

"I'm not hungry. Leave us." She directed that at me.

I hoped to start up with more questions, but lunch felt iffy enough that I went to the pickup desk and ordered to-go.

"Elizabeth!"

I turned at the familiar voice, already smiling.

Tamantha sat with Tom in the little entry hall, where people waited for their lunch pickup order. I'd heard they did the same for breakfast, but that was strictly rumor as far as I was concerned.

"What are you two doing here?" I asked.

"Picking up something to take home for supper," he said. "Tamantha's not up for me cooking tonight. We'll heat it up and be done."

"Just not real hungry," she said.

I'd seen how very uncharacteristic that was during our weekend trip to Fort Phil Kearny.

"How about you?" Tom asked.

"Having a late lunch with a couple people I'm talking to."

Tom raised one eyebrow in question.

I did my best to send him a *yes* answer without telegraphing it to Tamantha.

They called Tom's name.

I sat next to Tamantha as he went to the counter. "How was your report on our trip?"

"It was good. Except Jet Baranson kept holding up faces, like a baby."

"Holding up faces?"

"Making them on his phone, then holding up the phone so I could see them. Trying to make me forget what I wanted to say." Today's answer to pigtails in the inkwell of days of yore?

"But you didn't forget."

"Nope."

"Good for you."

Tom came back to us, bag in hand, as Hailey and Clayton approached ... then sailed past, slowing only enough for her to throw words at me, while he gave an apologetic nod.

"I've gotta get back," she said. "Gotta check on Fred White. You can get a ride to the TV station with them." She jerked her head toward Tom and Tamantha.

Unless she knew a cross-country shortcut I didn't know, she'd drive right past the station.

"Hey, you brought me—"

"You invited yourself."

"Because you—"

Tom cut me off. "We'll give you a ride, Elizabeth."

"Yeah, come with us," Tamantha said. "I wanna talk to you."

Chapter Twenty-Six

"**ANOTHER SATISFIED CUSTOMER?**" Tom asked once we settled in the truck after getting my order. His look informed me he knew I was looking into Hailey's parents' deaths at her request. "Didn't like all your questions?"

I grunted. Steamed, if I'm honest.

This young woman didn't need to gush thanks, but courtesy would be nice.

"I want to ask you some questions, too, Tom. About Davon Everett." O.D.'s younger son had been friends with Tom since they went to Two Rivers camp as kids.

He flickered a look toward the back seat. "I'll come by the station after I drop off Tamantha for her program at the library."

Fifty-fifty whether she was giving the program or in the audience.

"Thanks."

"I like it when you ask questions," Tamantha said from the back seat, setting herself apart from Hailey.

I swung around so I could look at her directly.

"Do you?"

She nodded, then amended it to, "Most of the time. Like you did at Fort Phil Kearny—like when you found out the reason they use its first name was because there was another Fort Kearny in Nebraska and even though one's named after the uncle and the other after his nephew, people get confused."

"When don't you like me asking questions?"

"When you're asking me. Because I already know those answers."

"Always? Because sometimes we don't know something that's going on inside us or how we feel about things until somebody asks us and we stop and think about it."

"Maybe," she granted. "I'll think about that."

As I turned back to face forward Tom kept looking at the road, allowing me only his profile, with fans of wrinkles at the corners of his right eye and the right side of his mouth.

"Can I ask you something—a question?" came from the back seat.

"Okay."

Swinging around again, I met Tom's gaze for an instant, warning me of what was ahead.

"Mike's back because he bought the TV station, right?"

"That's right."

"Not because you're dating him again?"

"Tamantha," her father scolded, "we talked about not asking questions that aren't any of your business."

"Elizabeth does."

"I ask questions that are everybody's business, because they're for the good of everybody who lives here, for our society. So, say, someone works for the county but he's not doing his job, you could say that's not my personal business, but it is the business of everybody in the county, because we all pay him. But everybody can't pay attention. So I ask on behalf of everybody."

"Because that's your job," she summed up.

"That's right."

"My job is to take care of Daddy. And Roxanne," she said of her horse. "But right now we're talking about Daddy. And sort of taking care of me, too, because I didn't like it when you dated Mike and stopped dating Daddy and I didn't see you as much, even though you explained about how we'll always be friends, no matter what. But it's even taking care of you, too, because you weren't as happy when you stopped dating Daddy. So it's my *job* to ask questions, to take care of everybody by making sure you aren't Mike's girlfriend."

"What if being Mike's girlfriend is what makes Elizabeth the happiest?" Tom asked, glancing in the rearview mirror.

"Does it?" she demanded of me.

"I don't know." I looked directly at her. "It's complicated."

She got the reference from a discussion during our trip. I saw her working through that. "My head hurts."

I knew exactly how she felt. Head and other parts.

Tom added, "And what about Mike? What about what makes him happy?"

That stumped her for a beat. Then she shook her head. "That's not my job. That's somebody else's job to ask questions to take care of him."

✧   ✧   ✧   ✧

THEY DROPPED ME off at the station, with Tamantha waving as they drove away.

Retroactive empathy swamped me.

She'd waved to Tom the same way when we left from Mrs. Parens' house eleven days ago for our girls' weekend to Fort Phil Kearny. Some girls go to spas. We went to a state historic site.

I'd seen him in my rearview mirror, the strong, straight, solitary figure of a cowboy standing beside his truck.

Except in this moment, I knew he had been all that, plus a mushy center watching his baby girl drive away.

The trip happened because Tamantha had drawn a promise from me to take her and Mrs. Parens to the site of a historic fort on the east side of the Big Horn Mountains.

I suggested we wait until warmer weather—maybe July—but was vetoed. I also pointed out I was needed in the short-staffed newsroom for the foreseeable future. That didn't earn me an excused absence, either.

I don't know which of them pulled the strings, but a delegation of Diana, Audrey, and Jennifer said I needed to get away for the weekend.

None of them laughed as they said it, either, despite all of them knowing I would be worked even harder by Tamantha and Mrs. Parens than I was at the station and have a whole lot less to say about what I did.

So, that Friday, I drove them in my SUV east across the Big Horn Basin, over the Big Horn Mountains, then south down their eastern slope to Sheridan. We stayed at a chain motel—Mrs. P and Tamantha in one room and me granted the privacy of my own room. Tamantha came prepared and swam before bed in the indoor pool.

Early—very early by my standards—the next morning, we headed to the fort, midway between Sheridan and Buffalo.

At this time of year, visits were by appointment only, but apparently Mrs. Parens had a standing invitation, because they said they'd welcome her with open arms whenever she chose to come and for as long as she chose to stay.

They meant it, putting together a lunch for us, staff, friends, and colleagues, making this an all-day affair.

We tramped around the grounds that had once been Fort Phil Kearny.

The head guide knew almost as much as Mrs. P. They'd had a lovely time trading half sentences that the other understood, then looking at me with pity for my ignorance, before explaining to Tamantha, whom they forgave based on her years.

They needn't have bothered. She also knew more than I did and almost as much as they did.

Here's the TV news version. There was a treaty protecting this area as belonging to various tribes. Then gold was discovered in Montana. Gold hunters determined the fastest route was heading north off the Oregon Trail and along the eastern slope of the Big Horns on what they called the Bozeman Trail after the guy who started it.

The tribes took use of this trail across their territory amiss.

Gatherings at Fort Laramie, in the southeastern quadrant of what became Wyoming, tried to iron out the issue.

At the same time, bigwigs back east sent troops under Colonel Henry Carrington to build forts to protect gold-seekers and others using the trail.

In fact, Carrington went through Fort Laramie during one of the peace meetings in 1866 on his way to erecting Fort Phil Kearny and two smaller outposts.

Several tribes *really* took this amiss.

There had been … let's call it jockeying … among the tribes.

The ones who'd ended up with the territory the Bozeman Trail pushed through said hell, no. We met with a descendant of one of those warriors, who shared their oral history, earning Tamantha's intense interest.

The tribes who'd been jockeyed out of that territory aligned more or less with the army.

Stalemate.

Except a lot went on during this stalemate, including people dying, Fort Phil Kearny being essentially under siege during its entire existence, a major ambush of soldiers, a daring ride for help through snow and dark.

At dinner that night, Tamantha talked and asked about what we'd seen. During dessert, I said, "I read earlier that the ambush at Fort Phil Kearny was the worst defeat of U.S. forces until Custer. And then the army named a different fort after the guy who led his men into that ambush."

I might have let disapproval seep into my tone.

Tamantha frowned and turned to Mrs. P. "Why did they do that?"

"History is rarely clearcut, because it is made by people, who also are rarely clearcut. The man they later named a new fort after in 1867 was considered a brave and good officer during the Civil War. That fort was established months after his death and feelings were quite raw about those events."

"They should have named the new fort after one of the guys he led into the ambush," Tamantha said sternly. But then she went silent for a moment. "When I ask questions, my friend's mom says *It's complicated* a lot. Is that what she means? A guy can be brave and good one time, then mess up another time?"

I tucked the insides of my cheeks between my teeth. Mrs. P said, "Indeed."

"Okay." She pushed away her empty dessert plate. "We can leave now and I can swim in the pool for an hour and forty minutes."

She was off by a few minutes—she hadn't calculated time to pay the bill, which fourth graders rarely concern themselves with.

I told Mrs. P I'd take this pool watch, since Tamantha had declared her intention also to swim in the morning and I preferred to skip that time slot. Mrs. P accepted, but then remained straight-backed in a chair beside my chaise.

"Tamantha is a remarkable child," she said.

No argument from me.

"She demonstrated a pivotal developmental moment, from expressing her inalterable moral code in desiring the fort be named after one of those commanded into the ambush, rather than the commander, to expressing the recognition of mitigating and ephemeral factors that affect such decisions."

"History is rarely clearcut?" I murmured. Also, *it's complicated*.

"Indeed."

"Yet," I argued, "you pointed out a while back that the push up the Bozeman Trail and building of forts coincided with railroad construction reaching southeastern Wyoming and—lo and behold—the forts were abandoned and troops withdrawn after construction pushed farther west.

"Not clearcut, but downright suspicious that someone somewhere had the influence to get those troops sent to build forts—and die, not to mention to kill Native Americans—while the railroad continued relatively unscathed."

"We must accept that we cannot know with certainty every twist and turn of history, including our own."

Whoa. That *including our own* phrase came out of left field.

No question, Emmaline Parens was talking about *my* history.

I stuck with Wyoming's. "You weren't so *laissez faire* the first time you told me about the Bozeman Trail forts."

"If you recall our conversations in detail, I am confident you will realize my position is consistent. One can look at events of the past and arrive at theories, while remaining open to revamping, even abandoning, those theories as new information or new viewpoints come to light."

Still standing in the KWMT parking lot, I abruptly recognized I was very cold.

Chapter Twenty-Seven

TOM RETURNED, AS promised.

I met him by the door and escorted him past the old breakroom.

Ahead of us, Mike emerged from a one-on-one with a custodian. Seeing people come out of the news director's office smiling was disconcerting, but I could get used to it.

Mike sent off the custodian with a handshake and a couple more words, said hello to Tom, winked at me, then welcomed in a fifty-ish woman I vaguely knew did something for advertising. As he closed the door, we saw a hand-printed paper sign that said *Mike, Majority Owner* taped over the official sign.

I gestured Tom toward our new break room.

"Like what you've done with the place," he said.

The last time he'd seen it—not long ago by the calendar—we'd confronted a murderer.

"Amazing how much cozier it can feel when you don't arrange furniture to take into account a murderer possibly going berserk. Want anything?"

He declined, hooked his hat on the back of a chair, but took a seat on the couch.

I poured myself water and took the chair with his hat.

"Tom, I know you don't like us poking into these things, but I hope you'll help with background. You seemed to like the Newhalls—"

He interrupted. "I respect you and the others trying to find the truth. But there are people I'm not willing to suspect, while you are. And I worry about you. And the rest."

"I can look out for myself. I have a lot of experience—"

"At murder?"

I had to admit, "That's more recent. But I'm still not going to put myself or the others in danger." Honesty compelled me to add, "Not on purpose."

He eyed me. "Ask your question. Or questions, knowing you."

"I want to know more about Isaiah Everett. I know you've been good friends with his brother Davon for a long time."

Slowly, he nodded. "You think folks are locked into their views of Kim and Lewis—he did it or he didn't—so you're going farther back. Smart."

He didn't wait for a response.

"Isaiah was a good bit older than Davon and me. What I knew of him mostly came through Davon. Seeing his brother's mistakes, along with O.D. keeping a better eye on him, helped Davon avoid the same ones."

"What kind of mistakes did Isaiah make?"

"Got in a lot of trouble in school—when he was there. Had DWUIs. Sad thing was he seemed to be turning around. Kim's influence, without a doubt. And with the baby, it was like it woke him up. Then, right after Hailey was born, he went driving drunk one too many times and killed himself. Clayton Rayger was real lucky it didn't kill him, too."

"Tell me about them—those three and Wylie Easley."

He lifted one shoulder, playing down what he had to say. "Like I said, I saw them from afar."

"And through Davon."

"Yeah, but he saw them from afar, too. Plus … I don't know."

I tipped my head to consider him. "I just realized that as good as you are at keeping your mouth shut and staying deadpan when you choose, when you do talk, it's almost all the truth because you're a lousy liar."

"That's why I keep my mouth shut," he said.

I laughed. He grinned at me.

Pasting on a frown, I said, "You also are beginning to sound like

Mrs. P. Wanting me to learn my way through an inquiry when I'm just trying to stay upright with all that's going on here at KWMT, along with the hopes of this young woman that her father didn't kill her mother, and figuring out who stole her horse's tail."

He held up both hands in brief surrender. "Davon was kind of excited about being an uncle. He didn't really know Kim. He didn't see much of Isaiah after he started seeing Kim. Without hearing direct from his brother, he saw it all—including Kim—through O.D.'s eyes. You know O.D. and Isaiah...?"

I nodded.

"Davon saw Isaiah as choosing Kim over his people."

His own words? Or O.D.'s?

I thought of O.D.'s comments about his grandmother choosing her art over her people. Had that primed him to be harsh to his son? He clearly mourned Isaiah. Would he have done things differently if he could?

He did seem to do them differently with his granddaughter.

"As for Clayton and Wylie," Tom continued, "Davon called them shadows, trying to gain substance from the reflections of Isaiah and Kim.

"Said Clayton never took responsibility. Anything bad happened, he let Isaiah take the blame. Nothing was ever Clayton's fault. Of course, that all came with a good dose of jealousy, with Davon wanting to be the one hanging around Isaiah.

"Saw Wylie as worse—pathetic. Not the word he used. Everybody knew Wylie had a thing for Kim. More he tried to hide it, more obvious it was. Probably the best thing to happen to him was the blowup with his brother. Shut him out of the family garage and sent him away from here. Found himself another life."

"Clayton stayed here, though."

"Yeah," he said, watching me. "Sure not for me to say that says something bad about the man."

"What about O.D.'s relationships with his sons?"

"Warming up with all the other questions first to get to this?"

I shot back. "You'll make me think you're more on guard about

O.D. because he and Isaiah didn't have a good relationship."

His dark eyes met mine. "You're right. They didn't. Better with Davon and his sisters. Better still with the grandkids. That's the O.D. I know."

"What about the Carey Maight paintings? I know O.D. values his grandmother's legacy. Do his surviving kids and grandkids?"

"They all respect the legacy. No question, O.D. the most."

"And Paytah?"

His hesitation was so small it could have been missed. "I'd say him the most of that next generation, along with Hailey. But killing Kim and Lewis over the Carey Maight paintings? No. Besides, then why not kill Hailey, too? Especially at the same time as Kim and Lewis. Doing it now wouldn't put the paintings in the Everetts' hands. Her possessions would go to her brother. Or Clayton if they get married. Not the Everetts."

"Unless she has a will that says otherwise."

"Does she?"

"She says she doesn't."

One side of his mouth lifted. "Lot of people you encounter lie about having a will?"

I waved that off. "O.D. doesn't have to inherit to get the paintings. Gavin and Clayton—you see either of them holding onto the paintings if they did inherit? More like selling at first opportunity. And who'd be first in line to buy?"

"That's a stretch."

"You like O.D."

"So do you."

He was right.

I shifted angles. "You hesitated over Paytah Everett. What are you not telling me? Something to do with the paintings?"

He studied me a moment. "Not Carey Maight's paintings directly. Paytah's an artist himself. People say he has real talent. But I don't see how that applies—"

"Right now, I don't see how *anything* applies or fits together or gets us anywhere."

He sat silent, waiting for me to get back on track after that snit of frustration.

"Okay," I said half to myself, "One of the first rules of investigating is to see what the crime accomplishes. In this case, it accomplished taking the paintings out of Kim and Lewis' sphere of influence and putting them completely in Hailey's control. At the same time removing the two major influences in her life, while O.D. became more of an influence."

"And Clayton Rayger."

I nodded. "If he or O.D. had been killed, I sure would look at the other as a prime suspect."

"But what purpose would it serve? Hailey's not selling the paintings."

"No," I agreed. "Even though it seems like she could use the money."

He nodded slowly. "Jack's hoping to hire her back full-time, but she's holding off until Gavin goes to college, assuming he does go. She's worried about him, wants to be available."

"I can see why she's worried. He's got a lot of anger."

His gaze sharpened. "You don't think that boy—"

"Hey," Mike said from the doorway. "Diana's ready to shoot the interview."

Chapter Twenty-Eight

"WHAT DO YOU have to offer Cottonwood County other than the ability to play football?" I asked Mike on camera.

"Well," he drew it out, deadpan "that *is* the most important. Even though I'm not playing anymore. But I bring my caring about this place—loving it and knowing it. While I also love and know Chicago, from my years with the Bears and now reporting in the best sports city around...."

Yeah, Mike would do fine.

We talked about this unusual situation. About his plans for employee ownership. About his start in TV here. About his growing up here. About his finding a home and success with the Bears.

Diana shot him in front of the courthouse. At the rodeo grounds. At the high school football field. By a fence with cattle behind it on his land—nobody in Chicago had to know those weren't his cattle, but belonged to the rancher who leased Mike's land. Everybody in Cottonwood County already knew it.

We had way, way more than we needed, but as he continued to stand by the fence, while Diana scooched down, panned across the vista behind him before coming in on him in a zoom, I shot questions at him for fun. His favorite boots, flavor of pizza, color, season, holiday, book, TV show.

Some might make the cut, like "What's your favorite food?"— "Beef, of course, Chicago style pizza, and then snacks."

But most wouldn't.

Without her saying anything, I knew Diana was winding down.

I asked him, "Do you wear a cowboy hat in Chicago?"

"Depends on how I'm feeling. Out here, you wear them most all the time, because they're normal to everybody. In Chicago, I wear it because it's normal to me, even if it's not to everybody else."

I liked that. Staying who he was while not needing to make it a statement by wearing a cowboy hat all the time.

"Are you happy?" I didn't know I was going to ask that.

"Yes." His fast grin followed the answer. "I am happy."

I grinned back at him. Then remembered to gesture to Diana to quit recording.

"Of course," he added, "I could be happier if I could be two places at once—there and here, but that's something else I sorted out rookie year with the Bears. I carry home with me. I'd also be happier if you could be two places at once, too—here and there."

❖ ❖ ❖

DIANA AND MIKE went to work on the rough edit of the interview to send to Chicago. As they headed out—Diana for home and Mike for a meeting with James Longbaugh—they told me his station loved it.

I answered a call from Linda Caswell at my desk as I put the final polish on Leona's intro to a wire piece on river rights in Nevada.

"I'm afraid it's a mixed result, Elizabeth," Linda said.

"It all helps."

"I didn't find any artists in the area currently using horse-hair brushes. However, I do have a name and contact information for a woman who taught the technique, twenty, thirty years ago around here. She's now retired to New Mexico. With it being so long ago, I didn't know if that would help, but since it's the only tangible information I found..."

I took it with thanks, not mentioning I'd almost forgotten the horse-tail thief.

"Are you making progress?" she asked.

"Not directly."

"Ah. So you are looking into the Newhalls' deaths."

I swear, that movement in the Wyoming air I described, also

zipped rumors faster than sound.

"Yes. For my sins."

"Not a lot of progress there, either?" She took my grunt as intended. "Well, they do intersect in both involving Hailey," she said tentatively.

"True. And her great-great grandmother, Carey Maight. What I really need, Linda, is a better glimpse behind the curtain. What people said about her. Insights."

She encapsulated that in a word. "Gossip. I'm really not the one—"

"I know you're not. And why I'm friends with so many discreet people is beyond me, but you are my friend and you will share with me more than Mrs. P or O.D. will for their various reasons. Please."

"It was all well before my time."

I waited.

"It was said that her second husband was a better parent and grandparent to Carey Maight's family than she was. He smoothed the way between her and her relatives. After his death she had the harshest disputes with her people, including O.D. Many thought her leaving the paintings to Isaiah was a deliberate slap to O.D." She sighed. "And then he died so young and Hailey inherited."

"With Isaiah and Kim not married did anyone challenge Hailey inheriting?"

Yes, I was thinking of O.D.

"Oh, no. Everyone knew Isaiah was her father. He was so incredibly proud and happy about the baby. Of course that wouldn't have been enough in a legal case. But I was a volunteer at the hospital and the day after he died, nurses were talking about how sad it was so soon after his baby's birth. And then they said it was a blessing he'd signed an affidavit of paternity and was named as the father on the birth certificate."

Along with matching what Wylie and Clayton said of Isaiah's attitude toward the baby, that would certainly have discouraged a lawsuit.

And, in my estimation, O.D. wouldn't have been trying to possess the paintings himself, but rather to control them.

He would say protect them.

Whatever you called it, he accomplished that through the friends and family agreement. Which Kim wholeheartedly agreed to during the years of her guardianship—at least according to O.D.

✧   ✧   ✧   ✧

I FINISHED THE piece, sent it to Audrey and Leona, then called the former art teacher in New Mexico.

"Oh, yes, that class was so interesting," she said enthusiastically. "I had to do a great deal of research and teach myself how to make the brushes before I could teach them. And then using them."

She gave no sign of seeing anything odd about someone she'd never met calling out of the blue to ask about a class she'd taught two or three decades before.

As a kid, I'd worked for the quintessential grizzled old newspaper man at my hometown paper. He'd said there were people who thought every aspect of their life and history was fascinating and they assumed it was to everyone else. He so clearly thought poorly of such people he shocked me by adding, "They're God's gift to journalists."

It still astonished me when people reacted that way. Grateful, but astonished.

"It's amazing what Carey Maight accomplished using those brushes," she continued, "I always heard she said they helped her, but honestly—"

"You made brushes—horse-hair brushes? In the class?"

"Yes. It's not horribly difficult once you get the knack. Of course, it helps if you've made your own brushes before and we had in a previous class, so most of them picked it up satisfactorily. I'm sure you could, too. I can send you—"

"Thanks, but, no. I'm not making brushes. But I'd be interested in knowing who was in your class that you taught how to make them."

"Of course. That way you can buy brushes from them. Though, if you make your own—"

"I do understand, but a list of those former students—as you say, they could make the brushes now—would be so helpful."

"I'll have to check my records." She trilled a laugh. "And I'm afraid my records fit the stereotype of artists. But I will see what I can find, if you really need it. Because I have every confidence you could make them—"

"I really need the list. Thank you, so much."

AUDREY SAID THEY didn't need me for the Ten and I should go after the Five.

I stopped at the Sherman Supermarket on the way home for supplies for the morning.

Diana, Jennifer, Mike and I had gone round and round about the timing for a gathering, complicated by Mike's meetings, Diana's assignments, Jennifer's work shifts, my hating mornings, and all of us needing to be at the museum tomorrow night, where we'd be using their function room for Mike's official meeting with employees.

My hatred of mornings lost.

I wandered the store on an unfamiliar quest for breakfast fare beyond coffee and eggs.

In a nod to Mike's second-favorite food group being snacks, I added cheese curls.

Supplies were all I came away with.

Penny wasn't working.

I WENT TO bed in anticipation of the early alarm coming.

It didn't work.

It never works.

I fell asleep quickly. Then woke quickly.

Staring at the shadow-dappled ceiling, thinking about Kim and Lewis Newhall's deaths, Hailey and Gavin Newhall's lives, KWMT-TV's prospects, my future.

Back to my mind going *tickety-tickety-tickety,* accompanied by pulsing pain.

I thought of Tamantha saying her head hurt this afternoon.

I knew exactly how she felt.

My arm flopped over the edge of the bed in despair or something like it. Certainly in headache.

After a moment, Shadow walked to my bed, ducked his head, then brought it up under my flaccid hand.

I dare you not to move your hand when a dog's used this maneuver to initiate self-petting. At least my dog.

He falls into the four-legged, dark, and handsome category.

When he initiates affection, he's statistically impossible to resist. That might be because I don't try.

I stroked his head.

From when he first let me touch him—a considerable time after he let me feed him—his coat improved dramatically. Scavenging for food had not been good for its color or texture, not to mention for providing flesh between coat and bones. Now my hand encountered silky fur, with no danger of being impaled by a protruding bone.

Despite dog-training videos, I can't claim credit for Shadow's training—he's mostly trained himself by accepting or rejecting my suggestions—but I can for his improved health. Also—I hope—for his renewed trust of humans.

My *tickety-tickety-tickety* head no longer hurt.

Nothing like a little self-satisfaction to ease a headache.

Although my elbow wasn't real happy with how I'd twisted it to get maximum contact with Shadow's head.

I rolled onto my side so I could reach him with my opposite hand.

He nudged my first hand, since it wasn't pulling its weight by petting him, too.

I stretched farther, putting both arms around him, hugging and petting.

There was a high probability I would fall out of bed onto my head. Or possibly onto my dog.

But despair was nowhere to be found.

Fair enough.

DAY SIX
WEDNESDAY

Chapter Twenty-Nine

I LET THEM in and made coffee. Diana, Mike, and Jennifer laid out supplies for our breakfast meeting, the ones I'd bought last night and ones they provided today, including a healthy breakfast casserole by Diana.

The cheese curls went first.

"You probably have the most to report again, Elizabeth," Jennifer said. "You start."

I groaned.

"Give her time to take on more coffee," Diana said. "Also, Elizabeth, I wanted to tell you Tamantha didn't go to school today."

She raised a hand, telling me to sit back, because I'd started to rise.

"Nothing serious. I drove the kids to school before coming here. The mother of one of Gary's classmates has a son in Tamantha's grade. Apparently, a bug is going around and she mentioned Tamantha and two others are the latest. I texted Tom already," she added in response to my pulling out my phone. "He says she feels punk, but her fever isn't real bad."

I texted him anyway, reminding him she'd said yesterday that her head hurt.

"I'll report first on gathering opinions from my contacts," Diana said. "It takes sorting, but as far as I can tell, there were no real rumors about problems between Kim and Lewis before the shooting."

"No *real* rumors?" I asked.

She grimaced. "Yeah. There's a fair amount of miraculous hind-sight. You know, *I never would have believed it, but now that I look back, I see the warning signs...*"

"What warning signs?"

"They were nice to each other. No kidding. That's been twisted into them needing to be careful not to upset the other person—Lewis in particular—or they'd go off. Nobody ever saw or heard an instance of that, but retroactively, some are sure there were signs."

She added more thoughtfully, "Even so, a good percentage of people still don't believe it. Higher than you'd expect with the pressure of the others claiming looking-back signs."

"What's your take, Diana? Do you think people legitimately re-membered warning signs after the Newhalls died?" Jennifer asked.

She leaned forward for a sip of cranberry juice, then sat another moment.

"No. I think some had recollections reshaped by later events. No one voiced suspicions about the Newhalls' relationship before the shootings. All those few can do now is claim they had the thought. But, honestly, most of those are folks who express every thought they have, so ... I come back to no, I don't think people saw anything ahead of the Newhalls' deaths."

I grunted acceptance of her reasoning and her conclusion.

A text from Tom came in. *A bug. Going around the class. Feeling punk. ...* Then he added, *Hope you don't get it.*

"As for anything going on between Kim and Wylie," Diana said, "a few said other people believed that, but no one would admit to believing it themselves. In other words, points away from it, but not definitive."

"Jennifer, you next?" Mike invited.

"You all already know about the horse-hair theft background I found yesterday." A not-so subtle reminder to not let that fall off our radar. She must have found a time to tell Mike about it yesterday, too. "On the Newhalls' shootings, I'm working through the records. Started with financial. Money's tight for Hailey. A lot tighter than it was when her parents were alive. There was an insurance settlement, but Hailey split it between college funds and a trust for Gavin.

"They sold the house for less than market, then used that and a lot of her savings to buy the place they're on now. She works piecemeal. Her savings are dropping fast."

"Clearly not selling paintings on the sly," Mike said.

Starting to come alive, I asked, "What about Clayton Rayger?"

"Not much on him. He must be an under-the-mattress type. From what I can find, he's not flush, especially after buying a truck not long ago. Since they moved to this place a couple years ago, his name's not on any bills—they're all in Hailey's name.

"I'm working back on the phone records now. Looks like I'll be able to see times of calls and texts. I'll make a timeline. But the sheriff's department didn't spring at the time for the higher cost software that would get the actual texts or locations. I could get deeper into the phone company's—"

"No," I said. Diana continued, "You're so close to starting the Northwestern program, you are not jeopardizing that."

I nodded vigorously, so Jennifer knew Diana spoke for both of us.

"Fine, but—"

"Keep working what you have. Timeline will be great. I can go next, unless you want to, Mike?"

"Go right ahead."

It wasn't a great haul.

I recounted the lunch with Gavin, the lunch with Clayton—and the fact I didn't get to eat at either. Then touched on what Tom said about the Everett family dynamics. For my finale, I emphasized Linda coming through with the contact who taught painting techniques with horse-hair brushes and how to make them and my conversation with the woman.

That was for Jennifer's benefit.

"When is she calling back?" the ingrate demanded.

I shrugged.

"What about Wylie Easley?" Jennifer asked. "Don't you think it's weird he was supposed to be looking around here for a second home, getting Kim's input, taking her out for coffee to talk about his choices, then ends up buying in Jackson?"

The same hint of dismissal, even disdain I'd heard from Walt.

I rather liked Jackson and no one could deny the Jackson Hole area was gorgeous scenery. But the Wyoming natives I'd encountered seemed to wish they could excise it from the state.

"Why do you think buying in Jackson instead of here's significant—other than revealing poor moral fiber?" I asked.

"Guilty conscience," she said immediately. "Couldn't bear being around reminders of what he did."

"But he's back here now."

"Short trip. More bearable."

"Or," Diana offered, "he had to come back for a specific reason."

Jennifer sat up. "Like he remembered a clue he forgot and he's got to destroy it?"

"Two years later, plus he's been here almost a week. What clue would take that long to destroy?" I asked.

"Maybe he can't get into where the clue is. Like the Newhalls' old house? He's waiting for an opportunity."

I tipped my head and raised one eyebrow. "Jennifer, check police reports. See if the new owners have reported anything."

"Got it."

"Let's also see if we can find out more about what he's been doing on this trip."

Diana raised one hand. "That's me. It's got to be easier than asking about what he did two and a half years ago."

Jennifer added, "I meant to say before, we found nothing on the black-market horse-hair boards about anything for sale from around here. And only a couple offers of light color, like Fred White's. The guys traced those and they're not around here."

"I didn't think they were traceable," Mike said. "That's the whole point of the dark web."

She simply looked smug.

"Can you look back and see if what was taken in the spate of thefts a few years back showed up for sale?"

My request took a layer of shine off her smug. "We can try. No guarantees. What about you, Mike?"

"I got a couple things from Gee," he said—way, way, too inno-cently. "Including a copy of the crime scene report on the Newhalls."

"Whoa!" Jennifer said.

"From your Aunt Gee?" Diana said. "Are you sure you had the right woman?"

"Maybe pod people took her over and—"

I interrupted Jennifer's speculation. "How did you do that? She's been so much more closed-mouthed about sharing information since Diana's honey became sheriff."

"Other way around," Diana said. "Became sheriff, then became my honey. Want to keep things straight because I know how highly you regard accuracy."

I focused back on Mike. "How did you do that?"

"I might have told her if she gave me the report, you'd marry me."

Diana choked on a bite of casserole. Jennifer sucked in a breath.

Chapter Thirty

"WHAT?" I SQUAWKED. But that was reflexive, because I could see the glint of mischief in his eyes like fireworks over Lake Michigan on the Fourth of July. I whacked him in the arm. "You are so full of it."

"Well, it would give her a major one-up on Mrs. P and you know how those two are."

I did. They sat on opposing banks of the meandering stream of my romantic life. Both guys knew it. And, as they defied all the guys-as-rivals cliches, they seemed to find this rivalry by proxy between the two older women amusing.

It made me want to swat both of them in the arm. With only Mike available, I swatted him.

"Ow," he fibbed. "Want to see this report or not?"

"You bet I do, since I'm being sold into matrimony like chattel in an ancient civilization."

"The good old days."

He saved himself from another swat by handing over a sheaf of papers.

"Jennifer—"

"Yeah. I'll scan them in and send everybody copies."

But I couldn't resist looking first.

As I skimmed the pages and passed them on, Mike talked between cheese curls.

"Aunt Gee also told me something that might explain Shelton's comment about a Redus hot streak."

"Don't stop there," Jennifer said indignantly. "Quit eating and tell us. And don't get cheese curl dust on the pages."

He swallowed. "The month before the Newhall shootings, Redus caught a call about remains found up at the Montana border. He wasn't happy with the paperwork it would take and was already saying they'd never figure out who it was—which Gee indicated meant he wouldn't try."

"I sort of remember that," Diana said, slowly. "The body was up on some out-of-the-way BLM road. A guy got lost, let his dog out for a pit stop, then the dog wouldn't come away from something off the road. It was a body. No ID. A Jane Doe. But it wasn't just *at* the border, it was smack-dab *on* the border.

"Redus couldn't have had much to do with it, certainly not enough to count as part of a hot streak, because they handed the inquiry over to Montana authorities."

Diana's remembrances gave Mike time to reach the dregs on the cheese curls.

"Yup, Redus palmed the case off on Montana authorities, according to Gee."

"*Hot streak.*" I huffed out a breath while still skimming. "Shelton was getting in a dig at Redus for getting another jurisdiction to investigate being part of his *hot streak*, while simultaneously yanking my chain by sending us on a wild goose chase."

"Mostly you," Diana said. "Wayne Shelton doesn't devote time to thinking up wild goose chases for the rest of us."

"*That* makes me feel all warm and glowy." I'd hit the end of the report, then returned to one spot. "You read the report, Mike?"

"Uh-huh."

I knew from his voice, he'd spotted it.

"Tell us," Jennifer demanded. She'd recognized Mike had something, too.

"First," Diana said, "let's note it confirms what you'd been told before, Elizabeth, about the *incomplete* gunshot residue. And the bullet trajectory being upward into Kim."

"Good points. Okay, Mike, share what's new."

"Time of death is wide open. At least in what Aunt Gee gave me.

The autopsy should have more, but she spared my delicate constitution and didn't include that. As I said, wide open."

"That's not new," Jennifer complained.

"Sure doesn't rule out Easley," I said. "He could have killed them, left, then circled back to *find* them. *Finding* them covers up any stray evidence left behind. It's why law enforcement looks so closely at whoever finds the body. Or, he could have arrived, killed them and been leaving when Gavin arrived.

"That wide open timeline also means Gavin could have done the kill, leave, circle back routine. Or he could have killed them before he left for school."

Mike whistled softly.

"You really think...?" Jennifer asked.

"We have to look at the possibilities. Like that the grief and anger in Gavin Newhall are a result of killing his parents. Hailey said he took a different bus home than usual. Why?"

"So someone else would find his parents," Mike said.

"That's horrible," Diana's murmur reminded me Gavin was in school with Jessica.

I added, "There's nothing in the report about Redus checking Gavin's story of his movements."

After a beat of rather depressed silence, Mike said, "But there is something else in the report. The gun that killed Kim and Lewis Newhall was definitely his."

"That's not new—"

He talked over Jennifer with a lurking grin. "The gun safe it was kept in was in the garage."

Diana and Jennifer looked from him to me.

I reminded them, "And Hailey said her mother reported that key was missing the month before the deaths."

✦ ✦ ✦ ✦

JENNIFER RUBBED THE side of her face. "What does that mean?"

"We have no idea—yet," Mike said.

"True," I said. "But it gives us things to think about. Let's look at this from another angle. Say we accept the report and Redus' conclusion as accurate. Why did Lewis Newhall kill himself?"

Three looks best summarized as *Duh*, focused on me. Jennifer added to her *Duh* look with, "Because he'd shot his wife."

"Okay. Say we accept Lewis Newhall killed himself out of overwhelming and instant horror at killing his wife. What I haven't heard is why Lewis Newhall might have killed his wife."

Instant silence.

The kind where you could hear the mental processes whirling and whistling, if you listened closely enough.

"He snapped," Mike said slowly and without conviction. "I know. Weak."

"That *was* what Redus' report said." By Jennifer's tone, that reduced its likelihood.

"Snapped why? Over what?" I asked.

"The other man. He thought Kim was seeing—or doing more than seeing—Wylie Easley." As she spoke, Diana held her hand out and waggled it, like a plane dipping first one wing then the other, in commentary on her own suggestion.

"Don't dismiss that so fast," Mike said. "It can make a man more than a little crazy."

A flick against a nerve had me looking at him sharply, but he'd tacked on no personal subtext. I breathed out.

"No suicide note," Jennifer said, clearly following her own path. "But that's part of snapping, isn't it? Not thinking things out, not preparing. Just acting."

"Still, there has to be a trigger—no pun intended," Mike said. "I say again, why dismiss the other-man factor so fast?"

"Beyond their reputations as a happy, solid couple?"

I flashed back to my thought after class, when O.D. Everett knew about my having visited Mrs. P earlier that day, how fast even the most innocuous item spread across the county. How much faster would the not-innocuous tale of a supposed upright member of the community fooling around with a former classmate spread?

Unless, somehow, Kim and Wylie kept it a secret.

How would they do that in Cottonwood County?

Go somewhere else.

"Was Kim out of town in the month or two before she died?"

"Ah. An out-of-town assignation," Diana said.

"I'll check my gossip sources," she volunteered.

Jennifer added, "Phone and financial records should show something if she did. I'll go back further than the couple days before the shootings."

"And I'll ask Hailey, but it's a long shot, considering everything we've heard about Kim and Lewis."

"Doesn't that come to us mostly from their daughter?" Mike countered.

Diana shook her head. "It's what everyone says. I know, I know. *Everybody says* is not evidence. But consider what Tansy at the café said about how Kim and Wylie were at their first coffee. Plus—"

"Penny said they weren't fooling around."

Diana acknowledged Jennifer's addition. "That's major. Plus, there were no rumors about them. None. How would Lewis have ever found out?"

"She told him," Mike said.

We three females shook our heads. Diana said, "If she consorted with Wylie Easley—and I don't think she did—she was so careful there were no rumors. The reason to do that was to make sure her husband didn't find out. So it makes no sense to then tell him."

"Heat of the moment," Mike suggested, though without enthusiasm. "They're arguing. She blurts it out. He pulls out the gun—"

I jumped in. "Ah. Where did he pull the gun from?"

"You've been waiting for that, haven't you," Mike said ruefully.

I flashed him a grin. "Gun was kept in the locked gun safe in the garage. The key by the back door—on the way to the garage—was missing. Lewis' key was in their bedroom."

Jennifer's head bobbed in an emphatic nod. "That would mean they were arguing in the house, he went to the bedroom, got this gun safe key, went out to the garage, then came back and shot her between the kitchen and the living room. She just stood there waiting? After seeing him get the gun safe key?"

"If anything, she'd follow him out to the garage, trying to talk sense into him," Diana said. "If he snapped, the shooting should have been there."

"Unless he had the gun in the house for another reason," Mike argued. "Like he planned to shoot Wylie when he showed up."

"Back to how did he learn or come to think Wylie was worth shooting? Penny said there was nothing going on. We know that doesn't stop gossip necessarily, but Diana also said no rumors."

"Maybe the key was back on the peg by the door—"

"Found in the silverware drawer," I objected.

"—or he moved his key to the peg beforehand, so Kim would think he'd just walked out, when in fact, he grabbed the key, went to the garage, got the gun and shot her before she realized."

"That sounds like premeditation."

"Not necessarily. Did it beforehand for other reasons then took advantage when he snapped."

I flipped through the report to copies of crime photos—some of them. Had to wonder if Gee took out the ones of the bodies.

But blood stains still showed.

"Kim's body was closer to the back door than Lewis'," I said. "So he'd have to walk past her, then turn around and shoot her, while she stood there."

"He hid the gun, had it in his pocket or shirt or down beside his leg," Mike said.

I tipped my head and raised the uphill eyebrow, acknowledging that as a long shot.

"We can't rule out Mike's scenario," I acknowledged.

I went through the photos again. Gee also left one in of the keys on pegs by the back door ... along with a smear of what looked to be blood on the door frame beside them.

"That one caught me, too," Diana said. "Wylie Easley did more than look at the bodies."

Jennifer clicked her tongue. "They didn't go for fingerprints? That's basic."

"Redus," Mike said.

"There's a chance his sloppy investigation wasn't solely laziness." I had their attention. "Redus had access to the paintings."

"You think he could have—?" Diana started.

Mike interrupted. "Wait. How do you figure he had access? They had to break down the door to that closet."

"Hailey did say they broke down the door, but did they really have to? Start at the beginning. Hailey said her mother said nothing about the key to the painting closet being missing when she talked about the gun safe key missing a month before the shootings. So the painting closet key, presumably, wasn't missing.

"The first time we hear it was is *after* the shootings. And the source is Foster Redus, who, by the way, said in the report that no paintings were missing. Two possibilities. He lied or he told the truth. Let's start with lying."

"That fits," Jennifer muttered.

"The key's there. Redus takes it when no one sees him and keeps it, with the intention of helping himself to a painting or two. Then he sets up the hue and cry that the key is missing. Before he can take any paintings, though, O.D. insists on an inventory—perhaps when Gavin saw them in animated discussion. Foiled, Redus puts the key in the silverware drawer."

"But it was found with the key to the gun safe, which was missing the month before," Diana said. "Did Redus happen to pick the same hiding place? And if he did and saw the gun safe key, why didn't he make that public? All he had to do was hold onto the painting closet key and nobody would know anything except his excellent investigative work turned up the gun safe key."

"All good questions. The easiest answer would be it didn't fit the scenario he'd already declared was the solution and he couldn't be bothered."

"You said Redus couldn't take any paintings before O.D. insisted on the inventory. But what if O.D. was in on it?" Mike theorized. "And that's what was going on when Gavin saw them meeting."

"Possible. Hailey did another inventory when they moved the

paintings to where she lives now. Unless O.D. was able to mislead that inventory, too…"

"If Redus was involved in stealing paintings, alone or with O.D., he would have blown the money," Jennifer said. "But his spending matched what he got from blackmail. No sign of income from selling stolen paintings."

"Excellent, Jennifer," Mike said, not bothered that it shut down his theory. "Okay, what if Redus was telling the truth and the painting closet key didn't go missing until after the shootings?"

"Then we have a lot more possibilities. Someone took the key before the shootings, but the Newhalls didn't notice. They did notice and they were killed to keep them quiet. They were killed so they couldn't stop the killer from taking the key. They weren't killed for the key, but the killer took it after killing them. Someone who wasn't the killer took the key after they were dead."

"You've been thinking about that, haven't you," Diana said.

"Yeah," I confirmed a bit grimly.

"One more possibility," Jennifer said, "the key has nothing to do with the killings."

Chapter Thirty-One

JENNIFER HAD LEFT. Mike was in the bathroom.

I said to Diana, "I meant to ask what people around town are saying now about the Newhalls?"

She shook her head. "Not a lot. A lot has happened since then around here. Most of it having to do with you."

"Hey."

"Okay, most of the *solving* of it having to do with you. Though your personal life, what with living in a dead woman's house—"

"I bet a bunch of people are in houses where people died."

"—and romantically connected to the two most eligible men in the county. Unless you count Cas Newton—"

"Linda's *nephew?*" I objected.

"—who is a bit young for you," she continued placidly. "Though you do seem oddly friendly with him."

I groaned.

She laughed. "Honestly, it's good-natured. They find you a bit ... exotic. Which makes you fun to watch and talk about."

A second groan.

"Though what I'm wondering is how you feel about Mike."

"Don't you start, too."

"I mean how you feel about Mike not being the one and how you feel about how that makes him feel."

"I don't feel—"

"Bull." She relented, maybe because we heard Mike approaching. "But about what they're saying about the Newhalls ... It's not sport.

They're genuinely sorry Kim and Lewis are gone and worried for Hailey and Gavin."

✧ ✧ ✧ ✧

HAVING PARKED IN the KWMT-TV lot so the morning sun flooded my SUV, helping the inside temperature stay tolerable, I turned off the engine to make my phone call. If the SUV started to lose the temperature battle, I'd restart it in a heartbeat.

"Hello." His phone manner had improved from his usual, *What?*

"Hi Dex, it's Danny."

He'd called me by that play on my last name since becoming a background source for me. It provided a modicum of misdirection to bosses or coworkers who might wonder who he was talking to, especially in instances when the FBI lab higher-ups didn't want explanations given to reporters.

The nickname endured even now that they wouldn't much care what a consumer affairs reporter in Sherman, Wyoming, knew and— probably more important—Dex's brilliance earned him more elbow room.

"Are you in Washington?"

"No. Afraid not. I'd let you know if I was. I'm in Wyoming."

"Oh, yes," he said with enough vagueness that I suspected it would take him a while to remember my move here … if he had attention to spare to retrieve the memories.

"I'm looking into a case where there's talk about the bullet trajectory being odd. I'm hoping you can fill in gaps for me, in a practical, non-scientific way for the lay person."

"Practically speaking, trajectory is dependent on where the bullet initially goes into motion and where it ceases motion." I'd gotten that far on my own. "I should say, rather, when it connects with the victim, because it can continue in motion after initial impact, traveling through the body in what is called in the vernacular a through-and-through or traveling within the body and—"

"Yes, of course. But—"

I talked over some of what a bullet could do inside a body, but hadn't stopped the train of his thoughts.

"It can also pass through other materials before reaching the victim, which alters trajectory. As well as distance and—"

"Dex. Dex? In this specific case I want help with something—" That turned down his spigot on possibilities to listen to me. "The initial finding said it was murder-suicide, and a source said the trajectory from shooter to victim was slightly upward, although the shooter was at least six inches taller than the victim."

"The shooter's position?"

"Standing, according to the report. It also says the victim was standing or moving toward the shooter—not standing on a chair or coming down stairs or anything that would make her temporarily taller. I suggested shooting from the hip, but one source said the GSR on the shooter's clothing didn't fit."

"That trajectory is an anomaly that would need to be explained."

"They also said the GSR was not all over the shooter's hand. There were patches where it barely showed."

A pause while he no doubt reviewed all the cases he'd studied and all the possibilities his brain could produce—a much larger sample.

"Without seeing the evidence, including the crime scene photos, the positioning of the bodies, and the testing protocol, I could not go further than to say that could be a second anomaly."

Was it worth potentially earning Gisella Decker's unending ire to send the materials to Dex?

In a rare twist in our roles, Dex interrupted my thoughts. "There is an aspect to factor in, Danny."

"Yes?"

"An instructor of mine posited the rule that three anomalies always warrant further examination."

Did the victims' daughter's certainty the experts had it wrong count? Or...

I told him about the theft of Fred White's tail and the tenuous connection to the shootings through Hailey.

"I had never heard of that." His enthusiasm came from learning something new. I'd place a hefty bet Dex would soon be an expert on horse-tail thefts. "However, I would not count that as an anomaly with confidence in this instance because of the separation of time and characteristics of the incident."

That's what I wrestled with, too, though my thoughts ran more along the line of *I don't see how it fits.*

"What about you, Dex? How many anomalies do you accept before saying a situation warrants further examination?"

"I accept none."

That was my Dex.

✧   ✧   ✧   ✧

THINGS WEREN'T RUNNING as smoothly today as the previous few, since Audrey had to have a dental procedure and Mike insisted she take the day off to be sure she made tonight's meeting.

I had to agree it wasn't a great idea to have someone half loopy running the assignment desk or producing two shows.

Walt and I were patching together the assignment desk for the day, a part-timer had the production job for the Ten, and Bruce, a Thurston loyalist, would handle the Five, accompanied by a lot of grumbling.

Mike's Chicago station ran the interview early in the day, with different segments planned for several other of their eight daily newscasts. He had interviews with Needham and Dell today and now other outlets were chasing him for interviews.

With all that on Mike's plate, plus one-on-one meetings, and a conference with James before tonight's station-wide meeting, I had to stick closely to the KWMT grindstone.

✧   ✧   ✧   ✧

OF COURSE, THERE was always a little time for talk of murder, when Jennifer came by my desk and said, "I found a couple references to those unidentified remains."

"Unidentified remains—? Oh, you're thinking Redus' hot streak? I think Shelton was having fun with me."

"So you don't want to see what I found? You don't care who she ended up being?"

"Of course I want to see what you found. Who was she?"

"A woman from California."

"Hiker? Tourist who got lost?"

Jennifer pointed to my inbox, which flashed that I'd received five files, all articles from the *Independence*. "Doesn't sound like a hiker or a lost tourist, but read for yourself."

One established the fact of the remains being found, including their location, potentially dividing the investigation between jurisdictions.

One covered the Montana authorities taking over the investigation the next day. Adding that the clothes found were not consistent with hiking or camping.

One updated with Montana authorities after a week with no progress. None they were willing to share, anyway. It included how little information they had to go on. Then added the standard line that they were pursuing all avenues available to them.

As if law enforcement ever said, *Nah, we're going to skip a couple obvious avenues, just because.* Those sorts of phrases drove journalists nuts, but had to be included. Both to cover bases for the public and to keep from giving law enforcement an excuse to be even less forthcoming than it usually was.

One reported smart detective work by the Montana jurisdiction involving clothing and shoes—especially brands and labels—leading to an identification. They would release the ID after notifying next of kin.

The last, which included a formal headshot of a woman in her sixties with determinedly red hair who did not look at all like a hiker or tourist, came three days later, in the second week of July. The remains were those of Bernarda Garmin, from California. She'd been reported missing by friends. She had no immediate family.

Those who reported her missing said they hadn't known she'd planned to come this way. So nobody connected her with the unidentified remains.

The final article also said they'd found her car.

"What I don't get is Needham making such a big deal out of their detective work. They found her car, for Pete's sake. Talk about a big, fat clue," Jennifer said.

I checked back for time references. "The way it's written, the car was found after they ID'd her. And Needham wouldn't have slipped up on something like that."

"I suppose."

"What I don't get is they don't cite a cause of death. Maybe all the medical reports weren't in yet. Can't imagine Foster Redus doing that much work if he'd had the case. Her friends were fortunate it went to Montana."

She sighed. "Well, it's a dead end, but it does explain Shelton's hot streak comment."

"Closing off a dead end helps, too, and—"

"Jennifer!" Walt called from the assignment desk. "How do I recover the A Block that just zapped off my screen?"

She dropped a printout on my desk. "Here, I made a copy of her photo."

With thanks, I tucked it into my bag.

"I also checked police reports on the Newhalls' old house. Nothing reported."

Back to the grindstone for both of us.

Chapter Thirty-Two

DIANA GAVE ME my next reprieve.

"Can you follow me to the high school, then give me a ride back here?"

"Sure."

I was up and pulling on my outdoor clothes.

"You don't want to know that the kids and I are doing an intricate vehicle shuffle? I'll leave it with them, Jessica will drive to the library, then pick up Gary after football practice, do a food stop, and get them both home. I'll use the Newsmobile for my next assignment, then Mike will drive me to the ranch after the meeting tonight."

She never called it *her* ranch. She considered it held in trust for her kids as their inheritance from their father, who'd died in a ranch accident when they were little. Refusing to sell, Diana rented out the land and went to work to support her family.

"To get a break from Bruce for a while, I'd follow you to the dump."

"It's not quite that bad."

At the high school, I parked next to her. She slid into my passenger seat as I read Tom's most recent text saying Tamantha was about the same and thanks for checking. Again.

Okay, he didn't include again, but I could hear it. I hadn't texted *that* much.

Diana asked, "Do you mind waiting until Jess comes out for the key?"

"Of course not. Gives me a chance to tell you about reading the crime scene report again. Did you get the files from Jennifer?"

"Yep."

Her daughter sauntered up to my SUV before we could say more.

"Hi, Elizabeth. Hi, Mom. Key?"

"Couple things first. Get in." With Jess in the car, Diana said, "Remind Gary he has to clean the Bunkhouse. Today."

"He'll just whine about it. Though I don't know why, when he had the choice of days—,"

"For the same reason you whined about doing it when it was your turn. And you need to shell the bag of walnuts I showed you, so I can get the cake done for Gary's class bake sale."

With that sounding like the end of their information exchange, I restarted our conversation as Diana gave her daughter the key. "That so-called crime scene report is a travesty."

"Oh, God," Jessica said with the long-suffering only a teenager can achieve, "if you're going to talk about horrible murder stuff, I'm leaving."

"I am," I said firmly.

Diana swung around to make eye contact with her daughter. "Don't forget, those walnuts need to be finished before I get home tonight. Unless you want to—"

"No way am I baking for him," Jessica huffed. She swung her legs out of the vehicle.

"Bye, Jess. As I was saying, since that idiot Redus didn't even check Gavin's account of taking a different bus from school and was later than usual—"

Jessica stalled, one hand on the open door's handle.

"Gavin? Gavin Newhall? That's who you're talking about?" she demanded. Her voice started to slide up. "Like he needs an *alibi* for when his parents died? That's *crazy*. You can't—"

"Hold on, Jessica," Diana said. "Do not yell at Elizabeth."

That didn't come close to the kind of being yelled at I'd endured from groups as diverse as politicians, protestors, and pet advocates.

"Close the door," I told her. If she stopped letting the cold in, I was fine with the volume. "You know Gavin Newhall, Jess? Are you dating him? Have a crush on—"

"*No.*" She packed disgust for my ignorance into that. Did that mean she was still in touch with my nephew, J.R., since they'd met this summer? But she did close the door.

"Her friend, Lacey, had the major crush on Gavin in their freshman year," Diana said.

"She is not *dating* him. Or have a *crush* on him." From lofty, Jessica's delivery slid to mundane. "Not really. Not anymore. And he's not dating at all. He hardly talks to anybody. But he does *not* need an alibi. There's no way—"

"In an investigation, everybody needs an alibi. To eliminate them if not to—"

"Well, you can eliminate Gavin, because he was with Lacey that day."

Diana turned toward her daughter. "You never said that before."

"It never came up before."

I knew Diana well enough to know she didn't think her daughter spoke the whole truth. But she wasn't going to push her now, because it was a full-fledged discussion all on its own.

"Let's talk to Lacey," I said to Diana.

Jessica turned to me. "What? Now?"

"Yes, now."

At the same time. Diana said, "No, not now. I have to get back to the station for an assignment, you have to finish pulling the newscasts together, and we both have to go to Mike's meeting with employees."

She was right. Darn it.

"We'll do it tomorrow."

We drove back, with me telling her about Bernarda Garmin, even though it didn't help us any.

❖ ❖ ❖

MIKE HAD THE museum rearrange folding chairs from a classroom setup to a circle. Actually, more of a lumpy oval.

He sat at the end, with James on one side of him and me on the other. Leona and Walt were among those who filled in nearby chairs.

Others sat along the sides and back, then created a second, partial ring at the back and one side.

Standing by the door, Mike talked to people as they came in, until James Longbaugh suggested we start.

Mike said briefly how glad he was to see so many KWMT staffers here and how excited he was about the possibilities, then turned it over to James to explain how the employee ownership element would work.

There'd been a few questions. But I suspected most wanted to read the material closely before next week's promised follow-up.

James turned the meeting back over to Mike.

"For most of you this is home," he said. "You're not looking to move away from Cottonwood County. I—"

"So you think you have us pinned down. Don't need to do anything for us?"

"Iverton," Mike said to the reporter with the right blend of reproach and fondness. "Not only do you know better, but since you'd all have a share, you'd all have a say. You know how that works. Your family's been in the grazing association for how many years? So you know exactly how it works, people getting together to make it better than it would be if each worked alone."

"KWMT as TV's version of a grazing association?"

Mike grinned. "Pretty much. You can look at what we'll be facing as herd management, too. Only instead of breeding you guys to create the next generation—"

That got a big laugh. Then he extended it by adding, "Though if any of your kids want to sign up…"

Without stepping on the heels of the laugh, but before it faded completely, he said, "But we do need young blood. I'm not telling you anything you don't know when I say we're a small market. Maybe the smallest. We don't have a draw for young talent. If anything, working for us, means more intermediate steps to get up to where most of them want to get. Or—"

"Tell me about it," Audrey grumbled.

"—*think* they want to get," Mike finished, looking right at her.

"You're in the big-time," she shot back. "Why shouldn't some of us want that, too?"

"No reason if you really do want it and don't think it's what you're supposed to want. As for me, buying the station sure feels like planting my roots here deeper than ever."

He gave her a moment to respond, then smoothly picked up, "To get that young blood, we've got to offer something they won't get in bigger markets. Think of it as ongoing education or mentoring. You'll all be involved."

Iverton slowly stood. "Taking on young, raw kids. *Mentoring* them. It sounds like we're going to be training our replacements."

"There's an element of fact in what you say. They will be your replacements—eventually. Unless you're all planning to work to death."

"Sounds like you could be working us to death," Leona said.

I leaned forward to see her face better. She wasn't attacking. She'd said what others were thinking and giving Mike the opportunity to address it.

Okay, forcing him to address it.

"Look, it's going to take work to figure out a balance so too much doesn't fall on people. And at different times, with different young staffers things are going to shift around.

"A few of you remember what it was like when Artie was news director. That's the general idea. Never heard you complain about how it was under him, Iverton. In fact, your stories about it helped sell me on this idea."

That was a brilliant stroke.

"And you all know Elizabeth. She's going to be spearheading the effort."

Instead of admiring his brilliant line, I should have been girding my loins.

Quickly, I said, "I'm not going to be another Artie, for those of you who remember him, but I'm confident we can work together to smooth out wrinkles."

Bruce huffed his disbelief. The producer was one of three Thurston loyalists I'd tabbed as potential roadblocks.

One had been a pleasant surprise recently, almost like he'd broken out of an evil spell and now sheepishly rejoined the land of the living.

Bruce, not so much.

I looked directly at him. He continued to look down.

"I'll be calling on each of you for ideas as well as your cooperation." No chance of my words magically making everything better, but they started setting out expectations. "We'll pair up with folks by area of expertise and by shift, to get these kids accustomed to working all hours."

That drew a few chuckles. My phone vibrated. I shifted away from the sensation. Mike shot me a quick, questioning glance. I tossed back a no-worries response.

"But first," I said, "we need to get these recruits."

"That's right," Mike picked up. "I'm talking to as many of Artie's contacts as I can, but I could use more. If any of you remember who he talked to at specific colleges, come see me after we're done here. And if you have contacts of your own or new ideas of how to reach out, I'd like to hear them."

In the silence he left for anyone to jump up with a great idea—nobody did—my phone vibrated again, knocking against the button on my pocket and making a slight ticking sound no one beyond Mike could have heard.

He flicked an eyebrow up, but otherwise kept his attention on the group.

"Iverton, you know first-hand how Artie worked the program, tell the rest of us what you know."

"He just did it. It wasn't a *program*," he complained. Then he started to tell us how it worked.

A third vibration of my phone. I reached in my pocket to turn the thing off.

A name jumped off the screen at me—Tamantha.

I looked at three brief messages.

The first, from Tom, said, *NOT an emergency. Tamantha feeling poorly, hopes to talk to you soon.*

The second, from Tom, said, *She says to tell you she's asking for you like*

Beth asked for Marmee in Little Women when she had scarlet fever. This is not scarlet fever. NOT an emergency.

The third, from Tom's phone, but clearly not typed by him said, *When are you coming? I feel DREADFUL.*

I felt Mike's attention on me. When another staffer corrected Iverton on when a specific event happened under Artie's reign—a good sign of engagement—I tipped the screen so he could read it.

"Serious?" he asked under his breath.

"Not an emergency," I quoted under mine.

After a beat, he came back with, "Want to go?"

My mind whirled with balancing wants, responsibilities. My heart said, "Yes."

"Go."

I was up, outerwear bundled in my arms, and halfway to the door before anyone noticed.

Iverton interrupted himself to say. "Hey, where are you going, Elizabeth? If you're going to be responsible for this—"

"Go," Mike said to me aloud. I kept moving. "We're *all* going to be responsible for this. Elizabeth has a—"

Our eyes met a second as I pulled open the door.

"—family emergency. Which brings up another area nobody's taken stock of yet—more staffers, even young ones we'll be training and teaching, will pick up some of the workload you've all been carrying. Having more bodies means we can spread it out more and that means we can adapt better when emergencies hit—"

The door swung closed behind me, cutting off another great point by Mike.

Chapter Thirty-Three

A FOURTH MESSAGE came in from Tom. *This is not serious. Don't come. Call after the meeting.*

I called from the SUV. "I'm on my way."

"Elizabeth, you don't need to come—"

"That's not what Tamantha said. Besides, as I said, I'm on my way. Making one quick stop."

"Could you make it two?"

"Of course, what do you need?"

"Orange popsicles. I don't get them anymore, not since she said they're for babies."

"She's sick and she wants comfort food. Got it."

"Thanks. Door's open when you get here."

I HAD ONLY the popsicles and a couple bags of cookies—because you never know—when I reached the checkout line.

Penny was working tonight.

While the man in front of me paid, I reached for my wallet in my bag and encountered the printout Jennifer had given me.

"Bye now, Well, hi there, Elizabeth. Thought you'd be at that meeting. Lots of excitement—"

On impulse, I showed her the photo. Perhaps with a thought of distracting her from my unusual purchase of orange popsicles. "Did you ever see—"

"—with him buying it. Though some expecting miracles when they already got one. These orange popsicles always did make her feel better—"

So much for distracting her. I refused to react to her knowing I'd bought popsicles for Tamantha Burrell.

"—from when she was the smallest and smartest little thing. Asking about the friends and family. Lots—"

Her momentary focus on the printout told me we'd just shifted from Tamantha to the woman in the photo.

Jennifer's dead end wasn't dead. Well, the woman was, but the line of inquiry wasn't, not with her asking about Friends and Family of Carey Maight.

"—and lots of questions about that. Like I'd gossip."

She said it with a straight face. To my great credit, I held onto my straight face, too. Though, in a way, she didn't gossip. She gathered information and disseminated it, true. But with beneficial purpose and never to show off that she knew more than her listener, even though she almost always did.

"Didn't tell her a thing. Not about Carey Maight—acted like I'd never heard of her—not about who around here has her paintings. Not any of it. Saw her pick up real estate brochures. Didn't—"

"Carey Maight? Real estate—?"

"—stop her questions. Not one second. That one could talk the hind leg off a mule. Bye now. Well, hi there, Bella…"

I accepted my dismissal with dignity. This time.

Even if I'd managed to hold Penny's attention, I didn't have time to push her. I had another stop. Before the popsicles melted.

❖   ❖   ❖   ❖

EVEN WITH THE two stops, I made it to Tom's ranch north and west of Sherman in record time.

I might be picking up Diana's heavy-on-the-gas-pedal driving style.

When I opened the door to Tom's ranch house—both in style and fact—I heard Tamantha's voice declaring the green blanket was all wrong. In another child I'd call it whiny. For Tamantha, I substituted querulous.

Shadow—the purpose of my second stop—looked up at me. I released him with a word and he loped straight to Tamantha's room.

"*Shadow*," she croaked.

By the time I followed, with a quick detour to the fridge's freezer compartment, Shadow was on the bed, with his head on her lap. Several blankets covered the bed, including the derided green one. More pooled at the foot of the bed, apparently preceding the green one in ignominious dismissal.

"Looks like Shadow likes the green blanket," I said. "You'd have to roust him out to get it off now."

"Elizabeth," she said with a little catch of satisfaction—relief?— that brought a big catch to my throat. "You came."

Tom sat on a chair under the window. I sent a how-is-she look to him.

"Some fever. Not serious." His words drew a frown from his daughter. He saw it and expanded, "We're watching it."

Who knew. Tamantha Burrell was an I'm-sick-diva.

Only one way to deal with this.

I threw off my outer clothes with more emphasis than necessary and sat on the side of the bed left open by my dog. "You poor, poor thing." I reached out to hug her.

"She might still be contagious," Tom said.

Too late. She was in my arms, hers around my neck.

"I don't feel good, Elizabeth." She sounded younger than I'd ever heard her sound.

"I know, sweetheart."

"I might feel better if you get in bed with me and talk to me."

"Tamantha—" her father started.

We paid him no mind. In a moment, I was propped against the headboard with the covers over my lap, she was propped against me and Shadow had reclaimed his spot on the other side of the bed with his head at a convenient angle under her hand.

"There, that's better."

"Uh-huh. Daddy said you were at a meeting and wouldn't come."

"Couldn't come now," he quietly defended himself against her implicit accusation of cruelty to dreadfully sick daughters.

"I was at a meeting, but I did come, didn't I."

She sighed out deeply in satisfaction and snuggled deeper. "Yes."

I looked over her head to her father. He shook his head slightly, answering a bevy of questions from was this serious to did he mind to was she asleep.

She proved him right about the last one when her voice came, sounding a bit more like herself. "Were you asking questions?"

"Not this time. I was mostly listening to other people's questions, answering a few."

"Tell me about the questions." I bit back a smile at the familiar authoritarian undertones to the croak.

First, we sent Tom on a popsicle retrieval errand. She consumed that, then fell asleep to the bedtime story of KWMT-TV's new ownership model.

Chapter Thirty-Four

TOM LEFT THE door of her room open and gestured for me to precede him down the hall.

Shadow stayed where he was, declining an invitation to go out.

"That green blanket's a winner with my dog," I said. "I'll get it cleaned—"

"It washes. She usually wants it when she's sick. Not this time."

Under his calm sense, I caught a whiff of *my baby's growing up.*

"Now she'll want it because it's Shadow's."

His eye wrinkles flickered. "Yeah. And no video taught him that. Coffee?"

I accepted. Mostly to watch him make it. He doesn't hurry, but no motion's wasted either.

"Sorry to drag you out here," he said. "I thought if I messaged you what she said that would satisfy her. Obviously, I was wrong."

"I like the sound of that. Say it again."

He ignored that except for the compression of the lines around his mouth and eyes as he suppressed a grin.

He looked tired. A different kind of tired from working all day on the ranch. "Then she wanted to see what I'd written and she had her message typed and sent before I knew it. It's not like her."

"She's an illness diva. That's what my mom calls it."

He half-snorted a chuckle. "I like your mom."

"She likes you."

We looked at each other a long moment. Both of us knowing the unspoken part of this—my dad would be overjoyed if I became half of a couple with Mike. It wasn't only because Mike played for the Chicago Bears and Dad was a huge Bears fan—though that sure counted for something.

Dad wanted things easier, smoother for me. Mom thought I needed trouble, challenges.

This man—and his daughter asleep down the hall—would provide those.

I looked away from him.

"Mom mostly applies the illness diva label to guys in the family," I picked up as if nothing had come since my previous words. "But Tamantha qualifies. They're so used to charging full speed ahead that when something stops them, they not only feel bad, they're affronted by feeling bad. And they can't be a little sick. It has to be *big*—" I threw out my arms. "—*important* sick."

"Only the guys in the family, huh?"

I ignored his implication. "Is Tamantha always like this when she's sick?"

"Pretty much."

"Hope she doesn't get sick often."

"Not as much as when she was younger." His mouth shifted with what I'd swear qualified as a reminiscent smile. "Those first school years, kids are a germ factory."

"And you didn't mind, you strange, strange man."

"Never wanted her to get sick, but if she did ... We read a lot of books together in those years."

"You took care of her whenever she was sick, her mother didn't?"

He turned, rinsed his mug, as if it weren't just a motion to avoid meeting my eyes. Instead of putting it in the dishwasher, he undercut his alibi by moving to the pot—mug in hand—and lifted it in invitation. "More?"

"No thanks, I'll never sleep."

"I will." He poured himself another dose. "Being a parent's like cowboys who used to ride night herd. You drift when you can, but keep a sensor or two on all the time for picking up signals."

I nodded, said nothing.

After two more sips, he said, "Mona wasn't good with Tamantha being sick or fussing. Not from the start."

I did not point out Mona Praver-Burrell hadn't been good with Tamantha—period.

"I'd scoop her up and keep her snug in her room. Kept the peace with Mona. She'd still say she couldn't bear to be in the house with a sick baby. Had to get out of there. Smoky bar was a lot healthier." That he said without inflection. "It was our time, Tamantha and me. From the time she was a little thing."

He looked at his hands. Hands that no doubt once held all there was of his daughter.

"After the divorce, Mona didn't give me a minute extra visitation—"

Not because she wanted to spend time with her daughter, herself. I'd seen that. It was about using Tom's love for Tamantha as a weapon against him.

If the woman weren't already dead, I could be tempted.

"—until Tamantha got sick. Then she couldn't hand her off fast enough. She tried having Mrs. George—our neighbor here who looks after Tamantha now and then—take care of her once. But Mrs. George told Mona a few home truths and she'd never have her back."

"You not only didn't mind taking care of Tamantha when she was sick, you were glad to have the extra time with her."

"Had to fight it sometimes, or I could've turned her into a hypochondriac. Probably let her stay home from school an extra day just about every time."

"That's it. You're out of the parent Hall of Fame," I said. "Because clearly, she'd be president by now instead of when she grows up if you hadn't given her a handful of extra days in bed over the years. And socially—yeah, the girl has no confidence at all."

He grinned. "Don't mind losing the Hall of Fame status, but holding her back? If I thought … Even though we did spend those days reading. Me reading to her to start, then her reading to me, if she felt up to it."

Thomas David Burrell used to scoop up his sick or fussy daughter and close out his wife—before she was ex and after.

Yet, here I was. Called to the sick bed.

He hadn't closed me out.

He hadn't kept Tamantha to himself.

Mind you, she'd had a lot to do with that.

Still, the man had shared.

And then he'd actually talked about it.

ON THE COUCH, I fell asleep against him, the way Tamantha had fallen asleep against me.

But, first, my mostly self-told bedtime story was the ins and outs of the deaths of Kim and Lewis Newhall.

"Take it from the premise that it was a double murder, what do we have? They were shot with Lewis' gun. A gun normally kept in the locked gun safe in the garage. But a key to that gun safe was missing for a month.

"And then the key to the painting closet went missing after—No. Stick with the crime, first. What else do we know? They let the person in."

"Does that get you anywhere?"

"No, considering the shooter had to have access to the gun safe, too, so had to be the sort of person they'd let in."

"A friend," he said, not liking it.

"Or neighbor or relative or authority figure. And, no, that doesn't get us anywhere, either. I might as well go for the hat trick of getting nowhere." I dug out the grainy photo of Bernarda Garmin. "Do you know her?"

He shook his head. "Who is she?"

"Bernarda Garmin from California. Penny says she asked about Carey Maight paintings, including who owned them around here. I'd think she was a prime suspect, except Penny didn't give her any information—"

"Someone else did?"

"Possible. But even without the questions of would the Newhalls have let her in and how she got the gun, I don't know how we get past the fact that she was found dead the month *before* they were killed."

"That's a tough one."

"One other thing about her. She took real estate brochures. Like Wylie Easley, who, by the way could be a strong candidate for killing Kim and Lewis."

"Suppose he's a suspect because he found the bodies."

"Yup. Classic. Even though that makes Hailey grateful to him because it kept her brother Gavin from finding the bodies, as he would have if he hadn't taken a different bus. Possibly because of a girl. A girl he hasn't talked to since that day."

"Guilt."

"Yeah," I said grimly. "But over not being there to save his parents because he dallied with a girl? Or the kind of guilt he deserves in spades."

I held up a hand to stop words he didn't say.

"I know, I know … A kid. Anyway, the fact that his normal schedule would have had Gavin finding the bodies is one reason Penny says Lewis Newhall absolutely didn't commit murder-suicide. Along with *he just wouldn't.* I tell you, this whole thing feels like circles going around in my head. You get a couple things where you can start to see one thing leading to another … and then it comes back around to where you started, like a snake eating its head.

"*Snakes*—that's another thing. One of those circles is Carey Maight, who keeps coming up and coming up. Or maybe it's her and O.D. Or O.D. and Isaiah and Hailey. Or—"

He put an arm around me, drew me into resting my head against his shoulder.

"Tell me."

He listened in interested silence. I have no idea where I left off.

When I woke, from moonlight slanting across my face, I was curled on my side, covered by a blanket that hadn't been there before.

I crept down the hall, with the faint light from Tamantha's partially open door drawing a wedge on the floor and opposite wall. Not disturbing the door, I slid in quietly.

Tamantha was still congested, but sound asleep. So was Tom, on the chair. Only Shadow acknowledged my presence, his eyes following my movements without lifting his head, because that would dislodge Tamantha's hand.

"Good boy." I mouthed the words more than spoke them. Shadow's tail thunked softly.

I looked at Tom, remembering the second time I met him. In the jail. And how he went still. Thinking through what I said. Examining me. What I was made of. Whether I meant what I said.

So still.

I picked up one of the blankets from the floor at the foot of the bed—this one blue—and draped it over him. He blinked.

"Go to sleep," I whispered. "Everything's fine."

His eyes closed and he didn't awaken.

DAY SEVEN
THURSDAY

Chapter Thirty-Five

TOM SET OUT a new toothbrush and clean washcloth on the edge of the sink in Tamantha's bathroom for me.

After, I followed the coffee aroma to the kitchen, feeling half human, despite the decidedly morning hour.

"She slept through the night," he said while I sipped. "I let Shadow out a couple hours ago."

"Good. And thank you."

"Thanks to both of you for coming last night. And staying." He drank from his mug, then put it down. "I have something I want you to see."

"Okay."

"It's in my bedroom."

My brain jammed. Too many thoughts at once.

Hot damn.

Tom Burrell using that cheesy line?

Hot damn.

Who cares if it's cheesy?

Hot damn.

I kind of care.

Hot damn.

I thought better of him.

But ... hot damn.

I said, "Okay." It was the wittiest repartee I could produce at the moment.

"This way." He gestured almost formally. As if his compact ranch house had a lot of choices of which direction we might take to get to the bedroom.

I'd been down this hallway plenty. To use the bathroom. To go to Tamantha's room.

I'd seen his bed against the wall at right angles to the hallway, with wall lamps to either side for good reading light. The denim covered comforter always pulled up, though the pillows were as often jumbled as stacked upright. The plain wooden nightstand on the hallway side of the bed had two paperbacks—one open—on top and a shelf under-neath with a stack of ranching journals.

But I'd never been in his room before.

He'd been in my bedroom when we'd used it to gather people to clear underbrush on the way to solving a murder.

Not exactly rose petals and champagne.

"Go on in," he said from behind me.

I'd stalled on the threshold.

I headed for the end table. To distract from an awkward situation, I could always flip through ranching journals.

"Turn around."

If his voice had been husky, as it has been a few times in our histo-ry, that could mean something more.

This time it meant what the words said.

I turned around.

He tipped his head to the wall beyond the foot of his bed.

A painting.

A landscape.

A river winding through pines and peaks. In the river bed, rocks and tree trunks sharp and clear through the water in the foreground, but fading as the river moved on, obscured by distance and the reflection of the sky on the surface.

His land.

I don't know how I knew that, because it wasn't a spot I'd seen on the Circle B during rides with him and Tamantha.

The painting was by Carey Maight.

It had the same reality reaching out to the viewer from the mistiness as the portrait of Linda's ancestor. But so much more. It was about how a scene, a piece of land, could get into your blood.

Was that part of this painter's power, that she understood what got in your blood? That she knew how to get in your blood herself?

As I looked at it, there was something else. Something beyond the painter, beyond the painting ... Something about Tom.

Ah. Interesting.

"Why'd you hang it so it can only be seen from the bed?"

"Beginning and end of each day, it reminds me what this land is—a trust. It doesn't belong to me, but I belong to it."

"That sounds like—" I stopped a breath before the L word.

"It does." He tucked my hair behind the ear closer to him. "Not now, Elizabeth. But I'm coming to talk to you. Soon."

And then he kissed me.

First on my ear, then below it, then on my mouth, which I turned to him in a spirit of cooperation.

TAMANTHA CALLED OUT for her father.

Much improved, she wanted water, food, and a shower.

I stayed with her in the bathroom in case of sudden weakness, while Tom changed her bed to fresh sheets.

Back in bed, and with Shadow beside her again, she fell asleep.

I sat with her, giving Tom his chance to clean up and perform chores in the barn.

Watching her sleep, I thought about the last day of our trip with Mrs. P.

At our Sunday lunch, before the return trip, Tamantha took time after ordering to direct a look at me that made me feel like an object under a very intelligent microscope.

"I understand about how you were my friend first and even though you're not my daddy's girlfriend, you and I are still friends."

"Good." I said it firmly, while my brain screamed danger signals.

"Yeah, but you're not Mike's girlfriend now, either."

Never was his *girlfriend*. Nor Tom's. But this did not seem the time to confuse the throughline of her questioning. "No, I'm not Mike's girlfriend, either."

"He's not even around anymore."

Not a question. Didn't require an answer. Explaining things to this girl was hard enough. I wasn't going to voluntarily try to explain things she hadn't asked ... yet.

She slanted a look at me. "I know you like my daddy."

"Yes, I do like your daddy."

"You really, really like him."

"I really like him."

"Really, really like him," she insisted.

"I like him very much."

She looked toward Mrs. P. I couldn't read anything in the former teacher's oh-so-bland expression, so maybe there was nothing conspiratorial in the look.

"Okay," Tamantha said.

You'd think I'd take that acquiescence and run. Instead, it made me more uneasy.

A feeling borne out by meeting Tamantha's speculative look in the rearview mirror more often than was comfortable.

We'd have to be careful not to build up her expectations. Very careful.

When Tom walked me to my SUV, I sidestepped a kiss, shifting my eyes toward the window, where the curtain moved.

It was better to be careful. But I did miss the kiss ... along with my dog, whom I'd left as sickroom attendant.

Stopping the motion of closing my SUV's door, I said, "Tom, will your painting be in the exhibit Clara Atwood's putting on next year?"

"No."

"Do you know whose paintings are?"

"Mrs. Parens has a couple, several from other members of the Friends and Family group, but O.D.'s are the core."

"Not Hailey's?"

"No. Apparently, she said yes first. Then she changed her mind. Clara was unhappy because they'd invested in those postcards that featured a couple of paintings Hailey owns now. Real unhappy, until the others stepped up."

✧ ✧ ✧ ✧

THE WORST THING about spending the night on Tom's couch was I'd agreed to give Leona a break and take the anchor desk tonight.

This talking head needed extra concealer to be air ready. Could I get Jerry to use a soft filter on the two ancient studio cameras? Or back them up another three feet.

The best thing was I didn't have to go into KWMT until later than usual.

I'd showered and changed when my phone rang. Dell Yardley.

"Nice interview of Mike," he said.

"Thanks, Dell. Nice of you to take the time to call and tell me."

"Clara's working on her special exhibit."

He didn't notice the pause as I held back a laugh. "Surprised you're not headed back to Washington. You don't usually like to give a sub this much time to get comfortable in your job."

At the same time I said that, something he'd said started a new track in my brain.

"A week to Thanksgiving? With the only story the pardoning of those turkeys? They are welcome to fill in for another week. Especially since they are cycling through three green substitutes. None will be there long enough to get a foothold." He sailed on with, "I heard the network picked up a small section of the affiliate feed on your interview. Of course, *my* interview with him *originated* on the network. I also heard a couple of other things."

Paying the toll for him to share those *couple of other things*, I said, "Can't wait to see your interview."

"You will, tonight. And then in its entirety on a weekend magazine. Don't know which yet, because several want it."

"That's great, Dell." No need for him to know I was thinking about the good it might do Mike and KWMT, rather than him. Along with that other track in my head. "Do you know—?"

"It's expected, but satisfying. The Big Bosses like the humanizing touch of their White House correspondent talking with a sports guy. Do you know what else is great?"

I provided his favorite answer. "No, what?"

"Mike's station in Chicago is dying to hire you. Do not accept anything less than fifty percent more than you were making in New York."

"I won't. Because I'm not accepting at all. I have a job—and a life—here."

"You have to listen to the offer, Elizabeth. Even with Mike as your boss here—"

"No, I don't. And don't tell him about this, Dell."

"That is—"

"Don't."

"Fine, fine. Since you are adamantly opposed to restoring your career, I might as well tell you the other thing I heard. Wylie Easley is in a pickup, sitting in front of the house where the Newhalls were killed."

I immediately recalled the discussion with the others that he could have returned to town—and stuck around—because he was after something in the Newhalls' old house.

"How do you know *that*?" But I already had my bag and was headed toward the back door.

"Someone called Krista while I was giving an expert opinion on a new breakfast casserole recipe she tried. It needs more sage—"

"No," I heard in the background, at the same time, I said, "How long ago, Dell?"

"Immediately before I called you. It does, Krista. More sage will bring out the flavor of—"

"Thanks." I ended the call.

Chapter Thirty-Six

I KNOCKED ON the passenger window of the truck with Arizona plates parked across the street from the house the Newhalls had lived in.

I'd parked behind him, and walked up quietly along the sidewalk side. I could see him, alone in the truck, turned toward the house.

He jerked around at the sound, recognized me, spotted my SUV in the rearview mirror, lowered the window.

"Mind if I get in? It's cold out here."

I watched him think about telling me I could get back in my vehicle if I wanted to stay warm.

He unlocked the door.

"Good memories or bad?"

He gave me the back of his head as he looked toward the house again. "All bad about this place. The good ones are a lot older."

From when he was part of a foursome? Or before Kim met Isaiah?

He swung around to face me.

"You didn't come to the B&B to thank me on behalf of Hailey. You're nosing around into her parents' deaths."

Not a lot of acrimony in his tone. More presenting it as setting-the-record straight than accusing.

"She does thank you for keeping Gavin out. What we at KWMT are doing evolved—at her behest. We are looking at the investigation into Kim and Lewis Newhalls' deaths."

"What difference does it make? Kim's dead. I didn't really know her husband. Whether he did it or not..." Another of those practiced shrugs.

"Hailey does not believe her parents' deaths were the result of a murder-suicide. I'm sure you can understand it makes a great deal of difference to her whether her stepfather killed her mother and himself or not."

"Suppose it does," he said with studied casualness.

"Does it worry you that if it's looked at more closely with the idea that Lewis Newhall didn't kill his wife then himself, that you could be considered a suspect?"

"Me? I've never been a suspect," he said firmly. "The time of death let me out of the picture, even if it wasn't murder-suicide. They weren't killed right before I found them."

Was he that naïve? Or thought we were?

"What were you doing earlier that day?"

The look he arrowed at me said he wasn't naïve. Not stupid, either. He got the implication.

But he didn't fire up.

"I was driving around looking at properties in the county."

"With a real estate agent?"

"On my own. Narrowing down ones I'd talk to Kim about. With her input, I'd have picked which to see with the agent."

In other words, no alibi.

If Redus had done a half-decent investigation, he'd have checked for sightings of Easley at the time.

Might not have done any good, it was pretty darned hopeless. Nobody could prove he *wasn't* out looked at properties. Proving he *was* would be the needle in a haystack big enough to cover wide open spaces.

Redus also could have checked around the Newhalls' neighborhood. For Easley, for Gavin, for anybody.

He hadn't.

"You said they weren't killed right before you found them. What do you base that on?"

"Signs … Forensics, I guess."

I nodded my understanding. "Blood starting to congeal? Size of the blood pool, things like that? The problem is, the deputy's report doesn't include that." The crime scene photos Gee left out of what we saw would. But it wasn't my job at this moment to make him feel more secure.

Easley paled under his Arizona tan.

"Now that the lid's off this case, to not be considered a suspect, your best bet is to help us fully explore it to find who *should* be a suspect."

He didn't voice agreement to cooperate, but I took it as given.

I started by going back over his story the day of the Newhalls' deaths.

Nothing new.

He came to town to look for a second home with acreage.

He reconnected with Kim and met her and Lewis at the café a couple days earlier.

He stopped at their house that day to pick up Kim to take her for coffee and go over his real estate possibilities.

He knocked, called, then tried the door. Gavin arrived right after, and he kept him out.

Nothing budged or cracked from his previous telling.

I needed another entry point.

Abruptly, I asked, "Did you know Clayton Rayger's engaged to Hailey Newhall?"

"That a fact?" The lifting of his lip belied those uninterested words.

"Tell me about the four of you."

"I never knew Clayton that well. I was Kim's friend. He was Isaiah's friend. If we wanted to do things with our friend, we did them all together. We got along okay, but it seemed like it was the same with him as it was with me."

"What did you think of the relationship between Kim and Isaiah?"

A flicker of surprise showed before he damped it down. "I'm not against Native Americans, if that's what you're getting at."

"Only thing I'm trying to get at is insight on Kim and Isaiah's relationship."

"They were crazy for each other." Something came out around the edges of those words. That he'd been crazy for Kim, as Clayton said? Wylie quickly added more words to obscure whatever it was. "At the start, anyway. Don't know if it was her being pregnant or what, but in the months before Isaiah died, there were more arguments. Kim never said what they were about. She was too loyal to do that. Clayton might know from Isaiah."

In other words, Isaiah hadn't been as loyal as Kim was.

"Did you know about the Carey Maight paintings Isaiah inherited?"

A frown dug in between his brows. Remembering? Surprised by the question? Not liking that direction?

"Yeah. Everybody knew about that."

"Did you know Hailey would inherit, with Kim as guardian? Did Kim talk to you about that?"

"Nobody expected Isaiah to die. Least of all Kim."

He'd sidestepped. Drag him back and risk him clamming up?

I decided not to.

"Tell me about when Isaiah died."

"Going for ancient history, huh." His foray into lightness ended. "We were all at the little apartment Kim and Isaiah had. It was over the auto parts shop down the road from our garage. I heard about it and got them a deal. It wasn't much, but Kim turned it into a nice place. Cleaned like crazy in there, made curtains and pillows, stuff like that.

"Anyway, we were all there. The three of us drinking beer and shots. Not Kim, because of the baby. She and Isaiah had been fighting—that was clear from the tension between them when I got there, as well as him drinking even more than usual. Then he got a phone call and the sh—" He broke off, looking away from me. As if I'd never heard such language. "Stuff hit the fan. Isaiah said he had to go meet somebody.

"Kim didn't want him to go. She even cried—must have been hormones after being pregnant, because she was never much of a crier, even as a kid. He got more stubborn about it. She asked him if it was a woman. He wouldn't answer, which was stupid, because we'd all heard a woman's voice when he answered.

"Clayton tried to smooth things over, said it wasn't anything like Kim was thinking and she shouldn't worry and he'd make sure Isaiah didn't do anything stupid. It didn't reassure her any, because Clayton was stumbling drunk when he went after Isaiah.

"And now we all know how he passed out in the back seat. Relaxed enough to avoid serious injury, like drunks often do. Not Isaiah. The impact broke his neck and he died right away. Kim used to say that a lot—died right away, died right away. Like she was persuading herself of that. They say he didn't suffer."

The last statement was oddly flat. No reaction? Suppressing a reaction?

"Who was he going to meet?"

He lifted one of those impressive shoulders. "Nobody ever knew. Isaiah didn't tell Kim. Clayton said he didn't know."

That was clear. When Kim said Isaiah hadn't told her, it was gospel. When Clayton said Isaiah treated him the same way, it was subject to skepticism.

"What about Isaiah's phone?"

He took an extra beat. "You mean records on the phone? No idea. Don't know if they found it, checked it, or if it was smashed up. Never heard a thing about it."

"Nobody came forward?"

"No." He looked away. "It didn't seem to matter at that point. Sure didn't matter to Kim. Look, I gotta go."

"Wylie, why did you come back to town?"

"Family business." He'd had that ready.

"Are you going to stay long?"

"Have to see how things play out."

Pleasant wasn't getting me far. I added a point to my next question. "Looking at more property?"

The point poked him and the look he gave me qualified as unfriendly. "As I said, family business. Not that it's any of yours."

"Should I tell Hailey you'll be in touch?"

"Don't bother yourself. I'll get hold of her myself if that looks good."

"Do you plan to see Clayton?"

"Have to see how things play out," he repeated without interest.

"What are you doing here, Wylie?"

"Sherman's my hometown. Why shouldn't I—"

"Here. In front of this house."

"I told you. Memories."

"Bad memories. That doesn't seem like—"

"As I said, I gotta go."

Chapter Thirty-Seven

WYLIE EASLEY DIDN'T outright tell me to get out of his truck, but he came close.

Preferring being in the driver's seat—of my own SUV and metaphorically—I got out.

He drove off with a heavy foot on the accelerator.

I took my time heading back to my SUV.

The Newhalls' house had been a deep blue in the crime scene photos with bright white trim. It was now dark gray. Other than that it looked the same.

A peaked porch protected the centered front door. The drive on the left side of the house ran past a small, enclosed side porch toward the rear of the house, then to a two-car garage. A structure enclosed the short space between the porch and a garage side door. That must be the painting closet.

I crossed the street to the sidewalk for a closer look.

Would it be too creepy to walk up the driveway and…

"Hey. I'm on the phone with the police. If you trespass—"

I jumped back from the edge to the center of the sidewalk, but that didn't appear to be what stopped the fiftyish woman charging at me, phone in hand, from the front door of the house next door.

"You … You're that woman on TV. I watch you whenever you do one of those specials on a murder."

What is it in me—in many people—that immediately made me think, *What? You don't watch Helping Out! segments?*

I'm not an idiot. I didn't ask that.

"Yes, I am. E.M. Danniher. And your name is—?"

"Amy Cravaford. I live next door. You're looking into Kim and Lewis being killed? The new owners don't like people looking around, but they weren't around when it happened, were they. Not like me. I can help you get the guy who really killed them."

"It was ruled a murder-suicide."

"If you thought that was right, you wouldn't be here, would you."

She had me there. "Hailey hopes for more ... clarity."

"Thank heavens somebody is looking for clarity of *something*, because Lewis did not kill Kim. I told that deputy. And I told him who he should investigate, but he wouldn't listen. That was him—the one who found them—you were talking to, wasn't it? That Wylie Easley.

"That's why I got me phone out. To take his picture and call the police, but he took off before I could. Not that I need his picture. I'll never forget what he looks like. Saw him come that day. And then Gavin. And next thing I know, Kim and Lewis are dead. I'll never forget that."

✧ ✧ ✧ ✧

AMY CRAVAFORD HAD plenty of certainty, all based on feelings, not facts.

Kim and Lewis got along great. He never would have killed her. Hailey and Gavin were wonderful kids. The perfect neighbor family.

They chatted about things all the time.

Like that Wylie Easley had been pestering Kim and she was too nice to tell him to get lost. All that stuff about looking for property, just showing off that he'd made a lot of money in Arizona.

As if that would matter to a woman like Kim.

And Lewis Newhall was not jealous. No possibility in this universe. Because he knew Kim loved him and nobody else.

"Did you notice anything unusual—?"

"Only thing unusual that day was that man, that Wylie Easley coming around."

Then Amy—apparently unknowingly—undercut Wylie's status as a suspect by maintaining she saw exactly when he arrived, followed minutes later by Gavin. She'd been in her yard after returning from several hours of running errands and saw it all.

But she didn't hear anything.

Because the killings happened while she was gone.

✧   ✧   ✧   ✧

JENNIFER GREETED ME at the station, "You've got to talk to Audrey."

Let loose of Leona's strictures, Audrey had gone a little wild on the hard news.

I talked her down from an analysis of money policy influencing political trends in Eastern Europe. We did get in a short piece on experimental cattle breeding in Finland, bookended by tying it to local efforts.

We were already behind and it was one of those news days.

There wasn't one big story to focus on, but a lot of smaller ones that accumulated gloom.

You've heard the Mathew Arnold quote that journalism is literature in a hurry? Sometimes journalism is minutiae in a hurry.

I told Jennifer about Penny recognizing the photo of the dead woman—and her asking about Carey Maight paintings.

"That's got to mean something," she said hopefully. "What?"

"Something, yeah. No idea what. And with anchoring tonight…"

"Yeah. Work's really getting in the way. I'll tell Mike, you tell Diana when she gets in."

Jennifer also caught me for ten minutes later in the afternoon for updates.

"The guys didn't find any listings for the horse hair from those earlier thefts. Can't be absolutely sure it wasn't offered for sale—not this long after—but we didn't find any. I'd say better than eighty-five percent chance it wasn't offered for sale."

Why wouldn't thieves sell their booty?

Obvious explanations included that the person or persons who stole it kept it or had a buyer already lined up.

Fred White did not have his tail stolen in that previous flurry of thefts. Would someone stealing horse hair to sell have skipped his prized light-colored tail and mane?

And why was his taken this time—still only his, with no other reports coming in—when there was no sign of it being on the market? Again, the thief kept it or it was a contract horse-tail theft?

And why did these incidents feel so different?

"Did you hear me?"

"What? Sorry, Jennifer. You were talking about the phone calls?"

"Yes. I'm working my way back through the Newhalls' phone logs. Lewis' cell called Clayton Rayger's cell the day of the shootings."

"That's worth asking him about."

"Before you get too excited, it looks like Hailey used his cell a fair amount, sending and receiving calls and texts. Unless he was contacting her girlfriends and hair salon on a regular basis."

"Safe to say it was her. Because if Clayton made calls like that, Diana's rumor sweeps would have picked it up. Not to mention Penny."

"True. The other thing I found was a couple calls from the same Palm Springs, California phone number to the Newhalls, one in early June, one in the middle of the month. They never called back. The phone number is no longer active. I have the guys checking who it belonged to back then."

"Keep at it," I said.

Which is what I needed to do to prepare for these newscasts.

I did take one other break.

MY SECOND VEHICLE interview of the day came in my SUV at the high school.

It took more to set up than my surprise appearance at Wylie Easley's car door. But that was Diana's doing.

She called and asked if I wanted to talk to Jessica's friend, Lacey—the one Jess said was Gavin's alibi witness.

Silly question.

Then she said, she'd be at the station in two minutes and we had to go right then to reach the high school before the girls left for a horse drill team practice.

I met her in the parking lot. She offered to drive in the Newsmobile. I declined. It wasn't quite as decrepit as it looked, except for its shock absorbers and seat cushions, which were worse.

So we rode in comfort while I filled her in on Tamantha, Easley, and Jennifer's work on the phone calls from two and a half years ago.

Having arrived, we sat in comfort while we waited for the girls to emerge and Diana explained there were conditions to this conversation. Jess was sitting in, too. And they could not be late for practice.

Jess sat behind me, but I could feel waves of wariness coming off her. Lacey sat behind Diana.

She had a round, sweet face with light brown hair losing its summer highlights. The strongest impression was of niceness, rather than *va-va-va-voom*.

Gavin might have better taste than I'd expected.

I eased in with, "Did Jess tell you what we want to ask you about?"

"Yeah. About Gavin and the bus from summer school."

"Did he say why he was on that bus? He wasn't usually, was he?"

"No. He said he missed his regular bus."

"You sat together?"

"No. It wasn't real full. We sat across from each other."

Remembering how they'd sat … A crush on him for sure.

"What did you talk about?"

"School and friends and … kidding around, you know? There are only a couple routes for summer school, so they're long. We talked about a lot of stuff."

"Was anything different from when you usually talked together?"

A deeper tinge of pink hit her cheeks. "It was the first time we'd really talked. At my stop, he said he might as well get off with me, because none of the stops went near his house."

The crush might have been mutual.

"He walked with me to outside my house and we talked some more and then he said he had to get home, he'd see me the next day, and then he jogged down the block and turned the corner toward his house."

Major crush.

Not only did she watch him leave until he went out of sight, she knew which direction his house was.

"How long did you and Gavin talk, Lacey?"

She shook her head. "I don't know. Not real long."

"Did you look at the time, maybe when you went inside?"

"No. But summer school was only until about one, so maybe around two?"

Far too vague to pin down a timeline. If Redus had checked at the time ... No use wishing.

"Are you sure you have the right day?"

Disdain layered over her niceness. "You think I'd forget? We heard about his parents later and ... I'll never forget. *Never.*"

"Tell them the rest," Jessica said, firm but understanding.

Lacey looked off to the side and blinked. "He hasn't talked to me since. Not even hello."

"He looks right through her like ... like—"

"It was my fault," Lacey completed in a whisper. "Like if he hadn't talked to me, he could have..." Her voice faded to a whisper. "Saved them."

"I wish you'd let me say something to him and—"

"No. He has enough to deal with. I won't add to it."

Diana leaned around to reach back to pat the girl's knee. "That's very generous of you, Lacey. You have to know it's not because of you or anything you did. If he does think that if he'd followed his usual routine he could have been there in time to change things, he's wrong. He'll accept it eventually."

"C'mon, Lacey, we have to go now. Done?" Jess challenged me.

"For now, yes," I said. "Thank you both. If we think of more questions, is it okay if Jess gives me your contact information, Lacey? And if you think of anything...?"

"I'll give it to you now."

That done, she looked up, from Diana to me.

"I just hope ... I hope you find out what happened, if it wasn't what they said, about his dad killing his mom and then himself, that would make such a difference to him. But even if that is the truth, maybe if you can show him it was that for sure, he'll…"

Heal.

That's what she had in mind.

But what about other possibilities?

Chapter Thirty-Eight

"**I STILL SAY** there are two possibilities behind Gavin's actions that fit the sloppy timeline work by Redus," I told Diana as I drove us back.

"You're telling me you think he could have—" She went with euphemism. "—done something he'd never heal from?"

She'd caught Lacey's healing vibe, too.

"Could have? Yes. Gavin Newhall could have run home, killed his parents, then circled back, and followed Wylie in the door. In that scenario, Wylie Easley wasn't as good at estimating time of death as he thought he was. Kim and Lewis would have been killed just before he arrived.

"Or Gavin could have killed them before he left for school. Took the different bus and all the rest to delay going home."

"Wouldn't someone at school notice different behavior? Wouldn't Lacey have?"

"Stranger things have happened than people not noticing. As for a girl in the throes of a crush noticing something else when the boy talked to her for the first time? Maybe not. And the other question— would a girl with a crush lie for him?"

"Not Lacey. Also, human nature being what it is, plenty would have retroactively noticed he'd acted strange that day if he'd given them any cause."

"That's a stronger argument than resting it on Lacey. But, even if he did what she said he did, we can't eliminate him. The times are too loose. *Not real long* doesn't help at all."

"I can tell you that talking for *not real long* for those girls could easily reach an hour. I hear all this stuff about kids today only messaging and not having face-to-face conversations. Not my daughter. But that doesn't help, either. You're right. The times are too loose."

We fell into a silence. Neither of us happy that we couldn't eliminate the kid.

After my version of *not real long*—based on TV news slots, not teenaged girls' conversations—I spoke.

"The way Jess reacted, I thought maybe she did have a crush on him." As Diana started to shake her head, I said, "I know. She seemed more ... protective of Gavin."

"Yeah. I suppose it was his parents getting killed and the association with her memories of Gary's death. I wish she would talk to me about it, but it's when she gets the quietest."

I rested my hand on her arm. "She knows she can come to you any time. But she's also learning to work things out on her own. That's good news."

"Keep telling me that," she said dryly. She gusted out a breath. "She does accept the justice component of what we do—even the necessity of it. But she sure doesn't want to hear the details."

"So cross detective off her list of potential careers. That's no tragedy."

"You're right. It's not."

✧   ✧   ✧   ✧

MIKE CAME INTO the studio the second the Five ended.

"Great work, everybody!"

He said a few words to each of the crew as they left. I sat at the anchor desk watching him.

He pulled up a spare chair beside me.

"We need a new anchor desk," he said with the air of someone adding to a mental to-do list.

"Thought you had a working dinner with James tonight to go over the employee ownership structure."

"I do. In an hour. Rather be talking clues with you and Jennifer and Diana, especially because I'll have post-dinner homework—a fun night of reviewing documents. With a gap before dinner, I stuck around to see a delivery they're uncrating on the loading dock. And that meant I got to see your anchoring work. You really are good, Elizabeth. There's nobody—"

"No."

"—we could possibly get to anchor—"

"No."

"—because nobody else—"

"I went through this with Audrey when Thurston went off the air. And it's turned out well."

He paled. "You can't—You can't expect me to tell Leona to anchor permanently. Not only will she say no, she'll kill me. You saw what happened the day I got here."

"You know, I do think you might be almost as afraid of Leona as you are of Mrs. P and your aunt."

"I'm not afraid of them. I respect them."

"That's good, Mike. You've been working on your ability to spin and that should help you greatly as an owner."

"Terrific. But in the meantime, where the hell am I going to get an anchor, much less a general manager and news director? They've got to be good to make the Artie program succeed."

"I have an idea about that. Instead of putting a lot of the burden on the news director, we supplement by rotating in top-notch journalists as guest instructors."

"Yeah? How are we going to get them in? Not by paying big bucks. If the news operation starts spending like—"

"Spoken like management *already*. But relax. To start, we call on connections—yours, mine, former proteges of Artie's. We use friendship, nostalgia, loyalty, the exciting chance to impart wisdom to fresh young talent ... and side-trips to Yellowstone Park, the rodeo, the Absaroka Mountains, a real working ranch, potluck dinners with the citizenry of Sherman, and all the other things their regular lives don't offer."

He'd started tapping into his phone a third of the way through my brilliance. I let him catch up.

"I like it," he said. "I really like it."

"Also, we—*you*—might find a news director by offering a lighter load in a laid-back atmosphere. Someone who still has the journalism juice, but is tired of the rat-race, wants the work for the work's sake and not the competition."

He looked intrigued. "Anyone in mind?"

"No. And it's going to require careful consideration."

"What about a general manager?"

"Out of my realm." A thought occurred to me. "But get Mel to get you in touch with the woman in Dallas who's worked for the Heathertons. Mel thinks highly of her. She might know people."

"That's right, he negotiated with her for your contract here. Great. I'll do that. About your contract—"

"Don't you dare try to change it."

"I was thinking of making it a lifetime agreement."

"Hah. I'm not getting tied to this place for the rest of my life."

"Aren't you? Maybe not the station, but Sherman? Cottonwood County?"

"I've grown fond of it of course, but—"

"That's what you're saying? You've *grown fond of it*. Seems like more than that."

"If you think you're talking about more than my contract with KWMT—"

"No. I know where I stand with you. Tom and I've talked a little." I groaned. "Really, a little. We haven't needed to talk much. It was clear early on how we each felt."

"About each other, you mean. That you like and respect each other." Annoyance, rather than admiration came through in those words.

"Yeah, we do. And how we each feel about you."

I couldn't respond to his sincerity with anything but the same.

"Mike, I truly do love—"

"I know. You love me. You're not in love with me. What about Tom?"

The question—from him—took the breath from my lungs. "I ... I don't know."

"While you do know with me," he said flatly. Before I could respond, he went on in his normal voice. "You'll get there, Elizabeth. I know it. With you and Tom ... Well, I've felt sometimes like I was a marriage counselor. I guess I kept hoping because you two disagreed. What I should have focused on was you already acted like a couple."

"Mike—"

"No." The word was harsh. The ones that followed weren't. "No need to say it. And no need to shed those for me."

He reached up with both hands and swept his thumbs under my eyes, pushing tears aside that I hadn't realized were falling.

His face became even more serious. "Don't do him wrong. If you realize you don't, then cut it off fast and firm."

"Mike—" I put a hand on his forearm.

"It's okay. Not good, but okay. The way I feel about you—Well, I want you to be happy."

"I want the same for you."

"Yeah. I know. So why do we both look miserable."

"I think ... I think because we both thought—hoped—for something different and then we realized it wasn't there. Not for us."

His expression shifted, a tinge of amusement showing through. "Maybe."

"I'll take that."

"I'd take it, too, if you consider a for-life contract."

I gasped. Part laugh, part sob, part amusement, part outrage. "You *weasel*—this was just to negotiate a contract?"

He laughed at my mostly mock outrage.

"Not all of it."

Then he kissed me. It tasted like a last time.

✧   ✧   ✧   ✧

I LINGERED AFTER the Ten. I pulled up Diana's original footage on the interview of Mike and watched it all the way through to when I gestured to Diana to stop recording.

It really was good. Darned near air ready without any editing.

I wound it back to see the last part again.

Seeing without the journalist filter on. Just a person. Who cared a lot about another person.

I watched Mike's face as I asked if he was happy and he answered.

I not only heard his answer, I saw it. I believed it.

However he felt about what might have been possibilities between us at one time, he was truly happy.

I found myself smiling at the screen.

Still smiling, I waited for the recording to end. It didn't.

Diana had kept the camera running, pulling back to a two-shot, as Mike talked about being even happier if he could be two places at once and about me being two places at once.

Then she'd come in close on me.

I could see my thoughts on that screen that I hadn't even been aware of at the time.

I didn't want to be two places at once.

Illinois remained the center of gravity for family, a touchstone.

But this was home now.

You must be patient, Elizabeth. Sometimes you must wait for the answers to come to you.

That's what Mrs. P said.

I could use more answers—a lot about the Newhalls and a big one not about them. I didn't know if I could be patient.

DAY EIGHT
FRIDAY

Chapter Thirty-Nine

THE PEN AND Ink shop was down the street from the offices of the *Independence*.

I did not stop to say hello to Needham.

No sense giving him leads on our inquiry, like we were talking to someone in his neighborhood.

Besides, Jennifer came with me, giving up her free time before a late shift. Didn't want to drag her on a detour.

The front of the shop displayed cameras in an old-fashioned cabinet on one side. The other side had modern round tables with stools for customers to fill out print and copy orders. Beyond them came a couple copy machines, then a door to a framed-in room.

The back right side had a work counter for framing, with art supplies on one part of the wall behind it and the rest devoted to samples for framing.

Clayton Rayger, wearing a backward ball cap, stood at the counter, contemplating a frame, matting, and family photograph laid out in front of him. He wasn't doing anything with them, just looking.

"Hi there."

He focused on Jennifer first, smiling—a strong enough smile to be obvious under the turned-down mustache.

His smile ebbed as he shifted to me.

"Hi, Clayton, remember me? E.M. Danniher. Hailey introduced us. And this is my colleague, Jennifer Lawton." Not waiting for him to confirm, I added, "I was so impressed with how you want to help Hailey by answering my questions. Can we buy you a cup of coffee?"

He looked around. No boss jumped up to say no.

"Yeah." He walked away from the project without a backward glance.

At the café, he also ordered a ham sandwich and macaroni salad on my tab.

"Clayton, first, we hope you can clear up a little matter for us. Does Hailey use your phone?"

"All the time. She's always got more important things to fill her pockets, I keep mine with me."

"Does she receive calls on your phone?"

His mostly hidden mouth seemed to lift. "Sure. Folks calling back without checking the number."

"Thanks."

"No problem." He bit into the sandwich.

That gave me plenty of time to flatter. "You're in a unique position to give us insight, since you've known all the people involved."

"Guess so." Another big bite.

"And that means you can help give Hailey what she most wants—answers about the deaths of Kim and Lewis."

"I don't know anything—"

"Not directly. But for background, to help us understand the situation and the relationships—nobody's better than you."

He chewed without comment. What more could you want as an invitation to proceed?

"Take the relationship between Isaiah and his father, especially how the paintings affected that. You were right there to see all that."

"O.D. always cared more about those paintings than his son—or his granddaughter. Isaiah said him getting the paintings as a baby warped his old man forever."

"They argued about the paintings?"

He chuckled. "Can't say argued. O.D. told him what he should do and how and when. Isaiah ignored him. Told him to go…" He let it die out. Sparing our sensibilities or to eat more salad.

"But I guess some of those lectures rubbed off on Kim, because after Isaiah died, she lined up right behind O.D. in all matters about the paintings. Like he was the only one who had anything worthwhile to say. Like I didn't know anything about painting and all."

"He thinks he should be the one telling Hailey what to do and how to do it with the paintings, poking his nose in."

Could that be a far more innocent explanation for why Hailey didn't follow O.D.'s advice on the inventory? Not selling paintings herself or worrying her nearest and dearest had, but declaring her independence from her grandfather?

The same could apply to her withdrawing her Carey Maight paintings from the exhibit.

"They're hers," Clayton continued, "Just like they were Isaiah's. Old man Everett has no say in them."

Satisfaction and something else came through in that.

"Did you discourage Hailey from having her paintings in the upcoming exhibit at the museum?"

His eyebrows slanted up. "Me? Why would I do that?"

"That would be my next question."

"No need to ask it, then, because, like I said, those are Hailey's paintings."

Direct wasn't getting me far with him. I softened my angle. "She said you make sure people don't take advantage of her, which she really appreciates."

"Yeah, well, she needed somebody looking for her after Lewis and Kim were shot. Lots of people telling her all sorts of things about what she should do and shouldn't do."

"Including O.D. about inventorying the paintings? Maybe you felt he pushed her too much?"

"He's always pushing her. Pretends he's not, but it's always there. What he thinks, what he wants. Same way with Kim and Lewis. Hailey gives in sometimes because it's easier. But after she thinks it through, she stands up for herself."

"Is that what happened with lending the paintings to the museum for the exhibit?"

"Guess so. Like I said, ask her. She knows her own mind."

He'd polished off the sandwich and salad. He and Wylie Easley certainly had appetite in common ... along with their connections to Kim and Isaiah.

"Did a woman named Bernarda Garmin approach you or Hailey about the Carey Maight paintings? It would have been the month before the Newhalls died."

He shook his head. "Never heard of her."

"She asked other people in town about them." She asked Penny, anyway. And based on that, she was a good guess for the woman who called the Newhalls. "Did Hailey mention her or—"

"Nope. Never did. Miss?" he called to the server. "Can I see the dessert menu?"

✧   ✧   ✧   ✧

WE LEFT CLAYTON still eating, having added a slice of cherry pie to my tab.

"That didn't help much," Jennifer said, once we cleared the door. "Did it?"

"Not much," I agreed.

Jennifer snorted softly. "Was she standing on her own two feet, knowing her own mind or was he protecting her from the world trying to take advantage of her?"

"Very well put."

"He's not bad looking for a guy his age." Her next words came faster. "But why would someone like Hailey want someone like him?"

"Like him in what way?"

"No ambition. He's been working at Pen and Ink forever. I re-member him from when Dad brought me there to frame a drawing I'd done for Mother's Day. He got all into the *composition* and *technique* and stuff—like I couldn't tell he was fake and I was in third grade. And he's still doing the same thing—"

I placed a hand on her arm.

Because coming toward us on the sidewalk was Wylie Easley.

He might have considered cutting across the street, but he was way too slow. I greeted him with a warm smile, pretending he hadn't practically banished me from his truck a day ago.

"Really glad to run into you this way, Wylie. I have friends who are looking for a vacation home in Wyoming. I can tell them about around here, but Jackson's the area they're most interested in. I know you have a place there."

"Just outside Jackson."

"I'm trying to get them to come here, but ... What made you decide to buy there instead of here?"

"Had a place I was interested in there, but thought I'd check here before a final decision. After Kim died, I bought the place there."

"You like it?"

"Yeah. Enjoy the social life, the galleries, winter sports, hiking, music. If your friends like any of that, they'll love it."

"How long were you looking before you found your place."

"Took a while. Must've been almost a month before I came here."

"Thanks. That's really helpful."

Not only had I softened him up, but he'd given us a bonus. One I knew Jennifer had spotted from the way she stiffened beside me.

As if continuing our conversation about Jackson, I asked, "Have you met a woman named Bernarda Garmin?"

"Not that I recall."

"With a place in Jackson to stay, what are you doing here now?"

"I told you—"

I cut off the impatient response. "Sherman's your hometown all the time. Why come now?"

He huffed out a breath through his nose. "My fool brother is why, all right? He can't run a business to save his soul and I'm trying to straighten it out without costing me an arm and a leg. Satisfied?"

"Yes." Or I might be if that was confirmed. Even if it was, he'd taken time out of his business-saving duties to sit in his truck and stare at the Newhalls' old house.

I downshifted abruptly. "As you know, we're looking into the deaths of Kim and Lewis Newhall at the request of their daughter, Hailey. Do you think it was murder-suicide?"

"No reason not to. It's what law enforcement said."

"Would you be surprised to know it was double murder?"

A vein at the side of his forehead jumped.

"I told you before, it doesn't make much difference to me. Wouldn't bring Kim back."

"You feel that way because you loved her?"

"Yeah, I loved her, but if you're trying to—"

"Were you having an affair with her?"

One of the benefits of Sherman's wide sidewalks was Wylie Easley's shoulder didn't even brush against me as he walked past without a word ... but with a look. Not friendly.

"Was that a yes or a no?" Jennifer asked dryly.

Chapter Forty

WITH AUDREY BACK to one-hundred percent, tonight's newscasts were rolling along. That left me time to pursue the Newhalls' deaths and Fred White's stolen tail hair.

Too bad I had no idea what to do next.

Could I have gotten more out of Wylie if I'd approached him differently? Or out of Clayton?

I sure hadn't gotten enough out of them combined to push us forward.

If in doubt, review.

For more than two hours, I wrote up notes of conversations, with follow-up questions boldfaced after each.

There wasn't much boldface.

The evidence of how stymied I was came when I reread the *Independence*'s coverage of the remains found the month before the Newhalls died.

Nothing new. Except this time I noted the name of the Montana sheriff who'd held the news conference revealing the name Bernarda Garmin. Since Jennifer had told us that up front, nothing new there, either.

Then I sat up straighter.

Not at what was in the articles, but what wasn't there.

A cause of death.

If it was an accident, why not say so? If it wasn't an accident...

I called that department.

I identified myself, and said I was calling about Bernarda Garmin's remains being found on the border about two and a half years ago.

I was transferred to someone who answered, "Sheriff Sauder here. What? Now that it's solved, you want the case back? I know that deputy who foisted it off on us is even less interested than he was at the time, because he turned up dead himself and—Wait a minute. I know that name. Danniher. You're the one who figured out who killed that deputy. Redford? Something like that."

"Redus." I'd given the station ID to the phone answerer, but with this decisive voice I wanted no confusion. "I'm not with the sheriff's department. I'm with KWMT in Sherman. Sounds like you all did some very neat investigating."

"Wasn't me. Young deputy got interested looking at the clothes. Said they weren't from around here. Started researching on the Internet, tracking them down. Too many places selling them for a little department like ours to sort through, even with her working mostly on her own time. But then she cross-referenced with the shoes and that came up with a manageable list of places with missing persons who fit the remains we had."

"That is impressive. We might want to follow up on that for a story."

"If you do, it'll be the first you folks have done on us."

I made a mental note to check that. It could be an interesting story even if they weren't in our viewer area, but I thought they were.

"Of course, you were fortunate—" I exaggerated it to let him know I was pulling his leg. "—that the lost guy's dog had a small bladder, and found the body. And then you came across her car."

There was a pause. An unexpectedly long pause.

"Why are you calling, Elizabeth Margaret Danniher of KWMT-TV?"

I opened my mouth, then closed it. When I opened it a second time, I said, "Something tickled the back of my neck about this. I'm fully aware that Redus' involvement in both isn't much of a thread to cause a tickle."

As for Penny saying Bernarda Garmin asked about Carey Maight's paintings, I doubted I could explain that contribution to the tickle unless he shopped at the Sherman Supermarket.

"Both?"

I explained Redus' role in investigating—or not investigating—two deaths the month after Bernarda Garmin's remains were found.

"Huh. I called Redus when we found out who she was."

"Let me guess. He blew you off."

"He expressed a complete lack of interest. Including that she was shot in the head."

"Caliber?" I asked automatically over the ka-thumping of my heart.

"Not sharing that. Will say, it was a handgun. Telling you that because something tickled at the back of my neck about it, too."

"The identification—?"

"No. That's solid. But ... You have no reason to know that area. Take my word for it, she could have been there months, years, decades without being found. Fact she was, well, that's one of those flukes. The lost guy whose dog found the body checked out six ways from Sunday. As for her vehicle, we didn't *come across it.* We went searching like for lost treasure. And it was hidden nearly as well as treasure."

"Hidden?"

"Group of us went by it twice until somebody caught something shiny from the corner of his eye. There'd been brush laid up against it, all over it. So, yeah, hidden. Though why I'm telling you this—"

"Tickles up the back of the neck. What was this woman doing here? Not Jackson. Not Yellowstone. Not Cody. Staying in a short-term rental, by herself, no family or friends in the area—"

"None," he confirmed.

"What brought her to that spot on the border?"

"And who?" he added.

WE DIDN'T HAVE answers for each other, or ourselves. What we did have was a meeting of the minds.

I asked if he had anything more than had been in the *Independence.*

"Can't say without looking at those articles again. Been two years and more. Besides—"

"I know, I know. You hold back details from the media. All in the interests of the investigation. Not to torment the media, not one little bit."

"Don't know about that. Sort of a two-birds-with-one-stone deal."

"An honest man."

We both chuckled, agreed to keep in touch, and ended the call cordially.

Impulsively, I called Shelton.

"I just got off the phone with a law enforcement professional who could teach you the benefits and methods of cooperating with the media," I told him.

His snort said the person must be a fool. When I told him the name, the tenor of his silence took it all back.

I briefly outlined what Sheriff Sauder said, ending with, "We're going to keep each other updated. He's smart, open-minded, and forward-thinking."

He got the implicit comparison. "He doesn't have to deal with you every day."

"Neither do you."

"Feels like it."

I detoured around that. "You could have saved time by telling me what he said. It must be in the case file."

He grunted. "I'll remember that, next time I want to save you time."

"In what way was the gunshot residue incomplete on Lewis Newhall? And how was the bullet trajectory that killed him off?"

"It often is in self-inflicted gunshots." So Alvaro had been quoting him.

"Yes, but specifically how? And was it really a contact wound?"

"Yeah, it was really a contact wound. Now, go away, Danniher. I've got work."

Chapter Forty-One

IF I GAVE my next contact the opportunity, she'd say the same thing—go away, I've got work.

I denied her that opportunity and drove to the Sherman Frontier Life Museum.

Then, with an airy wave to the volunteer at the front desk, I went directly to the back, like I had an appointment with curator Clara Atwood.

Wardell Yardley lolled in her office—as much as he could in that confined space. Clara allotted as little space as possible to non-display uses.

"Oh, no," Dell greeted me, while Clara remained intent on her computer screen. "Go away. We are leaving in minutes for a hideaway where I've been promised we will while away the weekend with hot toddies before a roaring fire. You shall not delay that pleasure an extra second, Elizabeth Margaret Danniher."

I ignored him.

"Clara, what can you tell me about Carey Maight?"

She looked up. "I'm with Dell on this. I can't possibly tell you about her in a few minutes."

"Okay, okay. I just..." Wished I knew what I needed to know. The woman kept showing up—heck, more like being crammed down my throat—but the mentions of her didn't go anywhere.

Grasping for something concrete, I asked, "Do you remember a woman coming to the museum, two years ago last June, interested in the works of Carey Maight?"

"C'mon, Danny, how's she going to remember—?"

Clara interrupted Dell. A notable occurrence because he had re-fined a trick of talking faster and with more authority if anyone tried to wrench the conversational reins from him to such a point that he was famed among the Washington media for being uninterruptable.

Also notable, because neither of them appeared to consider it anything out of the ordinary.

"Interested? She wasn't *interested*. She was salivating so hard over our Carey Maight painting, I worried about damage to it. Sandy at the front desk told her twice to back up from the exhibit, then called me. I was quite firm with her."

Dell grinned at her proudly. "Which would stop a rhinoceros in full charge."

"Barely caused a hitch in her step." Clara frowned. "Maybe that's why I remember her so clearly. She backed up from the painting, but only to pelt me with questions faster and hotter than you do, Eliza-beth."

I wasn't sure that was a compliment. When Dell chuckled, I knew it wasn't.

I ignored him. "Questions about what?"

"Provenance, mostly. She wanted to know all the ins and outs of the donation and the bona fides of the donor. I didn't tell her, of course. None of her business. Besides, who was she to question one of our donations?"

Provenance. Donors. "Was she with a museum? Interested in a show or—?"

"No museum curator would take that approach. Not to mention there are no museums with more than a single Carey Maight work. That's why this upcoming show is so important."

"Did you get her name or—"

"I didn't bother. She wasn't from around here. Maybe back East, although her accent wasn't right for that, either. Anyway, after she realized I wasn't going to tell her who donated and why and when and if they had more where that came from, she started down another line about sales of works by Carey Maight."

"Sales…" That sounded more like a collector.

"I told her not to hold her breath, that they were few and far between, and outlined the Friends and Family's agreement to discourage her further."

"Ever hear from her again?"

"No. I did see her the next day, in Renata Santo's office."

The real estate agent who'd died last winter. And whose house I now lived in.

Not only couldn't I ask Renata if she remembered the woman, but I also knew her former assistant, now an agent herself, was on vacation in Hawaii for two weeks.

I wondered if I could persuade the station's new owner that I needed to fly to Hawaii to interview her.

Have I mentioned it's November in Wyoming?

Unaware of my mental detour, Clara said, "But if that woman was looking to move here, she must have changed her mind, because I never saw her again."

Or the woman had her mind changed for her—permanently—by being killed.

I pulled out the printout. "Is this her?"

Dell got up and leaned over the desk, trying to get a look. "Is that from the local newspaper? Who is this woman? Does she connect to your fascination with Wylie Easley?"

She squinted at it, then pulled it close. "The resolution is terrible. It could be, but I can't be sure. She had huge sunglasses on and her hair was whipped around from the wind. Let's say eighty-percent."

"Where are you getting the Carey Maight paintings for the exhibit?"

Her brows jumped up. "It's not any secret. From the Friends and Family group, with the greatest number from O.D. Everett."

"Not from Hailey Newhall?"

"No."

"Doesn't she own the largest collection?"

"She might, but she declined to include any in the show after first saying she would."

"For what reason?"

"Said she'd decided it wasn't in the best interests of her collection and I couldn't get anything else out of her. Third time I asked, she hung up on me. O.D. doesn't seem to know, either. Made no sense."

"What is this about? What are you working on?" Dell demanded.

"Thanks, Clara." To him I said, "What does it matter to you? You're going to drink toddies with your feet up in front of a fire. Have a great time, you two."

At the door, I stopped. "What sort of work does Clayton Rayger do for the museum?"

"Framing. Him or someone from Pen and Ink."

Clara's final words followed me out. "I will say, that woman who came here knew quite a bit about Carey Maight."

✧　✧　✧　✧

RICHARD ALVARO LURKED by my SUV when I came out of the museum.

"Elizabeth," he half hissed, like an old spy movie. "Those things you asked the sergeant about earlier today? Gunshot residue results showed one big blotch, then smaller ones on Lewis' hand, where it wasn't the same dispersal pattern. It was a lot, lot lighter. Also, his wound angled down more than the medical people said they'd expect, but it was a contact wound."

Before I could thank him—which would have come after asking more questions—he was gone.

✧　✧　✧　✧

I RETURNED TO the station to discover Christmas had landed early, with Mike playing Santa.

Nobody needed help getting into the spirit.

Diana stroked a camera like a beloved pet. Jenks grinned so wide the Cheshire Cat looked like a grouch. Even Bruce, a Thurston holdout, pulled items out of boxes like a toddler, except he enjoyed what was inside more than playing with the box.

This must be what they'd been uncrating last night.

"They're not new, but I got a great deal and..."

Yes, Santa Mike's toy factory resembled TV news' version of Goodwill. Didn't matter. The used equipment was multiple generations newer than what we had.

Audrey breathed, "Porta-lights." She threw her arms around his neck and kissed him on the cheek.

"Better video and less weight to drag around. I could kiss you, too," Diana said.

"Please, don't. I want to stay on the sheriff's good side."

Audrey dug back into the packages. "And peanut mics."

"Couldn't round up many, but there are lavalier mics, too," Mike said. "Also, I have an idea so we're never caught unprepared."

Everyone stopped and looked at him.

"The station could spring for micro mics that go on phones, along with mini lights and tripods. I got a trial setup for Jennifer."

She held up her phone with a tiny mic protruding from it.

"I like that," Walt said simply.

As much as their delight delighted me, it also made me want to get the Heathertons back here to give them a piece of my mind for making their employees delighted to get second-hand equipment.

On second thought, no, I didn't want the Heathertons back, even for that.

Leona tugged Mike's sleeve. "You have to see this. The studio."

We followed her as she said, "I thought Jerry would take that studio equipment to his grave, like a pharaoh carrying his possessions to the next world. But he forgot it all the instant he saw this new camera."

We walked into the studio, but not far. Jerry sat on the floor, connecting cables to a big studio camera.

He had tears in his eyes and seemed to be talking to himself.

"I remember Dad talking about the TK-30 from the late Forties. Took two big trucks to transport two cameras and a microwave unit. Studio cameras he operated took three people to lift. He wouldn't have believed this. Not even a vacuum tube. And now light sensitive chips and..." He shook his head, unable to continue.

Choked up at the disappearance of the old or appreciation of the new? Maybe both.

Mike said, "I couldn't find a new pedestal, Jerry, but it's in the budget and I've got word out looking for one to complete the unit.

"This is ... A pedestal would be..." He waved toward boxes along the far wall. "And new lighting. I can do real four-point..."

Our weather guy, Warren Fisk, said, "I hoped for the software I told you about, Mike. I know it was only a couple days ago—"

"On the list for the next round, Warren."

He nodded in sad but gracious acceptance. "Does new lighting mean we won't have tearing on the blue screen?"

It's what we called it when the image of what was in front—usually Warren—seemed to spasm against the blue screen background.

"That's what it means," Jerry said with a beatific smile.

"It also means the camera will pick up every wrinkle," Leona said with satisfaction. She thunked Mike in the arm. "Once viewers get a good look at me, you'll *have* to replace me as anchor and *fast*."

✧   ✧   ✧   ✧

SHERIFF SAUDER FROM Montana sent a message I retrieved before leaving.

"Read over those articles again. There's one piece of information we got after that's not in the *Independence* and not something we're holding back. No sense in holding this back, because everybody in Palm Springs knows. Bernarda Garmin owned an art gallery."

Over Audrey's protests about needing her for tonight's newscasts, I grabbed Jennifer and directed her to start her guys right away on researching Bernarda Garmin, her art gallery, and any connection to Carey Maight paintings.

Then I went home to feed my dog and get to my Contributions and Inventions of Native Americans class.

✧   ✧   ✧   ✧

O.D. FINALLY SHARED information on Navajo code talkers in the

Pacific in World War II.

He went far beyond that, too.

The practice started with the Choctaw Telephone Squad in World War I. By the next world war, along with the Navajos, it included Cherokee and Comanche code talkers being used in Europe as well as the Pacific, by the Army, Navy, and Marines.

He also told us of Native American contributions to the space program, plus Navy ships named in their honor.

It was fascinating.

I could hardly wait for class to end.

When it did, students hung around. I waited them out, using the time to write messages to Jennifer, Mike, and Diana, suggesting we meet at my house the next day ... and asking Jennifer for more research.

When I finished, I saw everyone had left except O.D., Paytah, and me.

O.D. gave a slight jerk of his head to his grandson. The kid glowered, but left.

Chapter Forty-Two

WE WENT TO O.D.'s office.

He sat behind his desk and gestured for me to take the same chair I had before. First, I took another long look at the painting.

"The postcards the museum has to promote the exhibit, I understand those are from paintings Hailey owns? Ones she said could be in the exhibit, then withdrew?"

"Yes, the postcards are reproductions of postcards Carey Maight licensed a couple decades before she died. The quality does not do the originals justice. Have you had an opportunity to see more paintings by Carey Maight?"

"I have."

"Which do you care for the most?"

I snorted. "No art critic or scholar would approve of that question."

"That is why I ask it."

"A landscape that is in private hands," I said before I knew I meant to.

"Ah. It depicts a place that means a great deal to you."

I started to say the place meant a great deal to someone I knew and for that reason it meant a great deal to me. Instead, I said, "Yes."

He breathed out slowly. "That is her gift. To reach into a heart and stroke it with the tip of her brush. Each painting touches different people. Because different places touch different people."

"I was thinking about what you described as people shedding a skin," I said. "Perhaps she couldn't watch people going through that process because she saw beneath the skin already. To see one layer deep and to paint it must verge on the uncomfortable. To apply that ability to someone exposed as they shed one skin to grow into the next might be ... beyond uncomfortable."

"You are generous, Elizabeth. My mother said of her that she did not see the people in front of her, but only what was in her eyes to paint.

"I also have thought of our conversation. You said women can feel invisible inside their roles, feeling the core of the person is forgotten. Carey Maight, however, was all individual core. A core that left no surface to connect with those around her. Her family, her tribe. I asked elders about my grandmother when I was growing up. They told me of the white hunter who came in the old times."

His level gaze asked if I knew of that.

I nodded.

"They said my grandmother was no more of the white hunter's people than ours. She cared only for the painting.

"My grandmother's mother was known for her art in our people's traditions. Not the art of the white world. She never used what the white hunter sent." Amusement seeped in, though his voice and expression went more deadpan. "Except the horses."

"Would those horses have still been alive for Carey Maight to use hair from their tails for brushes?"

"Doubtful. Though it would be in keeping with her character. And the brushes were integral to her technique."

Ah, the source of Linda Caswell's quote.

"What about Paytah? Does he use horse-hair brushes?"

He didn't react to my introducing his grandson. "He has. Not always."

"He seems to admire his great-great-grandmother's landscapes over her portraits."

"He paints in his own style, not Carey Maight's." He'd answered a question I hadn't asked. That didn't make it the truth. "He does not steal horse's tails to make horse-hair brushes."

Sometimes the best you can do after you've ticked someone off is keep him talking.

He saved me the effort. "Did you know that after Kim and Lewis died, there was a key Hailey could not find? A key to where Kim stored the paintings by Carey Maight."

Did he not know about the gun safe key? Not care? Or not want to talk about that?

"Was something taken?" Why would the closet key be taken if not to steal paintings? "Are you certain no paintings are missing?"

"That does not come yet in this story," he admonished. I wasn't waiting weeks as we had for tales of the code talkers. "Kim told me a month before her death that a key to their gun safe was missing from where they kept keys by their back door. I asked if the key to the paintings was gone, too. She said it was not. She would not have lied."

"Did you tell the deputies that?"

"I did. Deputy Redus. I not only told him, but I asked him several times if he had pursued the matter. He became annoyed. And then, some months after, when they were moving to where Hailey and Gavin live now—" Was that grandfather tact or grandfather disapproval not to include Clayton? "—the key was found. Hailey said that meant it had been mislaid and never taken."

"I am certain the number of paintings is correct. I checked them against a list of the titles and sizes in the Friends and Family records. But Deputy Redus would not let me see the paintings. When they were moved, they were already wrapped."

Comparing lists? That sounded quite different from what Hailey described.

"Each of us in Friends and Family created a visual inventory when we established the group," O.D. said. "It is outmoded now. I have encouraged Hailey to create a new visual inventory with updated photography across multiple storage methods. She said she would. To my knowledge, she has not."

An inventory of wrapped up paintings, a resistance to updating? What did Hailey have against inventories?

Answer one, they would reveal she took a painting or paintings. But why hide that, when the paintings were hers? According to the agreement, she should offer them to the Friends and Family group first, but there was no legal penalty if she didn't.

If she *had* sold any, could she have fudged about the inventory to avoid O.D. chastising her?

Possible.

But, if she'd sold paintings, why was money tight? And why wasn't it in Redus' report? Unless she didn't tell him. Or he left it out.

Answer two of why Hailey might resist inventories—to protect Gavin or Clayton if they had taken paintings. Or she feared they had.

But why would she think that?

Besides, there were other possibilities.

Easley had access to the key in the time he was alone in the house. He said he didn't go much past the back door, but with the keys kept there, he didn't have to.

If he killed Kim and Lewis, he could have had lots of time to find the key, leaving behind the blood smear on the doorframe.

His access to the key to Lewis' gun safe—and gun—became more feasible now that we knew he'd been in Jackson, instead of Arizona, around the time Kim said it was missing.

And then there was Redus...

He certainly would have had access and time to snag a key from the peg by the back door during his so-called investigation.

But how would he have gotten Lewis' gun? And why no money trail?

I was aware of O.D. watching me.

"Hailey said the inventory showed nothing was taken," I said.

"I was not satisfied the inventory was sufficiently detailed to be certain either way." He shifted in his chair. "It is late, Elizabeth, and—"

"A few more questions. Did you tell Hailey to withdraw her paintings from the museum's exhibit?"

"No."

"Why did she?"

"I do not know."

"Did a woman named Bernarda Garmin contact you around the time of Kim's and Lewis' deaths?"

I'd succeeded in surprising him, though he quickly masked it.

"I do not know this woman. Now, we must end."

Chapter Forty-Three

ON THE DRIVE home, I left a voice message for Hailey, asking her to send me a copy of the visual inventory of Carey Maight paintings she owned. I also said we should talk.

I arrived home to find Thomas David Burrell sitting on my front porch. Not for the first time.

Though I think it was the first time with flurries falling. Also the first time he had my dog with him.

"Tamantha—?"

"Is fine. She's at my sister's. More than tired of my company." His mouth went crooked. "I'm told it's part of the growing independent process. After letting me baby her because she was sick, she needs to show she doesn't need me."

With his first words of reassurance, I'd unlocked the door and led them in.

"Have you been reading self-help books on parenting, Burrell?"

"Not lately."

I tipped my head, considering him. "Mrs. P," I concluded.

"Yep." He put his jacket on the back of a stool, with his hat atop it, hooked over the corner.

"Don't understand why you stayed out in the cold." Even to my ears, I sounded peevish.

"Not that cold." Which was Wyoming for *I hadn't frozen to death yet.*

"I feel like we've had this conversation before. You have a key, Tom. You could have come in, if not for yourself, for Shadow."

He lifted one shoulder. Our gazes met.

"You could have come in," I repeated. An entirely different tone. "I think ... I guess I feel more ... settled," I said as I fiddled with my keys before placing them on the small table by the entry to the bedroom hallway.

He cut me a look. Then he turned fully toward me, took a step. Stopped.

"What?" came out, when I wanted to ask, *Why didn't you keep coming?*

"You had to be sure Mike is okay. Had to see it for yourself."

"That's nuts. He's a big boy. He can—he *does*—take care of himself."

"Yep. But you didn't really believe it until now."

"That's—"

"The truth."

Diana said to me not long ago that I did know how I felt and if I'd get out of my way, the answer would be there.

As much as it galls me, she was right.

"Maybe a little true."

We kissed. Long and involved. But lazy in a way, too. Time all ahead of us.

With enough breath to speak again, Tom said, "I have proof you're sure and I know how much you like proof."

"What proof?" I tried to scoff, but he'd leaned in close, greatly impeding my scoffing technique.

He slid his right hand under my hair and around to the back of my neck, his thumb brushing lightly at my lips, until it was replaced by his lips.

He eased back for a breath and said, "Because now you'll make love with me."

And then he proved it.

DAY NINE

SATURDAY

Chapter Forty-Four

I EXPECTED IT to be awkward, tentative with Tom.

It wasn't.

Possibly it wasn't awkward because there wasn't time and there wasn't time because it was not tentative. At. All.

For once, I didn't even mind morning that much.

Lying beside him provided a very different perspective on his face. Not softer—the lines were too sharp for that. Perhaps less guarded.

"I need to tell Tamantha. If not now, soon." He left the choice to me.

"Now." I swallowed. "That means we're going to give this a try?"

"No." Several anatomically impossible things happened to me at his single word. Stomach dropped. Lungs dried up. Heart turned over.

Then he said. "We're going to love each other and make a family."

With tears in my eyes—from all the anatomical gymnastics, of course—I said, "I get it. You're the Yoda of Wyoming. There is no try."

"That's right."

He kissed me—we kissed each other.

"Do or not do. There is no try," he said against my lips while we replenished oxygen. "Because imagine what Tamantha would do to us if we failed."

Laughing—terrified, but laughing—our mouths came together again.

❖ ❖ ❖ ❖

WHILE TOM WAS on his phone with Tamantha and his sister, I checked mine.

No copy of the inventory from Hailey. No reply at all.

I called.

When she answered, I repeated my request.

"I … I'll have to think about that."

"You said you'd give us the material we needed—"

"But why would you need it?"

"It's too early to explain. Are you going to send it?"

She paused. "I'll have to think about it."

"Why didn't you allow any of the Carey Maight paintings you own to be included in the exhibit?"

"That has nothing to do with … anything."

"We need to talk."

"I have too much to do around here to come into town. Maybe next week."

"If you're serious about this, Hailey, you need to cooperate. You're hiding things—"

"I'm busy. I have to go."

We ended the call with, I suspect, neither of us thinking the best of the other.

❖ ❖ ❖ ❖

"TOM, I HAVE to run to the store for a few things—"

"You're going to have one of your murder gatherings." Perfectly flat. No disapproval.

"Yeah. And cheese curls are the latest brain food."

"Mind if I take a shower before I leave?"

"Of course not. I hope … If you can stay until I get back, we can have lunch. In fact, if you want to join us, I'm sure everybody would be fine with that."

He gave me a steady look. "Not yet."

In those two words, I heard thoughtfulness for Mike's feelings.

"Okay. I'll be back soon. This shouldn't take long."

"You haven't shopped on Saturday morning, have you?"

HE WAS RIGHT, I hadn't shopped on Saturday morning—or any morning—but it was nearing noon, so how bad could it be?

Bad.

Those of us who lived in town might stop at the Sherman Supermarket frequently, but for those out on ranches reached by the offspring of back roads and antelope trails, shopping was an event and a trek.

After steering my way around heaped shopping carts to the snack aisle, it dawned on me that this also was the Saturday before Thanksgiving.

Very bad.

"Elizabeth." I turned with a smile at Gisella Decker's voice.

"Hi. And Mrs. Parens. How are you both?"

Gee drove her neighbor here regularly for items their small store in O'Hara Hill didn't stock.

"Overrun by crowds. We told Diana—" Who cleared a clot of carts and joined us. "—we were debating going to lunch now and shopping later when we saw you. Problem is, there might be nothing left by then."

"Let's get out of this aisle to somewhere we can talk," Diana said.

We found refuge by the light bulbs. Not a big-selling item at the moment.

"Before we saw you, I was telling Gee and Mrs. Parens about our inquiry," Diana said. "Mrs. Parens, I was about to ask if Wylie Easley or Clayton Rayger were students of yours."

"They were not, nor were Kim or Isaiah or Lewis. I had taught older students when they began their academic career, then switched to younger students for a time, which coincided with their being in high school."

"What about Hailey?" I asked.

"She was a student of mine." She didn't even make me pull it out of her, but said, "A reliable student, though her passion was horses."

"Reliable's a good word," Gee agreed. "Never in any trouble. By the way, O.D. Everett was one of Emmaline's earliest students."

Diana and I responded with *Was he?* and *Really?*

Mrs. P said serenely, "I have great respect for O.D. Everett's mind and his accomplishments. He also has great passion for the heritage and future of his tribe."

Passion was not a word I'd jump to in connection to O.D., although deadpan did not equate passionless. If I needed another example, I could always look at Thomas David Burrell.

"He carries a great deal of his grandmother in him," Mrs. Parens continued. "If he did not, he would not have gone away to college or lived elsewhere before returning here. Yet he is connected to the tribe and its people as his grandmother never was. That produces blind spots in his view of her. Perhaps not in the matter of Carey Maight, yet certainly in his view of his grandmother.

"His grandmother's obsession molded her daughter, which in turn molded him. His mother was determined not to ignore him, as she felt her mother had done to her. While he might well have excelled regardless, one might attribute some measure to his mother's attention and expectations."

In other words, she pushed him.

"He also has you to thank," Gee said to Mrs. P, then turned to Diana and me. "O.D. wouldn't have gotten all those scholarships and opportunities if she hadn't gone to bat for him. Barely out of school herself, but she launched him."

This was among the fascinating aspects of their relationship—rivals, yes, but determined that the other got her due.

"Was he always interested in Carey Maight's art?"

"He did not include art among his academic pursuits," Mrs. P said.

I looked at Gee. She immediately said, "Not until after Carey Maight left the bulk of her paintings to Isaiah. Not long before Isaiah died, O.D. started the Friends and Family group. They give each other first crack if anyone wants to sell, so her works stay concentrated around here.

"Some worried it might depress the paintings' value. O.D. said it would do the opposite and he was right. He's bought what owners wanted to sell, giving them the going price, even as it's gone up and up. He has a good collection now."

"More than Hailey?" Diana asked.

We looked to Mrs. Parens for the answer. "The largest collection of Carey Maight works remains that belonging to Hailey. however it is stagnant, while O.D.'s collection continues to grow."

"Do you think he resents the paintings going to his son, then his granddaughter?"

She frowned. I'd treaded too close to asking her to gossip.

To cover, I mused, "As Gee said, he created the cooperative agreement, which brought together—loosely, but still together—a collection rivalling that held by his oldest son."

"He did. He was quite passionate—" That word again. "—that Carey Maight's legacy not be dispersed."

Was it significant she didn't dispute—by word or look—the characterization of O.D.'s efforts as a way to rival, even eclipse the paintings now held by Hailey?

Oh, yeah.

❖   ❖   ❖   ❖

WHEN GEE AND Mrs. P ventured back into the maelstrom, Diana held me back a moment, studying me. Then she said, "Tom."

"Tom? Tom Burrell? What about him?" My voice was good.

"What happened?"

"Nothing."

"Then why do you look like that?"

"I don't look like anything."

"Exactly. You're so blank it's unbelievable."

"That makes no sense."

Instead of chastised, she crossed her arms over her chest and grinned. "You and Tom did it."

I stuttered something. Then blurted out, "I just don't know if we're truly air ready. You know?"

"I do know. I also know sex isn't the solution—though it sure can be satisfying. And it's one big hurdle on the way to the solution. It means you're going to have to deal with your feelings for each other. And find out if you're air ready or not."

✧ ✧ ✧ ✧

TOM HELPED ME unpack my purchases as I told him about the craziness at the store and running into Diana, Mrs. P, and Gee.

As we sat down to sandwiches, I blurted, "Diana said our ... making love means we have to deal with our feelings. I didn't tell—"

"Diana being first makes sense."

"First." I groaned. "You think there's more commentary to come?"

"Think? No. Sure? Yeah."

I groaned again. "How can we stop—?"

"Can't." He took my hand. "Only way around it is to do what Diana said. Figure out our feelings. I know what I want, Elizabeth." My heart *ka-thudded* so hard it felt like the earth shook. "I want to be married to you for the rest of my life."

"What if I die first and you're a widower and—"

"Dog training videos."

"What?"

"You're trying to fix things that don't need fixing. The rest of my life, that's the most I've got to pledge. That's the least I'll pledge."

He wanted the same from me.

"The past—Aren't you a little afraid I'll turn into your ex?"

One side of his mouth lifted. "Nope. Not afraid of you turning into my ex, not afraid of me turning into your ex. You aren't either."

"Maybe not. But you once said to me it was more about questioning our judgment after the choices we made in exes."

"There's truth in that. But it's like points on your driver's license. You go long enough without making another boneheaded move, and you're back to zero."

"You silver-tongued devil, you."

He chuckled. Once. "What it comes down to is what we're afraid of more—making a mistake? Or missing out on the chance that it's *not* a mistake? While you work that out," he said, as if it were a foregone conclusion I'd arrive at the same point he was at, "your murder-tracking crew should be here soon. Not this time, but if there's another of these, mind if I join?"

"You want to?" That rocked me almost as much as my uncertainty.

"Uh-huh." Without looking away from me, he kissed me.

Chapter Forty-Five

"**Not a whisper** of a rumor about Kim meeting Wylie or anybody outside of town," Diana reported as soon as we settled around the snack-laden coffee table.

Jenifer practically bounced in her seat. "That's okay, because I found something in the phone records."

"On Kim being out of town?" Diana asked. "Meeting with Wylie? Was she in Jackson?"

"No, no, and no. But—"

"Hold up, Jennifer," Mike said. "Why did you ask about Jackson, Elizabeth?"

Together, Jennifer and I recounted yesterday's conversation with Wylie.

"...so, if Kim was making phone calls from Jackson at the same time—"

Jennifer cut me off. "She wasn't. That's what I said. No out-of-town calls by Kim at all the month before she died. But there was one call ... Bernarda Garmin called the Newhalls on June 21."

"So Bernarda Garmin is likely the person Gavin heard his parents talking about having called and asked about the paintings. She's tied in with Carey Maight's paintings and that's the pool we're swimming in." Sometimes I felt like that was the pool I was pushed into. By Mrs. P for starters and O.D. consistently.

"It's even better than that. Because the other thing I found out is the art gallery Bernarda Garmin owned in Palm Springs specialized in western women artists. Plus, the guys found a couple references to the gallery having sold paintings by Carey Maight. One from way back, about twenty-five years ago, and one a few months before she died."

"That's fantastic, Jennifer. Any photos or—"

"Not yet. I have the guys digging deeper."

"Great job," Mike added. "But where'd she get paintings to sell? You think somebody cheated on Friends and Family?"

"We'll know more if Jennifer's guys can get data on what sold," Diana said. "But I hate to be a downer, but may I point out that we have another victim and still no answers? I know we say it gets messier before it gets clear, but we still seem to be accumulating mess."

I grimaced at the accuracy of that.

Jennifer was unbowed. "One other thing Wylie said yesterday was he was in Jackson when Bernarda Garmin was killed. Well, he didn't say it that way, but that's what it amounts to. Easy enough for him to drive here to meet her. And did you notice he mentioned galleries in Jackson?"

I nodded.

We had to fill in that bit, too.

At the end, Mike said, "Okay, as Diana pointed out, we've got another victim, who do we have as suspects?"

"Start with the most obvious," I said. "Lewis Newhall."

✧　✧　✧　✧

"WHAT?" JENNIFER'S WORD was an objection, not a question. "That's what this whole thing's been about—proving he didn't kill Hailey's mother, then himself."

"That's not what it's about. It's about—"

"Okay, okay. It's about finding the truth. I know. But—"

"The truth could include that it was Lewis."

"What about the gunshot residue?" Diana said.

Jennifer turned that point into a bandwagon. "Yeah. What about that?"

"That's a question we haven't answered yet and need to keep working on."

"Redus could have screwed up the collection of evidence somehow, Mike suggested.

I turned toward him. "That's an interesting point."

He half grinned. "Of course it is. Knew it all along. Just waiting for the rest of you to catch up with me."

Jennifer threw a cookie at him. He caught it left-handed and continued the motion to his mouth, tossing it in.

"You're seriously thinking Redus?" Diana didn't need an answer before continuing, "It would be tidy. No need for an arrest or trial. No need for the legal system at all."

Mike whistled. "Redus didn't just screw up the investigation and evidence from laziness or arrogance? He did it to cover his tracks?"

"That would be incredibly sneaky," Jennifer said with something like awe.

"He sure proved he was willing to make money illegally," I pointed out.

"Could be really hard to prove he did it," Diana said. "And without public acknowledgement..."

We all knew it wouldn't satisfy Hailey. She wanted the world—particularly her brother—to know absolutely that his dad didn't kill their mother then himself.

"The forensics—" Jennifer started.

"Wait," I interrupted. Splinters of thoughts went from spinning to starting to congeal in clumps. "Forensics ... Wait a minute..."

One clump in particular.

Not right away. It took ... well, I don't know how long it took.

I became aware of the silence around me.

That one clump held its shape. Another almost ... No. It wobbled away.

I looked at my friends, all looking at me.

"Tell us, Elizabeth," Diana said.

"How do you know—?"

Mike interrupted with a grin. "Because of my favorite phrase, at least when you say it. *Wait a minute.* We did. We waited a minute and now we want to hear."

"Turn it around," I said.

No one responded, so I added a finger drawing of a semicircle in the air, to indicate going from the beginning to the end, then back.

"Turn what around?" Jennifer asked.

"The sequence of what happened. What Redus and the others *said* happened. *And* it explains the forensics."

"That's good to hear, but you need to give a few more hints, Elizabeth," Diana said.

"We always say—everyone always says—the killings of Kim and Lewis. What if it was the killings of Lewis and Kim?"

After a pause, Diana said, "The order of who was killed?"

I sat forward. "Exactly. What if Kim wasn't shot first?"

"You mean *she* murdered *him*? But the physical evidence—Kim was shot from a distance, Lewis had a contact wound. And gun powder residue on his hand—" Jennifer cut off her own objection. "Incomplete."

"Not that Kim killed him, either. Not murder-suicide at all. Double murder, as Hailey said all along. The killer shoots Lewis first—catches him by surprise, puts the gun against his head and pulls the trigger."

"Contact wound," Mike said.

"Instinctively, Kim tries to get to Lewis. The killer puts the gun in Lewis' hand, with his own still on top and shoots her, while partially holding up his sagging body."

"So the trajectory is up into Kim," Diana said.

"The gunshot residue?" Jennifer said.

"The killer having a hold on the gun explains incomplete gunshot residue on Lewis, while leaving enough to satisfy Foster Redus—blast his lazy hide. Maybe Lewis reached up when he first felt the gun. It would be a totally normal reaction. That would have made it easier."

"So Lewis didn't do it," Jennifer said with satisfaction.

"That scenario would take awfully damned fast thinking and reactions," Mike said.

"If it were spur of the moment, yeah. That *would* take incredibly fast thinking and reacting."

"You think it was planned," Diana said.

"Seems likely."

"But the gun?" Jennifer objected. "Kim and Lewis were shot with his gun."

"Which was kept in a gun safe that many people knew about, with a key kept on a peg by their back door, so anybody who'd been to the house would know where it was. And that key was missing."

"Just one question," Mike said. "Who?"

Chapter Forty-Six

"OKAY, LET'S GO back to what was happening that day," I said. "What things changed that might have sparked the killer to act then."

"They decided to give Hailey and Clayton their blessing—quasi-blessing according to Gavin," Jennifer said. "To withdraw their objections, anyway. Gavin hears them discussing it the night before, then confirming it in the morning."

"Could that have triggered the kid somehow?" Mike asked. "Jealous of his older sister? Angry she got the attention, the paintings, everything."

"We have to be open to all possibilities. We know from when he was on the bus that killing them before Wylie got there, then circling around would have been tight, but possible. Before school is more open, especially with the loose time of death."

"But for a kid to kill his parents, then go to school like nothing happened? Unless…?" With the single word, Mike asked if Gavin's behavior at school that day fit with *nothing happened*.

Diana shook her head. "Nothing from the school, friends, coaches, teammates that had him acting different in any way. Not until he got home."

Shaking us all out of that visual, I said, "Let's keep going with suspects. Someone who murdered both of them, setting it up so Lewis looked like the killer."

"Wylie Easley," Jennifer said. "He'd want to make Lewis look bad. And what you were talking about with a trigger, well, the trigger could have been Kim rejecting him, making it clear he didn't have a chance with her because of Lewis. He acted out on that."

"That is really good, Jennifer."

"There's a possible scenario," Diana said. "He goes there, tries to win her over one last time. She says no or her husband tries to throw him out—or both. He shoots Lewis, then her."

"Why shoot her when he wanted her to run away with him?" Mike asked.

"Some men do kill the women they supposedly love," Diana said.

"And if he shot her husband in front of her and she was a witness, he kind of had to," Jennifer said.

"But the way Elizabeth described things happening fast to account for the evidence, he shot her right away, immediately after shooting Lewis. No time to try to get her to run away with him. More like he'd gone there with that plan," Mike said.

"Maybe he'd already asked and been rejected. He went there that day thinking if he wasn't going to have her, nobody would," Diana said.

I nodded slowly. "And then he conveniently found their bodies, explaining away trace evidence, blood, fingerprints. Though it might not have been as convenient if Redus had tested him for GSR."

"Or done a halfway decent investigation," Jennifer said.

"**WHAT ABOUT O.D.** Everett?" Mike said.

I thought of Tom saying the rest of us could suspect people he wouldn't. He was right. "O.D. is not in the clear."

"Why?" Diana asked.

"Because he parsed his words right into being suspected. When I asked if Bernarda Garmin contacted him he said, *I do not know this woman.* Not what I'd asked. He could maintain he *didn't know* her—not the way you really know someone—yet she could have contacted him. No reason for him to do linguistic gymnastics unless he's hiding something."

"You think O.D.—?"

"Or he's protecting someone. Most likely Hailey or Paytah, but protecting from what is another question. I'd say O.D. doesn't think Paytah had anything to do with the deaths of Kim and Lewis."

"How can you know that?"

"Because when I asked about Paytah, O.D. defended him strongly against any implication he might have stolen horse tails to make brushes. If O.D. feared accusations of murder against his grandson, he wouldn't have worried about horse-tail thefts."

"What about his granddaughter?" Mike said.

"I admit, it's a stretch to suspect Hailey. Seems self-destructive to get us involved if she killed them."

"But?"

"But I keep remembering the shift in her when I said that she had loved Lewis very much and she'd replied that he'd loved her very much. Could it have been an unconscious admission of guilt. A kind of double guilt. Not just that she'd been involved, but that she felt guilty, because the man *had* loved her."

"Maybe it's not protective," Mike said. "O.D.'s not exactly neutral about those paintings. Could have thought Kim wasn't taking care of them the way she should. Or didn't trust Hailey would handle them the way he wanted. The agreement's voluntary. Nobody could force her— or her mom—to stick with it. Plus, he didn't approve of Kim."

"He changed his mind. He appreciates Kim let him build a rela- tionship with Hailey."

"On Kim's terms," Diana said.

"And he's said what a good father Lewis was to Hailey Newhall, better than his son could have been."

"So he says. Now," Diana said.

"Okay, say O.D. was so protective of or obsessed by the Carey Maight collection owned by his granddaughter that he killed her parents so—what?—he had more influence over her? If so, why then? Wouldn't it have been a more effective tactic when she was younger and more swayable?"

"He just got the idea," Mike said. "Or his feelings built up until he couldn't take it anymore."

"Or he heard about a woman with an art gallery being in town.

And figured she was making a deal with Hailey or Kim and Lewis," Diana suggested.

"She was already dead when they were killed. If the purpose was to stop a deal, her death accomplished that." I said that fast enough that they all knew I'd thought about this.

"He wouldn't know that if someone else killed her," Jennifer said immediately.

Mike shook his head. "Two murderers, both apparently motivated by the collection of Carey Maight's works? That's a stretch."

"It's possible," Jennifer insisted. "He could have killed Bernarda Garmin, then figured that didn't really solve the problem, because if Kim and Lewis were open to selling, it would have been hard to keep killing gallery owners and get away with it. Better to go to the source."

"That's a fair point," Diana said. "And there was O.D.'s meeting with Foster Redus. What was that about?"

Jennifer jumped on it. "Maybe he hired Redus to scare the woman off. Redus got carried away and killed her. O.D. knew she was gone, but not that Redus killed her. So he's thinking she could come back. Along with the possibility of other people trying to buy paintings. And then he thinks the way to handle it is to kill the Newhalls. But by now he doesn't trust Redus, so he does it himself."

Mike started to say something. She waved her hand, stopping him.

"Or he hires Redus to scare them, but Redus goes too far."

"As much as I'd like it to be Redus, who else?" Mike asked.

"Clara Atwood," Jennifer said of the museum curator. "Bernarda wasn't the only one super interested in Carey Maight's paintings."

"What argues against her is she wants to display them publicly. Killing the Newhalls wouldn't advance that," I said.

Jennifer accepted the logic. "True."

"But talking about Redus made me think … Let me check…" I let it hang while I scrambled to pull up one of the files Jennifer had sent me. "Got it. Sheriff Sauder in Montana announced the identity of the remains found as Bernarda Garmin the day after Kim and Lewis were shot."

"Why is that important?" Diana asked.

Mike held up a finger. "Maybe whoever killed Bernarda knew Kim and Lewis could connect him or her to that first murder."

"Lewis and Kim..." I muttered.

"Yeah, you talked about that already. How everybody says Kim and Lewis."

I heard Jennifer's words without really listening to them. I was too busy hearing and seeing things fall into place.

Mrs. P talking about the archives of three women...

That's why...

Turning around the scene ... parsing words ... talent ... it's complicated ... decisions changed ... the woman from California ... old friends...

And that's how...

I blinked. Saw the coffee table partially cleared.

How long had I been out?

I looked around. They were all looking at me.

"Welcome back, again," Diana murmured. "Bring us anything?"

"Yes. Not everybody says Kim and Lewis. Not every time."

Chapter Forty-Seven

"WHAT DOES THAT mean?" Jennifer asked.

"It means it makes a difference if you say Kim and Lewis or Lewis and Kim. And that means we've got a lot to do. A lot. Phone calls to make—" Including one to Dex. But not on my phone this time. "—a visit to the neighbor. That's you, Diana. Mike, you need to go to the Easley Garage to use your pull as hometown sports hero. And I need to get Hailey and Gavin to Fred White's corral. Before the sun sets."

"Wait. Explain first," Mike demanded.

Before I did that—briefly—I called Hailey.

"I've decided against sending you the inventory," she said as soon as she heard my voice. "There's no connection to my parents' deaths."

"Fine." For now. "Are you at your place?"

"Yes."

"Alone?"

"No, Gavin's around somewhere."

"I'll be there shortly. Don't go anywhere. We need to talk."

UNEXPECTEDLY, MY PHONE rang as I drove to Hailey's place.

Unexpected, because none of the phone calls the others were making should come back to my phone.

For example, a return call from Dex at the FBI lab at the wrong moment could really mess things up.

But this call was from the retired art teacher in New Mexico.

"I can't believe it myself, but I actually found that class roster. It was in a box with cards from my kids from—"

"That's great. And I'm sorry to cut you off. But I'm in a time crunch. Can I tell you who was in that class?"

And I did.

"Why, yes." She sounded miffed that I'd had her find the roster for seemingly nothing.

But it wasn't for nothing. I hadn't known at the time I'd asked her to look.

"Make a copy and hold onto it. That's important evidence."

I CAUGHT A break.

Hailey was standing alone in the corral, other than Fred White. She held long reins as the horse moved around her.

As she pivoted with him, she spotted me at the gate.

"You can come in," she said. "I'm nearly done walking him down."

"That's okay. I'll wait."

"Come in." This was an order worthy of Tamantha. "It's good for him to be exposed to people more and he's more open to it now that lunging him's worked out some jitters."

Great. I was a test case for a jittery horse.

On the flip side, if she moved to the far end of the corral, I did not want to have to shout what I needed to say.

Fred White whipped around at the gate screeching open.

With it closed behind me, I stood still, resisting the urge to slap my forehead. The gate rivaled the noise my desk chair made. If I'd heard this gate before...

"Okay, come ahead now." Hailey's attention stayed on the horse. She unhooked the long reins from the halter.

I moved slowly.

She came toward me. Fred White didn't.

"We have an answer for you, Hailey." I did not get into details, like whether we could prove it to the satisfaction of a court. That might— or might not—come later. "Your father—Lewis—did not kill your mother. Or himself."

Instead of celebrating that she'd been right, she stopped dead and asked, "How do you know?"

Fear? Was that what I heard?

Or was I mistaking that for determination to contain her emotions.

Either way, I pretended she'd asked what happened, and closed the gap between us.

"The killer took the key to Lewis' gun safe and his gun in June. He kept the gun—" After using it on Bernarda Garmin. But we'd get to that later. For this step, I gave Hailey the bare-bones *how* of her parents' deaths. "—until that day. Your parents let him in your house, they were walking toward the kitchen, relaxed, trusting, when he pulled the gun out, put it to Lewis' head and shot him. It was a contact wound."

She sucked in a breath.

Fred White turned his head, watching us.

"As he started to fall, the killer put the gun in Lewis' hand, his own around it, and shot your mother, who was trying to reach Lewis, after hearing the gunshot, turning, and seeing her husband slump toward the floor. That's why the trajectory was up—Lewis was on his way to the floor despite the killer trying to hold him up, while your mother was still standing. The killer covered Lewis' hand with his own and pulled the trigger the second time."

That explained the blotchy gunshot residue. The killer's hand partially covered Lewis'.

Hailey's first sob cut across the stillness.

Fred White stepped closer to her, then closer.

Hailey covered her face with her hands, her sobs audible.

The horse gently nudged her shoulder. Touched the top of her head, then nudged again at her arm.

Hailey dropped her hands and the horse pressed his face against her shoulder in a kind of hug. She returned it with one arm, but focused on me.

Broken by sobs, she said. "Who did this? My parents—"

A shout stopped her words. "Hey! What are you doing to her?"

My head jerked up. Gavin Newhall, coming from the shed. I really needed to pay closer attention as this unfolded.

"C'mon in here, Gavin." I called.

"No. Just leave her alone and get the hell out of here."

"Your sister needs you."

Hailey helped my cause in that instant with a shaky sob-call of "Gav..."

He swore under his breath.

Fred White alerted to the gate again. When Gavin entered and started toward us, Hailey reached up to hold onto the equine hug, but Fred White backed away. She grasped the halter, her focus on her brother.

"Gavin, she knows Dad didn't kill Mom. She knows it and she has proof. Tell him, Elizabeth."

I let the shock of her words hit him, then followed with, "Why'd you cut off and take Fred White's tail, Gavin?"

Hailey's head snapped toward her brother.

He didn't look at her or me. He did snarl, "You're crazy."

The jury was out on that, but I wasn't wrong.

"Why?" I repeated.

"I didn't steal any horse's tail."

"You did. Not the ones two and a half years ago. But Fred White's, you did. You came in here at night a little over a week ago and cut off his tail. You're one of the few people he wouldn't react to. One of the few people he trusted enough to let them cut his tail without kicking. *Used* to trust enough."

I saw something in Hailey's eyes.

She'd wondered if Gavin did it, somewhere below where she'd let herself recognize it.

"What did you do with the jeans you left a piece of on the fence? That must have been a shock when Hailey found the fabric the day you were putting up cameras. A random thief wouldn't have climbed the fence, because they wouldn't have known the gate creaked. But you knew, so you climbed the fence. Didn't want anyone at the house to hear it? Or to keep Fred White from spooking?"

"I didn't do it." But Gavin's head was down.

"Fred White says you did."

Hailey looked at her horse's face, the whites of his eyes showing as he huffed and tried to back away ... from Gavin.

She released the halter. Fred White jerked back, watching him.

Hailey spun on her brother. "Why? Why would you do that? For the money? If you need money—"

"Shut up. Just shut up about money."

"If it's not money, then ... To hurt Fred White? I can't believe that. You've known him almost all your life. You've loved him. To do that to him and leave him uncomfortable and—"

"Not him—*you.*"

She recoiled. "Me? Why?" It was an entirely different question. Small, hurt.

"So you'd shut up. So you'd damned well shut up. Stop talking. Stop pushing. Stop wondering. And just let it be in the past. Instead of going on and on and on about it. Hitting me in the face with it. Never letting me forget. Just *forget.*"

"We can't forget. We can't ever forget."

"You—*You* can't forget. And you won't let me forget. So I cut off your horse's tail. To shut you up about—About..."

He couldn't finish it.

"I never knew you were so angry," she said.

He'd been on the edge of breaking down, but she'd handed him the rope to back away from that edge—anger.

"Yeah, well, that just shows I'm my father's son and you better get the hell away from me because I could be capable of the exact same thing."

That lit her fuse.

"He did not. And you—You can't get rid of me. I'm not going anywhere, you ... you..." In rapid succession, his sister threw up her hands in recognition that words failed her, punched him in the shoulder, then grabbed him into an ungentle hug.

He remained stiff with heartbroken anger turning his backbone into a ramrod.

Two beats. Six. Eleven. Nineteen.

And then he gasped.

The breath he'd been holding—possibly since his parents' deaths—erupted from his throat. "I can't…"

He muttered that over and over.

Hailey hugged him tighter. "Cry, damn you. Nobody deserves to cry more than we do."

"I can't … He … He…"

"No. He didn't. He *didn't*. He loved her. He loved you. He loved me. He didn't do it, Gavin. Someone shot them both. Murdered them. Shot Dad, put the gun in his hand, then shot Mom, when she tried to get to Dad to help him. *That's* who they were. He didn't kill her. She tried to help him. They were together. At the end. Just the way they were with us. All of us."

He sagged.

She went with him to the dirt, still holding him. "We're going to find who did it. We are. Because it wasn't Dad. The murdering scum took his name, his reputation. And took the future—took our future as a family—but we aren't going to let him take our past. Not anymore. You, me, Mom, Dad. We're a family. We were and we are. We have that back. We have that back."

The boy cried.

Chapter Forty-Eight

"WHY FRED WHITE'S tail?" I asked Gavin, pretending not to notice him wiping his face on his jacket sleeve, now that both of them were upright. "I mean, I know why Fred White. To get maximum effect in the effort to distract your sister. But of all the things you could have done, why steal a horse tail?"

"I don't know. Because it happened before, I guess."

Defensive. Good. Just what I wanted.

"You were thinking about Hailey driving you nuts because she insisted your father didn't kill your mother and himself. You just wanted her to be quiet, because you'd made a nice shell around your feelings. People backed off. Didn't question you about how you felt, didn't make *you* think about how you felt. You could be numb, if you stayed really still and silent inside that shell. But there was Hailey banging at it. Making you think, making you feel, making you remember. How your dad and mom were together, how they talked to each other, the things you heard them talking about, like the person who called about the paintings..."

I trailed it off, because I saw the bubbling of something toward the surface in his eyes the same way it had when he'd brought that up before.

Hailey gave me a hard, questioning look. I spread my fingers, patting the air, telling her to wait.

When Gavin spoke, his voice came sing-song, distant.

"They were talking about the paintings. I went in the kitchen for an apple. Mom took it from me, washed it, cut it into slices the way she did even though my braces were off. And they kept talking. Nothing secret. Just continuing what they were talking about, knowing I wasn't interested. It was more about the paintings. That woman who called—"

Woman. He hadn't said that before when he gave us the fact of the call. Only that a *person* had asked about the paintings. But in the memory of his parents' conversation, *woman.*

"—and maybe they should check, just in case. Because how could she have known so much? She'd described that small one of the dry creek so well, including the streak, where the horse-tail brush got overloaded and—"

His head jerked up. "The horse-tail brush. I was going to ask Mom what that was about, but she handed me the apple and I started eating and I wasn't interested enough to stick around."

A micro-flinch. Regret. One of nearly infinite moments when we pass up an opportunity to be with those we love, to hear them say one more thing, tell one more story. Until they're gone. No more moments, no more opportunities, no more stories.

"Later, I looked it up. I was supposed to be researching some stupid paper for school, and I couldn't take another minute of it, so I looked up about what Mom said. I saw about some artists using horse-hair brushes and read articles on people stealing horse hair."

"When was it, Gavin? Do you remember?" I asked.

He shook his head. "It could have been any time between that phone call and when ... And when..."

From behind his hard shell, he'd flung the harshest words at the world. Now, he didn't know how to voice the ambiguity. I hoped we could give him new words. Soon.

"Did you know Wylie Easley? Either of you?"

Dual head shakes.

Then Gavin added, "Mom and Dad met him at the café. I don't know exactly when."

"Right," Hailey said. "She told me on the phone they were doing that. Two, three days before..."

"Wait," Gavin said abruptly. "That phone call was while I was working on that first paper I had in summer school. So that had to be middle of June. But they were still talking about the paintings right before..."

They'd both stalled on the same word. Their lives would forever be divided into before and after their parents' deaths.

"We had a baseball tournament that weekend and practically everybody in town came, remember, Hail? After we won the final on Sunday, we had the picnic."

Hailey slowly nodded. "Mom had made so much and she didn't want to pack it all up to go home and go bad, so she put it out and invited everybody. Sandwiches and chicken and salad and chips and brownies."

They smiled at each other. Ordinary smiles. No tears or anger or— in this moment—grief.

They might never remember this moment again, but I would. Seeing them start to reclaim part of what had been taken from them.

"That's when they talked about the call from the woman, remember?"

His sister slowly shook her head.

He nodded, more emphatic. "I was getting brownies and they were telling people about the phone call from that woman about Carey Maight paintings."

"Who were they telling?" I asked.

He shook his head. "It was a group. A bunch of adults, talking, and I was there because the brownies were on the picnic table behind them."

"Anybody you remember?" Before he solidified his non-memory with another headshake, I tossed out possibilities, hoping for a spark. "Your teammates? Their families? Your coach? A teacher? Your next-door neighbor? An aunt—?"

He stopped shaking his head. "O.D. was there. So were you," he said to Hailey. "Beside him."

She frowned fiercely. "I remember being there and the picnic and people talking, but not about a phone call or Carey Maight. There was something else, though ... They were talking about a body found earlier and the identity was going to be released soon, but she wasn't from around here and nobody knew who she was, until somebody in Montana figured it out and—Oh." She looked at me. "Wylie Easley was there. So, I *did* meet him. I'd totally forgotten. But now I remember him saying something about there were a whole lot of people in the world beyond Cottonwood County. Snotty, like the rest of us weren't smart enough to know that. And—right—that deputy was there. Redus. That's why he was familiar. I thought maybe I'd seen him around, you know? But I'd just seen him a couple days ... before."

No smiles now.

✧ ✧ ✧ ✧

I LEFT THEM alone. We had some time before the next round.

Giving them privacy was one reason. Also, freezing my body parts was not on the agenda.

In the SUV, I cranked up the heat. The warmth seeping into me coincided with water sliding down my cheeks.

I wasn't technically crying.

Before getting in my vehicle, moisture on my eyelashes froze. Now it melted thanks to the automotive heater.

Where had the moisture come from?

Tears.

I called my parents.

"Mom, Dad. If anything happens to any of us and if we're not on the best ... If we're ... you know, scratching at each other, I want you to know I love you. No matter what. And how grateful I am that you're my parents. To never doubt that. No matter what."

"We know that," Dad told me.

"What's going on?" Mom asked me.

"Cat, tell her we never doubt that she loves us."

"We never doubt it. What's going on, Elizabeth?"

Before I had to answer, Dad said, "I have to go. Told J.R.—" One of my nephews. "—I'd help him change the oil in his mom's car. He's about got it on his own, but likes somebody on hand. But if you want to talk more, Maggie Liz..."

"I'm good. Thanks, Dad. Give J.R. a hug for me."

"Will do."

Mom said nothing until after I heard a door close in the background.

"What's really going on?" she asked.

I broad-brushed Hailey Newhall's situation, adding a bit more detail on her relationship with Gavin.

She expelled a breath. Understanding, sympathy, and a little impatience, if I had the recipe right.

"Sounds like you have that handled."

"Handled? Not at all. We got Gavin to fess up to his sister about cutting her horse's tail, but the underlying case that he was trying to get her to ignore that's tormenting them both? *Not* handled."

Not yet.

"You're working on it."

"Yeah, I am. We all are. But—"

"You'll get there. What about your personal situation. Is that handled?"

Oh. That.

"It's ... You could say it's sorted out." I felt a reminiscent aching burn in my body and a smile spreading across my face. Sure was glad we weren't on video. "But the way it turned out ... I know Dad thought things might go another direction."

"Mike's direction instead of Tom's. Yes. Your father likes Mike a great deal. Always did as a player and now..."

"I know." It came out part groan.

"But I don't think your father will be as disappointed as you expect. Besides, I don't see Mike Paycik cutting off ties with the Dannihers over this."

As if he had that option once the Dannihers decided he was part of the clan.

"What about you, Mom?" I asked impulsively. "What do you think?"

"It's your life and your heart. I never had an opinion," she lied. She had opinions on everything. And then a corner of the truth peeked out. "Though I had a suspicion after visiting Sherman."

She paused, demanding that I ask. So I did. Just to speed up the process. "What was your suspicion?"

"First, that you would go your own way. Always have, always will. Even when some of us thought you let that snake Wes turn your life upside down without retribution or—"

"Mom. Ancient history."

Satisfied she'd made her point, she continued, "Second, that your relationship with Mike was too smooth for your taste or your own good. Not with Tom. And that will keep both of you on your toes. You and Tom rub up against each other. Friction and fire. Combined with respect and love, it's a great combination for you."

I flashed back to a moment in my back yard last summer when they'd been visiting. Mom and Dad had disagreed about something— could have been the future of the world or what kind of pie for dessert—and lobbed a few pithy, point-filled comments. With other couples I'd heard do similar exchanges, the next round would escalate matters. Sharper, possibly more personal.

Mom and Dad looked at each other and smiled.

"So," Mom's voice concluded through the phone, "I'm not the least surprised you and Tom finally got out of your own ways to make this happen."

Of course she wasn't.

"You are going to have adventures being a momma to Tamantha."

"We haven't talked about—" Well, Tom had, but ... "We aren't on the verge of marriage or anything. So I wouldn't be—"

"You think a marriage license matters to that girl? You're about to be a momma."

"I—"

My protest dropped. I'd just spotted a pickup on the highway, headed this way.

Was it the one I wanted to see?

"Gotta go, Mom. I'll talk to you later."

Chapter Forty-Nine

I GOT OUT of the SUV and back in the corral in record time.

My hurry flustered Fred White, which worked to my advantage. Hailey left her brother to calm the horse.

I got in Gavin's face, practically front to front. He stepped back. I followed, talking low enough that Hailey wouldn't hear. I looked right into his eyes. "Get in the shed. Right now."

"What? No. Why? I'm not—"

"Do it. Watch and listen. Call the sheriff's department if I say—" I scrambled for something. "Tanglefoot. Or if I'm not in a position to say anything."

"What the hell—? I'm not—" He broke off, as he spotted the pickup. Still on the highway, but slowing for the turn. "You think he—? I'm not going anywhere. I can—"

"What I hope to God you can do is be a grown-up with a head on your shoulders. And be our ace in the hole. Move. Fast. Before he sees you."

Indecision suspended him another beat. But I held his stare, letting him see.

He jerked around toward the shed.

"Tanglefoot," I repeated. "Stay out of sight."

❖ ❖ ❖ ❖

HAILEY DIDN'T SPOT the arrival until he'd parked and was nearly to the corral gate.

"Speak of the devil," she murmured.

"You called me, said to come out here?" Wylie Easley said to me.

"Stay outside the gate," I said. "The horse is spooked."

"Is this the one—Sorry. I should have said hello, Hailey. I've been meaning to get in touch."

"Oh?" she said chillingly.

He released his grasp on the metal, as if her chill communicated through gate and gloves into his flesh.

But he was a salesman. "I'm Wylie Easley. You probably don't remember—"

"I remember."

"I appreciate what Elizabeth here told me about you thanking me for making sure your brother didn't see—"

He said more, but the sound of tires turning fast off the highway onto the gravel and dirt covered it.

Wylie was the last of us to turn his head toward the sound.

The truck stuck a landing inches from Wylie's—he'd have to get in the passenger side.

Clayton jumped out, strode toward the gate.

"Clayton, what are you—?"

The newcomer seemed to take the beginning of the protest as a greeting, saying briefly, "Wylie," while his attention was on Hailey and me inside the corral. "What's going on here?"

"Oh, Clayton." Her voice wobbled.

She took a step toward him. I grabbed onto the back of her jacket. "Stay here with me, Hailey."

She looked around in surprise.

"I don't want to be alone in here with Fred White nearly as much as he doesn't want to be alone with me. And you stay there, Clayton. Hailey wants to tell you things, but we can do it from here."

"What things?" he asked.

"About my parents. And—"

"And Fred White's tail," I interrupted.

"Gavin," Hailey said, then stalled.

Clayton picked up her meaning, though. "Gavin took Fred White's tail? And he must have done those other horses, too."

I said, "We're sure that theft is not related to the ones two and a half years ago. We're—"

Boy, the pickups were coming fast now.

This one sped in and squealed to a stop. O.D. Everett's brakes needed work.

Clayton and Wylie turned toward him as O.D. came out of the truck at his top speed—no match for Clayton's, but different from his usual measured walk.

"Hailey. Are you all right?"

"I am. What are you—?"

I cut in. "She's fine. Stay where you are, O.D." Which was with the bulk of his pickup between him and the other two men. "All of you stay where you are. We're all going to have a little talk now."

Hailey turned her head toward me, the muscles of her jaw working as if she fought to keep them from sagging.

My attention was for the three men.

"Gavin told us about the woman who called Kim and Lewis about the paintings."

"What woman?" Wylie asked.

"Gavin stole horse tails for her?" Clayton asked.

I kept going. "That was the month before they were killed. Her name was Bernarda Garmin. She owned an art gallery in Palm Springs.

"Gavin also remembers a conversation about the death of the woman and her connection to Carey Maight paintings at the baseball tournament picnic the weekend before Kim and Lewis died. You were all there. You went with Hailey, right, Clayton? You stood next to your granddaughter, O.D. She remembers you there, Wylie."

Clayton and Wylie looked at me, then each other, then back to me. O.D. looked only at Hailey.

Hailey said, "Why are you interested in that woman? Mom was right. She didn't know what she was talking about. The landscapes aren't on the market. Once in a while, a portrait comes up for sale and O.D. won't always pay what the sellers want, so that might be available to another buyer. But not with the landscapes. He buys all of those."

I pitched my voice to the men.

"That was one of the problems for the killer, wasn't it? The very few Carey Maight paintings that are for sale on the open market."

So unlike those historic photographers Mrs. P told me about, who could make copies from their negatives. That, along with being in mostly private hands, was what made Carey Maight's archive so different.

"Were you the one who got Bernarda Garmin to come here, O.D.? Did you buy paintings from her? Were you the one who told Hailey not to allow any of her collection to be in the upcoming exhibit?"

Hailey pulled in a breath. I gave her another hand signal to be quiet.

O.D. said nothing.

I didn't let it slow me.

"But the most immediate problem for the killer was that Kim and Lewis might connect the dead woman with the woman who'd called Kim. And that was going to happen fast if they heard she owned an art gallery, which would happen as soon as the sheriff in Montana released her identity."

I FELT THE crackle of reaction.

But it was quickly suppressed.

As a compact car, followed by another truck pulled in, I knew the surprise at my knowing that much wouldn't be enough to break this open.

But the new arrivals might be.

With the three men's pickups clogging the area in front of the gate, these two vehicles parked closer to the highway.

"We've got it," Diana shouted to me getting out of her truck and gesturing for Jennifer to join her. "He was there."

The three men turned toward her.

"Don't get too close," I called to Diana and Jennifer.

"What do they have?" Easley demanded.

Diana and Jennifer climbed up to stand in the bed of Diana's truck. The height carried their voices, while the cab offered a modicum of potential protection. More than Hailey and I had in the corral.

The killer left the gun used on Kim and Lewis to sell the murder-suicide story, but that didn't mean he couldn't have another one.

"What the hell is going on?" Clayton asked, those eyebrows peaking over his nose.

"Yeah," Hailey said from beside me.

I didn't answer.

"Dex says your scenario works," Jennifer said. "Rechecking ballistics tests should also show there wasn't enough on Lewis' hand to account for two shots, not to mention the blotchiness."

Good thing, since I'd already presented my scenario as fact to Hailey.

"And the Newhalls' neighbor, Amy Cravaford, says, yes, the suspect was at the Newhalls' house at the right times for stealing the gun in June and committing the murders in July."

"What the hell?" Wylie shouted, having picked up the refrain from Clayton.

He took a step toward Diana's pickup.

"Don't," Jennifer commanded, holding her phone aloft. "I'm live-streaming this around the world."

As relieved as I was to have those pieces of confirmation, I did not want to start by tackling the major hurdle of the murders of Kim and Lewis Newhall.

Work him up to it. That was the plan.

Jennifer gave me the opening when she also called out, "The guys found another record of Bernarda Garmin selling a painting attributed to Carey Maight."

O.D.'s gasp was only half finished when I said, "Did she know they were forgeries, Clayton?"

Chapter Fifty

I **HAD TO** hold onto Hailey's coat again. This time to help keep her upright.

"No, no, no, no."

She hadn't been hiding things from me. She'd been hiding them from herself. Gavin. And Clayton.

But I didn't have time for heartbreak. Or to acknowledge how quickly she accepted the implicit accusation as fact.

He didn't notice at all.

"I don't know what you're talking about." He tried to shut me out. "Hailey, this woman's crazy. I—"

"Give it up, Clayton. Didn't you hear? The neighbor saw you in the Newhalls' garage—where the gun safe was kept—at the right time for taking the gun to shoot Bernarda Garmin.

"We know you took the key. Easy enough to slip it off the peg by the back door, maybe when you were there with Hailey. Nobody saw you do that. But when you went back, alone, when Kim and Lewis weren't there, the neighbor noticed. If Foster Redus had asked basic questions—but you were lucky there. Amazingly lucky."

"Amy—the neighbor—wasn't asked after Kim and Lewis were killed," Diana said, "and she didn't connect it because of the time gap and you'd always been in and out of their house. Less frequently since you and Hailey got together, but not enough to raise her suspicions."

"You must have counted on that," I added.

"That's—"

"We also know you forged Carey Maight paintings. That's why you talked Hailey out of putting any of the paintings in the exhibit."

"I didn't do that. That's not what happened—"

"It is," Hailey whispered. No one heard her but me.

I kept going. "The same way you persuaded her to do the half-hearted inventories. Never letting O.D. see the paintings. But the exhibit was the big danger to you. The original paintings or your forgeries of them would be on public display. Pairs of paintings where there should be only one. How long before the buyers or the museum realized they'd been scammed?

"We know you learned how to make and use horse-hair brushes in an art class. All these years later, your instructor remembers how good you were at making the brushes ... and at mimicking Carey Maight's style."

"He said one night that he could do that," Wylie said abruptly. "He was roaring drunk and bragging and he started to talk about painting like Carey Maight and Isaiah decked him. He stopped taking art classes after that."

"Keeping your skill under wraps," I picked up. "Using your talent only for the forgeries you sold."

"Yeah, I have talent, but I wouldn't do what you're saying."

His eyebrows were almost vertical over his nose. I remembered my impression of a singer being soulful. What I hadn't recognized in that instant was the singer was performing.

"Was it a falling out of confederates with Bernarda? She came here demanding you produce more paintings than you could paint without getting caught? Or had she realized what you were doing and came to confront you? Or—"

"Neither," O.D. said unexpectedly. "She'd seen paintings on the market. Became curious. Tracked down the Friends and Family group, wanted to know about this source of Carey Maight paintings, because she had buyers wanting more. Didn't seem to believe we hadn't sold any."

Indignantly, I thought it would have helped if he'd told us that before now.

If Clayton knew what Bernarda Garmin was trying to do, it would have made him more determined to get rid of her before she could talk to anyone else. Like Kim or Hailey. Because if they compared notes with her...

"So, she kept digging," I said, as if I'd known O.D.'s piece all along. "She went to the supermarket, the museum, a real estate office, asking questions. Not a stretch to think she went to where art supplies are sold. Nasty moment for you when she came into Pen and Ink, asking questions, Clayton.

"Fast thinking to agree to set up a time to meet her, probably telling her you weren't free to talk then, but you had things to tell her. A quick trip to the Newhalls' house, to get the key and the gun, and you were prepared for that meeting."

"I wouldn't do that. Hailey, you know I wouldn't."

I yanked his attention back to me, because I'd caught the sound of another pickup, coming fast—what other way was there around here?

"You weren't as lucky or as careful with killing Bernarda. First-time jitters? Must have really rocked you when the Montana authorities identified her. They also did a really good job with extracting DNA.

"You could explain away any of your DNA at the Newhalls'. After all, even with their disapproval of your relationship with Hailey, you still went there for parties, family events. But Bernarda Garmin ... How are you going to explain your DNA being found around her?"

Across the distance, I saw him trying to remember exactly what he'd done, touched.

Without turning my head, I tracked the latest pickup turning, having slowed enough to not call attention to itself.

"I met her. So what. Like you said, she came into Pen and Ink. She wanted to know about Carey Maight paintings and Hailey was working so much then I wanted to spare her meeting this pushy woman. You remember that really, really tough spell you had at the ranch, Hailey—lost that horse and you were devastated."

From the corner of my eye, I saw her face, struck by the memory.

"So, yeah, I met with her. But I wouldn't kill anybody. You know that, Hailey. You love me, I love you. You know that."

The newest pickup truck, now in my main field of vision, had a

light rack and Cottonwood County Sheriff's Department markings.

It stopped sharply, and Richard Alvaro got out—staying behind the open door, with his gun drawn.

"Hands up. Everybody stay where you are," he ordered.

"Deputy, Jennifer has a cell phone in her hand," Diana called.

"Okay. Thanks. Now, what's going on here?"

Before anyone could answer, a new vehicle—this one a luxury SUV—pulled in.

Mike got out with his hands up, showing Richard they were empty. He looked at the deputy, but he was telling Diana, Jennifer, and me when he said, "Easley's brother confirmed Wylie's here to try to dig the business out of a hole. He was here two and a half years ago to offer to do the same thing. Wylie was telling the truth."

"Of course I was. *He* killed them," Wylie shouted. "Clayton. He killed them all."

No argument there. But Clayton Rayger hadn't confessed.

He had gone from never hearing of Bernarda to meeting with her. I might wish I could have moved him another step to the killing, but if Hailey was wobbling...

All in all, I wasn't sorry to see Richard Alvaro.

And without my saying Tanglefoot.

Gavin Newhall had proven to be a grown-up with a head on his shoulders.

✦ ✦ ✦ ✦

HANDCUFFED AND BEING ducked into the official car, Clayton Rayger yelled.

"Tell them, Hailey. Tell them. You love me, I love you. That's what counts. We can work through the rest of this."

Chapter Fifty-One

OUTSIDE INTERVIEW ROOM One at the Cottonwood County Sheriff's Department, Hailey and I stood with Shelton and Sheriff Russ Conrad.

Diana, Jennifer, Gavin, Mike, O.D., and Wylie were in the waiting area.

Clayton Rayger sat in the interview room with Deputy Alvaro, who read him his rights and asked a few introductory questions.

I argued my case to Shelton and Conrad. "You'll never get him to say it. But he said he thought he and Hailey could work this out. Let her go in there. He *will* talk to her."

Hailey jerked around. "Yes. I want to talk to him. I want to know—" She grabbed my arm. "With you. You come, too. You have to."

I could have kissed her.

Shelton gave me an I'll-get-you-for-this look, as if I'd coached her. But he's no fool. Neither is the sheriff.

With Richard retiring unobtrusively to a corner of the room, Hailey and I took the chairs opposite Clayton.

I doubted he knew anyone was in the room except Hailey.

He reached across the table toward her. She kept her hands in her lap.

"Hailey. Hailey, you have to listen to me. This is all a screwup. You know that. You love me and I—"

"I have to understand, Clayton. Tell me what happened. Did you copy paintings? Why? How did that start?"

That was the one thing I'd suggested to her, that she start by asking about the paintings.

Shelton had told her the most important thing was to keep Clayton talking, no matter what he said, no matter what she had to swallow.

A tall order.

Clayton's eyebrows pitched up. "That doesn't matter. What matters is how we feel about each other, what we have and—"

"She needs to understand, Clayton. You heard her say that." I broke in before she let him see he'd already lost her. I heard Tom's voice recounting Davon Everett's impression. *Nothing was ever Clayton's fault.* "Even if it means telling her the truth about Isaiah. How he drew you into it when you were a kid."

"He did," he said. "He dragged me into it. He said it would just be copying a couple paintings to help out after Kim had the baby and all those expenses. He couldn't do it himself—" A flick of disdain. "—because he couldn't draw a stick figure to save his life. But I could. I could make it look just like Carey Maight's."

Some vestige of honesty surfaced. "Maybe not when someone who really knew looked close. But for most people, yeah, my work was as good as hers. I could use horse-hair brushes. That was the key. With the horse-hair brushes my paintings passed for hers, easy. The thing was, he planned to sell the real ones. I was smarter than that."

"Th-thank you for telling me." Hailey swallowed. "You must be very talented."

"I am. That's why—"

"But Isaiah died. Did you go ahead on your own?

Hailey followed up my question immediately with, "Did you?"

"Not for a long time." He said that as if it made him virtuous. "It wasn't until Kim married Lewis and he built that closet that she took them out of storage from somewhere. I didn't even know where."

"But you did take paintings out when things got tight, including about two and a half years ago," I said.

"How'd you know that?" he demanded between slitted lids.

"You needed more horse-hair brushes. The stolen horse tails, that was you. Resupplying what you needed in order to sell more paintings.

But you must have slipped that time, because Bernarda Garmin had a lead she followed to here, to the family. When you met, did she ask for more paintings? Or was she going to expose the others as fakes?"

"I'm not saying anything. I know my rights."

Of course, he didn't have to answer me. But his eagerness to persuade Hailey it had all been for love of her ... and his eagerness to put the blame elsewhere kept him going.

I prompted him with, "You said Isaiah dragged you into it..."

"Yeah, yeah, he did. Took it for granted I'd do that for him—the paintings. Dragged me out that night to meet the Garmin bitch. I didn't want to go. He was drunk, I was drunk, it was a crappy night. I just wanted to stay with Kim. Not let that Easley leech get all over her like a fussy grandmother. But Isaiah said we had to go. And nothing would stop him.

"And then we're out there, trying to get it over faster, driving and the wind coming and coming. And the snow. And then it was like it just picked my truck up. One second on the road and the next up in the air, then rolling and rolling. I could see crap in the back tumbling in the air like a freakin' zero gravity ride or something. And I gripped and gripped as hard as I could, just holding on. Until we came down, with the windshield clear as anything, but snow and dirt and tumbleweeds all smashed into the side and back ... And it finally stopped. Stopped. Dead. Isaiah was dead."

Almost a whisper, I said, "He was dead in the back seat."

Hailey started to whip her head around to me, but I clamped my hand on her thigh under the table and she froze.

"Yeah. Yeah, he was."

After a breath-held moment, he slowly looked up at me.

"What good would it have done? None."

He meant telling the truth.

It would have done Hailey Newhall a great deal of good.

✧   ✧   ✧   ✧

"WERE ANY OF the works you sold really by Carey Maight?" I asked.

"The first one. It was little and way, way back in that closet, I had to take almost all the other ones out to get to it. I almost missed it myself, so I was sure Kim would never notice. But it wouldn't let me go, worrying about it.

"So I painted one that looked like it. First try was bad. But by the fourth try, I had it. I put it in where the real one had been and nobody noticed anything."

He took pride in that.

"After that, I only took a painting out in order to ... to *study* it. What's sold are my paintings."

So, Hailey's collection didn't hold forgeries, except the one. But the exhibit still could have given away what he'd done. If a holder of one of his forgeries saw the real thing listed in the exhibit ... He couldn't risk that.

"I was real careful. I knew old man Everett watched the market. After Isaiah died, he tied the local ones up tight. I used a guy I know in California to get them in galleries. Always needs money. He wasn't supposed to go back to the same place twice, but he must have. Because that Garmin woman sold three and was looking for more. But as long as she didn't know my name, she couldn't tell it.

"Besides, it wasn't really forging. Painted the same places, maybe, but it's like those old guys working in the style of another painter. That's all. *In the style of.*"

"Did you use old canvas? Did you age the paintings? Did you sign her name?"

"It was for Hailey." In other words, yes, he did those things. "All for Hailey. And Gavin."

"Gavin?" It jerked out of Hailey. "How do you figure——?"

"I pay expenses at the house, too. That helps keep a roof over his head."

"Not regular, you don't." Her words came fast. The depth of his betrayal would take time to absorb, but this was ordinary. Something she knew. "Not utilities or food or anything, while you live there rent-free."

To give her time I asked, "How'd you get in there, the painting closet?"

He looked toward the left side of the interview room door. If he'd been in the Newhalls' kitchen, he would have been staring right where the keys hung.

"I had a key. But with that woman nosing around I got rid of the copy I'd made. Just in case."

He shifted his focus to me. It had to be easier than looking at his fiancée.

"Even with it being my paintings that sold, it would be just my luck if Kim noticed … Every time I saw her or Lewis, I thought they were about to say they'd found out. But I didn't want to make them suspicious by staying away, either. It was better when they disapproved of Hailey and me, because that explained everything and I didn't have to see them so much."

"Until…" I prodded.

"Until they called me. It was all going to be patched up, they said. Only I knew it wasn't true. Why else would they call and say they needed to talk to me. Without Hailey. Just the three of us. Patch it up? Right. Like that's what they meant after all that talk at the ballpark about the woman calling them about the paintings and that Montana sheriff releasing her identity soon. They *knew*. They'd sent her to me for God's sake. Told her to talk to me at Pen and Ink because I'd known Isaiah and could tell her she was wrong that he'd planned to sell paintings. When her name came out, they'd tell everybody…

"After, it was better. With Hailey and me. It was really, really good. She needed me and I was there for her. I make her happy and that's what was most important to them, so…"

So … what? Hailey should be satisfied he'd murdered them both and set it up so Lewis took the blame? In fact, he'd killed all three of her parents. Her father, her mother, and her stepfather. And then he wooed her.

"It wasn't like I was hurting Hailey. It wasn't taking a thing away from her. In fact, it was giving her more, because the paintings were still there, were still hers, and what I used the money for were things we did together and that's what she wanted."

He left a pause. After a couple beats, he glanced up, perhaps to see if my expression gave him the agreement I'd failed to voice. I kept my expression as unreadable as my silence. That wasn't what he wanted—needed. Possibly because, somewhere deep, he didn't believe his rationalizations.

His gaze bounced away.

I took him back to where he felt safer. "So, after that one small painting at the beginning…"

"I didn't have to take any more original paintings," he said almost eagerly.

"But that all ended when Bernarda Garmin came to town," I said softly.

"That damned woman sniffing around. I took care of that—" Stealing a gun, murdering a woman, hiding a body, secreting a car, all encapsulated in the innocuous phrase *took care of*. "I thought it was over. But everybody was talking about her. Then Lewis called, said I needed to go over there. We needed to talk. I still had the gun—"

"You'd taken Lewis' gun?" I wanted him to say it.

"I needed it for that woman." He said it like that should have been obvious. "After, I figured if they found her fast and connected her to Carey Maight paintings.…"

They would also discover she'd died from a bullet fired from a gun owned by Lewis Newhall, whose stepdaughter was connected to Carey Maight and could be affected financially by the market for those works. If Redus had done a decent investigation, they *would* have.

If that had happened, would Hailey have believed Lewis committed murder-suicide out of shame, remorse for supposedly killing Bernarda? Would she ever have come to the station looking for answers?

"I was going to return it that day. Had it in my pocket when Lewis called, said to come over. I didn't want to have to do it. But then he started asking had I heard about that poor woman and Kim looking at me all serious and … and I had to do it. I had to."

He looked at Hailey from the corner of his eye.

"I would've told you about the paintings after we got together. But not with Kim and Lewis so against me. Once we were married, then I could have told you. And everything would've been fine. After all, they're your paintings and—"

"After you killed my parents? After you *murdered* my parents?"

He was too deep into his excuses to hear her.

"They wouldn't let it alone, just like that bitch. And they were getting closer. Closer all the time."

Hailey stood without pushing back her chair. I caught it before it tipped over. She didn't notice. "God, I wish you'd been the one to die that night in the wreck and my father lived."

"He wouldn't have treated you or Kim as good as I did. Always helping out. At least until Lewis came along and pushed me aside."

As we left the room, I saw her walk had changed. Not completely, but less weighted.

Clayton shouted after Hailey, "You have to understand. I love you. Have loved you all your life. From the moment I first held you—first baby I'd ever held."

Like Emma and Mr. Knightley ... gone horribly wrong.

Chapter Fifty-Two

DIANA, LEONA, WALT, Audrey, Jennifer, Jerry, and I went to dinner at the Haber House Hotel as Mike's guests. All the newsroom was invited, but the KWMT-TV staff has a strong bent toward going home for dinner. One of the perks of living in Sherman, Wyoming.

They didn't miss much conversation, because our meal was repeatedly interrupted by people saying hello to Mike, congratulating him on buying the station, suggesting programming, and asking for discounts on their advertising rates.

He handled it with impressive aplomb.

Though he did not object to doggy-bagging his dessert when the rest returned to the station for the Ten, while he, Diana, Jennifer, and I went to my house.

We'd gone over what Clayton said at the station in detail, when Jennifer asked me, "How did you figure out the horse-tail thefts?"

"That's the frustrating part. I got close to it earlier, thinking the difference from the previous thefts wasn't the horses or their tails, but the people. Specifically, Hailey. Not a target last time, the only target this time. But I didn't push it far enough or it might have clicked earlier."

"You didn't have the information to push it," Diana said.

I wasn't so sure. But my mind had been otherwise occupied.

Jennifer said, "I get why she was a target this time—Gavin was trying to distract her. Keep her from digging into what he didn't want to face. But why wasn't she—or Fred White—a target last time?"

"Because Clayton was the thief then, making brushes to forge more paintings. He wouldn't steal her horse's tail, but he'd kill Kim and Lewis."

"Lewis and Kim," Diana murmured.

"Right. He took the painting closet key, then realized that with everyone on the alert after the killings, he couldn't get to that painting closet at the Newhalls' house without raising all sorts of alarms with neighbors, with law enforcement, maybe even with Hailey. He had to bide his time until they moved the paintings to the new place."

"You think it was his idea at the start or Isaiah's?" Diana asked.

"It's a guess, but I'd say Isaiah. He'd have known Clayton had artistic talent. Isaiah could easily have pointed him toward the class on making and using horse-hair brushes. Isaiah owned the paintings, knew more about them, and—as everyone says—he was the leader. Plus, it makes sense if Bernarda Garmin reached out to the owner of the paintings. Might have given him the idea.

"After Isaiah died, Bernarda thought that ended her potential source of paintings. Then a Carey Maight painting showed up. Followed by more as Clayton got more confident. Remember, not all of them went through her gallery, so it took quite a while for her to realize there were more Carey Maights on the market and track them down."

"Did she know they were forgeries?" Jennifer asked.

"We can't know that. But give her the benefit of the doubt, based on her reputation and what she told O.D.—she had a market for the paintings, so she tried to find more."

Jennifer asked, "Do you think he ever really loved Hailey?"

"Maybe as much as he could," Diana said. "And as a sort of second chance with Kim?"

"And Isaiah," Mike muttered. "What made you start Clayton talking about the crash, Elizabeth?"

"Always thought it was better than fifty-fifty it was him driving. His truck, after all. Both men drunk. Isaiah was the leader. Did that make him more likely to drive or to make the other guy drive while he took a nap in back? Plus, Clayton talked about drag marks. Presented that as proof that he tried to help Isaiah. But it struck me they could also be the result of him repositioning Isaiah—putting the blame on him for the wreck."

I shrugged. "It was worth a shot. When Clayton talked about gripping and gripping—that's what you do to the steering wheel when you're driving, not when you're stretched out, asleep or passed out in the back seat. Plus the things he described seeing were from the driver's seat. Not the back seat."

"They can't charge him this late for that, can they?" Mike asked.

"Doubt they'll try with double murder to pursue."

"Besides, that's part of what lost him Hailey, so he'll keep paying for it," Jennifer said with satisfaction.

"Hope he pays for it in court, too," Mike said.

"They should go for premeditation. He didn't *just happen* to have the gun with him that day. He wasn't going to return it. Kim and Lewis called him to come over—that was the *worst* time to return the gun. He'd've wanted a time they weren't there to look over his shoulder and see him returning it."

Mike pushed his hair back off his forehead and swore. "He took the gun with him, with the murder-suicide already planned."

"That's not the sort of thing you come up with on the spur of the moment, as we've said all along—well, at least lately," Diana said. "That's really..."

"Cold," Mike said.

"Awful," Jennifer said.

"Such a betrayal," I said.

"And all based on the supposition that they'd found him out when, in fact, they were trying to make peace in their family. What a horrible waste," Diana said.

"Although he was probably right they'd have figured it out when Bernarda's ID was revealed," I said.

"Poor Hailey," Jennifer added.

She was right.

Hailey Newhall didn't deserve this. Any of it. Having her parents murdered. Having her fiancé be the killer.

She'd known something was wrong. At some level.

She'd felt it, like a river of wrongness eating away at the bank where she'd prepared to build her life.

Unconsciously, she'd assigned all the wrongness to her brother—she would have to deal with that, as well as the direct horror of her fiancé's guilt—yet she'd come to me.

She'd needed the truth that much.

Now that she had the answers that formed the truth, she would experience their pain. She'd retreat for a while, but that was okay. Sometimes you had to get back to where the ground was so solid under your feet that nothing could undercut it.

Then you could start venturing out again, looking for a new spot to last you a lifetime.

I knew that, first hand.

I'd been wrong the day Hailey told me about her parents, thinking she'd come to me for something far different from consoling.

Like me, she found consolation in the truth, in knowing what happened and at least a little of why.

We'd given her the horror. But we'd also given her the truth that would let her get past it.

"Pass the cheese curls, will you?" Mike asked Diana.

I pulled my thoughts away from the investigation and back to these people I loved.

Epilogue

MAYBE CLAYTON RAYGER does care for Hailey to some degree.

Once he went through a couple lawyers—each telling him his goose was cooked—he pleaded guilty.

There will be no trial.

That should help. Along with something I remembered from the first time we met, when I asked her about who lived at the ranchette. She'd said, *My brother and me. My fiancé lives there, too.*

Those small words, revealing priorities.

Hailey sold the ranchette. She is working full-time for Jack on that big spread. Gavin is living with a teammate's family in town, though he visits her regularly. I hear they spend long hours on horseback together with very few words spoken.

Fred White, on the ranch with Hailey, has started letting Gavin around him again.

❖   ❖   ❖   ❖

AS THE STATION'S new whatever-the-heck-I-was, I made one executive decision the day after Clayton Rayger's arrest.

I told Jennifer to have her way with the KWMT-TV website.

"Really?"

I couldn't read her response. "Do you not want to do it because you won't have enough time before you leave for Northwestern after New Year's?"

"I will *make* it enough time. I can do whatever I want?"

Hours later, as we worked on the special about the case, Mike asked, "What did you tell Jennifer? She's some weird combo of fierce and ecstatic."

"Is she?"

"Elizabeth—"

"She's doing what needs to be done to the KWMT website."

"Oh." He relaxed. "You're right. That does need to be done."

"And she'll do a great job."

"And she'll do a great job," he agreed. I moved toward the door. "I get ecstatic part, but why fierce? It's not like I told her she couldn't— Wait a minute. How much is this going to cost? Mel will—Elizabeth? Where'd you go?"

WE ALL HAD Thanksgiving dinner at Diana's house, as the best place to set up a table to accommodate Diana, her kids, Russ Conrad, Mike, Jennifer (who also had Thanksgiving dinner with her family), Mrs. P, Aunt Gee, Tom, Tamantha, and me. With a ban on talking about the investigation.

After dinner, while Mike, Diana, and I dried the last dishes, he said to her, "I'm hoping we can do something special for you, but Mel says it will have to wait a year."

I bit back a grin. I couldn't wait to tell Mel he was the KWMT financial boogey man.

"Smaller cameras, lighter lights, better mics—I'm a happy girl, Mike." She patted his arm.

"How about a new Newsmobile."

"What?" The squeal came from me, not Diana. "That would be amazing. Wonderful. How soon—It would have shock absorbers, right?"

But both Mike and I were aware of Diana's silence.

"I suppose I knew we'd have to replace it at some point," she finally said.

"We do. We really do," Mike said. "When Mel saw how old it was, he did a lot of grumbling about liability. I told him you'd never sue the station, but..."

She sighed, produced a half-hearted smile and said, "I'm sure whatever you get would be great."

"You'll shop with me for it, Diana."

"Look at it this way, Diana," I said, "you can get the only news van to go from zero to sixty in under two seconds."

TAMANTHA ASKED JESSICA if she and I could use her room to talk.

"You're Daddy's girlfriend now." From Tamantha it was more edict than question.

But I was ready. Tom had told me he'd talked to her.

"We're dating," I said.

"Not like on TV. You don't go anywhere and you're with all of them a *lot*."

Tempted to point out movies and TV shows showed couples forming from within a group, I pulled back from the dangers of arguing with Tamantha Burrell.

"We will. Eventually."

"Eventually." She disapproved of the concept. "You should skip all that and get married."

"Married? How do you—?" Tom wouldn't have said anything about *that* to her. "We're not. Don't—"

"I know you're not, because Daddy said he'd tell me first. But you should," she explained with great patience. "It would make everything easier. I could call you Mom and I can be in your wedding."

That surprised me.

Tamantha was not the kind of girl who dreams of weddings. For one thing, she doesn't need a wedding to be queen for the day. She rules every day.

"You want to be in a wedding?"

"I do cartwheels."

That surprised me, too.

Not that she could do them, but that she'd indulged in a non sequitur.

"The aisle in our church would be a great place to do cartwheels.

Right down the center."

Okay, not indulging in a non sequitur. She'd *sequitured* that in her own mind just fine, only I didn't recognize the connection until she revealed it.

"What makes you think we'd—there'd be a wedding at your church?"

Her eyebrows lifted. "Do you have a church?"

"My Mom and Dad do—my family does—in Illinois."

"Does it have an aisle down the middle?"

I've described to her father the power of questions, their ability to pull words out of you. I wasn't immune. I felt the draw to answer like a tuft of dog hair sucked toward a vacuum. A process I observe regularly since Shadow came into my life.

An image of Tamantha and my mother pooling resources to plan a wedding—*my* wedding—gave me the strength to dig my fingernails in and resist the pull.

"Your father and I are not talking about getting married." That was true. *We* weren't. *He* was, a little, but not *we*.

"Why not? You're both awfully old."

"That's why," I shot back.

She shook her head. "Mrs. P says nobody should quit living until they're dead. So you better hurry up."

WE'D BEEN SUMMONED to the sheriff's office for the day after Thanksgiving.

Mike, Diana, and me. I hoped not including Jennifer meant they didn't know how talented she was at ... what she did.

They said invited. I counted it as a summons.

It seemed unfair to Mike to spend his last hours in Sherman before his return to Chicago this way, but he didn't seem to mind.

Russ Conrad, behind his desk, and Wayne Shelton, seated to his right, awaited us with mugs of coffee and a tray of cookies.

Pepperidge Farm Double Dark Chocolate Milano.

As we sat three across on the opposite side of the desk, I peered at

Shelton. He didn't look back.

I looked at Diana. She gave an infinitesimal shrug. She hadn't shared my predilection for those cookies with Russ.

Mike took a cookie and ate it.

"Thank you for coming. Yes, please, help yourselves to the cookies and coffee. We hope with this informal exchange, we might find a better working relationship. We are communicating with Sheriff Sauder and expect to connect the cases."

Conrad's gaze zipped to and away from Diana, but plenty long enough to know that their non-working relationship was a-okay.

Then he said, "We would like to know—as we work on the case files—what started you on Clayton Rayger."

Mike and Diana looked at me to speak.

"Clayton said Lewis and Kim, when he was talking about them getting shot."

They waited.

I waited.

Shelton exploded a breath. *"That's* your evidence?"

"I'd say his confession's *your* evidence. But that was our way in, the key to focus on him. Other things fell into place then."

"A couple words? And not exactly *I did it.*"

"In a way, it was exactly that. He was the only one who did that— referred to Lewis and Kim, instead of Kim and Lewis. He did it when he was talking about the shootings, not other times. That told us a lot."

"Because he knew Lewis was shot first," Russ said softly.

Diana beamed at her love. I settled for, "Exactly."

Shelton huffed.

After a moment, Conrad said, "What I'm about to tell you is strictly off the record. The Newhall case was one of three that Sergeant Shelton presented to me when I first came here as cases closed under the previous sheriff that he wasn't satisfied with."

"But you didn't do anything about them?"

Diana frowned at my question, Conrad didn't falter.

"We discussed at length what it would take to reopen each case, especially in light of limited investigative time, money, and forensic resources. With the Newhalls, we concurred that efforts by us to stir the pot would clamp the lid tighter. In other words, our best opportunity would come if something else interrupted the stasis."

"God knows you're good at that." Shelton peered over his mug at me, then made a half circle with it to include the others. "The lot of you."

"Yes." Conrad swallowed from his mug. "You certainly interrupted the stasis."

"I'd say Hailey Newhall did that."

Shelton said, "There's folks that can't believe a thing's happened because they worked hard not to see signs. Once it's happened, they can't take on the load of guilt for ignoring those signs. Then there's folks that can't believe it because everything they knew and saw—really saw—says this couldn't have happened the way they're being told it did."

"And that," I picked up, "was what was expressed by those who knew the Newhalls best."

"Was that what made you think it was double murder?" the sheriff asked.

"Less thinking it *was* double murder. More lining up *wasn'ts* for it being a murder-suicide."

Shelton nodded.

At something I said.

In front of witnesses.

And then he added, "Wasn't a word about trouble between them. Sure wasn't talk of divorce or custody. Wasn't cheating going on. That hits the big factors in domestic murders, but it doesn't end the *wasn'ts* in this case. Wasn't any sign of financial problems. Wasn't depression or other mental health issues. Wasn't heavy drinking or drugs where one or both might lose their heads."

"If you knew all that—" I started.

"Case was closed. Nothing was stirring."

"Until," the sheriff said smoothly, "you took it out of stasis."

Until we took it out of stasis ...

I had a sudden memory of Richard Alvaro standing in front of me.

Telling me the GSR was inconsistent, the shot trajectory at Kim was strange, the angle of Lewis' wound was off. Stumbling a bit over the telling.

And using the same word—*incomplete*—Shelton did.

That little stinker.

Playing me.

Richard coming to us had not been a triumph after all. I should have bruise marks between my shoulder blades from being shoved into this thing.

Shelton set the scene in our encounter at the supermarket, with careful avoidance of referring to murder-suicide and a tantalizing whiff of Redus. Then he sent in Richard. No doubt telling him not to just spill the information, to make me work for it.

The sheriff was probably in on it.

Gee, too?

I wasn't raising that possibility to Mike. He'd been so pleased about getting the police report from her.

I mentally called them all another name. Without the *little* in front of it and not *stinker*.

"Did you plant Richard at the high school?" I demanded of Shelton, hoping it sounded like I'd known all along.

That drew surprised looks from Mike and Diana.

Not from the two on the other side of the desk.

"That was happenstance. Otherwise, he would have bumped into you someplace. Can always count on the cookie aisle at the supermarket."

I scowled at that crack ... especially since he'd picked up another cookie as he delivered it.

"Any more questions?" Conrad asked.

"What are the other two closed cases Shelton isn't satisfied about?" My words were in response to the sheriff, but I looked at the sergeant.

"Wouldn't you like to know?" he said.

Stalemate.

For now.

✧ ✧ ✧ ✧

"I WANT TO be married to you," Tom Burrell said.

"Don't let your daughter push you."

"In this case, she and I are in complete agreement. Marry me, Elizabeth Margaret Danniher."

I kissed him. After a bit, we separated. "That's a big step. We can talk—"

"Now. Soon." He put a mug of fresh coffee in my hands.

He'd cooked eggs. I'd done toast. We'd eaten breakfast together like it wasn't almost noon on a Saturday.

And that was after going to bed before nine the night before.

Tamantha was at a birthday sleepover for a friend, followed by brunch bowling. "A rookie sleepover mom," Tom had said. "Means she has to get them all ready for the bowling alley. Always do the sleepover last."

See, these were things I didn't know. No way was I ready to be a stepmother, no matter what my mother said.

But for now, I was completely grateful to the sleepover rookie mom. Because it gave Tom and me a long, decidedly not lazy night and morning together.

I settled my hips back against the counter and used both hands to raise the coffee mug. "You're saying this in the morning?"

He grinned. "Figure I need you as defenseless as you get."

"Is this about Tamantha? Us living in sin? Bad example and all."

"No. You know she's doing cartwheels over this. More like visiting in sin, anyway."

He didn't mean metaphorical cartwheels. This new skill from the serious Tamantha delighted me.

"I don't want to give up my house."

"Don't want you to. Would like both houses to be *ours*."

I liked that. "We've both experienced the sour side of marriage and—"

"We haven't been married to each other. What happened with those other people won't stop us from making our own way."

I *really* liked relegating our exes to *those other people.*

"I want to think—"

"Rather you feel. C'mon. I'm taking you someplace."

HE INSISTED ON me bundling up even more than I would have on my own.

Refusing to tell me where we were going, he got me in his ranch truck, turned on the heater full blast, then drove off into a path between trees nobody would call a road.

And then it started climbing.

After several minutes of being plastered back in my seat like the uphill of a roller-coaster—and wondering what happened when we hit the peak—I said, "Tom?"

He stopped, turned off the truck, came around to open my sticky door, and held out his hand.

"Now we climb," he said.

"*Now* we climb? What've we *been* doing—?"

I didn't have breath for more, because he tugged me along with him. When I had to let go of his hand to climb with hands as well as feet, he held onto my hood like a parent with a toddler in a store ... or like an experienced mountain climber with a rookie and no equipment. Shouldn't there be sherpas for a trip like this?

We reached an edge of the trees abruptly and he stopped.

"There," he said, showing off he had breath to say anything, while I sucked in as fast as I could.

Then I saw and lost my breath again.

The trees had stopped because we stood beside a small river. Before us opened the path of the river, the trees skirting it, the tallest line of mountain tops in the distance, zigzagging against blue sky.

It was the scene in the Carey Maight painting in his bedroom.

I looked down.

Yes.

Just like the painting.

From any distance, the river hid what was below its surface. But here, at our feet, rocks and tree trunks shone through the clear water in vivid detail.

"Carey Maight painted this scene a hundred years ago." He jerked his head in a half shake. "Yet it *couldn't* have been here then. Not exactly the way it is now. The tree trunks, even rocks she saw, long gone. Water sees to that.

"Yet here it is. Same scene. Because life keeps coming. Whether you try to fight the water or let it wash over you, life keeps coming. From a distance, you see only the path of the water. But here, at our feet, we see the trunks, the branches, the rocks the water runs past and over.

"I'd been to this spot, but I never really saw it until I saw Carey Maight's painting of it."

Neither of us looking away from the scene, I slid my gloved hand into his. He curled his around it.

"The first time was in Mrs. Parens' house as a teenager," he said.

"When I dropped out of college—" He accepted I knew the story behind his giving up his basketball scholarship when his ex-girlfriend pretended to be pregnant to get him to marry her. Only later, with the marriage disintegrating, did she actually become pregnant with Tamantha. "—Mrs. Parens called me to her house. I expected the lecture to end all lectures. But she left me alone with that painting."

He lifted his head, looking toward the jagged line of treetops.

"It helped." The now-familiar twitch of lines at the corners of his mouth and eyes prepared me. "And then she came back and gave me the lecture to end all lectures about leaving school. I didn't listen. But, despite that, over the years we became … friends. And every time I went to her house, we sat in her office with that painting."

I thought of Linda saying I stared at the painting of Rupert Senior whenever I went to her house.

"Mrs. Parens gave me the painting—no, that's not right. She gave it to Tamantha to give to me—after Redus went missing and rumors started I'd killed him. Reminding me that what you can't see by looking at the horizon can be clear and solid at your feet."

He put his arm around my shoulders, pulling me in tight to his side and his warmth while still letting each of us take in the scene.

"You and Tamantha," he said. "You're the clear, solid foundation at my feet."

I had no words.

✧ ✧ ✧ ✧

THE DESCENT WAS easier, but not easy.

I hadn't wanted to leave that spot, yet was happy to see the truck.

He opened the stiff passenger door, then moved toward the back, checking a strap holding a shovel in the bed to make sure it was secure.

Without getting in, I watched him for a long moment.

"Tom?"

He turned his head toward me, not stopping what he was doing, just a quick, casual look.

That changed.

First, his hands went still. Then the rest of him, the way he did when he was serious about something.

He turned completely toward me. Slow, steady, like he didn't want to scare off a wild animal that could take off any second. That would be me.

"Yes?" He wasn't asking why I'd said his name. He was asking if *yes* was what I was saying. "Figures you'd settle this with a question."

"Well, what about you, Burrell? Asking *yes?*"

He'd reached me.

We didn't touch. Not quite. Not yet.

"Which you haven't answered yet," he said.

I looked up at him now that he was close, taking shelter together in the shadow from the brim of his hat.

"Yes," I said. No question.

Looks like I'm getting married.

Soon.

The End

For news about upcoming books, as well as other titles and news, join Patricia McLinn's ReadHeads and receive her twice-monthly free newsletter.

www.patriciamclinn.com/readers-list

You can buy this book and all my others, including print editions and audiobooks, from my online store. I've added direct-to-you buying options to better control how my books reach you, while having lots more elbow room to give you special bundles, early offers, and exclusive bonuses.

Patricia's Bookstore
shop.patriciamclinn.com

Thank you for reading Elizabeth, Tom, and Mike's story! I hope you enjoyed it.

Please! Do not ruin the surprises for other readers.

I greatly appreciate your enthusiasm and your reviews, all the more if you will please leave out of your reviews:

- That Elizabeth and Tom become a couple
- That Mike buys KWMT
- That the murder-suicide, isn't one
- Or the solution to the mystery. (I know you wouldn't! But one reviewer did in an earlier book—in the headline—so I'm playing it safe.)

Elizabeth, Tom, and Tamantha prepare to celebrate their first Christmas together, with the joys and complications of forming a new family. But that's not all Elizabeth has on her plate for the holidays.

Someone's put a wish on the Christmas Wishing Tree set up at KWMT-TV that has her name on it … and it's a weird one.

Come join the gang as they celebrate, ring those sleigh bells—and find answers in this holiday novella.

Holiday Bullets

Enjoy **Air Ready**? (Hope so)

Elizabeth and friends ask if you'll help spread the word about them and the Caught Dead in Wyoming series. You have the power to do that in two quick ways:

Recommend the book and the series to your friends and/or the whole wide world on social media. Shouting from rooftops is particularly appreciated.

Review the book. Take a few minutes to write an honest review and it can make a huge difference. As you likely know, it's the single best way for your fellow readers to find books they'll enjoy, too.

To me—as an author and a reader—the goal is always to find a good author-reader match. By sharing your reading experience through recommendations and reviews, you become a vital matchmaker. ☺

The Caught Dead in Wyoming series

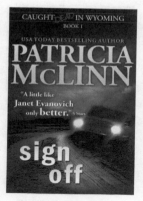

SIGN OFF

Divorce a husband, lose a career … grapple with a murder.

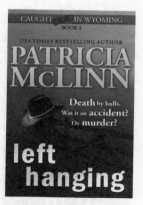

LEFT HANGING

Trampled by bulls — an accident? Elizabeth, Mike and friends dig into the world of rodeo.

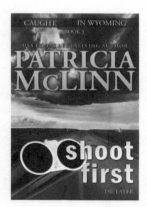

SHOOT FIRST

Elizabeth and friends delve into old Wyoming treasures and secrets to save lives.

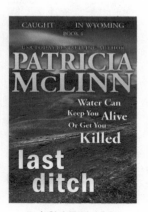

LAST DITCH

Elizabeth and Mike search after a man in a wheelchair goes missing in dangerous, desolate country.

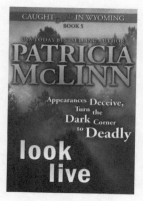

LOOK LIVE

Elizabeth and friends take on a misleading murder with help — and hindrance — from intriguing out-of-towners.

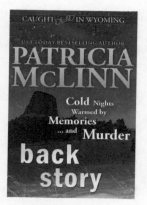

BACK STORY

Murder never dies, but comes back to threaten Elizabeth and her team of investigators.

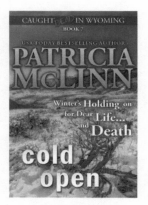

COLD OPEN

Elizabeth's search for a place of her own becomes an open house for murder.

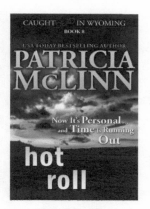

HOT ROLL

One of their own becomes a target — and time is running out.

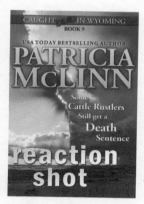

REACTION SHOT

Sometimes cattle rustlers still get a death sentence.

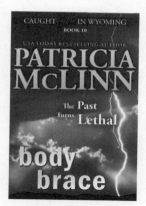

BODY BRACE

Everything can change, but murder still comes calling.

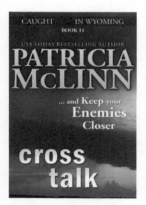

CROSS TALK

Prime suspect: The most annoying man in Sherman.

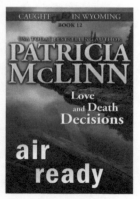

AIR READY

Love and death decisions.

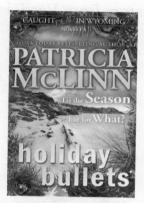

HOLIDAY BULLETS

A Christmas wish with Elizabeth's name on it.

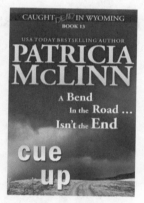

CUE UP

On the trail of murder.

More mystery from Patricia McLinn

Secret Sleuth series

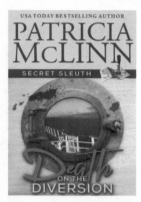

DEATH ON THE DIVERSION

Final resting place? Deck chair.

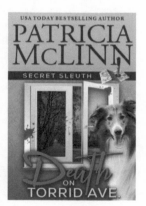

DEATH ON TORRID AVENUE

A new love (canine), an ex-cop and a dog park discovery.

DEATH ON BEGUILING WAY

No zen in sight as Sheila untangles a yoga instructor's murder.

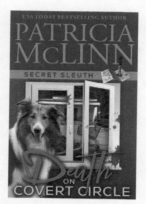

DEATH ON COVERT CIRCLE

A supermarket CEO meets his expiration date.

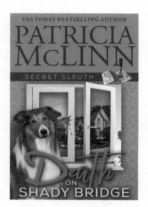

DEATH ON SHADY BRIDGE

A homicide cold case heats up.

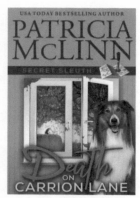

DEATH ON CARRION LANE

More murder is brewing in Haines Tavern.

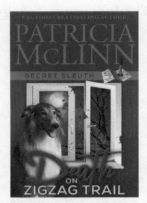

DEATH ON ZIGZAG TRAIL

A spooky legend twists grave matters.

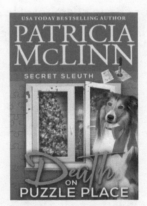

DEATH ON PUZZLE PLACE

Season's greetings: Whodunit?

The Innocence Trilogy

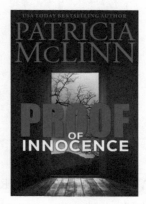

PROOF OF INNOCENCE

She's a prosecutor chasing demons. He's wrestling them.
Will they find proof of innocence?

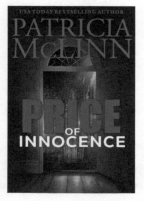

PRICE OF INNOCENCE

To solve this murder Detective Belichek will risk everything — his
friendships, his reputation, his career, his heart … and his life.

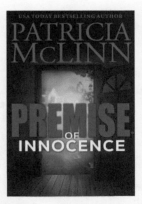

PREMISE OF INNOCENCE

The last woman Detective Landis is prepared to see is the one he must save.

Explore a complete list of all Patricia's books

patriciamclinn.com/patricias-books

Or get a printable booklist

patriciamclinn.com/patricias-books/printable-booklist

Patricia's Bookstore (buy online directly from Patricia)

shop.patriciamclinn.com

About the Author

Patricia McLinn is the USA Today bestselling author of more than 60 published novels cited by readers and reviewers for their wit and vivid characterization. Her books include mysteries, romantic suspense, contemporary romance, historical romance, and women's fiction. They have topped bestseller lists and won numerous awards.

She has spoken about writing from London to Melbourne, Australia, to Washington, D.C., including being a guest speaker at the Smithsonian Institution.

McLinn spent more than 20 years as an editor at The Washington Post after stints as a sports writer (Rockford, Ill.) and assistant sports editor (Charlotte, N.C.). She received BA and MSJ degrees from Northwestern University.

Now living in northern Kentucky, McLinn loves to hear from readers through her website and social media.

Website: patriciamclinn.com
Facebook: facebook.com/PatriciaMcLinn
Pinterest: pinterest.com/patriciamclinn
Instagram: instagram.com/patriciamclinnauthor

AMORE E GRIFFONIA

Poesie

Federico Riccardo

a Cipi

INTRODUZIONE AL TESTO

Integratore alimentare a base di estratto di semi di Griffonia titolato al 20% in 5-HTTP (5-idrossitriptofano). Indicazioni: i semi di Griffonia sono utili per mantenere il normale tono dell'umore e favorire il benessere mentale. Modo d'uso: Assumere una o due compresse al giorno prima dei pasti con un po' di acqua o altra bevanda.

Ingredienti: Griffonia (Griffonia simplicifolia (DC.) Baill) semi e.s.* tit.** al 20% in 5-idrossitriptofano (5-HTTP), addensanti: cellulosa e fosfati di calcio, agenti antiagglomeranti: biossido di silicio e sali di magnesio degli acidi grassi.

Avvertenze: Non superare la dose giornaliera indicata. Tenere lontano dalla portata dei bambini al di sotto di tre anni di età. Gli integratori alimentari non vanno intesi come sostituti di una dieta variata, equilibrata e di un sano stile di vita.

Ma il mio indirizzo è "Via del Sopracciglio destro"

Con rispetto parlando

e altre parti

altre parti di me…

(Francesco de Gregori)

SONO DIVENTATO ADULTO

Sono diventato adulto

quando ho cominciato ad aggiungere al mio lessico parole come:

pompino, sega, fottersi.

Ma anche fattura, bonifico e compenso.

E ancora: depennare,

procrastinare,

coadiuvare.

Poi Svitol, trapano, chiodo, avvinazzato, trentenne, infausto, morituro.

F24,

mantecare, revisionare, appellarsi,

includere,

serpeggiante, quindi serpeggiare,

bresaola,

postepay, day off, smart working,

incastrare, valutare, organizzare, sbeffeggiare, tinteggiare, sentimentale, impossibilitato,

moralista,

drenante, riposante, conclusione, incremento, bibliografico, ermeneutica, bacheca, shitake, kataifi, aloe, notturno, neonatale,

prepartita, contropartita,

pro forma, formalità,

svolgere (al posto di "fare"),

fermentare, defecare, copulare, seno, bestemmia,

Piripicchio e Piripacchio (per esempio quando devi organizzare i tavoli del tuo matrimonio e dici in modo ilare: ...*mentre invece Piripicchio e Piripacchio li mettiamo lì*),

quotidiano, stagionato,

crudité,

ricci di mare,

rito civile.

Sono diventato adulto

quando ho tolto dal mio lessico parole come:

pisello, bigiare, limonare.

Interrogazione, evidenziatore, panino.

Ma anche paghetta.

E latte, prosciutto, partita, tipa, cafferino, caffettino, sigarettina,
cannetta, pokerino, fantacalcio, risiko, rosico, cameretta.

Sbatti.

Infamata, pesante, mafia.

Infine la birra, il chinotto, l'estathè, kit-kat.

Calippo.

Vacanza.

Gol, palo, fallo, vita di merda

Mammina, papone,

fra, bro, zio, disastro

la mia fidanzata, i miei brutti voti,

serata

figata

bella!

Quante parole ancora abbandonerò

Quando sarò vecchio.

Quante poche ne avrei volute dire,

Quante ne dirò di meno

Quando sarò morto.

PERÒ

Però me lo potevi dire

dire cosa?

Per esempio: che quando dobbiamo cucinare le patate è meglio mettere la carta da forno

e che se ti dimentichi di inserire l'acqua la caffettiera si brucia

che il tappino del dentifricio va rimesso al suo posto dopo aver lavato i denti

e che per togliere il residuo incrostato nella teglia sarebbe meglio lasciare un po' d'acqua calda

con un filo di detersivo per i piatti

che ti dà fastidio l'odore dei croccantini del cane in cucina

che l'acqua è meglio nella bottiglia di vetro

che hai paura delle mosche

e che io sono automaticamente la persona designata a scacciarle.

Che hai paura delle zanzare

e alle 3 di notte, non importa che io stia dormendo, mi svegli e devo cercare una pantofola.

Mi potevi anche dire

dire cosa?

Che non sopporti l'odore dell'aglio

e il soffritto si fa solo di cipolle

e che ti soffermi più di un'ora in bagno la mattina

e quindi io devo svegliarmi prima e fare quello che devo fare in bagno.

«Che devi farci in bagno?»

Leggo *Internazionale*:

è così corta una settimana per leggerlo tutto intero.

Sai che altro mi dovevi dire?

Cosa, sentiamo, cosa?

Che sei adorabile da impazzire

che tutte le volte che ti svegli e mi cerchi, e quindi come prima cosa allunghi la mano e trovi il mio petto,

mi scappa quel sorriso che non conosco

e me ne stupisco,

quel sorriso che si confonde tra le briciole sul tavolo,

il fondo d'acqua nel bicchiere,

la confettura di albicocche,

lo zucchero di canna,

lo stupore nel pensare che il meteo questa volta aveva indovinato,

le pastiglie di griffonia

due a testa!

l'annullamento totale della ragione

l'amore

si fa soprattutto

a colazione.

MI CHIAMAVI GRIFFONIA

Mi chiamavi Griffonia

ed era amore a colazione

l'idea più dolce

la bomba atomica.

E ogni gesto era studiato con minuziosità,

con dedizione.

Mi ripetevi infinite volte

di non lasciare le briciole sulla tovaglia,

di non lasciare le orme per terra,

che questa non è casa nostra

che tutto il mondo è casa nostra

che tutta la vita è uno spettacolo

dalla durata sì o no di venti minuti

se vissuta bene

se montata bene.

Mi chiamavi Griffonia

perché con me stavi meglio di due giorni prima

ti stava stretto dare e basta

adesso era d'obbligo avere

non ti sembrava possibile condividere finalmente

la tua serotonina

non era giusto attentare alla felicità

tirata a sorte come il numero di una schedina

che tanto tutte le strade portano

inesorabilmente a una biforcazione.

Te ne sei accorta quando hai fatto l'autostop

di quanto sia fatale una non-direzione.

ATLETICO

1991 – 2001 – 2011 – 2021

Attraverso il mio tempo

come un cane

che saltella

da un cerchio

all'altro.

PRATICAMENTE I CANI

Praticamente i cani

in tenera età

si allenano ad abbaiare con una pallina in bocca

per far sì che non cada giù.

Possono sollecitare in questo modo il padrone

che, magari, distratto,

non ci stava badando poi tanto.

Questo tipo di allenamento

-abbaiare con la pallina in bocca –

è una prova

ma è fine a se stessa

non è che un esercizio di stile

una volta imparato non serve più

eppure si apprende

così, per naturale propensione,

come fare la cacca

o guadagnarsi la giornata.

Ti insegna a fare due cose contemporaneamente

-da una parte chiamare, dall'altra esser pronto

come una statua di Brancusi, con sopracciglia inarcate-

alla disperazione di un umano furibondo

che può incazzarsi come un alano o adottarti per sempre.

PAT

Pat l'vorrei che tu Lapo ed io

in questa quarantena silenziosa

ci mettessimo a fare tutti insieme

in un appartamento campagnuolo

il nostro Decameron pieno di sogni

e *poesie d'amore prima dello schianto.*

Cucino io per tutti

tu realizzi componimenti

Silvia Giulia dirige il gruppo a suon di giochi

«Questa sera Lupus in fabula siore e siori!»

Francesco e Claudia in stanza a far l'amore

Giacomo lo facciamo ragionare sull'infinito

e il suo ruolo non lo cambiamo assolutamente

perché c'è sempre bisogno di un filosofo durante una carestia.

La mattina presto si va tutti a fare sport

alla distanza di un metro, si intende, uno dall'altro

pranzo leggero con pochi carboidrati

-altrimenti ci vien sonno e non possiam creare-

pomeriggio ognuno alla sua arte

la sera attorno al fuoco a raccontarcela

e il tempo corre

e noi così leggeri.

La notte tenebra e coccolosa

farà da sfondo ad una luna dolce

che esploderà in mille pezzi di riso soffiato e latte

e tutti noi vi sguazzerem felici

come bambini dentro la pallestra.

Chissà che quando poi finisce tutto

ci avremo preso gusto a stare insieme

tanto da non voler tornare al nostro posto

che il posto dove stare sarà questo.

LA CITTÀ È MORTA

La città è morta.

Sembra quasi Agosto

non ci trovi niente e nessuno

nemmeno me.

Io sono qui

chiuso in questo appartamento

a gestire, disorganizzare, lasciar andare.

Nel mio balcone un cartone di pizza abbandonato a se stesso.

Nel balcone accanto

un tipo losco

fuma

lo saluto:

mi guarda.

Lo saluto di nuovo:

ricambia.

E ogni minuto che passa

mi avvicino

alla morte

con o senza virus

con o senza malasorte.

Inutile come sempre

la disperazione.

Siamo qui per un altro motivo,

non per osservarci discutere.

È la fine del mondo

ogni giorno

e non te ne sei accorto.

I CORVI

Ho fatto un sogno:

salivo su un palcoscenico.

Al momento di parlare

-era un qualcosa di Ionesco, mi pare-

non mi si apriva la bocca:

murata.

Non che l'assurdo mi aiutasse

in questa situazione bislacca.

In compenso

sono apparso nei sogni di mio padre

in mezzo al bosco freddo

mi cercava disperato e non mi trovava

e gli ero davanti.

Qui sì che uscivano le parole che volevo.

Ma i corvi ci coprivano entrambi.

I corvi che non vanno a dormire.

Che strani giorni, amore mio

più cerco il contatto col mondo

più il contatto non arriva.

Sembra di vivere a metà

tra possedere i mezzi

e impossibilità.

Mi distruggo in mille modi differenti

e non c'è la prospettiva di un rimedio.

MURO BIANCO, FOGLIO BIANCO

No, è che...

Ero qui, seduto ad aspettare niente

con un foglio bianco davanti

che poi bianco è un modo di dire

che poi pure foglio è un modo di dire

mica è un foglio vero:

è un programma di videoscrittura prodotto da Microsoft,

distribuito con licenza commerciale.

Quando torni?

Sì, poi sicuramente torni e c'hai voglia di fare la doccia

e io aspetto ancora qui seduto, come un deficiente.

Ma cosa sto seduto a fare?

«Ma alzati! No? » mi dirai tu

-guarda è già tutto scritto, tutto perfettamente studiato

nei minimi particolari dentro la mia testa –

mi dirai: «alzati no? Sei qui seduto da tutto il giorno! »

E allora mi devo alzare

per due motivi:

il primo è che me l'hai chiesto tu

il secondo è che mi sono rotto i coglioni

e ti inizio a vomitare addosso tutte le cose che non sono andate nel verso giusto oggi,

tutte quelle che proprio qui ce le ho,

che non riesco nemmeno a scriverle.

«E allora trovati un altro lavoro no?

Dici sempre che vuoi scrivere e poi non scrivi più»

Ma tu non dovevi farti la doccia, ti chiedo io.

Ma guarda che ti tiro un pugno che… che.

Mi volto e sono tutto solo.

Alzati, mi dico.

Guarda che non c'è nessuno qui e tu hai le allucinazioni, mi dico.

Sarà che fisso tutto il giorno 'sto muro bianco che mi viene da bestemmiare

muro bianco, foglio bianco

un giorno ti dipingo tutto, sia te che l'altro.

Alzati, no?

SEGRETO

Con il mio segreto vado in onda e mi espongo oltremodo

così forte da aver paura di avertelo raccontato.

Tremo.

Come un uomo nudo in mezzo al ghiaccio.

Un dente di bimbo, che non vuole avvicinarsi all'ingresso della scuola

perché freddo

perché sbaraglio

perché di fronte alla crudeltà dei compagni di classe infami.

Nascondo il mio sguardo inadeguato

e sogno una stanza buia

persiane chiuse

per dimenticare

quello che ho detto.

IO E TE SOGNAVAMO LA STESSA COSA

Io e te sognavamo la stessa cosa

di diventare piccoli piccoli

in un piatto di pesce crudo

e fare il bagno nel guazzetto.

Io e te sognavamo

di realizzare la parodia di Matrix

ingoiando pastiglie di griffonia

e giocavamo a muoverci come Neo

assuefatti da un prodotto fitoterapico.

Io e te sognavamo la stessa cosa:

di trascorrere la sera in un baretto con gli anziani

a criticare i giovani d'oggi

e le loro bevande zuccherine.

Ma sognavamo anche

di rimuoverci a vicenda i più umilianti difetti

come brufoli con una pinzetta

e di mandarli via con lo sciacquone.

Sciocchi noi,

sciocchi annoiati perfezionisti

da quando siamo così belli come il sole

non ci immaginiamo più come roba commestibile.

LA CASA

La casa si svuota

Silenzio signori!

L'occulta presenza seduta in cucina

non è più cosa nostra.

Venne di notte il Grande Mangiatore

e non fece una piega

quando gli chiesi: «Tu chi sei?»

Mi urlò che voleva amore.

E gli diedi del cibo

in sua sostituzione.

Ora è Maggio,

il polline è al suo culmine,

ancora non hanno deciso

chi vincerà il campionato dell'ipocrisia.

E mia madre è solita piangere

ma oggi forse non lo farà

oggi forse resisterà.

E studio tutto quello che è questa casa

Fredda, senza televisione.

IMPERFEZIONE (TITOLO PROVVISORIO)

Come la goccia rimbalza

dal bicchiere sulla tovaglia

come le frasi fuori luogo

alla fine di un discorso

si diffonde dalla finestra

fino a perdersi sul pavimento

questa polvere sporca

di ipocrisia e fallimento.

Decide dove andare,

senza salutare,

nasconde il previsto

crea l'imprevisto

«Fai sempre così»

«Scusami se esisto»

Io sono

l'abitante di questa casa,

il suo Don Chisciotte,

la sua mania.

Io conosco

dove arriva quel lenzuolo

e il fondo

della tazzina del caffè.

Io luccico

ad ogni complimento ricevuto.

Io muoio

come la luna

quando il lupo va a dormire.

Io muto ad ogni punto di domanda

ma ogni punto di domanda

come sempre

parte da me.

NELLA MIA ORA GIUSTA

Come un topo

che nell'ora giusta

esce dal tombino

a leccare la notte rimasta

quella che non appartiene più

alla velocità degli autobus in scadenza,

ai tossici di carboidrati,

ai rumorosi tacchi che rimbombano

l'asfalto secolare ma rinnovato dalle amministrazioni.

Come la blatta

che nell'ora giusta

si struscia e si arrapa

sulla superficie della cucina

partorendo continuamente i suoi schifosi eredi

e mandandoli al fronte

subito, appena nati

a contaminare l'arredamento,

a patire la fame,

così, senza chiedersi nemmeno se sia giusto farlo oppure no.

Così anche io

nella mia ora giusta

mai fuori tempo e luogo

non appena mi si concede uno spiraglio

per raccontare le situazioni che voglio

miste a quelle che mi tengo buone

per la prossima volta – l'ultima forse?-

esco solo quando mi è concesso

e paraculo – come un artista-

quando gli altri sono andati a dormire.

LA LUCCIOLA

Ti ricordi quella sera al parco

la lucciola!

Mostro scintillante

che vegliava sul mio sesso

(e sulla tua lingua su di esso)

danzando discreta, minima, nuda, sottile, piccola piccola.

Hai alzato lo sguardo per seguirla

mi adori quando interrompo

per farti osservare le meraviglie del parco.

E noi che lo stavamo profanando

(e noi che lo continuiamo a fare)

E tutto questo scompare o rimane?

E tutto questo

guarda che bello godercelo adesso

senti che fresco

senti che caldo

sto venendo.

È TROPPO TARDI

Pensavo prima

mentre mangiavo la pastasciutta

che non so allacciarmi le scarpe.

Ho sempre desiderato

fare il tranviere,

e avere la possibilità un giorno di togliermi la giacca e tornare

indietro.

Non si può fare l'artista invece

lo si può essere e basta

l'occhio mezzo aperto guarda il conto corrente

la bocca dice un sacco di fesserie impronunciabili

Anche quest'oggi, vedi

si sta alzando un polverone

volano le offerte del supermercato

la città va in pausa

io rimango.

È troppo tardi

per il cartellino

i lampioni si accendono

di notte succede sempre qualcosa, anche quando dormi.

Che poi la notte è quella cosa buia, sanguinolenta

che dormire è solo l'ultima delle meraviglie che ti concede.

SOLDI

Non avevo preso appuntamenti per quel giorno

ero completamente disoccupato.

Sei spuntata dal nulla,

come spuntano dal nulla gli arcobaleni quando non ha piovuto.

E allora, prima ancora di rivelarmi il tuo dolore

ti ho chiesto: «Ne parliamo davanti a una birra? »

Non avevo nemmeno la patente

quindi sei venuta tu, qui, in macchina.

Pioveva

ed eravamo senza ombrello

ci siamo ripresentati perché ci conoscevamo a stento.

La pioggia è aumentata

e siamo finiti in un posto che puzzava di morte,

hai ordinato due Margarita,

mi hai accennato ad una vita con un altro:

Potevo essere io, ho pensato.

Dio, quanto beve, ho pensato subito dopo, quando hai letteralmente scolato l'ultima goccia di quel putrido bicchiere

con l'innocenza di chi dice una cosa sporca, una bestemmia in una cappella durante una visita scolastica

Mi hai detto: «Io voglio fare i soldi»

E lì ci stavo, ti ho guardata

non sarei mai riuscito ad aiutarti

quindi scusa

ma ci stavo,

e se mi sporgo dal foglio bianco

ti vedo che dormi sul divano

e sì, non ho neanche una banconota in tasca

ma mi ripeto: ci sto ancora.

UCCIDESTI IL FANTINO E IL CAVALLO

Quella volta che uscimmo

-erano anni che volevamo farlo-

andammo in Piazza del Duomo

a pirlare sulle palle del toro

e tu, col tuo vestito rosa

che lasciava vedere tutto

tutto quello che noi maschi volevamo vedere da sempre

e io lì potevo ammirarlo gratis, ma arrossivo: vergine!

Non ti accorgesti di aver tirato un calcio per sbaglio

a un fantino giocattolo in groppa al suo cavallo

continuasti a camminare come se niente fosse

e io provai sincera commozione

per il pakistano, che vendeva ora un giocattolo rotto

e per lo stesso giocattolo rotto, rantolante.

Capii in quel momento

che per me la poesia scavalca tutte le donne

e tutte le buone intenzioni

e tutte le promesse che ci facemmo finirono in quel momento

non senza una punta d'orgoglio

tanto che adesso non mi vergogno

di usare il passato remoto per questa cosa che ho scritto.

SIPARIO

C'è ancora gente che prova a capire

per esempio, uscendo da una sala teatrale o al cinema

si alza e dice: «Non ci ho capito nulla»

e innesca polemiche contro il personale di sala,

chiede il biglietto indietro, chiede la spiegazione.

e il personale di sala, che è lì perché non può stare altrove,

è pure costretto a dire: «Non c'entro nulla io»

Al punto che gli si ribatte: «Eh no, voi c'entrate eccome»

Questi che vogliono capire sono i peggiori

e non perché non abbiano capito

bensì perché capire ormai è irrilevante

capire è fuori moda, incostituzionale.

Lo sapete infatti chi ha capito? Chi non ha davvero capito.

La gente che non ha capito, invece, non deve vergognarsi

Perché è a lei che noi parliamo

e anche se non ci capisce

e anche se non ci capirà

poco importa, anzi meglio così:

è meglio non essere capiti

che non capire che non c'è niente da capire.

IL VUOTO

Vorrei che per un giorno

sparissero i compromessi

mi basta un giorno,

ma deve essere un giorno lungo

una giornata di sole trascorsa al mare

con un chiosco di panini alle mie spalle

e in un giorno senza compromessi

il programma è semplice:

i panini del chiosco devono essere tutti i panini del mondo

da quello burro e marmellata a quello con la frittata di nonna

e il mare deve essere il mare più bello del mondo

con la sabbia e gli scogli, con i pesci e i molluschi.

Ma forse non è un compromesso questo?

La bellezza stessa non è un compromesso?

Non è un rifiuto di qualcos'altro in nome di questo?

Allora cancelliamo il mare, il chiosco, i molluschi:

cancelliamo tutto.

Che rimane?

Il vuoto.

Ecco, il mondo senza il compromesso.

QUARTO DI LUNA

Davanti a me ho un quarto di luna:

un pallino biondo perso nel buio

di un cielo che

non possiede confini.

Ne catturo il suo caldo,

sporco odore

di luna rassegnata

a controllare le nostre perversioni,

di luna puttana che

ci scruta e ci sputa addosso

l'aria inquinata e corrotta di città.

E vorrei correre con la mente

e arrivarci

per bruciarmi con lei

per fondermi con il suo candore.

Patata,

Chicco,

Pane,

Dio?

Sei tu solo un punto lontano e indifferente

o la stella che risveglia il mio animo bambino?

TALK TALK

Ho deciso: esco di casa

affronterò il sonno della ragione

con grazia, delicatezza, senso critico

schiverò i lombrichi, le blatte, i sorci, i ladri, i genitori

e tutto il resto delle paure

che mi porto dietro dalla culla.

Sia ben chiara una cosa però,

a coloro che da tempo si interessano

alle mie vicissitudini:

non lo faccio certo

per la presunta bellezza che si trova nel mondo.

Io non credo nella bellezza del mondo.

Non credo nel Dio magico che si sveglia e disegna una
montagna

(cosa c'è da credere nella bellezza di una montagna

se poi

un truffatore ci pianta una pista da sci?).

In un'altra cosa credo

piuttosto

- ed è per questo che ho deciso: esco di casa-

io credo

nelle coincidenze, nella fortuna

e nella sfortuna, mia e degli altri,

nel balletto delle concatenazioni

nel distruggere

così si crea bellezza: distruggendo,

e non creando ex novo,

spaccando piuttosto il bicchiere in otto parti.

Questo il segreto

questa l'arte

questa la bellezza:

spaccare

incendiare

uccidere

criticare.

Questo mi porto dentro

e così

lo porto fuori.

Ci vediamo al bar.

ALTRO CHE POLLO

Quando la notte

fa spazio al silenzio

e le luci di casa si spengono

-perché la notte non ha senso illuminarla-

le volontà mie carnali aumentano

la mano sfiora il cazzo

ma interrompo poco dopo

perché mi sento inquieto.

Apro il frigo,

mangio un pollo

muoio

bevo

rido

urlo

mi tocco di nuovo:

vengo.

Finalmente

vengo

e ti ripenso

se fossi con me adesso

altro che pollo

sarebbe sesso.

5 MINUTI

5 minuti

trascorsi

davanti alla porta

dubbi se uscire

per fare la spesa

o rimandare

evitare

per non incrociare

sguardi trasversali

di anonimi individui

individualisti corrucciati

stipati

in esistenze precarie.

Là fuori

non c'è nulla di invitante

crollano con me certezze

e il mio animo poetico

si sofferma

a quegli amori appena sbocciati

separati

da una quarantena infame

e lui a lei magari:

«Ti avrei dato il mio corpo

e invece

ti è rimasto il pensiero»

MI CHIEDO: CHE COSA TI AMO A FARE?

Mi chiedo: che cosa ti amo a fare?

se poi mi rispondi: ti amo anche io.

Mi chiedo: che cosa ti amo a fare?

se ormai è risaputo, scontato, poco efficace.

Ma poi ti vedo girare per casa

con quelle cosce

e con quei capelli che ti crescono a vista d'occhio

e quel sorriso che rompe le crepe della mia resistenza.

Mi chiedo: che cosa ti amo a fare?

Ecco che cosa ti amo a fare.

Mi chiedo – ah, mi sto ripetendo?

te ne farai una ragione, la poesia è tutta così –

mi chiedo

Sì, mi chiedo: che cosa ti amo a fare?

se poi da un momento all'altro

come dicono quelli

naufragheremo nell'ignoto dell'abbandono.

ma poi ti vedo leggere Bauman sul divano

con l'ingordigia di chi non ne ha abbastanza

di questa vita e di come la raccontano.

Se tutto ciò che hai da raccontare

potesse leggersi nei tuoi tatuaggi

senza badare a vite parallele

saremmo sì, incompleti ma felici

perché quello che hai da dire è stato scritto.

E io per te, poeta e traduttore

di tutto il mondo cui mi vuoi guidare

alla ricerca della miccia continua

che tiene accesa questa rappresentazione.

Ti devo ancora far conoscere

tutti i vini che non abbiamo bevuto

tutte le piazze vuote delle città d'Europa

e tutti i boschi nei quali passeggiare.

Abbiamo tempo da perdere ancora

senza la frenesia di volerlo recuperare

Mi chiedo: che cosa ti amo a fare?

Ecco che cosa ti amo a fare.

C'È DA CHIAMARE L'IDRAULICO .

C'è da chiamare l'idraulico domani mattina

per riparare un tubo sotto il lavello

e come al solito quando lo chiamerò starà guidando.

Gli idraulici

quando sono lì a smontare e rimontare cose incomprensibili
non rispondono al telefono,

rispondono solamente quando stanno guidando

e quasi ti senti responsabile

che magari si schiantano contro un altro furgone

e tu rimani in attesa a parlare con l'airbag scoppiato

Poi si presenterà

manco gli avrò detto il giorno e l'ora in cui deve venire

ma lui verrà lo stesso

anzi

verrà in ritardo

sarà tutto sporco

tutto bianco!

Lascerà per terra un secchio con tutte le cose

nere

quelle filamentose che sembrano i capelli di una vecchia morta,

con le dita unte mi sposterà le sedie della cucina,

mi dirà che c'è tutto da rifare

l'impianto, le cose, che non so neanche ripetere

mi dirà che sono 200 euro solo per l'uscita

e il preventivo di tutto quello che sarà me lo dicono quando tornano

-perché nel frattempo sono diventati in tre o quattro, tutti che vogliono i miei soldi, il mio caffè, la mia cucina, il mio lavello —

c'è da capire quante cose devono smontare e poi mi dicono

un altro giorno, mi dicono

quanto viene gli chiedo

te lo diciamo un altro giorno, mi dicono.

Io quel giorno sarò qui

a cercare ancora di indagare il senso della vita

a non trovarlo, un'altra volta

a sentirmi martellare dal senso di colpa

di una pagina vuota

e allora troverò nei discorsi dell'idraulico

forse

la mia via di fuga

per cui ben venga lui

e la sua combriccola di arrapati

a toccacciare i tubi della cucina

spero mi lascino un po' d'acqua così potrò mettere a bollire per loro una pastasciutta.

GIOSTRA

Mi guardi strano:

sono nudo sul tappeto, tra i peli del cane.

Quella di ieri sera sul divano

la chiameremo "la Nostra Sbornia"

ma ora mi trovi sempre più annegato

a testa in giù, tra i sensi di colpa

e non c'è niente di più eccitante

che invitarti a un altro giro di giostra.

TI HO IMMAGINATA VECCHIA

Ti ho immaginata vecchia

ma io non c'ero.

Forse ero già morto?

E quindi tu vedova

e alimentata dal ricordo,

sedevi su un bellissimo divano ad angolo

portavi

dei capelli corti regolari e oggettivi,

dei vestiti precisi e sottili

alla moda,

come sei sempre stata,

fumavi le sigarette strette e lunghe

e sfogliavi una pagina di libro con lentezza invidiabile.

Eri nel pieno della vecchiaia, quando ti ho immaginata

ma eri donna, veramente donna

ora che potevi permetterti di criticare

un autore, un vino, un fazzoletto di seta

ora che tutti se ne erano andati

e anche il giudizio degli altri,

che da giovane tanto faceva paura

contava meno dell'unghia del mignolo

o del tramonto ingannevole:

eri quella che si direbbe una persona sicura

eri vecchia, bellissima.

TI PREGO, NON TOGLIERMI I MOSTRI

Ti prego non togliermi i mostri

e le lattine di coca cola

e il pollo arrosto

e il prosciutto di Parma

e i pacchetti di Skittles

e i biglietti dei concerti

e la collezione di fantasmini della Kinder

e gli scontrini

e i dvd di Fellini messi in ordine per anno

e le poesie scritte sulla lista della spesa

e il farro soffiato a colazione

egli indirizzi mail sui post it

e il liquore dopo cena

e *Internazionale*

e il bicchiere di vino bianco da cucina bevuto alla goccia
mentre faccio sfumare

e la mia voglia di lavare i piatti

e la tristezza delle giornate da solo

e la sigaretta quando sento la stanchezza alle ginocchia

e le serie tv

e il mio arrivismo

e il mio disordine

e la mia scarsa attenzione

e la mia bellezza

e la mia inquietudine

e la mia nostalgia.

AMARE

Amare

è non avere paura

di dire all'altro che ha un pezzo di carne incastrato tra i denti

o di sentirsi dire che i propri amici sono dei trogloditi

e di confermarlo, comportandosi peggio di loro.

Amare

è non provare disgusto delle sue puzze,

quando viene condiviso il bagno per la troppa fretta

o del suo alito, quando appena svegli,

come mai prima, vorrebbe riempirti di baci.

Amare è soltanto un momento

quel momento scomodo dell'esistenza

rapido e fuggente, impalpabile e verace,

quel momento in cui tutta la miseria fuoriesce

gli occhi diventano oggettivamente quello che sono

quanto schifo si prova ad essere se stessi!

È quello il preciso istante del sogno.

Non avere paura

se in quella macchina urli il tuo racconto:

«Sono frustrato. Sì, è così! »

Non avere paura

della tua impotenza sessuale

di voler sprofondare nella sabbia mobile del tuo materasso.

Non avere paura della merda

quando viene sputata in modo simile a una sentenza di
tribunale,

è quella la vita che nei suoi grammi di sporco

si presenta implacabile sulla bilancia.

Amare è questo

è anche di più

è voler dare quando tutto sembra contrarsi

è vincere sugli psicologi dell'ultima ora

è il primordiale comportamento dell'uomo

contrapposto alla ragione di un'età senza ragione.

Amare

questo so fare

quando ripenso ai miei errori

alla convenzione

alla sottomissione

alla violenza

al decadimento

fisico e mentale

alla bruttezza

all'obesità

alla magrezza

alla stanchezza.

Amare

contro tutto il mondo, finalmente.

Amare

pur di dover essere "niente".

IO E TE IN MACCHINA

Non esco da questa macchina

neanche se vi fosse

un bisogno improvviso di partigiani,

neanche se piovessero banconote dal cielo

neanche se dicessero: hai mezz'ora di vita

non andrei dai genitori a salutarli

resto qui, ora e sempre

soprattutto perché sta nevicando

abbiamo bevuto vino che riscalda

abbiamo mangiato del pesce pesante

abbiamo fatto l'amore e siamo ancora bagnati.

Non uscire da questa macchina

è un atto politico

una questione di vita o di morte

la prima rivoluzione del mondo.

LECCAMI

Leccami!

In un qualsiasi bosco

bambini

andavamo a raccogliere le more

e puntualmente rimanevano sulle dita

quegli strascichi appiccicosi di frutta.

Così

mi toccavo la faccia

e ti dicevo: «Leccami»

Se torno ancora una volta

indietro nel tempo, senza astronave

rivedo capelli spontanei

e denti storti e ingialliti.

Rivedo addosso lo zucchero di tutto il mondo

quale sesso scegliere?

quale personalità mi si addice?

Rivedo te con un cesto al tuo seguito

e trecce arrotolate come una trama di eventi

occhi neri e malizia perpetua

e gonna bianca e alito fresco.

Ti dico: «Leccami»

ancora una volta

e tu con me decidi

che è un messaggio in codice

un mestiere nuovo

una benedizione

una condanna definitiva.

LA MEMORIA DEL FRIGO

La notte porta consiglio

ma io di notte torno bulimico

quelle lenzuola sono affettato misto

e piena di formaggio è la testa.

Ti cerco nelle briciole

ti cerco nei fondi di caffè

ti cerco nell'alito notturno

ti cerco nel mio frigorifero.

MAMMA

Così, parlottando, tra una delusione e l'altra,

si è ritrovato libero

felice nella sua stessa malizia

ha vomitato un po'

(quella è una cosa normale,

figurati!)

e mi ricordo ancora come fosse ieri

le corse sotto al portone

e l'odore di neomercurocromo

perché si sbucciava, il piccolo, e piangeva

anzi gridava.

Dai, lo possiamo dire

lo diciamo?

È felice!

Felice perché si è staccato dal cordone!

E che ci voleva poi a dirlo?

Solo che ora lascia un po' quel senso di vuoto nel letto

e, dipende da come ti metti, se osservi bene puoi anche notare l'orma del suo corpicino che è rimasta lì, come quando si sdraiava e leggeva libri così complicati, ermetici, in volgare.

Tanto la verità è una, sola e indissolubile

e la sa solo la mamma

e consiste in una cosa solamente:

questa è e rimane per sempre

casa sua.

Postfazione

di Simone Sciamé

Di poesia non ne capisco granché, quindi non me ne vogliano
le persone che invece di poesia ne masticano e se la spalmano
con il burro ogni mattina sulle fette biscottate. Quando leggo
una poesia rivedo nella mia mente una scena de *L'attimo
fuggente* di Peter Weir in cui il professor Keating – interpretato
da un memorabile Robin Williams – invita Neil Perry a leggere
l'introduzione di *Comprendere la poesia* di Jonathan Evans
Prichard, professore emerito. Lo studente – un giovanissimo
Robert Sean Leonard – si infila gli occhiali e legge: «Per
comprendere appieno la poesia dobbiamo anzitutto conoscerne
la metrica, la rima e le figure retoriche e poi porci due
domande, uno, con quanta efficacia sia stato reso il fine poetico
e due, quanto sia importante tale fine. La prima domanda
valuta la forma di una poesia, la seconda ne valuta
l'importanza». Mentre Neil Perry legge, il professore disegna
un grafico sulla lavagna cercando di determinare la perfezione
e l'importanza della poesia, come suggerito da Prichard. Al
termine dell'introduzione, il professor Keating si prende due
secondi di silenzio ed esclama, davanti allo sgomento dei suoi
alunni, queste parole: «Escrementi. Ecco cosa penso delle
teorie di J. Evans Prichard. Non stiamo parlando di tubi, stiamo
parlando di poesia. Ma si può giudicare la poesia facendo la hit
parade? Gagliardo Byron, è al quinto posto, ma è poco
ballabile. Adesso voglio che strappiate quella pagina» e in
un'altra lezione, che si lega con un *fil rouge* a questa
conclusione, dice: «Ecco, quando leggete non considerate
soltanto l'autore, considerate quello che *voi* pensate».
Con queste parole ben impresse nella mente ho cominciato a
leggere *Amore e Griffonia* di Federico, e ciò che ho letto aveva

poco a che fare con il *pensare* e molto di più con il *sentire*. È stato come essere in stato confusionale davanti a un quadro astratto. Non ne capisco granché, come vi ho detto, ma so per certo cosa mi piace leggere, cosa cerco. Vado in cerca di un pensiero intimista, di un fotogramma incastrato nel tempo, di un commento tossito dalla terza fila di un teatro. Mi piace che la poesia mi sorprenda come la frase saggia di un bambino. E ciò che distingue la poesia dalla narrativa non è la formula espressiva, è lo sconfinamento della ragione, l'incontro con la propria follia, il pensiero trasversale. *La memoria del frigo*, ad esempio, secondo me ne è la rappresentazione plastica. Le prime parole di *È troppo tardi*, sono poesia. Il ribaltamento del pensiero collettivo in *Sipario*. Cosa pretendiamo dalla poesia, se non che crei scenari nella nostra mente, che ci punzecchi l'animale dormiente dentro di noi, che rimetta in moto un flusso energetico recondito? Federico fa questo, in sostanza. Tratta le parole come un mezzo, non come un fine. Ci solletica l'orecchio con il suono, ci stuzzica il palato col sapore, crea spazi quadridimensionali nella nostra immaginazione, intercetta qualcosa che non sapevamo di covare dentro noi stessi. Capite bene che questo processo di emersione (o di immersione) che si genera grazie alla lettura non ha che fare con la meccanica espressiva o con la *ratio*. Non si può quantificare e non si deve giudicarla con un principio razionale. Queste poesie sono la dimostrazione che Prichard aveva torto.

Possiamo dire, con umiltà, che è poesia preoccuparsi dell'incolumità dell'idraulico mentre parla con noi al telefono durante la guida. È poesia non uscire da un'auto come atto politico, per continuare a fare l'amore. È poesia, così com'è arte, tutto ciò che ti tramortisce, tutto ciò che ti fa sentire infinitamente piccolo, ciò che ti eleva e che ti atterrisce, ciò che ti smuove le viscere. Questo è quello che ho capito leggendo *Amore e Griffonia*.

Infine, credo di aver capito di aver letto una raccolta di poesie nel momento in cui un aforisma ha creato un ponte che collega il foglio a quello che ho sempre pensato per tutto questo tempo, e cioè che *non si può fare l'artista invece lo si può essere e basta.*

RINGRAZIAMENTI

Vorrei evitare l'effetto "tesi di laurea", ma una postilla dedicata alle persone che più di altre hanno reso possibile la realizzazione di questo libro è necessaria. Meritano quindi di essere menzionati Mico Argirò, Giulia Borzumati, Marzia Gallo, Greta Passeri e Marinella Vescovini.

E poi ancora: Carlo Sabbatucci per il grande aiuto nella resa grafica. Umberto Bonavires per aver realizzato la splendida immagine di copertina (Instagram: @dobsart). Simone Sciamé per aver scritto la postfazione.

Ringrazio Marinella Brioschi, senza di lei non ci sarebbe stato né Amore né Griffonia. E ringrazio Cipi, per avermi suggerito a suo modo di pubblicare questo libro.

Amore e Griffonia è il diario intimo, riservato e tragicomico dei miei ultimi due anni (2020-2022), trascorsi tra quarantene, traslochi, lavori nuovi, lavori vecchi e tanta meditazione sulla vita. È un libro completamente autopubblicato. Se ti è piaciuto, regalalo a una persona speciale. E non dimenticare di scrivere una recensione, in totale libertà di pensiero, sulla pagina Amazon del libro o dove ti pare.

Io mi chiamo Federico Riccardo, sono un autore indipendente. Mi trovi su Facebook alla pagina "Federico Riccardo –Autore" o su Instagram (@federicoriccardo). Grazie per aver acquistato e letto il mio libro.

Printed in Great Britain
by Amazon

79416140R00051